C000053852

PIERRE COUSTILLAS is Pro... University of Lille. His many publications include volumes on Gissing, Hardy, Conrad and Kipling. He is editor of the *Gissing Journal*, co-editor of Gissing's Collected Correspondence (9 vols, 1990–   ) and general editor of Kipling's stories in the Bibliothèque de la Pléiade.

GEORGE GISSING

The Day of Silence and Other Stories

Edited by
Pierre Coustillas
University of Lille

J.M. Dent
London
Charles E. Tuttle Co.
Rutland, Vermont
EVERYMAN

First published in Everyman in 1993

Introduction and other apparatus © J.M. Dent 1993

All rights reserved

Made in Great Britain by
The Guernsey Press Co. Ltd, Guernsey, C.I.
J.M. Dent
Orion Publishing Group
Orion House
5 Upper St Martin's Lane
London WC2H 9EA
and
Charles E. Tuttle Co., Inc.
28 South Main Street
Rutland, Vermont
05071, USA

No part of this publication may be reproduced, stored
in a retrieval system, or transmitted, in any form or by
any means, electronic, mechanical, photocopying,
recording or otherwise, without the prior permission of
the copyright holder.

This book if bound as a paperback is subject to the
condition that it may not be issued on loan or
otherwise except in its original binding.

ISBN 0 460 87242 7

Everyman's Library
Reg. US Patent Office

CONTENTS

A NOTE ON GEORGE GISSING

Born in Wakefield in 1857, George Gissing was the oldest of five children. His father, a pharmacist, died when he was thirteen. In 1872 Gissing won a scholarship to Owens College, Manchester. He was a brilliant student, but his prospects were blasted when in 1876 he was caught stealing from the college cloakroom. He had hoped to use the money to reclaim a young prostitute, Nell Harrison, with whom he had fallen in love. After serving one month's imprisonment, he left for America, where he stayed for a year and began to publish short stories. Back in England in 1877, he lived with Nell, whom he married in 1879. The marriage was unhappy, the couple separated and Nell died in 1888. During these years Gissing survived on the proceeds of private tuition and some journalism. His first novel, *Workers in the Dawn* (1880), initiated a series of books that dealt powerfully with the poverty and degradation of the London poor: *The Unclassed* (1884), *Demos* (1886), *Thyrza* (1887) and *The Nether World* (1889). After this series he travelled on the Continent and his fiction expanded in other directions, more often adopting a middle-class setting, though never abandoning the subject of poverty. *The Emancipated* (1890) was followed by the novels that made his reputation: *New Grub Street* (1891), *Born in Exile* (1892), *The Odd Women* (1893), *In the Year of Jubilee* (1894) and *The Whirlpool* (1897). In the 1890s he also published many short stories. In 1891 he married Edith Underwood, who bore him two sons, Walter and Alfred. This second marriage proved as disastrous as the first and Gissing left Edith in 1897. Though he now had a considerable reputation as a novelist, he never achieved financial security. He did, however, enjoy the friendship of such writers as H. G. Wells, and from 1899 till his death in 1903 he lived (mostly in France) with Gabrielle Fleury, an admirer who had offered to translate his work. Among his notable later books were his critical study of Dickens (1898), his travel book *By the Ionian Sea* (1901) and the partly autobiographical *Private Papers of Henry Ryecroft* (1903). Gissing died – of lung disease – at the age of forty-six. He had written twenty-two novels.

CHRONOLOGY OF GISSING'S LIFE

Year	Age	Life
1857		22 Nov: born in Wakefield, Yorks, eldest child of Thomas Waller and Margaret Bedford Gissing
1859	1	15 Sept: William Gissing (brother) born
1860	3	25 Nov: Algernon Gissing (brother) born
1861		
1862	4	
1863	5	to 1870: attends local schools in Wakefield. 27 Oct: Margaret Emily Gissing (sister) born
1864	6	
1865	7	
1866	8	
1867	9	4 April: Ellen Sophia Gissing (sister) born
1868	10	
1869	11	
1870	13	28 Dec: his father dies
1871	13	George and his brothers sent to Lindow Grove School, Alderley Edge, Cheshire

CHRONOLOGY OF HIS TIMES

Year	Literary Context	Historical Events
1857	Flaubert: *Madame Bovary*. Dickens: *Little Dorrit*	Indian Mutiny Matrimonial Causes Act
1859	Darwin: *The Origin of Species*. G. Eliot: *Adam Bede*. Wagner: *Tristan und Isolde*	War of Italian liberation. Palmerston's second Cabinet.
1860	G. Eliot: *The Mill on the Floss*. Collins: *The Woman in White*	*Essays and Reviews*: rational attack on religious orthodoxy
1861	Dickens: *Great Expectations*. Meredith: *Evan Harrington*	US Civil War begins Death of Prince Albert Pasteur's germ theory of disease
1862	G. Eliot: *Romola*. V. Hugo: *Les Misérables*	Bismarck becomes Prussian Chancellor. Married Women's Property Act
1863	Gaskell: *Sylvia's Lovers*. Death of Thackeray. Manet: *Luncheon on the Grass*	
1864	Dickens: *Our Mutual Friend*	Geneva Convention (Red Cross)
1865	Elizabeth Gaskell dies	Russell's second Cabinet Assassination of Lincoln; end of American Civil War
1866	Gaskell: *Wives and Daughters*	Field's transatlantic cable. Derby's third Cabinet
1867		Second Reform Act
1868		Feb: Disraeli's first Cabinet Dec: Gladstone's first Cabinet
1869	Lecky: *History of European Morals*	
1870	Death of Dickens. Wagner: *Die Walküre*	Forster's Education Act Gladstone's second Cabinet Franco-Prussian War. Opening of Suez Canal
1871	G. Eliot: *Middlemarch*. Hardy: *Desperate Remedies*	Paris Commune

Year	Age	Life
1872	14	Enters Owens College, Manchester, and becomes one of its brightest students
1874	16	
1875	18	Winter: meets Marianne Helen Harrison (b. 1858), a young prostitute, known as Nell, whom he attempts to redeem
1876		31 May: caught stealing money in the cloakroom of Owens College. 6 June: convicted and sentenced to one month's imprisonment. 7 June: expelled from College. Sept: sails to America
1877	19	Teaches for two months. Mar–Jul: writes and publishes short stories in Chicago. Sept–Oct: returns to England. Settles in London, where Nell joins him
1878	20	Completes his first novel, which a publisher rejects. Gives private lessons until 1888
1879	21	Jan: meets Eduard Bertz, a German social refugee. Apr: receives a small inheritance. 27 Oct: marries Nell
1880	22	Publishes *Workers in the Dawn* at his own expense, shortly after his brother William's death. Through Frederic Harrison, the Positivist leader, is in touch with Turgenev, who asks him to write articles for *Vestnik Evropy* (*The Messenger of Europe*)
1881	23	
1882	24	Separates from Nell. Completes 'Mrs Grundy's Enemies' (never published)
1883	25	
1884	26	Jun: *The Unclassed*
1885	27	
1886	28	Mar: *Demos*. First journey to France. Jun: *Isabel Clarendon*. Meets Thomas Hardy
1887	29	Apr: *Thyrza*. 23 Jun: meets Edward Clodd
1888	30–1	28 Feb: Nell dies. Sept–March 1889: stays in Paris, then Italy. Nov: *A Life's Morning*

Year	Literary Context	Historical Events
1872	W. W. Reade: *The Martyrdom of Man*. Butler: *Erewhon*	Secret Ballot Act
1874	Hardy: *Far from the Madding Crowd*. Monet: *Impression: Sunrise*	Disraeli's second Cabinet
1875		
1876	G. Eliot: *Daniel Deronda*. Meredith: *Beauchamp's Career*	Victoria becomes Empress of India Invention of telephone. Bulgarian atrocities
1877	Ibsen: *Pillars of Society*. Zola: *L'Assommoir*	Russo-Turkish War, 1877–8 Edison's phonograph
1878	Hardy: *The Return of the Native*	Earliest use of electricity Congress of Berlin
1879	Ibsen: *A Doll's House*. James: *Daisy Miller*	London telephone exchange
1880	Disraeli: *Endymion*. Death of G. Eliot and Flaubert. Dvorak: *First Symphony*	Gladstone's second Cabinet Invention of bicycle Transvaal declares itself a republic
1881	Ibsen: *Ghosts*. James: *The Portrait of a Lady*	
1882	Besant: *All Sorts and Conditions of Men*. Gilbert and Sullivan: *Iolanthe*	Phoenix Park murders F. Forest invents the combustion engine Married Women's Property Act
1883	Nietzsche: *Thus Spake Zarathustra*	
1884	Moore: *A Mummer's Wife*. Burne-Jones: *King Cophetua and the Beggar Maid*	Third Reform Act Fabian Society founded
1885	Meredith: *Diana of the Crossways*. Gilbert and Sullivan: *The Mikado*	Fall of Khartoum Salisbury's first Cabinet
1886	James: *The Bostonians*. Stevenson: *Dr Jekyll and Mr Hyde*	Liberals split on Home Rule Feb: Gladstone's third Cabinet Aug: Salisbury's second Cabinet
1887	Hardy: *The Woodlanders*. Strindberg: *The Father*	Victoria's Golden Jubilee
1888	Kipling: *Plain Tales from the Hills*. Mrs H. Ward: *Robert Elsmere*	

Year	Age	Life
1889	31–2	Apr: *The Nether World*. Nov–Feb 1890: travels to Greece and southern Italy
1890	32	Mar: *The Emancipated*. September: meets Edith Underwood
1891	33–4	Jan: moves to Exeter. 25 Feb: marries Edith Underwood. Apr: *New Grub Street*. 10 Dec: Walter Gissing (son) born
1892	34	Feb: *Denzil Quarrier*. May: *Born in Exile*
1893	35	Apr: *The Odd Women*. Jun: moves to Brixton. Begins to write short stories regularly for periodicals
1894	36–7	Sept: moves to Epsom. Dec: *In the Year of Jubilee*
1895	37–8	Apr: *Eve's Ransom*. Dec: *Sleeping Fires*
1896	38	Jan: *The Paying Guest*. 20 Jan: Alfred Gissing (son) born. 20 Nov: meets H. G. Wells
1897	39	Feb: leaves Edith. Apr: *The Whirlpool*. Sept: separates from Edith and travels to Italy. Nov: *Human Odds and Ends*
1898	40	Feb: *Charles Dickens: A Critical Study*. April–May: returns from Italy via Germany and settles in Dorking. 6 Jul: meets Gabrielle Fleury. Aug: *The Town Traveller*
1899	41	May–June: joins Gabrielle in France. They settle in Paris. Oct: *The Crown of Life*
1900	42	Apr: spends the whole month in England. Late May–mid-Nov: stays at St Honoré-les-Bains
1901	43–4	May: *Our Friend the Charlatan*. Jun: *By the Ionian Sea*. Late Jun: enters the East Anglian Sanatorium, Nayland, Suffolk, where he remains until early Aug. Dec: moves from Paris to Arcachon
1902	44	Jan: Edith sent to an asylum. Jul: moves to Ciboure, near St Jean-de-Luz
1903	45–6	Jan: *The Private Papers of Henry Ryecroft*. Jul: moves to Ispoure, near St Jean-Pied-de-Port. 28 Dec: dies at 1.15 p.m. 31 Dec: is buried at St Jean-de-Luz
1904		Sept: *Veranilda*
1905		Jun: *Will Warburton*
1906		May: *The House of Cobwebs*

Year	Literary Context	Historical Events
1889	Stevenson: *The Master of Ballantrae*. Gilbert and Sullivan: *The Gondoliers*	London Dock Strike
1890	'Mark Rutherford': *Miriam's Schooling*	Parnell scandal First 'tube' railway
1891	Hardy: *Tess of the D'Urbervilles*. Morris: *News from Nowhere*. Tchaikovsky: *Nutcracker*	Free elementary education
1892	Kipling: *Barrack-Room Ballads*	Gladstone's fourth Cabinet Panama scandal
1893	Crackenthorpe: *Wreckage*	Foundation of Independent Labour Party
1894	Moore: *Esther Waters*. Hardy: *Life's Little Ironies*	Collapse of the three-decker novel Lord Rosebery's Cabinet
1895	Hardy: *Jude the Obscure*. Conrad: *Almayer's Folly*	Trial of Oscar Wilde. Jameson raid Salisbury's third Cabinet
1896	Wells: *The Wheels of Chance*	
1897	Conrad: *The Nigger of the Narcissus*. Tate Gallery opens	Victoria's Diamond Jubilee First aeroplane flight
1898	Shaw: *Plays Pleasant and Unpleasant*. Rodin: *The Kiss*	Fashoda incident Discovery of radium
1899	Wilde: *The Importance of Being Earnest*. Elgar: *Enigma Variations*	Boer War starts
1900	Conrad: *Lord Jim*. Wells: *Love and Mr Lewisham*	Relief of Ladysmith and Mafeking
1901	Kipling: *Kim*	Death of Victoria Accession of Edward VII
1902	James: *The Wings of the Dove*. Conrad: *Youth*. Butler: *The Way of All Flesh*	End of Boer War Balfour's Cabinet
1903	Shaw: *Man and Superman*. Conrad: *Typhoon*	
1904	Conrad: *Nostromo*	Anglo-French Agreement Rutherford: discovery of radioactivity
1905	James: *The Golden Bowl*	Campbell-Bannerman Prime Minister
1906	Galsworthy: *The Man of Property*	Sweeping Liberal victory at General Election

INTRODUCTION

Despite the considerable interest in George Gissing's life and works in the last four decades – witness the steady flow of biographies and critical studies, of new editions and translations of his novels – his short stories have received very little attention from publishers and critics. Ten years ago Robert L. Selig deplored the situation, observing that in his opinion 'the author's short stories deserve to rank among the best of the late Victorian era'.[1] Whereas *The Odd Women*, his feminist novel, has been dramatized successfully and is available in three paperback editions, and *New Grub Street*, an acknowledged masterpiece, can be obtained from as many publishers, none of his four main collections of short stories is currently in print.

Not that admirers have been wanting. A.H. Bullen, Gissing's own publisher in the 1890s, was one of them. In his *Guide to the Best Fiction* (1913), Ernest A. Baker declared *Human Odds and Ends* and *The House of Cobwebs* to be 'very significant and representative fragments' which show 'how admirably Gissing could work on a small scale'.[2] Christopher Morley admired the latter collection so much that he claimed to read it 'again and again at midnight with unfailing delight'.[3] In the novelist's lifetime his stories found favour with editors as far away as New Zealand, and they have enjoyed an extraordinary vogue in Japan since the interwar years.

It was as a short-story writer that Gissing made his debut in literature, some three years before he turned to the novels on which his reputation mainly rests. The *Chicago Tribune* published his first story, 'The Sins of the Fathers', on 10 March 1877, and it was sheer material need that forced it and another twenty into existence. Young Gissing, after being expelled from Owens College, Manchester, had been packed off to America, where it was hoped that he would live down the disgrace that his quixotic attempt to redeem a young prostitute had brought upon him. The stories that appeared in the Chicago press, for the most part anonymously or pseudonymously, constitute the first group of the 115 or so which he wrote for newspapers and magazines until his death in 1903. Inevitably, as he was then nineteen, they are prentice work, more valuable as an index to their author's tormented state of mind than a promise of the indelible mark he was to leave on late Victorian fiction. None of these stories remains uncollected – they may be read in *The Sins of the Fathers* (1924), *Brownie* (1931) and *Lost Stories from America* (1992) – but some additional tales which are known to have been written in Chicago may still emerge from oblivion if a file of the paper containing them ever turns up.[4] Exile, robbery, imprisonment loom large among other gloomy themes in those early tales that testify to Gissing's vain struggle to forget and be forgiven his youthful folly. He now and again ventured into thematic areas unconnected with his own predicament, for example the eerie in 'Brownie', or indulged in the jocularity that we associate with him as a schoolboy. A fictionalized backdrop of the few months he spent on the fringe of the Middle West literary bohemia is supplied by the well-known chapter of *New Grub Street* in which Whelpdale gives a spirited account of his American adventures, but Gissing is not known to have ever looked back light-heartedly upon his first encounter with starvation, a lost soul wandering on foreign ground.

The second group of his short stories extends over the years 1878–84 – from the time of his first, unpublished novel to the publication of *The Unclassed*, his second novel, admired by both George Meredith and Thomas Hardy. Only two of the nine stories in this group appeared in Gissing's lifetime, 'Phoebe' and 'Letty Coe', which George Bentley somewhat reluctantly accepted for his popular magazine *Temple Bar*, feeling guilty after purchasing the rights of, but failing to publish, Gissing's naturalistic novel 'Mrs Grundy's Enemies'. Try though he did to vary his subjects and force his naturally pessimistic self to take a more sanguine view of life, Gissing only met with rejections. Neither a gleefully farcical story like 'My First Rehearsal' nor the brisk social comedy of 'My Clerical Rival' was deemed acceptable. The tales of this second group were eventually collected in four volumes of varying length, *An Heiress on Condition* (1923),

Stories and Sketches (1938), *Essays and Fiction* (1970) and *My First Rehearsal and My Clerical Rival* (1970).

   Masochistically Gissing convinced himself in the early 1880s that he had no gift for short fiction, and for seven years – the seven years Bentley took to publish 'Letty Coe' – he concentrated on novels, making his name known among the intelligentsia and those well-educated young men without money, not uncommon in his fiction, who read his books in the copies they borrowed from libraries. No one familiar with his fine series of working-class novels, culminating with *The Nether World* in 1889, was aware of his failure to dispose of equally characteristic but shorter stories. It was the accident of a visit to Glastonbury, the ancient Somerset country town celebrated for its tor and its Arthurian associations, that tempted him to try his hand again at short stories likely to win the approval of magazine editors. The acceptance of 'A Victim of Circumstances' in 1892 proved decisive. He now realized that if he returned to London, after a couple of years in Devon, he could capitalize on his reputation as author of *New Grub Street* and *Born in Exile*, his two strongest books to date. An unexpected request for a story (which was to be 'Lou and Liz') 'like the Bank Holiday scene in *[The] Nether World*'⁵ confirmed his feelings. It came from Clement King Shorter, who edited the *Illustrated London News*, the *English Illustrated Magazine* and the *Sketch*, and was bent on improving the cultural tastes of the new readers turned out by the board schools.

   Gissing was prepared to meet the challenge if it entailed no lowering of his artistic standards. With the assistance of William Morris Colles, his literary agent, he embarked on a second career. From then on many of his short stories were commissioned by editors, chiefly C.K. Shorter and Jerome K. Jerome. The demand reached such a peak in 1895 that he thought he must learn to refuse (and occasionally did refuse) the least tempting offers for the simple reason that he might, in those days of small novels and ever shorter short stories, never be able to write any more full-length novels like his last two three-deckers, *The Odd Women* (1893) and *In the Year of Jubilee* (1894). Yet he readily admitted that this kind of work, to which he soon became accustomed, even though it required an altogether new technique, suited him well. Furthermore, shorter pieces were less incompatible with a disorderly domestic life than protracted novels. If the dedicated artist that he remained to the end mildly regretted having entered upon the commercial path, his 'Account of Books' attests that the sharp rise of his income in the mid-1890s is largely explained by the fees he received from editors. His short stories were read by a much wider audience than his novels. His work was printed in a variety of publications – popular newspapers and *avant-garde* quarterlies, as well as illustrated monthlies and stylish publications that were content to capture an audience of connoisseurs. The very last piece he completed, a few days before the outbreak of his fatal illness, and just when the ending of his historical novel *Veranilda* was at long last in sight, was a short story urgently requested by the *Daily Mail*, 'Topham's Chance'. With a few exceptions, all those which make up the third and by far the most important group were distributed haphazardly among four volumes, three of them posthumous, which have delighted generations of book-collectors, *Human Odds and Ends* (1898), *The House of Cobwebs* (1906), *A Victim of Circumstances* (1927) and *Stories and Sketches* (1938).

Ranging chronologically from 1893 to 1903, the present selection first glances back to the days when Gissing made of working-class life his main study. Indeed the link between 'Lou and Liz' and *The Nether World* was specified by the editor of the *English Illustrated Magazine*, although the gloomy atmosphere of the bank holiday merry-making in the novel has lifted. The narrator is amused rather than distressed by the rowdiness of the scenes in which Lou, Liz and the latest common-law wife of Bishop/Willox join to unravel his precise status in the eye of the law. Respectability is a relative value, and the cawing rooks of Rosherville Gardens that witness this episode look wiser than the squabbling holiday-makers they watch. The story also links up with *In the Year of Jubilee* (1894), in which Gissing was to review official celebrations and popular rejoicings with the soberness of hindsight. Its natural complement is 'One Way of Happiness', whose setting he had studied at close quarters in the 1880s when he would occasionally seek rest from metropolitan turmoil in Eastbourne. Bank holiday crowds had long since robbed him of the political and social illusions he had entertained in his radical days. Thus his alter ego Osmond Waymark in *The Unclassed* admits that his former 'zeal on behalf of the suffering masses was nothing more nor less than disguised zeal on behalf of [his] own starved passions'.[6] By the next decade he had come to consider the people more serenely, however, as appears in 'The Day of Silence', an admirably conducted tragedy of lowly life ; his compassion could still be as easily roused as his condemnation of human folly. Yet another facet of his response to the *mores* of the people is revealed in the only story reprinted here that is notable for its suspense, 'Fleet-Footed Hester', with its apparently happy ending. The discreet classical allusion to Atalanta in the title echoes the classical metaphors and similes in his proletarian novels.

The love interest which prevails in 'Lou and Liz' and 'Fleet-Footed Hester' has ramifications in a few of the other tales. Mr Whiston, the 'scrupulous father', may look startlingly different from John Rayner, Hester's future husband, but Gissing points with ironic subtlety to their one common characteristic – an undue concern for conventions which, in both stories, nearly has the better of emotional impulses. Class-consciousness, traced again in a different milieu, crops up obtrusively in 'An Inspiration', and is just as much of an obstacle to emotional fulfilment ; it is also present in the only other story which concludes, rather wryly, with the prospect of a union, 'The Fate of Humphrey Snell'. The poor herb-gatherer has a personality of a kind which rarely meets with approval, and we leave him precariously happy and under sufferance largely for reasons that smack of social prejudice. A misfit he was and he remains in a world where frustrations are in proportion to the consciousness of misery fostered by education – for as Gissing, with a note of self-pity, remarked in *New Grub Street* : 'To the relatively poor (who are so much worse off than the poor absolutely) education is in most cases a mocking cruelty.'[7]

Of the quandaries that stem from the conflict between poverty and aspirations, however unclearly formulated, a few touching examples are offered. Among the male characters elderly Mr Tymperley, the shabby-genteel prototype, is driven by his pathetic discretion to feign philanthropy only to be ultimately unmasked by dire necessity. Christopherson, the gentle, obsessive book-collector, is brought to choose between a chance of his wife's survival in a rural, bookless environment and the prospect of his own withering away through lack of cultural nourishment. As for Humplebee, a victim of good fortune and a temperamental relative of Humphrey Snell, he has been too sorely tried not to see himself smilingly as a born loser. But the female characters have greater resilience, for — with the exception of the anti-phrastically named Miss Jewell — the narrator of 'A Daughter of the Lodge' encourages us to view May Rockett as a profitably chastened young woman with a modest future, while Miss Rodney's triumphant nature sublimates all her difficulties into a capacity for creating 'a sort of order in [her] little corner of the world'. So that everything is not for the worst in the worst of all possible worlds. By the side of the bleak tragedy related in 'The Day of Silence' and of the half dozen stories that end on a neutral note there are as many that allow of hope for the struggling underdogs that populate the scene. Foolishness and social oppression may well still be endemic in this late Victorian world — Gissing had a knack for spotting them — but generosity is not altogether absent from it. Above all, we are led to ponder the sanity of revolt — whether conscious and reasoned, or instinctive and bred by the humdrum working of the social organism. An urgent need for emancipation, a hankering after a larger life are perceptible throughout and, quite naturally, are felt more distinctly by women.

Yet Gissing's position was not that of a radical feminist. As Sandra Enzer has noted, 'he advocated neither militancy nor covert rebellion against traditional male supremacy'.[8] There is rich evidence in 'Their Pretty Ways', for instance, that he held trenchant opinions on a certain type of frivolous, spendthrift Victorian wife he had observed round his suburban home, but about the time he wrote this story, he had already convinced himself that hope lay in female emancipation through better education, even though this would entail a phase of sexual anarchy. He was sensitive to the effects of inadequate training on the individual, on family life and on society at large. The irrational or shallow women he introduced into his stories of the 1890s are by no means an extinct race in his two post-1900 novels of modern life, where he continued to pity the socially handicapped and emotionally starving spinster so aptly sketched in 'The Foolish Virgin'. For the boredom that time causes to descend on married life he saw no better remedy than a sound, liberal education. In retrospect, his level-headed approach to the problems of married life is more valuable from both literary and historical standpoints than the shrill pessimistic vignettes of a trendy female writer like George Egerton or even the romantic class-ridden pictures of Hardy's *Group of Noble Dames*.

The thematic affinities between the short stories and the novels, especially *The Nether World, The Odd Women, In the Year of Jubilee* and *Our Friend the Charlatan*, are striking — alongside Gissing's refusal to sensationalize or sentimentalize. The ideal, he knows, is as unreachable as a shooting star. The young man who had composed 'An Ode to Truth' at Owens College remained a truth-teller to the end of his life, as well as a demanding artist. He delighted in his craftsmanship. Irony, humour, pathos are the dominant notes; a commendable restraint can be noticed throughout. Nor is there any monotony in the studiously subdued narrative voice. Deliberately written in a minor key, with an artistic discipline only approached by his three 1895 novellas, *Eve's Ransom, Sleeping Fires* and *The Paying Guest*, his short stories are memorable for the perfect subserviency of plot to character. Above all, whether crepuscular like 'Christopherson', or matutinal like 'Fleet-Footed Hester', they have meaningful beginnings and quietly summarizing endings. No good short story can be effective without such assets.

Pierre Coustillas
University of Lille, 1993

Notes to the Introduction

1. Robert L. Selig, *George Gissing* (Boston: Twayne Publishers, 1983), p. 112.
2. London: George Routledge & Sons, 1913, p. 118.
3. *Modern Essays*, selected by Christopher Morley (New York: Brace and Company, 1921), p. 316.
4. Indeed, an entry in Gissing's *Commonplace Book*, edited by Jacob Korg (New York Public Library, 1962), shows that other early stories from his pen still have to be traced in the *National Weekly*, a grandiosely entitled but trashy paper, no number of which is known to have survived for 1877.
5. Diary entry for 30 March 1893, *London and the Life of Literature in Late Victorian England: The Diary of George Gissing, Novelist*, edited by Pierre Coustillas (Hassocks: Harvester Press, 1978), p. 300.
6. Edited by Jacob Korg (Hassocks: Harvester Press, 1976), p. 211.
7. Edited by Bernard Bergonzi (Harmondsworth: Penguin Books, 1968), p. 70.
8. Sandra Solotaroff Enzer, 'Maidens and Matrons: Gissing's Stories of Women', *Dissertation Abstracts International*, August 1978, p. 894-A.

BIBLIOGRAPHICAL NOTE

'Lou and Liz' was first published in the *English Illustrated Magazine*, August 1893, pp. 793–801, with illustrations by Dudley Hardy. It was collected in *A Victim of Circumstances* (1927). The story was begun on 17 April 1893 and completed two days later. On 30 March Gissing had received a request for a short story like the Bank Holiday scene in his novel *The Nether World* (diary) from C. K. Shorter, the editor of the *English Illustrated Magazine*. He left his Exeter home for a few days in late March and early April and went up to town, visiting Rosherville Gardens at Gravesend, where he was to set the most part of the story. Location of manuscript unknown.

'The Day of Silence' first appeared in the *National Review*, December 1893, pp. 558–67. It was reprinted in *Living Age*, 30 December 1893, and collected in *Human Odds and Ends* (1898). Gissing wrote it 19–22 August 1893. The story was sold by his literary agent, William Morris Colles, who called it 'an inimitable piece of work' (7 November, diary). In his reply Gissing confessed that the story was a favourite of his. The manuscript is in the Beinecke Library, Yale University.

'Fleet-Footed Hester' was originally published in the *Illustrated London News*, Christmas 1893, pp. 26–33, with illustrations by Dudley Hardy, and collected in *A Victim of Circumstances*. Composition lasted three days, 27–9 July 1893. Commissioned, like 'Lou and Liz', by C. K. Shorter, but in his capacity as editor of the *Illustrated London News*, the story was begun immediately after an early morning trip to London in order to explore the City and see the 5.50 newspaper train off at Waterloo Station. The title of the story varied during composition between

'Fleet-foot Hester' and 'Fleet-Footed Hester'. Location of manuscript unknown.

'In Honour Bound' was first printed in the *English Illustrated Magazine*, April 1895, pp. 79–88, with illustrations by Chris Hammond. It was reprinted in *Living Age*, 25 May 1895, and collected in *Human Odds and Ends*. Gissing wrote it 22–4 December 1893, the last of a series of six short stories commissioned by G.K. Shorter. Location of manuscript unknown.

'Their Pretty Ways' was first published in *Lloyd's Weekly Newspaper*, 15 September 1895, p. 6, and collected in *George Gissing: Essays and Fiction* (1970). Gissing wrote the story on 4 October 1894 and posted it in the evening to William Morris Colles, who had received requests for two short stories from his pen – one from Jerome K. Jerome for the *Idler* ('Simple Simon', May 1896), the other from Thomas Catling. Because Gissing kept no accurate record of publication for 'Their Pretty Ways', the story was apparently lost for years. Gissing made a number of minor alterations on the typescript and at proof stage, changing 'Their Pretty Way' to 'Their Pretty Ways'. The version printed here is that which appeared in *Lloyd's*. The manuscript is in the Lilly Library, Indiana University, but the typescript version is apparently lost.

'The Fate of Humphrey Snell' was originally published in the *English Illustrated Magazine*, October 1895, pp. 3–10, with illustrations by Fred Barnard, and collected in *A Victim of Circumstances*. First entitled 'The Vision of Humphrey Snell' on 11 October 1894, it was completed after a week's intermittent work in partial fulfilment of a request from C. K. Shorter for three short stories. Gissing was gratified to see the 'excellent frontispiece' by Barnard and congratulated him on it. Location of manuscript unknown.

'An Inspiration' first appeared in the *English Illustrated Magazine*, December 1895, pp. 268–75, with illustrations by Fred Barnard, and was collected in *Human Odds and Ends*. It was written 1–3 November 1894. Like the preceding story it was commissioned by C. K. Shorter on 17 September 1894. Location of manuscript unknown.

'The Foolish Virgin' was printed in the *Yellow Book* for January 1896, pp. 11–38, and was collected in *A Victim of Circumstances* as well as in a number of *Yellow Book* anthologies. The story, commissioned by John Lane for his prestigious quarterly, was begun on 30 October and completed on 5 November. Location of manuscript unknown.

'One Way of Happiness' was originally published in the *English Illustrated Magazine*, June 1898, pp. 225–32, with illustrations by Gunning King, and collected in *A Victim of Circumstances*. Gissing wrote it 19–24 March 1896, in partial fulfilment of a promise made to C. K. Shorter in October 1895 to let him have three more short stories for his magazine. Location of manuscript unknown.

'A Freak of Nature' first appeared, in a bowdlerized version entitled 'Mr Brogden, City Clerk', in *Harmsworth Magazine*, February 1899, pp. 39–43, with illustrations by F. S. Wilson. Written 7–8 March 1895, the manuscript was sent immediately to William Morris Colles, who offered it to Beckles Willson, the editor of the projected Harmsworth monthly publication tentatively entitled *The London Magazine*. Gissing was paid promptly and, after a fruitless enquiry in September 1895, apparently forgot about the story, a typed copy of which was produced for Willson. When Harmsworth's monthly was at last launched in 1898, the new editor, Cecil Harmsworth, retitled it and cancelled substantial portions of the latter part of the narrative, ignoring the author altogether. After discovering the manuscript in the Kenneth Spencer Library, University of Kansas, the present writer published the story in its original form with an introduction in *A Freak of Nature or Mr Brogden, City Clerk* (Tragara Press, 1990). It is the version reprinted here.

'A Poor Gentleman' was first published in the *Pall Mall Magazine*, October 1899, pp. 177–87, with illustrations by F. H. Townsend, and collected in *The House of Cobwebs* (1906). The story was commissioned by the *Pall Mall Magazine* through James B. Pinker, Gissing's new literary agent, in November 1898. In his reply to Pinker, dated 30 November, Gissing promised to write a story of no less than 5,000 words when he had completed his novel *The Crown of Life*, and was able to do so 19 January – 4 February 1899. Location of manuscript unknown.

'Humplebee' originally appeared in the *Anglo-Saxon Review*, March 1900, pp. 7–18, and was collected in *The House of Cobwebs*. It was composed in mid-August 1899 in Switzerland, and placed by James B. Pinker in late January or early February 1900. Location of manuscript unknown.

'The Scrupulous Father' was first published in the New York *Truth*, December 1900, pp. 302–12, and reprinted in the *Cornhill Magazine*, February 1901. It was collected in *The House of Cobwebs*. Writing 5–10 June 1899, Gissing then sent his manuscript to James B. Pinker on 16 June, requesting him to try and sell it on both sides of the Atlantic. Luck assisted author and agent when, in February 1900, the editor of *Truth* asked Gissing to contribute to her magazine. Location of manuscript unknown.

'A Daughter of the Lodge' first appeared in the *Illustrated London News*, 17 August 1901, pp. 235–7, with illustrations by F. H. Townsend, and was collected in *The House of Cobwebs*. The actual writing took three days, 10–12 May 1900. This story was entitled 'The Rash Miss Tomalin' when Gissing sent it to James B. Pinker on the day of its completion. It was intended for the *Universal Magazine*, whose editor wanted a contribution from Gissing. On 29 September, as no news of publication had yet reached him, he wrote to Pinker, observing that the heroine's name would have to be changed, it having been used recently in his novel *Our Friend the Charlatan* for a character originally called Miss Kickweed. Ultimately, the *Universal* having ceased publication, the heroine's name was changed to Rockett. In May 1900 Gissing suggested to his agent that he might try to place 'A Daughter of the Lodge' with an American magazine, but there is no sign that the attempt was successful. Location of manuscript unknown.

'Christopherson' was originally published in the *Illustrated London News*, 20 September 1902, pp. 419–20, and collected in *The House of Cobwebs*. It was written in late February or early March 1902, completed by 6 March. A corrected typescript, now apparently lost, was returned by Gissing to James B. Pinker on 20 April, but the story was not disposed of until the summer. On 4 September he sent back to his agent a corrected proof, which he cut as the editor wished. Location of manuscript unknown.

'Miss Rodney's Leisure' first appeared in *T.P.'s Weekly*, Christmas 1903, pp. 1–5, and was collected in *The House of Cobwebs*. Gissing reported to Gabrielle Fleury from Arcachon on 6 March 1902 that he was writing this story, and he posted a corrected typescript of it to James B. Pinker on 19 April. He learnt on 9 October that the story was accepted. The leading character was inspired by a young woman – a fellow patient – with whom he became acquainted while under treatment at the East Anglian Sanatorium, Nayland, Suffolk, in the summer of 1901. Miss Rachel Evelyn White (1867–1943) was Lecturer in Classics at Newnham College, Cambridge – 'a very vigorous type, who will serve me one of these days. Humorous, erudite, smokes cigarettes – the friend of everybody one can mention'. [Letter to H. G. Wells, 25 June 1901, in *George Gissing and H. G. Wells*, ed. Royal A. Gettmann, London, 1961, p. 181. See Pierre Coustillas, 'Two Letters to a Fellow Invalid', *Gissing Newsletter*, November 1968, pp. 9–12, and James Haydock, 'Miss White a Source for Miss Rodney?', *Gissing Newsletter*, January 1969, pp. 7–11.] Location of manuscript unknown.

LOU AND LIZ

The great bell at Westminster was striking nine.

Sunlight streamed into the garret window, bathing a robust, comely girl, who stood half-dressed before a looking-glass and combed out her tawny hair. In bed lay another girl, seemingly asleep, and on the pillow beside her perched a baby boy of eighteen months, munching at a biscuit.

'Now then, Liz!' cried the girl who was dressing, as she took a hairpin from between her lips. 'Goin' to loy there all d'y? Wike up, do!' She began to sing in a strident voice, ' "J'yful, j'yful will that meetin' be, – when from sin our 'arts are pure and free."* Jacky, give mummy one on the 'ead. Liz, git up! 'Ow d'yer suppose we're goin' to git to London Bridge by eleven?' Again she sang: ' "You can 'ear 'em soigh, an' wish to doy, an' see them wink the other eye, – at the man that browk the benk at Monty Car – lo!"* Say, Liz, did you 'ear Mr Tunks come 'ome last night? Same old capers; fallin' down all the time he was goin' up— Wike up, I tell yer!'

Liz raised her head with a drowsy laugh.

'Stop yer jaw, Lou! What a chatter-mag you are!'

A rejoinder came in the shape of a pincushion, aimed sharply at the remonstrant. It missed Liz, and hit her child full in the face. The room rang with an infantile shriek of alarm and pain. In a moment Liz had jumped out of bed, had hurled back the missile with all her force at Lou, and in the same breath was trying to soothe the baby and to revile her friend. This time the pincushion knocked over the small looking-glass, which shattered upon the floor. For five minutes there was tumult – screaming, railing, scuffling; the storm of recrimination only ended when Lou discovered in her pocket – amid keys and coppers and dirt – a broken stick of chocolate, which she presented as peace-offering to Jacky.

''Ow'm oi to do my 'air?' asked Liz, as she stood in her night-gown and ruefully regarded the broken glass.

'Oi'll do it for you,' Lou replied, giving her own locks a final slap.

'An' now we've got to buy Mrs 'Uggins another glawss!'

'Don't fret yer gizzard about that. I can get a measly little thing like this for sixpence. What's the odds s'long as y're 'eppy!* – "The man that browk the benk at Monty Car – lo!"'

'I dreamt it was rinin',' said Liz, as she drew the blind aside, and looked with satisfaction at the cloudless sky. 'Somethin' loike weather, this, for a Benk 'oliday. Say, Lou, you might give Jacky's face a wipe whilst I'm dressin".'

Discord between the two (it happened about once every half-hour when they were long together) always ended in a request for some favour, urged by the younger girl and cheerfully granted by her companion.

They were nothing akin to each other, but had shared this garret for about a year. Liz worked at home, making quill toothpicks, and earning perhaps a shilling a day; Lou was a book folder, and her wages averaged eleven shillings a week; their money, on a system of pure communism, went to discharge their joint expenses. Alone, Liz could barely have supported herself and her child; as it was, they made ends meet, and somehow managed to save a few shillings against a Bank-holiday.

Lou wore a gold wedding ring, and round her neck, hidden by her dress, hung a little wash-leather bag which contained a marriage certificate. It was her firm belief that on the preser-vation of these 'lines' depended the validity of her marriage. Three years had elapsed since, at the birth of a child, her husband saw fit to disappear; the baby died, and Lou went back to her old calling.

Liz wore a brass wedding ring, and had no marriage certificate to show. She was known as 'Mrs Purkiss,' but was entitled only to 'Miss.' As to Jacky's father, his disappearance was as com-plete as that of Lou's husband.

In their way they had suffered not a little, these two girls. But the worst seemed to be over. With admirable philosophy they lived for the day, for the hour. Liz was never burdened by a

sense of gratitude to her friend; to Lou it never occurred that
she herself was practising a singular generosity. They laughed
and sang, squabbled and abused each other, drank beer when
they could afford it, tea when they couldn't, starved themselves
occasionally to have an evening at the Canterbury or at the
Surrey* (the baby, drugged if he were troublesome, sleeping
now on his mother's lap, now on Lou's), and on a Bank-holiday
mingled with the noisiest crowd they could discover.

To-day they were going to Rosherville.*

Jacky wasn't very firm on his feet; considering the child's diet
and his bringing up in general the wonder was that he trod this
earth at all. He weighed very little, and the girls were so much
in the habit of carrying him about wherever they went, that they
rarely grumbled at the burden.

It would have pleased them best to go down to Rosherville by
steamer, but that cost a little more than the journey by train,
and every penny had to be considered. Their tickets, both
together, came to three-and-sixpence; eighteen-pence apiece
remained for refreshment at the Gardens. Dinner they took with
them – bread and slices of tinned beef; for tea, of course, there
would be 'srimps and creases.' Before and after, those great
mugs of ale which add so to the romance of Rosherville.

What an Easter! Day after day, scarce a shadow across the
sun. And so deliciously warm that one had been able to save no
end of money from firing. On Good Friday they had lain in bed
until dinner-time – 'doin' a good sleep,' as Lou said; the rest of
the day they spent in patching up their hats and jackets. On
Saturday, it was work again. Sunday, another good sleep, and
an afternoon ramble just to show that they had some Easter
finery, like other people. And now had come the real holiday.
They were in wild spirits. On setting out, they ran, and leapt,
and shouted. Lou, as the elder and stronger, took Jacky up on
her shoulder, and rushed off with him, singing the great song of
the day, about the man who, etc.; – the man's feat, by the by,
signifying to Lou nothing more nor less than a successful
burglary, perpetrated at some bank in a remote country where
the police were probably deficient.

It rejoiced them to get far away from the familiar region, and
to indulge their gaiety amid a revelling throng. They had few
acquaintances they cared about. With the people who knew her
story Liz could not be altogether at ease; the morality of her

world pressed anything but heavily upon her, yet she was occasionally aware of slights and covert judgments. Lou, again, though strong in the possession of her amulet, was too proud to invite people's pity in the character of a deserted wife, and her sharp temper had before now subjected her to insults. 'No wonder y'r 'usband run aw'y an' left yer,' was a natural retort from any girl whom Lou's tongue had wounded. Except, of course, from Liz; who, however angry, could not permit herself that kind of weapon. This necessity of mutual forbearance made a strong link in their friendship. And the fact that Lou considered herself her friend's superior, morally and even socially, doubtless helped to keep them satisfied with each other.

Everything was fresh to them; even familiar posters acquired a new interest seen in the light of holiday. A wrestling lion and a boxing kangaroo, large and vivid on hoardings by the railway, excited them to enthusiasm. 'Look at it landin' 'im one in the jawr!' cried Liz, pointing out the kangaroo to Jacky, with educational fervour. And the monkey-faced little fellow seemed to understand, for he leapt on his mother's knee, and smote his sticky little hands together.

The grounds at Rosherville were a pretty show in this warm spring weather. Fresh verdure had begun to clothe the deciduous trees, and the thick-clustered evergreens made semblance of summer against a bright blue sky. From the cliffs of quarried chalk hung thick ivy; up and down and all about wound the maze of pathways, here through a wooded dell, there opening upon a lawn of smooth turf, or a terrace set with garden shrubs and flowers. Liz had never been here before; Lou not for several years. First of all they must needs scamper from place to place, uttering many an 'Ow!' of rapture. The bear-pit entertained them for long; so did the aviaries. But at length the sight of many people thronging about a liquor bar reminded them that it was nigh dinner-time. They found a spot within the area of beery odour, and sat down to eat and drink.

Jacky was encouraged to sip from the ale-mug; his wry face moved the girls to shrieks of laughter, interspersed with 'Pore dear! What a shime!' and the like exclamations. In her bag Liz had brought a bottle of milk; it was churned into acidity, but the infant, after his alcoholic thwartings, imbibed it eagerly. Bits of meat, too, he consumed, and lumps of heavy cake; and, by way of dessert, coloured sweets in considerable mass. The girls would have deemed it downright cruelty to refuse him any eatable thing that he appeared to relish.

Two or three hours went by. The pair encountered no acquaintance and gave only brief encouragement to exhilarated youths who sought to make themselves agreeable. Rough banter, even a dance, they were quite ready for, but Lou's amulet and Liz's child forbade them to pursue flirtation beyond a certain discreet limit. When Jacky began to wail from weariness, indigestion, and need of sleep, they came to a rest within sight of the dancing platform, where a band made merry challenge to crowding couples; Liz, very red and perspiring, sat down with the baby on her lap, and tried to hush him into slumber.

A sudden exclamation from her companion caused her to look up. Lou was standing with eyes eagerly fixed on the round platform, her lips open, her face and attitude expressing some intense excitement.

'Liz!' she ejaculated. 'If there ain't *my 'usband*!'

In an instant the other girl was on her feet. The child, left to roll upon the grass, made an unregarded outcry.

'Where is 'e? Which is 'im, Lou?'

'That fellow in the brown pot 'at dauncin' with the girl in a blue dress. Down't yer see?'

'I see!' – Liz quivered with sympathetic agitation, and balanced forward on her toes. 'What are you goin' to do?' she added, in quick undertones.

The other made no reply. She took a step forward, looking like some animal about to spring. Her fists were clenched at her sides.

'Are you quite sure?' asked Liz, following her.

'Sure? D'you think I'm a bloomin' fool?' was the fierce answer.

'Down't make a row, Lou!' Liz entreated, looking anxiously at the people around them. 'You always said you didn't care nothin' about 'im.'

'I ain' goin' to mike no row. Shut up, and go an' look after the child.'

She approached the dancers. It was several minutes before the man on whom her eye was fixed came out from amid the stamping, whirling, and shrieking throng; his companion in the blue dress followed him. Lou went steadily up to him, met his look, and stood expectant, without a word.

He wore the holiday attire of a rowdy mechanic; had a draggled flower in his coat, and in his mouth the extinct stump of a cigar. He was slim, and vulgarly good-looking; his age appeared to be not more than thirty. The flush on his cheeks told of much refreshment, but as yet he had not exceeded a fair Bank-holiday allowance. Only for a moment did the sight of Lou disconcert him; then he gave a broad grin, and spoke as if no encounter could have pleased him more.

'Thet *you*? Why, you've growed out of knowledge.' He turned to the blue dress, and said, 'Old friend o' mine, Sal. See y' again before long.' Then, going close up to Lou, 'You've growed that 'endsome, I shouldn't 'ardly 'ave known you. Let's have a bit of a stroll.'

He caught her by the arm, and drew her towards a part where there were fewer people.

'That's 'ow you tike it, is it?' said the girl in a thick voice, her eyes still fixed upon him.

'I always said you was good-looking, Lou, but to see you now fair tikes my breath away, s'elp me gawd! What 'a' you been doin' with yourself all this time?'

'What 'a' *you* been doin', that's what *oi* want to know?'

The delinquent affected compunction. He lowered his voice.

'I couldn't 'elp myself, Lou. Times was 'ard. I went off after a job an' I meant to send you somethin' to go on with, s'elp me I did. But it was all I could do to get grub for myself an' a fourpenny lodgin'. I've thought about yer d'y and night, an' 'oped as you wouldn't come to no 'arm. I knew your uncle 'ud look after you—'

Lou at length found her tongue, and for several minutes used it vigorously, but without creating a public disturbance. The man – she knew him by the name of Bishop – cast uneasy glances round about; he saw that his late partner remained at a distance, but that a girl with a child in her arms was following them.

'Who's that?' he asked at length, indicating Liz.

'It's a friend as I live with,' Lou answered, sharply. 'She knows all about *you* – no fear.'

'An' d' you mean to say as you 'aven't found another 'usband all this time?'

The reply was a fresh outburst of wrath. When it had spent itself, Bishop said in a wheedling voice:

'I behaved bad to you, Lou; there's no two ways about that. But I didn't mean it, an' I've always wanted to make things right again between us. 'Ev a drink, old girl. I've got something to say to you – but 'ev a drink first, and your pal, too. Let's be friendly together. There ain't no use in making a bother. I cawn't 'elp lookin' at yer, Lou. You're that 'endsome, I wouldn't 'a' believed it.'

In spite of everything, this flattery was so pleasant to Lou's ear that she had much ado not to smile. Old feelings began to revive as she regarded the man's features, and his insinuating talk tempted her to forget and forgive. Such an event as this was in harmony with the joyous nature of the day. Abruptly she turned round and beckoned Liz to approach.

'Moy oye, what a bebby!' exclaimed Bishop, as if in admiration. 'You don't mean to say as that's yours, Lou?'

'If you want to know,' Lou answered, sullenly, 'mine didn't live only three weeks.'

'Pore little thing! I'm sorry for that. But it's all for the best, I dessay. Come an' let's 'ev a drink. Let's be friendly. What's the odds, s'long as it all comes right in the finish.'

Liz, meanwhile, was suffering much mental disturbance. From the first moment, she had dreaded lest Lou and her husband should be reconciled: that would mean a parting with her friend, and how was she to get on alone? Obliged to disguise her uneasiness, she kept in the rear of Bishop, and glanced now at him, now at Lou. It became more obvious that the deserted wife was exulting in what had happened; her eyes had a strange gleam; she tossed her head, and walked with much swinging of the arms.

Bishop persuaded them to sit down on the grass whilst he fetched liquor from the neighbouring bar.

'Are you goin' back to him?' Liz asked of her friend in a hurried whisper.

'Me?' was the scornful reply. 'What d'you tike me for?'

'But you're goin' on as if you meant to.'

'He's my 'usband, I s'powse, ain't he?' Lou rejoined with a fierce glare.

'I wouldn't drink with a 'usband as had served me like 'e has.'

'Shut up!'

'Shut up yerself!'

The quarrel was interrupted by Bishop's return with two

foaming pint mugs. They were speedily emptied and replenished.
Liz quaffed the beverage without delight, for she saw that her
objection only had the effect of making Lou stubborn in
disregard of wrongs. One of the many concertina players who
rambled about from group to group suddenly shrilled out a
summons to dancing.

''Ev a turn, old girl ?' said Bishop, who, as he sat, had already
stolen an arm about Lou's waist.

After due show of snappy reluctance, the girl consented, and
with dismay in her heart Liz saw the pair twirl away. This was
Bishop's opportunity for private speech. After again assuring
Lou of his penitence for past injury, he told her that in a day or
two he was to begin work on a job at Woolwich, a job likely to
last for some months, with good wages; he had lodgings out
there already. His proposal was that Lou should return with
him this evening. They would go together, at once, to her home,
carry off her belongings, and to-morrow find themselves
comfortably established as man and wife once more. The fiery
colour in Lou's cheeks betrayed her mood of eager excitement,
the disposition to forget everything but this unhoped-for chance
of resuming her dignity of wifehood. Yet she could not, in fact,
lose sight either of the risk she ran (for Bishop would as likely
as not forsake her again when he grew tired of her), or of the
distress she would inflict upon poor Liz. The dance, the seductive
murmurs of her partner, told strongly in one direction; but
every thime she cast her eyes on Liz and Jacky, fears and
compunctions renewed their grasp upon her.

Just as breathlessness was compelling her to pause, she
became aware that her friend and the child had disappeared.
She stopped on the instant and looked in every direction;
nowhere amid the moving clusters was Liz discoverable. She
must have gone off in a sulk. Lou resented this behaviour. It
diminished her anxiety on the girl's behalf, and when Bishop
continued to urge an instant departure she sauntered slowly
away with him.

But Liz had not purposely withdrawn. Sitting disconsolate on
the grass, she happened to catch sight, at a distance, of that
young woman in blue, with whom Bishop had first of all been
seen. A thought flashed through her mind; she caught up Jacky
and darted in pursuit of the conspicuous person.

Not, however, to overtake her readily, for in front of them

was the Baronial Hall (name redolent of the old Vic.* and of the Surrey Theatre), and the blue-clad girl vanished through its portals before Liz could come up to her. Within was the high scene of Rosherville riot. A crowd filled the long room from end to end, a crowd that sang and bellowed, that swayed violently backwards and forwards, that stamped on the wooden flooring in wild fandangoes, and raised such an atmosphere of dust, that on her attempt to enter, Liz began to cough and felt her eyes smart. Jacky, terrified by the din, burst into a howl, here inaudible. But the blue dress was once more in sight, and Liz would not relinquish her purpose; she crushed onward, until an opportunity came of touching and addressing the object of her pursuit.

'Miss,' she said, speaking close to the young woman's ear, 'would you mind tellin' me somethin'?'

She of the blue robe seemed to be alone, but was stamping, like those around her, to the nearest concertina, and had a look of supreme good-humour on her blowzy countenance.

'What d'you want to know?' she shouted back.

'That gentleman as you was dancin' with out there on the platform—'

'What of 'im?'

'Is he a friend of yourn?'

''Course he is. Known him since't I was a choild.'

'But you don't know 'is wife, do you?'

''Course I do.'

'What — my friend Lou?'

The reply was a stare of astonishment.

'His wife ain't no Lou!' exclaimed the young woman. 'Her name's Marier. What d'you mean?'

Liz uttered a shriek of delight. She had hoped to discover something to Bishop's discredit, but nothing so good as this had struck her imagination.

'If you'll come along o' me,' she said, 'I'll tell you somethin' as you'd ought to know.'

Readily enough the stranger followed, and with a struggle they got into the open air. In the conversation that ensued, Liz learnt that the man of whom they spoke was not in reality named Bishop, and that he could not be legally Lou's husband. Some ten years ago he had married in his true name of Wilcox, and his wife, with four children, lived at Enfield. More than once he had left Mrs Wilcox to her own resources; but she, having a little shop, did not suffer much from her spouse's neglect.

Liz had now to rush in pursuit of her friend; the stranger, much interested by what she had heard, accompanied her. But Lou was by this time far from the spot where she had danced with her nominal husband.

'She'll have gone off with 'im!' cried Liz, in despair which was not wholly selfish. 'Where's the w'y out? If I 'edn't this baby to carry! I cawn't go no faster!'

Tears began to trickle down her cheeks, where dust had mingled muddily with perspiration. She saw before her a life of loneliness and want. The homely garret would have to be forsaken; she must shelter herself and Jacky in some miserable hole, – well if it didn't end in their going to the workhouse. Oh, why had she been so snappy with Lou! Perhaps that very last bit of quarrel had decided her friend to go off without remorse. Yet, even amid the distress, Liz experienced a brief, intermittent comfort in the reflection that, after all, Lou was not really a married woman, that the 'lines' of which she so often boasted were worthless, and her gold ring no better than one of brass.

Her companion offered to take a turn at carrying the child whilst they hurried on in search. They made for the exit, and asked if such a couple as Lou and the brown-hatted man had been seen to depart in the last few minutes; answers were vaguely negative. Back again into the gardens; hither and thither amid the folk who were enjoying themselves – drinking, dancing, love-making, shooting in the rifle gallery, watching acrobats and niggers on the lawn, and a performance in the open-air theatre. Liz seemed to herself the only unhappy creature in this assembly of thousands. Presently it occurred to the pair that one or other of them ought to have remained at the exit; they had forgotten this. Liz, utterly wearied and woe-begone, stood still and let her tears have their way.

High up on the tops of the tall elms, nesting rooks uttered their 'Caw, caw' undisturbed by the uproar of humanity in lower regions. Grave, domestic rooks, models of reason and virtue in comparison with the rampant throng they wisely ignored.

Ultimately, half an hour after the beginning of their search, Liz and the blue girl found themselves near the spot whence they had started; and there – there in the very place where they had danced to the concertina – stood Lou and Wilcox-Bishop. Liz, now again with Jacky in her arms, bounded forward.

'Lou! Dear old Lou! Thenk Gawd! Come 'ere and let me tell you somethin'.'

'Where have you been?' cried the other impatiently.

'Lookin' for *you*, everywheres. Ow, Lou! Don't 'ave nothin' to do with 'im.' She spoke in a subdued voice, not to be heard by passing strangers. 'He ain't what he calls himself! He ain't *your* 'usband!'

The man had drawn near, not without a look of misgiving, for he saw the young woman in blue regarding him ominously, and observed Liz's agitation. There followed a lively scene, brief, dramatic. Wilcox, made heedless by long impunity, and overcome by amorous temptation, had loitered about with Lou merely because she was unwilling to go away without seeing Liz; he had met no one except the blue girl who could imperil his project, and it seemed to him most unlikely that she would have an opportunity of learning what he was about before he got safely off. It was true that he had work at Woolwich, and he saw no risk in living there with Lou, whilst he kept up communication with his legitimate wife at Enfield, whose little shop was too valuable to be definitely forsaken. But the unexpected had befallen. Face to face with him were three accusing women, one of them furious, the second exultant, the third scandalised. Useless to attempt denial; evidence could now be obtained against him at any moment. He stood at bay for two minutes, then, with a burst of foul language, turned tail and fled.

Lou would have pursued him. She was beside herself with rage, jealousy, humiliation. But already a little crowd of amused observers was gathering, and followed her with whoops as she started after the escaping man. Upon these people Liz suddenly turned in wrath, asked them what business it was of theirs and so brought them to a standstill. Her voice had a restraining effect on Lou; she also stopped, turned, and glared savagely at the spectators, who fell back.

'See 'ere, Liz,' she said, 'you can do as you like; oi'm goin' 'ome.'

'So'm oi,' was the answer.

Jacky had been roaring incessantly for the last quarter of an

hour, and would continue until he fell asleep. The day was
hopelessly spoilt. Wherever they went in the Gardens they would
feel that people were pointing at them and talking about them;
the blue girl would of course make known their story. So they
moved dolefully towards the exit, exchanging not a word.

When they were out in the high road Lou paused.

'You don't think I meant to go with him, do you?' she asked
fiercely. ''Cause if you do, you're bloomin' well wrong. Think
I'd a' gone back to a feller like that?'

There followed a string of violent epithets. Liz, though
convinced that only an accident had saved her friend (and
herself), was politic enough to protest that of course she had
never feared anything so foolish; and when this assurance had
been repeated some fifty times, the injured girl began to take
comfort from it. Her wrath turned against the man once more.
She would be revenged upon him; she would go to the police-
station, and have him 'took up'; he should be sent to prison like
the bigamist they had read about in *Lloyd's* only a week or two
since.

'Where's a p'liceman?' she exclaimed, looking about her. 'He
ain't far off yet, an' I'd like to see him copped, and took off with
'andcuffs.'

The policeman was not difficult to discover, but for all that
Lou did not carry out her menace. She railed copiously but
decided that it would be better to go to the 'station' when they
got home, and make her charge with all formalities. Meanwhile
Jacky kicked, struggled, and roared in his mother's arms.

''Ere, give 'im to me,' said Lou at length, when her companion
was all but dropping in exhaustion. ''Ow can y' expect to enjoy
yerself when you 'ave to tike babbies out! We 'aven't had no
tea, nor nothin'. Come on, an' let's git 'ome.'

They missed a train at Rosherville Station, and had to walk
to Gravesend. The return journey was miserable, for very few
people were going back at this early hour, and none of the
accustomed singing in the carriage helped to restore their spirits.
Relieved from personal anxieties, Liz could now sympathise
with her friend's distress. They squabbled as a matter of course,
and the necessity of postponing talk about what had happened
until they were alone again exasperated the tempers of both.

By eight o'clock Jacky lay fast asleep in bed, and Liz was
preparing tea. Lou had not entered; she went off somewhere by

herself, promising to be back before very long. Within the house was perfect quietness; down in the street an intoxicated youth roared out a song which contested popularity with that concerning the bank-breaker of Monte Carlo – an invitation to a bride to take her marriage trip 'on a boycyle mide for two.'*

Three hours later Lou was still absent. Liz grew fearful once more. But perhaps her friend had really visited the police-station, and was detained there all this time by the gravity of her business. At half-past eleven there was an unfamiliar step on the stairs, ascending noisily. Liz threw open the door, called out, and was answered with a laugh which she recognised, though it had a strange note. Lou had not spent her evening with the police.

In the light of early morning Jacky's clamour for breakfast awakened the two girls. Having given the child some cold tea (left in the pot all night), and a hunch of bread, Liz spoke to her companion. For a while there was no answer, but presently came muffled words.

'Say, Liz, you won't let on to nobody about it?'

'Not oi! I tike my *hoath* I won't, Lou.'

A pause, then Lou's voice was again heard.

'I woke up in the night, an' thought I'd burn them marriage-lines. But I won't neither. I'll keep somethin' to show.'

'Oi should, if oi was you. You was married, all the sime.'

'But I can git married again now, if I want.'

'Course you can,' Liz replied, half-heartedly.

'All right. Let's do another sleep. What's the odds s'long 's y're 'eppy?'

And they dozed till it was time to get up and begin the week's labour.

THE DAY OF SILENCE

For a week the mid-day thermometer had marked eighty or more in the shade. Golden weather for those who could lie and watch the lazy breakers on a rocky shore, or tread the turf of deep woodland, or drink from the cold stream on some mountain side. But the by-ways of Southwark languished for a cloud upon the sun, for a cooling shower, or a breath from its old enemy, the east. The cry of fretful children sounded ceaselessly. Every window was wide open; women who had nothing to do lounged in the dusk of doorways and in arched passages, their money all gone in visits to the public-house. Ice-cream men found business at a standstill; it was Friday, and the youngsters' ha'pence had long ago come to an end. Labourers who depended upon casual employment chose to sleep through the thirsty hours rather than go in search of jobs; a crust of bread served them for a meal. They lay about in the shadowed spots, shirt and trousers their only costume, their shaggy heads in every conceivable attitude of repose.

Where the sun fell the pavement burned like an oven floor. An evil smell hung about the butchers' and the fish shops. A public-house poisoned a whole street with alcoholic fumes; from sewer-grates rose a miasma that caught the breath. People who bought butter from the little dealers had to carry it away in a saucer, covered with a piece of paper, which in a few moments turned oily dark. Rotting fruit, flung out by costermongers, offered a dire regale to little ragamuffins prowling like the cats and dogs. Babies' bottles were choked with thick-curdling milk, and sweets melted in grimy little hands.

Among the children playing in a court deep down by Southwark Bridge was one boy, of about seven years old, who looked healthier and sweeter than most of his companions. The shirt he wore had been washed a week ago, and rents in it had obeyed the needle. His mother-made braces supported a pair of trousers cut short between the knee and ankle, evidently shaped out of a man's garment. Stockings he dispensed with ; but his boots were new and strong. Though he amused himself vigorously, he seemed to keep cool ; his curly hair was not matted with perspiration, like that of the other youngsters ; the open shirt – in this time of holiday coat and waistcoat were put away to be in a good condition when school began again – showed a body not ill-nourished, and his legs were of sturdy growth. A shouting, laughing, altogether noisy little chap. When his shrill voice rang out, it gave his playmates the word of command ; he was ready, too, with his fists when occasion offered. You should have seen him standing with arms akimbo, legs apart, his round little head thrown back and the brown eyes glistening in merriment. Billy Burden, they called him. He had neither brother nor sister – a fortunate thing, as it enabled his parents to give him more of their love and their attention than would have been possible if other mouths had clamoured for sustenance. Mrs Burden was very proud of him, and all the more decent women in the court regarded Billy with affectionate admiration. True, he had to be kept in order now and then, when he lost his temper and began to punch the heads of boys several years older than himself ; but his frank, winsome face soon overcame the anger of grown-up people.

His father, Solomon Burden by name, worked pretty regularly at a wharf on the Middlesex side, and sometimes earned as much as a pound a week. Having no baby to look after, his mother got a turn of work as often as possible, chiefly at warehouse-cleaning and the like. She could trust little Billy to go to school and come home at the right time ; but holidays, when he had to spend the whole day out-of-doors, caused her some anxiety, for the child liked to be off and away on long explorations of unknown country – into Lambeth, or across the river to the great London streets, no distance tiring him. Her one fear was lest he should be run over. To-day he had promised to keep well within reach of home, and did so. At Mrs Burden's return from a job in Waterloo Road he was found fast asleep on the landing. She bent over him, and muttered words of tenderness as she wiped his dirty face with her apron.

Of course, they had only one room – an attic just large enough to hold a bed, a table, and Billy's little mattress down on the floor in a corner. Their housekeeping was of the simplest: a shelf of crockery, two saucepans, and a frying-pan supplied Mrs Burden with all she needed for the preparation of meals. Apparel was kept in a box under the bed, where also was the washing-basin. Up to a year ago they had had a chest of drawers; but the hard winter had obliged them to part with this.

When Mrs Burden unlocked and opened the door, the air within was so oppressive that she stood for a moment and drew a deep breath. The sound of the key wakened Billy, who sprang up joyfully.

'Ain't it been 'ot again, mummy!' the boy exclaimed. 'There was a 'bus-horse fell dead. Ben Wilkins seen it!'

'I a'most feel as if I could drop myself,' she answered, sinking upon the bed. 'There ain't no hair to breathe: I wish we wasn't under the roof.'

She stood up again and felt the ceiling – it was some six inches above her head.

'My gracious alive! It's fair bakin'.'

'Let me feel – let me feel!'

She lifted him in her arms, and Billy proved for himself that the plaster of the ceiling was decidedly warm. Nevertheless, sticks had to be lighted to boil the kettle. Father might come home any moment, and he liked his cup of tea.

As she worked about, the woman now and then pressed a hand to her left side, and seemed to breathe with difficulty. Sweat-drops hung thick upon her face, which was the colour of dough. On going downstairs to draw water for the kettle she took a quart jug, and after filling this she drank almost the whole of it in one long draught. It made her perspire still more freely; moisture streamed from her forehead as she returned to the upper story, and on arriving she was obliged to seat herself.

'Do you feel bad, mummy?' asked the child, who was accustomed to these failings of strength when his mother came home from a day's work.

'I do, Billy, hawful bad; but it'll go in a minute. Put the kittle on – there's a good boy.'

She was a woman of active habits, in her way a good housewife, loving moderate cleanliness and a home in order. Naturally, her clothing was coarse and begrimed; she did the coarsest and grimiest of work. Her sandy hair had thinned of late; it began to show the scalp in places. There was always a look of pain on her features, and her eyes were either very glassy or very dull. For thirty years – that is, since she was ten years old – struggle with poverty had been the law of her life, and she remained victorious; there was always a loaf in the house, always an ounce of tea; her child had never asked in vain for the food demanded by his hearty appetite. She did not drink; she kept a guard upon her tongue in the matter of base language; esteemed comely by her equals, she had no irregularity of behaviour wherewith to reproach herself. Often enough at variance with her husband, she yet loved him; and Billy she loved more.

About seven o'clock the father came home; he clumped heavily up the stairs, bent his head to pass the doorway, and uttered a good-natured growl as he saw the table ready for him.

'Well, Bill, bwoy, can you keep warm?'

'Sh' think so,' the child answered. 'Mummy's bad again with the 'eat. There ain't no air in this bloomin' 'ouse.'

'Kick a 'ole in the roof, old chap!'

'Wish I could!'

Solomon flung off his coat, and turned up the sleeves of his shirt. The basin, full of water, awaited him; he thrust his great head into it and made a slop over the floor. Thereat Mrs Burden first looked, then spoke wrathfully. As his habit was, her husband retorted, and for a few minutes they wrangled. But it was without bitterness, without vile abuse. Domestic calm as understood by the people who have a whole house to themselves is impossible in a Southwark garret; Burden and his wife were regarded by the neighbours, and rightly, as an exemplary pair; they never came to blows, never to curses, and neither of them had ever been known to make a scene in public.

Burden had a loud, deep voice; whether he spoke angrily or gently, he could be heard all over the house and out in the court. Impossible for the family to discuss anything in private. But, like all their neighbours, they accepted such a state of things as a matter of course. Everybody knew all about everybody else; the wonder was when nothing disgraceful came to listening ears.

'Say, Bill,' remarked the man, when he had at length sat quietly down to his tea, 'how would you like to go in a boat to-morrow afternoon?'

'Shouldn't I just!'

'Old Four-arf* is goin' to have a swim,' Burden explained to his wife; 'wants me to go with him; and I feel it 'ud do me good, weather like this. Bunker's promised him a boat at Blackfriars Bridge. Shall I take the kid?'

Mrs Burden looked uneasy, and answered sharply.

'What's the good o' asking when you've spoke of it before the boy?'

'Well, why shouldn't I take him? You might come along, too: only we're a-goin' to strip up beyond Chelsea.'

This was kindness, and it pacified the wife.

'I couldn't go before six,' she said.

'What's the job?'

'Orfices near St. Bride's – Mrs Robins wants 'elp; she sent her Sally over to me this mornin'. It'll be an all-day job; eighteen-pence for me.'

'Bloomin' little, too. You ain't fit for it this weather.'

'I'm all right!'

'No, you ain't. Billy just said as you'd been took bad, an' I can see it in yer eyes. Have a day at 'ome, mother.'

'Don't you go fidgetin' about me. Take Billy, if you like; but just be careful. No puttin' of him into the water.'

''Tain't likely.'

'Cawn't I bathe, dad?' asked Billy.

'Course you cawn't. We're going to swim in the middle of the river, Jem Pollock an' me – where it's hawful deep, deep enough to drownd you fifty times over.'

'The other boys go bathin',' Billy remonstrated.

'Dessay they do,' cried his mother, 'but you won't – so you know! If you want for to bathe, arst Mrs Crowther to lend you her washin'-tub, and fill it with water. That won't do you no 'arm, and I don't mind if you make a bit of a splash, s'long as you don't wet the bed through.'

After all it was a home, a nesting place of human affections – this attic in which the occupants had scarcely room to take half-a-dozen steps. Father, mother, and child, despite the severing tendency of circumstances, clung together about this poor hearth, the centre of their world. In the strength of ignorance, they were proof against envy; their imaginations had never played about the fact of social superiority, which, indeed, they but dimly understood. Burden and his wife would have been glad, now and then, of some addition to the weekly income;

beyond that they never aspired. Billy, when he had passed the prescribed grades of school, would begin to earn money : it did not much matter how : only let the means be honest. To that the parents looked forward with anticipation of pride. Billy's first wages ! It would warm their hearts to see the coins clutched in his solid little fist. For this was he born, to develop thews and earn wages.

It did not enter into their conception of domestic happiness to spend the evening at home, sitting and talking together. They had very little to say : their attachment was not vocal. Besides, the stifling heat of the garret made it impossible to rest here until the sun had long set. So, when tea was finished, Billy ran down again into the street to mingle with his shouting comrades ; Mrs Burden found a seat on the doorstep, where she dozed awhile, and then chatted with bare-armed women ; and Solomon sauntered forth for his wonted stroll 'round the 'ouses.' At ten o'clock the mother took a jug to the neighbouring beerhouse and returned with a 'pot' – that is to say, a quart – of 'four ale', which she and Solomon drank for supper. The lad was lying sound asleep on his mattress, naked but for the thin shirt which he wore day and night ; the weather made bed-clothes a superfluity.

Saturday morning showed a change of sky. There were clouds about, and a wind blew as if for rain. At half-past six Solomon was ready to start for work. Billy still slept, and the parents subdued their voices lest they should wake him.

'If it's wet,' said Mrs Burden, 'you won't go on the river – will you ?'

'Not if it's thorough wet. Leave the key with Billy, and if we go you'll find it on the top of the door.'

He set forth as usual : as he had done any day these eight years, since their marriage. Word of parting seemed unnecessary. He just glanced round the room, and with bent head passed on to the landing. His wife did not look after him ; she was cutting bread and butter for Billy. Solomon thought only of the pleasant fact that his labour that day ended at one o'clock, and that in the afternoon he would perhaps have a swim. Mrs Burden, who had suffered a broken night, looked forward with dreary doggedness to ten hours or more of scrubbing and cleaning, which would bring in eighteen-pence. And little Billy slept the sleep of healthy childhood.

By mid-day the clouds had passed, but the heat of the sun was tempered; broad light and soft western breeze made the perfection of English summer. This Saturday was one of the golden days of a year to be long remembered.

When he came home from work, Solomon found Billy awaiting him, all eagerness. They went up to the attic, and ate some dinner which Burden had brought in his pocket – two-pennyworth of fried fish and potatoes, followed by bread and cheese. A visit to the public-house, where Billy drank from his father's pewter, and they were ready to start for Blackfriars Bridge, where Solomon's friend, Jem Pollock – affectionately known by the name of his favourite liquor, 'Four-half' – had the use of a boat belonging to one Thomas Bunker, a lighterman. It was not one of the nimble skiffs in which persons of a higher class take their pleasure upon the Thames, but an ungainly old tub, propelled by heavy oars. Solomon and his friend, of course, knew that the tide would help them upwards; it wanted about an hour to flood. He was a jovial fellow, this Jem Pollock, unmarried, and less orderly in his ways of life than Sol Burden; his nickname did him no injustice, for whenever he had money he drank. A kindly temper saved him from the worst results of this bibulous habit; after a few quarts of ale he was at his best, and if he took more it merely sent him to sleep. When Solomon and Billy found him on the stairs at the south side of the bridge he had just taken his third pint since dinner, and his red, pimply face beamed with contentment.

'Come along there!' he roared from below. 'Brought that bloomin' big son of yours for ballast, Sol?'

'He can steer, can Bill.'

'He won't 'ave a chawnce. There ain't no bloomin' rudder on this old ship.'

Billy stepped into the boat, and his father followed; but their friend was not yet ready to depart. The cause of his delay appeared when a lad came running down the stairs with a big jar and a tin mug.

'You don't s'ppose I'm a-goin' without a drop o' refreshment,' Pollock remarked. 'It's water, this is; the best supplied by the Lambeth Water Company. I've took the pledge.'

This primitive facetiousness helped them merrily off. Billy sat in the stern; the men each took an oar; they were soon making good way towards Westminster.

Their progress was noisy : without noise they could not have enjoyed themselves. The men's shouts and Billy's shrill pipe were audible on either bank. Opposite the Houses of Parliament they exchanged abusive pleasantries with two fellows on a barge ; bellowing was kept up until the whole distance between Lambeth Bridge and that of Westminster taxed their lungs. At Vauxhall Jem Pollock uncorked his jar and poured out a mugful of tawny ale, vastly to the boy's delight, for Billy had persisted in declining to believe that the vessel contained mere water. All drank. Solomon refused to let Billy have more than half a mug, to the scorn of Jem Pollock, who maintained that four-ale never did anything but good to man, woman, or babe.

At Chelsea the jar was again opened. This time Pollock drank an indefinite number of mugs, and Solomon all but quarrelled with him for continuing to tempt Billy. The child had swallowed at least a pint, and began to show the effect of it : he lay back in the stern, laughing to himself, his eyes fixed on the blue sky.

A sky such as London rarely knows : of exquisite purity – a limpid sapphire, streaked about the horizon with creamy cloud-lets. All the smoke of the city was borne eastward ; the zenith shone translucent as over woodland solitudes. The torrid beams of the past week were forgotten ; a mild and soothing splendour summoned mortals to come forth into the ways of summer and be glad.

With the last impulse of the flowing tide they reached the broad water beyond Battersea Bridge, where Solomon began to prepare himself for a delicious plunge. The boat could not be left to Billy alone ; Pollock was content to wait until Burden had had the first swim. Quickly stripped, the big-limbed fellow stood where his boy had been sitting, and of a sudden leapt headlong. Billy yelled with delight at the great splash, and yelled again triumphantly when his father's head rose to the surface. Solomon was a fair swimmer, but did not pretend to great achievements ; he struck out in the upward direction and swam for about a quarter of a mile, the boat keeping along with him ; then he was glad to catch hold of the stern. Pollock began to fling off his clothes.

'My turn, old pal !' he shouted. 'Tumble in, an' let's have a feel of the coolness.'

Solomon got into the boat, and sat naked at one of the oars, Billy managing the other. Five minutes saw Jem back again : he had wallowed rather alarmingly, a result of the gallon or two of ale which freighted him. Then Burden took another plunge. When he had swum to a little distance, Pollock whispered to the boy:

'Like to have a dip, Bill?'

'Shouldn't I just! But I can't swim.'

'What's the odds? Go over the side, an' I'll 'old you by the 'ands. Orff with yer things sharp, afore yer fawther sees what we're up to.'

Billy needed no second invitation. In a minute he had his clothes off. Pollock seized him by both arms and let him down over the side of the boat. Solomon swam ahead, and, as the tide had ceased to drift the boat onwards, he was presently at some distance. With firm grip, Pollock bobbed the child up and down, the breadth of the tub allowing him to lean cautiously without risk.

Then the father turned to look, and saw what was going on. He gave a terrific shout.

'Damn your eyes, Jem! Pull him in, or I'll—'

''Old yer jaw,' roared the other, laughing. 'He's all right. Let the kid enjoy hisself – cawn't yer?'

Solomon struck out for the boat.

'He's a-comin'!' said Pollock, all but helpless with half-drunken laughter.

'Pull me in!' said the child, fearful of his father's wrath. 'Pull me up!'

And at the same moment he made an effort to jump upon the gunwale. But Jem Pollock also had bent forward, and the result of the two movements was that the man overbalanced himself. He fell plump into the water and sank, Billy with him. From Burden sounded a hoarse cry of agony. Already tired with swimming, the terrified man impeded himself instead of coming on more quickly; he splashed and struggled, and again his voice sounded in a wild shout for help.

There was a boat in sight, but far off. On the Battersea side a few people could be seen; but they had not yet become aware of what had happened. From the other bank no aid could be expected.

Pollock came to the surface and alone. He thought only of making for the boat, as the one way of saving Billy, for he had no skill in supporting another person whilst he himself swam.

But the stress of the moment was too much for him: like Burden, he lost his head, and by clutching at the boat pulled it over, so that it began to fill. A cry, a heartrending scream, from the helpless child, who had just risen, utterly distracted him; as the boat swamped, he clung madly to it; it capsized, and he hung by the keel.

Billy was being wafted down the river. Once or twice his little head appeared above the water, and his arms were flung up. The desperate father came onwards, but slowly; fear seemed to have unstrung his sinews, and he struggled like one who is himself in need of assistance. Once more his voice made itself heard; but Pollock, who was drifting with the boat, did not answer. And from the drowning child there came no sound.

A steamer was just putting in at Battersea pier – too far off to be of use. But by this time some one on the bank of the old church had seen the boat bottom upwards. An alarm was given.

Too late, save for the rescue of Jem Pollock. Burden had passed the boat, and was not far from the place where his child had gone down for the last time; with ordinary command of his strength and skill he might easily have kept afloat until help neared him; but he sank. Only his lifeless body was recovered.

And Billy – poor little chap – disappeared altogether. The seaward-rushing Thames bore him along in its muddy depths, hiding him until the third day; then his body was seen and picked up not far from the place whence he had started on his merry excursion.

This disaster happened about four of the clock. Two hours later, Mrs Burden, having done her day's work and received her pay, moved homeward.

Since noon she had been suffering greatly; whilst on her knees, scrubbing floors and staircases, she had several times felt herself in danger of fainting; the stooping posture intensified a pain from which she was seldom quite free; and the heat in this small-windowed warehouse, crowded among larger buildings in an alley off Fleet Street, was insufferably oppressive; once or twice she lay flat upon the boards, panting for breath. It was over now: she had earned the Sunday's dinner, and could return with the feeling of one who had done her duty.

On Monday she would go to Guy's Hospital and get something for that pain. Six months had passed since her last visit to the doctor, whose warnings she had heeded but little. It won't do to think too much of one's ailments. But they must give her a good large bottle of medicine this time, and she would be careful to take it at the right hours.

She came out into St. Bride's Churchyard, and was passing on towards Fleet Street when again the anguishing spasm seized upon her. She turned and looked at the seats under the wall of the church, where two or three people were resting in the shadowed quiet. It would be better to sit here for a moment. Her weak and weary limbs bore her with difficulty to the nearest bench, and she sank upon it with a sigh.

The pain lasted only a minute or two, and in the relief that followed she was glad to breathe the air of this little open space, where she could look up at the blue sky and enjoy the sense of repose. The places of business round about were still and vacant, closed till Monday morning. Only a dull sound of traffic came from the great thoroughfare, near at hand as it was. And the wonderful sky made her think of little Billy who was enjoying himself up the river. She had felt a slight uneasiness about him, now and then, for Jem Pollock was a reckless fellow at all times, and in weather like this he was sure to have been drinking freely; but Solomon would look after the boy.

They would get back about eight o'clock, most likely. Billy would be hungry; he must have a bit of something for supper — fried liver, or perhaps some stewed steak. It was time for her to be moving on.

She stood up, but the movement brought on another attack. Her body sank together, her head fell forwards.

Presently the man who was sitting on the next bench began to look at her; he smiled — another victim of the thirsty weather!

And half-an-hour passed before it was discovered that the woman sitting there in the shadow of St Bride's Church was dead.

That night Jem Pollock went to the house in Southwark where Solomon Burden and his wife and his child had lived. He could hear nothing of Mrs Burden. The key of the attic lay on the ledge above the door; no one had been seen, said the neighbours, since father and son went away together early that afternoon.

In the little home there was silence.

FLEET-FOOTED HESTER

She was born and bred in Hackney – the third child of a burly, thick-witted soldier, who had married without leave. Her mother, a thin but wiry woman, took in washing, and supported the family. At sixteen, Hester had a splendid physique : strangers imagined her a fine girl of nineteen or twenty. It was then she ceased running races with the lads in London Fields, for she was engaged to John Rayner, a foreman at the gasworks.

In spite of her petticoats – she would not wear a frock that fell much below the ankle – Hester could beat all but the champion runner of that locality; the average youth had no chance against her. Running was her delight and glory. At the short distance she made capital records, and for 'stay' she could have held her own in a public school paper-chase.

Of course John Rayner put an end to all that. It was her running, witnessed by chance when they were strangers to each other, that excited him to an uneasy interest. He made inquiries, sought out her parents, wooed, won a provisional assent ; there was an understanding, however, that she should run no more, at all events, in places of public resort. Rayner's salary came to about two hundred a year ; when he married he would take a house of his own ; his wife must conform to the rules of civilisation. Hester willingly agreed, for, though she manifested no strong attachment, large prospects decidedly appealed to her, and she rejoiced in the envious admiration of girls who could not hope for a lover with more than thirty shillings a week.

Moreover, he was a man to be proud of. It would have been a calamity had Hester plighted her troth to some whipper-snapper of a clerk or artisan, some mortal of poor blood and stinted stature. John Rayner was her male complement : a stalwart fellow, six feet or close upon it, of warm complexion, keen eye, independent bearing. Intellectually, altogether her superior, but a man of the open air, companionable, full of animal passions, little disposed to use his brains in the way of improving a very haphazard education. As a lad he had run away from home – somewhere in the North – and he throve well simply because he did not become a reprobate; for John there was no medium. For him, to fall in love meant something beyond the conception of common men. His fiery worship puzzled Hester, who as yet was by no means ripe for respondent passion.

She looked what she was, a noble savage. Her speech was the speech of Hackney, but on her lips it lost its excessive meanness, and became a fit expression of an elementary, not a degraded, mind. At school she had learnt little or nothing, yet idleness, in her case, seemed compatible with purity; an unconscious reserve kept her apart from the loose-tongued girls of the neighbourhood. She respected her body, was remarkable for cleanliness, aimed in attire at ease and decency, never at display. It was but rarely that she laughed; the sense of humour seemed quite lacking in her. But no one lived from day to day with more vigour of enjoyment. She had the appetite of a ploughboy. Notwithstanding her neglect of cheap triumphs, a vigorous ambition ruled her life. She boasted of John Rayner's four pounds a week because it seemed to her a very large income indeed; she liked the man because he seemed to her much stronger, and better-looking, and more authoritative than other men with whom she came in contact.

For half a year all went fairly well. Hester had worked at a pickle-factory, but Rayner, disapproving of this, secretly paid her mother an equivalent of the wages, that she might be kept at home. An elder sister, who had hitherto helped in the laundry, went out to work, and Hester took her place; not a very good arrangement, for the girl would not trouble herself to starch and iron skilfully; but it was only for a short time. At seventeen Hester was to be married.

Then befell a calamity. Challenged to run against a lad who boasted himself to be somewhat in the race-course, Hester could not resist the temptation. Late one evening she stole forth and ran the race – and was defeated. Soon hearing of this breach of their agreement, John Rayner came down in wrath. Had Hester been victorious in her contest, she might have bowed the head and asked pardon; mortification made her stubborn and resentful of chiding. There was a quarrel, of characteristic vigour on both sides, and for a week the two kept apart. The good offices of Hester's mother brought them together again, but John was not his old self; he had become suspicious, jealous. Presently he began to make inquiries concerning one Albert Batchelor, who seemed to be much at the house. He objected to this young man – a paper-hanger's assistant, smelling of hair-oil and of insolence. Hester wrathfully defended the acquaintance: she had known Albert Batchelor all her life: his object, if any at all, was to make love to her sister; Mr Rayner must be a little less of an autocrat, notwithstanding his place at the gasworks and his ample pay. Language of this kind brought the blood into John's face; there was a second conflict, more vigorous than the former. Hester tore the ring from her finger, and flung it to the ground – they were in Victoria Park.

'Tike it, and tike yerself off!' she exclaimed, with magnificent scorn, 'I don't want nothin' to do with a man like you.'

'I'm glad to hear it,' was the furious answer. 'It's very certain you won't do for me! Just send me back my letters, and – and anything else you've no use for.'

'I'll very soon do that! And never show your bad-tempered face again near our 'ouse.'

John turned his back and marched away. His letters and presents were returned – in a very ill-made parcel – and the rupture seemed final.

'You're a fool, that's what you are!' observed Hester's mother. 'Now you may go to the pickles ag'in, and let your sister come back to the work as she didn't ought never to have left.'

'I'll go precious quick, and glad of it!' Hester made retort.

But she ran no more races and perceptibly a change had come over her. Old friends gave place to new girls of more pretentious stamp than those Hester had formerly chosen. She dressed with corresponding increase of showiness, began to frequent the Standard Theatre whenever she had money to spare, and 'carried on' with various young men. About this time her father died, which, on the whole, was a fortunate event, for he had grown of late too fond of rum, and might soon have been a serious burden upon the household which he had never exerted himself to assist. John Rayner heard the news, and one evening managed to encounter Hester in a street near her home. He spoke kindly, gently, but the girl answered only a few cold words and went her way.

A week later he saw her on Hackney Downs with Albert Batchelor. She was laughing noisily – a thing John had never known her do.

One night Hester stayed out so late that her mother threatened chastisement if the offence were repeated. That threat brought about another crisis in the girl's life. She left home, took lodgings for herself, and henceforth held little communication with her family.

For a space of two years John Rayner spoke not a word to the girl he loved, and in the meanwhile his circumstances underwent a notable change. First of all, owing to outrageous fits of temper, he was dismissed from his place as foreman; his employers offered him work in the carpenter's shop, a notable degradation. At first John scornfully refused, and left the works altogether; but in a few days – extraordinary thing in so proud a man – he returned as though humbled; he was willing to accept the inferior employment. Again he got into trouble, this time through drink; he was reduced to the smith's shop, and bore the disgrace without murmuring. Time went on; one day John fought with a fellow workman, and behaved like a wild beast. He had the choice given him of leaving the works altogether or 'going to the heap.' To go to the heap signified to labour as a loader of coke. John accepted his debasement, went to the heap, and toiled among the roughest men, making himself as one of them. He drank, and seemed to glory in the fate that had come upon him. To all appearances he was now a sturdy blackguard, coarse of language, violent in demeanour. He terrorised his companions; with him it was a word and a blow. His comely face had lost its tint of robust health; he wore grimy rags; his home was anywhere and nowhere.

Now of all these things Hester was well aware. An old friend of hers, a girl married at sixteen and widowed at twenty, knew John Rayner, and from time to time talked with him; this Mrs Heffron assiduously reported to Hester each calamitous step in John's history.

'It's because of you,' she kept repeating. 'If you was a girl with a 'art you'd go an' make it up with the poor man.'

'Me! A likely thing!'

'He's awfully fond of you.'

'How d'you know?' asked Hester, indifferently.

''Cos he always says he don't care for you not a bit.'

This, to be sure, was evidence. Hester mused, but would not discuss the matter. She talked a good deal just now of Albert Batchelor, whose employment kept him in South London, so that she saw him very seldom.

In the summer of this year Hester was just nineteen; she and Mrs Heffron went one Sunday morning into Victoria Park, taking it in turns to push a perambulator which contained the young widow's two-year-old child. At one point of their walk they passed a man who lay asleep on the grass; Hester went by without noticing him, but Mrs Heffron, suddenly casting back a glance, exclaimed in surprise—

'Why, that's Mr Rayner!'

Her companion stopped and looked. John lay in profound slumber, head on arm. He had dressed himself decently this morning and was clean. For nearly a minute Hester gazed at him, then made a summoning motion and went on.

'A precious good job I didn't marry 'im!' she said.

'It's all your fault, Hetty,' replied the other, looking back.

'No, it ain't. He'd have come low, anyway. He ain't half a man.'

Albert Batchelor proposed marriage to Hester for the third time, but she would give him no definite reply. That she encouraged him was not to be doubted. This autumn he spent a good deal of time in her company: she allowed him to say what he liked, and constantly smiled, but a characteristic reserve appeared in her replies – when she made any. Frequently Hester spoke scarce twenty words in the course of an hour's walk. In fact, a strange silence had fallen upon her life, and she shunned ordinary companionship. Her temper was occasionally violent, but the old ardours never appeared in her; she had quite ceased to talk of her feats as a runner. In beauty, however, she had by no means fallen off; her lithe frame seemed to have reached the perfection of development, and her face had more expressiveness, consequently more charm, than when it was wont to be flushed with the fervour of physical contest. No one attacked Hester's reputation; her talk was still pure, and to all appearances she went fancy-free.

On an evening of September, Batchelor and she walked in a

quiet road not far from her lodgings. Few people passed them, but presently they were both aware that an acquaintance approached, no other than John Rayner. He wore the coarse clothes in which he worked 'at the heap.' Hester fixed her eyes upon him; he saw her, but would not look, and carelessly he went by.

'Will you let him insult me like that ?' said the girl, in a hard voice, the moment after John had passed.

'Insult you ? What did he do ?'

'Why, he looked at me as insultin' as he could – you must a'seen it. You're a nice man to walk with anyone !'

Her face was hot; she stood still, pointing after John's figure.

'It isn't the first time, neither,' she added, with breathless rapidity. 'If you let him go off like that I'll never speak to you again !'

Mr Batchelor was not exactly a combative man, though he had serviceable thews, and on occasion could face the enemy. The present affair annoyed him for he suspected that Hester had either imagined or invented the insult from Rayner; perhaps she wished to see John punished for the sake of old times. For an instant he hesitated.

'Coward !' cried the girl, with a face of bitter contempt.

That was more than Batchelor could endure.

'Hoigh !' he shouted, running after Rayner, who had reached a distance of twenty yards. 'Hoigh, you ! – jist stop, will you ?'

The other turned in astonishment.

'Are you speaking to me ?'

'Yis, I em. What d'ye mean by insultin' this young lydy ? She says you looked at her insultin' and it ain't the first time neither. You jist come along 'ere an' apologise.'

John gazed at the speaker in bewilderment, then at Hester, who had moved a few steps this way.

'She says I've insulted her ?'

'Mind who you're calling she. Why, you're at it again, a turnin' up yer nose—'

'If you say another word to me,' said John fiercely, 'I'll leave you no nose to twist. Fool !'

He turned away, but at the same moment received a smart blow on the side of the face.

'That's your game, is it ?' John remarked, again glancing

towards Hester, who was leaning slightly forward, with eager gaze. 'Look out for yourself, then !'

His coat was off, and in less than a minute Albert Batchelor measured his length on the pavement. There sounded from the spectator of the fight a short mocking laugh. Up again, not much the worse, her champion made excellent play with his fists: blood was on Rayner's cheek. Unable to plant another knock-down blow, John had still the best of it. Crash, and crash again, sounded his slogging hits. At length he damaged his opponent's front teeth and brought him to his knees.

'Had enough, you fool ?' he asked.

Three or four people had assembled, and others were rushing up. A window in the nearest house flew open; women's voices were heard. The light of a lamp, shining full on Hester, showed her watching with fierce delight.

'I wouldn't give in, if I was you,' she cried, tauntingly, to Batchelor.

Nor did he. The gathering crowd made it impossible. Another round was fought; it took perhaps, two minutes, and, in that space of time, Batchelor received so severe a thrashing that he tottered to the house steps, and sank there, helpless.

'Don't try it on again, young fellow,' was John's parting advice, as he took up his coat and hustled through the throng.

At the same moment Hester went off in the opposite direction, an exulting smile in her eyes. Albert Batchelor never again sought her society.

On reaching home, Hester lit her lamp — it revealed a scrubby little bedroom with an attic window — took off her hat and jacket, and deliberately lay down on the bed. She lay there for an hour or more, gazing at nothing, smiling, her lips moving as though she talked to herself. At eleven o'clock she rose, put on her hat, and once more left the house. She walked as far as the spot where the fight had taken place. It was very quiet here, and very gloomy. A policeman approached and she spoke to him.

'P'liceman, can you tell me 'ow fur it is from 'ere to the corner of Beck Street ?' she pointed.

'Cawn't say exactly. Five 'undred yards, dessay.'

'Will you toime me while I run it there and back ?'

The man laughed and made a joke, but in the end he consented to time her. Hester poised herself for a moment on her right foot, then sprang forward. She flew through the darkness and flew back again.

'Four minutes, two second,' said the policeman. 'Not bad, Miss !'

'Not bad ? So that's all ! Find me the girl as can do it better.'

And she ran off in high spirits.

A few days after, as she came out of the pickle factory, Mrs Heffron met her with an item of news. John Rayner had left the gasworks, and, what was more, had resolved to leave England. He was going to the Cape ; might be off in a week's time.

'What's that to me ?' said Hester, snappishly.

'If I was you I wouldn't let a man like that go abroad. Mrs Crow's 'usband went to the Cape, and they've never heard of him again to this day.'

'He may go to the devil for all I care,' rejoined Hester, with unusual violence of phrase. And she walked away without heeding her friend.

They met again before long. Mrs Heffron's child was very ill ; the mother had nursed it two days and two nights ; she was worn out, and sent for Hester. The girl made herself useful, and promised to sit up half the night whilst Mrs Heffron slept in a room which her landlady put at her disposal.

'I've 'ed a letter from Mr Rayner to-day,' said the widow, in an exhausted voice, as they sat by the child's bed.

'Oh !'

'He's goin' to-morrow. From Waterloo, first train in the morning.'

'Best thing he can do, dessay.'

Mrs Heffron took the crumpled letter out of her pocket and gazed at it.

'My God !' she exclaimed mournfully. 'If it was me, Hetty, he wouldn't go.'

Hester flashed a look at the thin face, pallid with fatigue. She said nothing ; her eyes fell in abashment.

It was seven o'clock. Hester said she would go home for an hour, then return and watch over the child while the mother slept. But instead of going home, she walked to the nearest railway-station, which was Hackney Downs, and there, at the booking office, she put a question to the clerk.

'What's the first train from Waterloo in the mornin', please ?'

'Main line ?'

'To go to the Cape.'

The clerk laughed.

'Southampton, I suppose you mean, then, or Plymouth. Five-fifty; ten minutes to six.'

With this information, she presently returned to Mrs Heffron's lodging. It was arranged between them that Hester should sit up until two o'clock; the mother would then take her place. Mrs Heffron placed a watch on the mantelpiece, that her friend might call her, if necessary, when the time came. And at eight Hester seated herself, understanding perfectly what she had to do from time to time for the little sufferer.

Till midnight the child kept moaning and tossing on its bed. A dose of medicine given at that hour seemed to be of soothing effect. By half-past twelve all was quiet. Hester found the time go very slowly, for her mind was as feverish as the body of her little patient. One o'clock was striking; another hour—

How had it happened? From complete wakefulness she had sunk into profound sleep, without warning. It was the child's voice that wakened her, reproaching her conscience. She ran to the watch, and saw with great relief that it was only half-past two. Mrs Heffron must still be sleeping, poor thing. At any other time Hester would have let her sleep on, but now she was eager to get away. Half-past two – ten minutes to six; abundant time, but she must get away.

She called the mother, and told her what hour it was. They talked for a few minutes, then, with a promise to look in again that evening, Hester left the house.

Dark, and a cold morning; happily, no rain. Hester ran home, admitted herself with a latch-key, went silently up into her bedroom, and hurriedly made a change of dress. She put on her best things; a nice black straw hat, just purchased for the winter; a warm jacket, which showed the grace of her figure; a serge skirt; round her neck a boa of feathers, cheap imitation of a fashionable adornment. Then she stole forth again. It must be about three.

Deeply absorbed in her tumultuous thoughts, she walked at a quick pace as far as the crossing of City Road and Old Street. Here she spoke to a policeman, and asked him which direction she had better take for Waterloo Station. The reply was that she couldn't do better than go straight on to the Bank, then turn westward, and so to the Strand.

Very well; would he tell her what time it was? Just upon twenty-five minutes past five.

She staggered as though he had struck her. Twenty-five minutes past five? Then Mrs Heffron's watch had stopped. She saw in a flash of miserable enlightenment the misfortune that had befallen her.

'But,' she panted, 'I must be at Waterloo by ten minutes to six.'

'You can't,' replied the policemen stolidly – 'unless you take a cab.'

She felt in her pockets. Not a penny. In changing her dress she had left her purse behind; and she remembered that it contained only a few coppers.

'How far is it?'

'A matter of three miles,' was the leisurely answer. Five-and-twenty minutes: three miles. Without a word, without a look, Hester set off at her utmost speed.

Before reaching Finsbury Square, she pulled the boa from her neck, unbuttoned her jacket, loosely knotted the boa round her waist. As she came out into the open space between the Bank and the Mansion House, a clock pointed to one minute past the half-hour. She knew that it was now a straight run to the street which led out of the Strand towards Waterloo Bridge. But she must be prudent; agitation had made her heart beat violently; her breath came in painful pants; a 'stitch' in the side, and it would be all over with her.

So along the Poultry, along Cheapside, she ran with self-restraint, yet quickly, her hands clutched at her sides. Clanging hoofs upon the asphalt suggested to her that she might get a lift, but it was only a parcels-post van, the driver perched high above his flaring lanterns; it soon outstripped her. On she sped between the tall, silent houses, the closed shops. Only one or two pedestrians saw her, and they turned in curiosity as she bounded by.

At the crossing from Cheapside into St. Paul's Churchyard a policeman, caped and with bull's-eye at his belt, put himself sharply in her way.

'What's up? Where are you going?'

Hester would have flown past, but a heavy hand arrested her. The constable insisted on explanations, and she sobbed them out all the time trying to tear herself away.

'Waterloo – the first train – ten minutes to six – someone goin' away—'

The bull's eye searched her face – bloodless, perspiring – and pried about her body.

'Let me go, Sir! Oh, let me go!'

She had lost two or three minutes, but was free again. Like a spirit of the wind, the wind itself blowing fiercely along with her from the north-east – she swept round the great Cathedral, and saw before her the descending lights of Ludgate Hill. How grateful she was for the downward slope! Her breath, much easier just when the policeman stopped her, had again become troubled with the heart-throbs of fear. At Ludgate Circus there came out from Blackfriars a market-cart, which turned westward, going to Covent Garden.

'Will you give me a lift?' she called out to the man who drove it.

Imprudent, perhaps; she might run quicker; but Fleet Street looked like a mountain before her. The man pulled up in a dawdling way, and began to gossip. Hester leapt to a seat beside him, and urged him on.

There was sudden revelation of busy life. She knew nothing of the newspaper trade; it astonished her to see buildings aflare with electric light; carts drawn up in a long row, side by side, along the pavement; trucks laden with huge bales; men labouring as if minutes meant life or death, as they did to her; for she felt that if she missed the train, if John Rayner were whirled away from her into the unknown, there would be nothing left to live for.

'Can't you go quicker?' she said feverishly.

The man asked questions; he was a chatterbox. Presently a big clock before her, that of the Law Courts, pointed, like the hand of fate, to twenty minutes before the hour. Oh! She could run quicker now that she had her breath again. Without a word she sprang down, fell violently on her hands and knees, was up and off. Moisture upon her hands – blood, the street-lamp showed. But the injury gave no pain.

The cart kept up with her; she would have burst the sinews of her heart rather than let it pass.

St. Clement Danes – the Strand. Here men were washing the road, drenching it with floods of water from a hose. Another great place of business, with bales flung about, men furiously at work, carts waiting or clattering away. She passed it like an arrow, and on, and on.

Somerset House — Wellington Street — the lights of Waterloo Bridge.

Again a policeman looked keenly at her, stepped forward. She shrieked at him, 'The train! The train!' and he did not pursue. From the river a fierce wind smote upon her, caught her breath. Had she looked eastward she would have seen the dome of St. Paul's black against a red rift in the sky. To-day the sun rose at a few minutes past six; dawn was breaking.

Many workmen were crossing the bridge, and carts rattled in both directions. Her breast seemed bound with iron; her throat was parched; her temples throbbed and anguished. Quicker — but she could not, she could not! Men were staring after her, and some shouted. She saw the station now; she was under the bridge. A railway servant, hurrying on before her, turned as she overtook him.

'The train — which way?' she gasped.

'Five-fifty? All right; you'll do it, my girl.'

He showed the approach to the main line and Hester sped on. Up the sharp incline she raced with a mail-van. She saw the sparks struck out by the horses' hoofs. Behind came a newspaper cart, with deafening uproar.

The clock — the clock right before her! It was at a minute past the train time. Five minutes fast had she known it. On, in terror and agony! The outer platform was heaped with packages of newspapers, piles of them thrown back to await the slow train. A crowd of porters unloaded the vehicles, and rushed about with trucks. There was the sound of a jangling bell.

A long train, so long that she could not see the engine, waited with doors agape. No hurrying passengers; no confusion; trucks being briskly emptied into the vans, that was all. She was in time, but her eyes dazzled, and her limbs failed.

Then someone touched her. She turned. It was John Rayner. He had a rough new overcoat, a travelling cap, in his hand only a stout stick, and he looked at her with wide eyes of astonishment.

'What are you doing here?'

'I've come — I've run all the way—'

Her gasped words were barely intelligible.

'You came to see me off?'

Hester caught him by the hand in which he held his stick.

'Don't go ! – I want you ! – I'll marry you !—'

'Ho, ho ! Then you must go with me. I've done with this country.'

He drew his hand away, but kept his eyes fixed on hers.

'Go ? To the Cape ?'

'There's about one minute to get your ticket. I've got little enough money, but enough to pay your passage and leave us a pound or two when we get out there. Make your choice; a minute – less than a minute.'

She tried to speak, but had no voice. John darted away from her to the booking-office, and returned with her ticket.

'Come along; my traps are in here.'

He seized her by the arm and drew her along. She could not mount the step of the carriage. He lifted her in; placed her on the seat.

'But I haven't got no clothes – nothing !'

'I'll buy you some. We shall have two or three hours at Southampton before the ship sails. I say, how bad you look ! Hetty !'

An official came to examine the tickets; he glanced with curiosity at the couple, then locked them in together. Again a bell rang.

'Hetty !'

She was all but fainting. John put his arms about her, kissed her forehead, her cheeks, her lips.

'I've run all the way—'

Insensibly, the train began to move. Hester did not know that she had started until they were rushing past Vauxhall.

And behind them the red rift of the eastern sky broadened into day.

IN HONOUR BOUND

At the top of a dim-windowed house near Gray's Inn Road, in two rooms of his own furnishing, lived a silent, solitary man. He was not old (six-and-thirty at most), and the gentle melancholy of his countenance suggested no quarrel with the world, but rather a placid absorption in congenial studies. His name was Filmer; he had occupied this lodging for seven or eight years; only at long intervals did a letter reach him, and the sole person who visited his retreat was Mrs Mayhew, the charwoman. Mrs Mayhew came at ten o'clock in the morning, and busied herself about the rooms for an hour or so. Sometimes the lodger remained at home, sitting at his big table heaped with books, and exchanging a friendly word with his attendant; sometimes he had gone out before her arrival, and in that case he would have been found at the British Museum. Filmer abjured the society of men for that of words; he was a philological explorer, tracking slowly and patiently the capricious river of human speech. He published nothing, but saw the approaching possibility of a great work, which should do honour to his name.

Proud amid poverty, and shrinking with a nervous sensitiveness from the commerce of mankind, he often passed weeks at a time without addressing a familiar word to any mortal save Mrs Mayhew. He had made friends with his charwoman, though not till the experience of years taught him to regard her with entire confidence and no little respect. To her he even spoke of his studies, half soliloquising, indeed, but feeling it not impossible that she might gather some general conception of what he meant. In turn, Mrs Mayhew confided to him some details of her own history, which threw light upon the fact that she neither looked nor spoke like an ordinary charwoman. She was a meagre but trim-bodied little person of about the same age as her employer, clean, neat, and brisk, her face sharply outlined, with large good-humoured eyes, and a round mouth. A widow, she said, for ten years and more; childless; pretty much alone in the world, though she had relatives not badly off. Shamefaced hints made known to Filmer that she blamed only herself for her poor condition, and one day she confessed to him that her weakness had been drink. When first he engaged her services she was struggling painfully out of the mire, battling with old temptations, facing toil and hunger. 'And now, sir,' she said, with her modest, childish laugh, 'I feel almost a respectable woman; I do, indeed!' Whereat Filmer smiled pensively and nodded.

No life could be less eventful than his. He enjoyed an income of seventy pounds, and looked not for increase. Of his costume he took no thought, his diet was the simplest conceivable. He wanted no holidays. Leisure to work in his own way, blessed independence – this sufficed him.

On a morning of December (the year was 1869) Mrs Mayhew came to the house as usual, went upstairs and tapped at Filmer's door. On entering she was surprised to see a fireless grate, and on the table no trace of breakfast. Filmer stood by the window; she bade him good-morning, and looked about the room in surprise.

'I'm going out,' said the student, in a voice unlike his own. 'I didn't trouble to light the fire.'

She observed his face.

'But won't you have breakfast, sir? I'll get some in a minute.'

'No, thank you. I shall get some – somewhere—'

He went into the bedroom, was absent a few minutes, and returned with his overcoat.

'I wanted to speak to you, sir,' said Mrs Mayhew, diffidently. 'But if you are in a hurry—'

'No, no. Certainly not. I have plenty of time.'

'I am very sorry to tell you, sir, that, after next week, I sha'n't be able to come. But,' she hastened to add, 'I can recommend some one who'll do the work just as well.'

Filmer listened without appearance of concern; he seemed to have a difficulty in fixing his thoughts on the matter.

'I am going to take a little shop,' pursued the other, 'a little general shop. It's part of the house where I've been living. The woman that's had it hasn't done well : but it was her own fault ; she didn't attend to business, and she – but there's no need to trouble you with such things, sir. Some one advised me to see what I could do in that way, and I thought it over. The landlord will let me have the shop, and a room behind it, and another room upstairs, for twenty-eight pounds a year, if I pay a quarter in advance. That's seven pounds, you see, sir ; and I ought to have about twenty pounds altogether to start with. I've got a little more than ten, and I know some one who'll lend me another ten, I think.' She spoke quickly, a glow of excitement in her cheeks. 'And I feel sure I can make the business pay. I've seen a good deal of it, from living in the house. There's lots of people round about who would deal with me, and of course I could begin with a small stock, and—'

Her breath failed ; she broke off with a pant and a laugh. Filmer, after standing for a moment as if in uncertainty, said that he was very glad to hear all this, and that he would talk with her about it on the morrow. At present he must go out – on business – special and disagreeable business. But he would talk to-morrow. And so, without further remark, he went his way.

The next morning Mrs Mayhew saw that her employer was still in a most unusual frame of mind. He had a fire, but was sitting by it in gloomy idleness. To her 'Good-morning' he merely nodded, and only when she had finished putting the bedroom to rights did he show a disposition to speak.

'Well, Mrs Mayhew,' he said at length, 'I also have news to tell. I have lost all my money, and have nothing to live upon.'

Her large eyes gazed at him with astonishment and compassion.

'Oh, Mr Filmer ! What a dreadful thing !'

'Bad ; there's no disguising it.' He struggled to speak without dolefulness ; his limbs moved nervously, and he stared away from his companion. 'No hope, now, of writing my book. All over with me. I must earn my living – I don't know how. It's twelve years since I ever thought of such a thing ; I felt safe for my whole life. All gone at a blow ; you can read about it in the newspaper.'

'But – but you can't surely have lost everything, sir ?'

'I have a few pounds. About thirty pounds, I think. What's

the use of that ? I don't want very much, but' – he tried to jest –
'I can't live on ten shillings a year.'

'But with all your learning, Mr Filmer—'

'Yes, I must find something. Go and teach in a school, or
something of the kind. But I'm afraid you can't understand what
it means to me.'

He became silent. Mrs Mayhew looked up and down, moved
uneasily, played with the corners of her apron, and at last found
resolution to speak.

'Mr Filmer' – her eyes were very bright and eager – 'you
couldn't live in one room, I'm afraid, sir ?'

'One room ?' He glanced vacantly at her. 'Why not ? Of
course I could. I spend nearly all my time at the Museum.
But—'

'I hardly like to say it, sir, but there's something – if you
thought – I told you I was going to have a room behind the
shop, and one upstairs. I meant to let the one upstairs.'

He interrupted, rather coldly.

'Oh, I would take it at once if I had the least prospect of being
able to live. But what is the use of settling down anywhere with
thirty pounds ? To write my book I need at least two years, and
a quiet mind—'

'But I was going to say something else, sir, if you'll excuse the
liberty. I told you I shall have to borrow some money, and –
and I'm not quite sure after all that I can get it. Will *you* lend it
me, sir ?' This came out with a jerk, on an impulse of great
daring. 'If you would lend me ten pounds, I could afford to let
you have the room, and – and to supply you with meals, and in
that way pay it back. I'm quite sure I could.' She grew excited
again. 'If I miss getting the shop, somebody else will step in, and
make money out of it. I *know* I could very soon make two or
three pounds a week out of that business !'

She stopped suddenly, awed by the listener's face. Filmer, for
the first time since her knowledge of him, looked coldly distant,
even offended.

'I beg your pardon, sir. I oughtn't to have said such a thing.'

He stood up.

'It was a kind thought, Mrs Mayhew; but – I really don't
know—' His face was changing. 'I should very much like to let
you have the money. A few days ago I would gladly have done
so. But—'

His tongue faltered. He looked at the woman, and saw how her countenance had fallen.

'Ten pounds,' he said abruptly, 'couldn't last – for my support – more than a few weeks.'

'Not by itself, sir,' replied the other, eagerly; 'but money grows so when it's put into trade. I do believe it would bring in a pound a week. Or, at all events, I'm quite sure it would bring enough—'

She glanced, involuntarily, at the breakfast table, which seldom showed anything but bread and butter.

'In that case,' said Filmer, laughing, 'I should be a partner in the business.'

Mrs Mayhew smiled, and made no answer.

That day they could not arrive at a decision; but after nightfall Filmer walked along the street in which he knew Mrs Mayhew lived, and looked for the shop. That which answered to her description was a miserable little hole, where seemingly business was still being carried on; the glimmer of one gas-jet rather suggested than revealed objects in the window – a loaf, some candles, a bundle of firewood, and so on. He hurried past, and got into another street as quickly as possible.

Later, he was prowling in the same locality, and again he went past the shop. This time he observed it more deliberately. After all, the place itself was not so squalid as it had seemed; by daylight it might look tolerable. And the street could not be called a slum. Other considerations apart he could contemplate having his abode here; for he knew nobody, and never had to fear a visit. Besides the little chandler's there were only two shops; no public-house, and hardly any traffic of a noisy kind.

In his great need, his horror of going forth among strangers (for of course his lodgings were now too expensive to be kept a day longer than he could help), Filmer compromised with himself. By lending Mrs Mayhew ten pounds he might justly accept from her a lodging and the plainest sustenance for, say, ten weeks, and in that time he would of necessity have taken some steps towards earning a livelihood. Some of his books and furniture he must sell, thus adding to the petty reserve which stood between him and starvation. If it would really be helping the good woman, as well as benefiting himself, common sense bade him disregard the fastidiousness which at first had been shocked by such a proposal. 'Beggars cannot be choosers,' said the old adage; he must swallow his pride.

Waking at the dead hour of night, and facing once more the whole terrible significance of what had befallen him, not easily grasped in daytime, he resolved to meet the charwoman next morning in a humble and grateful spirit. His immediate trouble thus overcome, he could again sleep.

And so it came about that, in some few days, Filmer found himself a tenant of the front room above the chandler's shop. As he still had the familiar furniture about him, he suffered less uneasiness – his removal once over – than might have been anticipated. True, he moaned the loss of beloved volumes; but, on the other hand, his purse had gained by it. As soon as possible he repaired to the Museum, and there, in the seat he had occupied for years, and with books open before him, he tried to think calmly.

Mrs Mayhew, meanwhile, had entered exultantly into possession of her business premises; the little shop was stocked much better than for a long time, and customers followed each other throughout the day. In his utter ignorance of such transactions, the philologist accepted what she had at first told him as a sufficient explanation of the worthy woman's establishment in shop-keeping. To a practical eye, it would have seemed not a little mysterious that some twenty pounds had sufficed for all the preparations; but Filmer merely glanced with satisfaction at the shop front as he came and went, and listened trustfully when Mrs Mayhew informed him that the first week's profits enabled her to purchase some new fittings, as well as provide for all current expenditure.

Under these circumstances, it was not wonderful that the student experienced a diminution of personal anxiety. Saying to himself every day that he must take some step, he yet took none save that literal step which brought him daily to the Museum. A fortnight, and he had actually resumed work; three weeks, and he was busy with the initial chapter of his great book; a month, and he scarcely troubled himself to remember that his income had vanished. For Mrs Mayhew did not let a day pass without assuring him that his ten pounds – his share in the partnership – produced more than enough to represent the cost of his board and lodging. He lived better than in the old days, had an excellent supper on coming home from the Museum, a warm breakfast before setting out. And these things caused him no astonishment. The literary recluse sees no limit to the potentialities of 'trade'.

At length he remembered that ten weeks had gone by, and on a Sunday morning he summoned his partner to a conference. The quondam charwoman looked a very presentable person as she entered in her Sunday gown. Though she still did a good deal of rough work, her hands were becoming softer and more shapely. In shop and house she had the assistance of a young girl, the daughter of the people who occupied the upper rooms, and it was this girl – Amanda Wilkes by name, and known to her friends as 'Manda – who generally waited upon Filmer.

'Mrs Mayhew,' he began gravely, 'I begin to feel that I have no right to continue living in this way. You have long since paid me back the small sum I lent you—'

'Oh, but I have explained to you, sir,' broke in the other, who bated nothing of her accustomed respect, 'that money is always making more – indeed it is. It makes enough for you to live upon, as long – oh, as long as you like.'

The philologist drew a silent breath, and stared at the floor.

'Now *don't* trouble yourself, sir !' begged Mrs Mayhew, 'please don't ! If you can be content to live here – until—'

'I am more than content so far as personal comfort goes. But – well, let me explain to you. At last, I have really made a beginning with my book. If my misfortune hadn't happened I might have put it off for years ; so, in one way, perhaps that loss was a good thing. I am working very hard—'

'Oh, I *know* you are, Mr Filmer. I can't think how you do with so little sleep, sir. I'm sure I wonder your health doesn't break down.'

'No, no ; I do well enough : I'm used to it. But the point is that I may be a year or two on this book – a year or two, and how can I possibly go on presuming upon your great kindness to me—'

Mrs Mayhew laughed, and for the hundredth time put before him the commercial view of the matter. Once again he suffered himself to be reassured, though with much nervous twitching of head and limbs ; and after this he seldom recurred to his scruple.

Two years went by, and in the early months of the third Filmer's treatise lay finished. As he sat one evening by his fireside, smoking a delicious pipe, he flattered himself that he had made a solid contribution to the science of Comparative Philology. He was thirty-eight years old; young enough still to enjoy any honour or reward the learned world might choose to offer him. What he now had to do was to discover a publisher who would think this book worth the expense of printing. Long ago he had made up his mind that, if profit there were, Mrs Mayhew must share in it. Though his ten pounds had kept him alive all this time, yet clearly it would not have done so but for Mrs Mayhew's skill and labour; he felt himself vastly indebted to her, and earnestly hoped that he might be able to show his gratitude in some substantial form.

Fortune favoured him. His manuscript came into the hands of a generous scholar, a man after his own heart, who not only recommended it to the publisher in terms of enthusiasm, but expressed an earnest desire to make the acquaintance of the author. Filmer, no longer ashamed before his fellows, went forth from the hermitage above the chandler's shop, and was seen of men. He still had money enough to provide himself with decent clothing, and on a certain day his appearance so astonished Mrs Mayhew that she exclaimed tremulously:

'Are you going, Mr Filmer? Are you going to leave us?'

'I can't say,' was his nervous answer. 'I don't know yet whether I shall make any money by my book.'

He told her how things were tending.

'Oh,' she answered, 'then I'm sure you will soon get back to your proper position. After all, sir, you know, you oughtn't to be living in this poor way. You are a learned gentleman.'

Her voice was agitated, and her thoughts seemed to wander. The philologist examined her for a moment, but she turned away with a hurried excuse that she was wanted down stairs.

That day Filmer brooded.

In another month it was known that his book would be published; whether he profited thereby must depend upon its success. In the meantime, one or two fragments of the work were to appear in the *Journal of Comparative Philology*; moreover, the author himself was to read a paper before an erudite society. Overcoming false delicacy, he had made known his position (without detail) to the philological friend who took so much interest in him, and before long a practical suggestion was made, which, if it could be carried out, would assure him at all events a modest livelihood.

Amid all this promise of prosperity, Filmer was beset by graver trouble than he had known since that disastrous day, now two years and a half ago. He could no longer doubt that the prospect of his departure affected Mrs Mayhew very painfully. She kept out of his way, and when meeting was inevitable spoke the fewest possible words. More, he had once, on entering his room unexpectedly, surprised her there in a tearful condition; yes, unmistakably weeping; and she hurried out of his sight.

What could it mean? Her business throve; all appeared well with her. Could the mere thought of losing his companionship cause her such acute distress? If so—

He took long walks, musing anxiously over the situation. At home he shrank into himself, moved without sound, tried, if such a thing were possible, to dwell in the house and yet not be there. He stayed out late at night, fearing to meet Mrs Mayhew as he entered. Ludicrous as it sounded to a man who had long since forgotten the softer dreams of youth, Mrs Mayhew might perchance have conceived an attachment for him. They had now known each other for many years, and long ago the simple-minded woman used to talk with him in a way that betrayed kindly feeling. She, it must be remembered, did not strictly belong to the class in which he found her; she was the daughter of a man of business, had gone to school, had been married to a solicitor's clerk. Probably her life contained a darker incident than anything she had disclosed; perhaps she had left her husband, or been repudiated by him. But a strong character ultimately saved her; she was now beyond reproach. And if he were about to inflict a great sorrow upon her, his own suffering would be scarcely less severe.

As he crept softly into the house one night, he came face to face with a tall man whom he remembered to have seen here on several former occasions; decently dressed, like a clerk or shopman, forty years old or so, and not ill-looking. Filmer, with a glance at him, gave good-evening, and, to his surprise, the stranger made no reply; nay, it seemed to him that he was regarded with a distinctly unamiable stare. This troubled him for the moment, sensitive as he was, but he concluded that the ill-conditioned fellow was a friend of the family upstairs, and soon forgot the occurrence.

A day or two later, as the girl 'Manda served his breakfast, she looked at him oddly, and seemed desirous of saying something. This young person was now about seventeen, and rather given to friskiness, though Mrs Mayhew called her an excellent girl, and treated her like a sister.

'If you please, Mr Filmer,' she began, in an unusually diffident tone.

'Yes?'

'Is it true that you're going to leave us, sir?'

She smirked a little, and altogether behaved strangely.

'Who told you I was going to?' asked Filmer.

'Oh! – Mrs Mayhew said as it was likely, sir.'

Again she dropped her eyes, and fidgeted. The philologist, much disturbed, spoke on an impulse.

'Yes,' he said, 'I am going – very soon. I may have to leave any day.'

'Oh!' was the reply, and to his ears it sounded like an expression of relief. But why 'Manda should be glad of his departure he could not imagine.

However, his resolve was taken. He had no right to remain here. Prospects or no prospects, he would engage a room in quite a different part of the town, and make his few pounds last as long as possible.

And on this resolve he had the strength to act. Dreadful to him in anticipation, the parting with Mrs Mayhew came about in the simplest and easiest way. When he had made known his purpose – with nervous solemnity which tried to mask as genial friendliness – the listener kept a brief silence. Then she asked, in a low voice, whether he was quite sure that he had means enough to live upon. Oh yes; he felt no uneasiness, things were shaping themselves satisfactorily.

'Of course, Mrs Mayhew, we are not saying good-bye.' He laughed, as if in mockery of the idea. 'We shall see each other – from time to time – often! Such old friends—'

Her dubious look and incomplete phrase of assent – her eyes cast down – troubled him profoundly. But the dreaded interview was over. In a few days he removed his furniture. Happily the leave-taking was not in private; 'Manda and her mother both shared in it; ye. poor Mrs Mayhew's eyes had a sorrowful dimness, and her attempted gaiety weighed upon his spirits.

He lived now in the South-west of London, and refrained even from visits to the British Museum. The breaking-up of his life-long habits, the idleness into which he had fallen, encouraged a morbid activity of conscience; under gray autumnal skies he walked about the roads and the parks, by the riverside, and sometimes beyond the limits of town, but there was no escape from a remorseful memory. When two or three weeks had passed, his unrest began to be complicated with fears of destitution. But, of a sudden, the half promise that had been made to him was fulfilled: the erudite society offered him a post which, in his modest computation, represented all that a man could desire of worldly prosperity. He could now establish himself beneath some reputable roof, repurchase his books, look forward to a life of congenial duty and intellectual devotion. But—

His wandering steps brought him to the Chelsea Embankment, where he leaned upon the parapet, and gazed at the sullen river.

To whom – to whom did he owe all this? Who was it that had saved him at that black time when he thought of death as his only friend? Who had toiled for him, cared for him, whilst he wrote his book? Now at length he was able to evince gratitude otherwise than in mere words, and like a dastard he slunk away. He had deserted the woman who loved him.

And why? She was not his equal; yet certainly not so far his inferior that, even in the sight of the world, he need be ashamed of her. The merest cowardice, the plainest selfishness, withheld him from returning to Mrs Mayhew and making her that offer which he was in honour bound to make.

Yes, in honour bound. Thus far had his delicate sensibilities, his philosophical magnanimity, impelled the lonely scholar. Love of woman he knew not, but a generous warmth of heart enabled him to contemplate the wooing and wedding of his benefactress without repugnance. In a sense it would be loss of liberty; but might he not find compensation in domestic comfort, in the tender care that would be lavished upon him? But the higher view – a duty discharged, a heart solaced—

The next day was Sunday. In the morning there fell heavy rain: after noon the clouds swept eastward, and rays of sunlight glistened on the wet streets. Filmer had sat totally unoccupied. He made a pretence of eating the dinner that was brought to him, and then, having attired himself as though he had not a minute to lose, left home. Travelling by omnibus, he reached the neighbourhood hitherto so carefully shunned; he walked rapidly to the familiar street, and, with heart throbbing painfully, he stood before the little chandler's shop, which of course was closed.

A knock at the house-door. It was answered by 'Manda, who stared and smiled, and seemed neither glad nor sorry to see him, but somehow in perturbation.

'Is Mrs Mayhew in?' whispered, rather than spoke, the philologist.

'No, sir. She went out not long ago – with Mr Marshall. And she won't be back just yet – p'r'aps not till supper.'

'With – with Mr Marshall?'

'Yes, sir,' 'Manda grinned. 'They're going to be married next Saturday, sir.'

Filmer straightened himself and stood like a soldier at attention.

'To be married? – Mrs Mayhew?'

The girl laughed, nodded, seemed greatly amused.

'I should like to come in, and – and speak to you for a moment.'

'Oh yes, sir,' she smirked. 'There's nobody in. Would you mind coming into the shop?'

He followed. The well-remembered odour of Mrs Mayhew's merchandise enveloped him about, and helped still further to confuse his thoughts in a medley of past and present. Over the shop window hung a dirty yellow blind, through which the sunshine struggled dimly. Filmer hesitated for a moment.

'Who is Mr Marshall, 'Manda?' he was able to ask at length.

'Don't you know, sir?' She stood before him in a perky attitude, her fingers interlaced. 'You've seen him. A tall man – dark-looking—'

'Ah! Yes, I remember. I have seen him. How long has Mrs Mayhew known him?'

'Oh, a long, long time. He lent her a lot of money when she started the shop. They'd have been married before, only Mr Marshall's wife was alive – in a 'sylum.'

'In an asylum?'

'Brought on by drink, they say. There's all sorts of tales about her.'

The philologist eased himself by moving a few paces. He

looked from the pile of firewood bundles before the counter to a row of canisters on the topmost shelf.

'I'm glad to hear this,' at length fell from his lips. 'Just say I called; and that I – I'll call again some day.'

'Manda's odd expression arrested his eyes. He turned away, however, and stepped out into the passage, where little if any daylight penetrated. Behind him, 'Manda spoke.

'I don't think I'd come again, sir.'

'Why not?'

He tried to see her face, but she kept in shadow.

'Mr Marshall mightn't like it, sir. Nor Mrs Mayhew – Mrs Marshall as *will* be.'

'Not like it?'

'You won't say anything, if I tell you?' said the girl, in a low and hurried yet laughing tone. 'It made a little trouble – because you was here. Mr Marshall thought – ' a giggle filled the lacuna. 'And Mrs Mayhew didn't like to say anything to you. She's that kind to everybody—'

Filmer stretched his hand to the door, fumbled at the latch, and at length got out. It took some hours before his shamefaced misery yielded to the blissful sense of relief and of freedom.

THEIR PRETTY WAYS

As they were to be married about the same time, Henry Wager and Joseph Rush, friends from boyhood, agreed to take a house and share it together. After much consultation with their future wives, young ladies keenly sensible of social distinctions, they chose a house in Brixton – imposing, spacious, and convenient for double occupancy. It was perhaps unfortunate, to begin with, that Wager's resources – he had just begun business as a hop-merchant in the Borough – enabled him to spend more on furniture and decoration than his friend could reasonably afford, Rush being only cashier to a firm of wholesale cheesemongers in Tooley-street; but the buoyancy of prenuptial days permitted this detail to pass without remark. On their return from the honeymoon, the ladies embraced with effusion, and spent their first day at home in exclaiming delightedly at each other's domestic appointments, in admiring each other's wardrobe, and in forecasting a long lifetime of rapturous intimacy.

Mrs Wager had dark tresses, a tall, slender form, and somewhat acute features. She was nine-and-twenty. Mrs Rush, younger by five years, exhibited a fluffy growth of pale-brown hair, had a face of rather infantile prettiness, and frisked about with the grace of a plump lamb. Their names being Elizabeth and Theresa, they decided to call each other 'Muriel' and 'May'.

'They seem to hit it off very well,' remarked Wager to his friend, when, for a day or two, they had been witness of affectionate demonstrations. And Rush, whose temper was less sanguine, answered fervently, 'First-rate!'

As might have been anticipated, the earliest note of dissonance that sounded amid these ideal harmonies came from below-stairs. The ladies had engaged two servants, who were expected to devote themselves impartially to both their mistresses. Given a quartette of females, each of whom was but a little lower than the angels, this arrangement might have worked fairly well; in a Brixton household it naturally led to trouble in the first week. Coming home one evening in expectation of a quiet dinner, the husbands found a scene of disorder; each was taken apart by his tender spouse, and, spite of hunger, compelled to hear a catalogue of complaints against cook and housemaid. Practical men, they pooh-poohed the difficulty, talked about system and firmness and the like, and turned towards the dining-room with resolute joviality.

'Things'll work themselves right,' said Wager, carelessly, as he smoked with his friend afterwards. 'The girls have to get used to housekeeping. Take my advice, Joe, and don't pay much attention to this kind of thing. It isn't our department.'

Rush acquiesced, subduing his nervousness. He had begun to understand, for his own part, that housekeeping on the present scale was decidedly more expensive than his calculations supposed. That night, he and his Theresa put aside their lovers' babblement for dialogue of a less agreeable nature. Mrs Rush had but the vaguest idea of domestic economy. When her husband insisted upon speaking gravely of sordid matters, she pouted, rambled into all manner of irrelevant subjects, and at length, accusing him of never having loved her, burst into tears. Joseph, whose soft heart and irresolute will put him at a great disadvantage in junctures such as this, passed a restless night, and came down next morning with no appetite for breakfast.

The servant difficulty, more serious as days went on, was soon complicated with heart-burnings between the newly-married women, of which their husbands for awhile heard and suspected nothing. Friends and relatives called, and had their calls returned; a river of gossip was set flowing, and ere long showed a decidedly turbid course. To Mrs Rush's ears came remarks on the inferiority of her furniture and her dress, when compared with her darling Muriel's possessions. Mrs Wager heard it whispered that her sweet May was complaining of slights and injustices experienced in the common home. One evening, Joseph found his wife in her bedroom, with red eyes and flabby cheeks. She would not dine; she was not well; she — in short, she wished she might soon breathe her last.

'Come, come. What's all this about?' exclaimed Joseph, good-naturedly. And he referred to the state of her health. Already there was question of the state of both ladies' health — a fact which their husbands would not henceforth have much chance of forgetting.

'That woman has been horrid to me!' sobbed Theresa, after five minutes' entreaty that she would explain herself.

'That woman! Who?'

Joseph was astounded to learn that Mrs Wager had been thus designated. Half an hour's talk resulted in other disclosures which no less perturbed him. Impossible, his wife declared, to go on living thus. She was despised and insulted — openly, flagrantly! The servants (a new pair) regarded her even less than those who had been dismissed. And, with autumn advancing, she had not yet purchased a single article of new attire, whereas Mrs Wager had spent the last three days in shopping, and at least half-a-dozen parcels had been delivered for her. It was enough to make one think of suicide! Why had Joe married her, if he meant only to plunge her into degradation?

'Look at my dresses! Look at my old waterproof! And I feel ashamed to take my sister into the bedroom, with that mean carpet —'

Rush felt the perspiration rising to his forehead. This helpmate he had chosen promised to help him only too effectually in one particular — the spending of his income. But before the dialogue ended, he had promised that Theresa should have a ten-pound note to lay out in garments of the new fashion, that she might hold her own with Mrs Wager.

A week later Mrs Wager's state of health necessitated fresh visits to big shops across the water. Again parcels arrived, and again Joseph Rush found his wife possessed with thoughts of self-destruction. The two men had carefully avoided speaking to each other of the discords no longer disguised from them, and the result was that they talked much less frequently and less cordially than of old. Both had long since repented their domestic experiment, but they would not confess. Wager contrived to spend very little time at home. He had many friends, and was to a large extent resuming his bachelor life — of course, with the consequence that his wife grew bitter against him, and yet more against Mrs Rush. Joseph, less courageous, came home at regular hours, and bore the brunt of miseries. His wife ruled him through his fears. Mrs Wager, on the other hand, sought more subtly to manage her husband through his pride and his passions.

So it came to pass that, less than four months after marriage, Joseph Rush was driven to the inevitable step. Before speaking to his wife he made avowal to Wager that the expense of this mode of living was too high for him; he must find a separate abode.

'I shouldn't wonder if you're right, old fellow,' said his friend. Neither spoke of their wives' dissensions.

Had matters ended thus, it had been well. But on learning that she must go into a small house, whilst her rival would henceforth occupy the whole of this 'desirable residence,' Mrs Rush fell into a voiceless fury. She resolved not only to quarrel violently with her erewhile darling Muriel, but that her husband and his old friend should be set at variance – the fiercer the better. And this she brought about with little difficulty. When for two or three days the house had been thrown into furious disorder, Henry Wager and Joseph Rush sought a colloquy late at night. Hitherto, in talk with their wives, each had tried to make peace by defending the wife of the other against more or less virulent charges – a masculine method which, needless to say, made things worse by adding to the cauldron of strife the fresh ingredient of jealousy. But this time Wager began by saying abruptly –

'Look here, old chap, you must really put a stop to your wife's talk. She had been saying all sorts of ill-natured things about Lizzie. Of course, I know that it isn't easy – '

Rush, driven to desperation, broke in hotly –

'Why, confound it, Wager! I'm told that your wife has spoken abominably – to the servants, too – about Theresa. You certainly ought not to allow that. Your wife is very much older, and – '

Now it happened that Mrs Wager, having crept down from her bedroom to hear if possible what the men were talking about, heard this last remark through the keyhole. And it also happened that, as she stood listening and quivering with rage, Mrs Rush, who suspected that this was to be a night of crisis, also crept downstairs, and caught her enemy eavesdropping. In consequence the men presently became aware of angry voices in the hall. They moved to the door, and forthwith the two couples were involved in loud reproof and recrimination. Where both women had determined that their husbands should come into conflict, such issue was inevitable. The old friends said harsh things to each other, made charges and comparisons not easily forgiven. Had their social standing been one grade lower, they would have come to blows. For this they had too much self-respect; but it was impossible that they should live together for another day under the same roof. Next morning Rush took his wife into temporary lodgings, and in a week or two their goods were removed to a modest house half a mile away. The men of necessity corresponded, but they would not meet (out of shame as much as anger), and did not see each other again for a long time.

Though removed from contact with her rival, Mrs Rush still endeavoured to vie with her at all events in pursuit of the fashions. The little house and the solitary servant ate into her soul; but her dress when she received visitors, and that in which she showed herself abroad, became little inferior to Mrs Wager's equipment. When Joseph declared that ruin stared him in the face, his wife fell into hysterics, and shrieked about the state of her health. In the fulness of time this plea became no longer valid, but with the birth of a child Joseph found the demands upon his purse still increasing. Mrs Wager also had a baby, and common friends reported the magnificence of its layette. Again and again Rush yielded, until, one morning of late summer, his old friend Wager unfolding the newspaper at breakfast, uttered a horrified exclamation.

'What is it?' asked his wife, who by this time had learnt the limits she might not pass in resistance to her husband's will, and, on the whole, was better for it.

'Why, good heavens! Joe Rush has been arrested for embezzlement!'

Had she dared, Mrs Wager would have screamed with delight. Ha! there was an end of that odious Theresa and her pretensions to cut a figure! But Wager's eyes counselled a decent dissimulation.

'Oh, never! I must go and see that poor, silly creature – '

'You must do nothing of the kind,' replied her husband, sternly.

Nor was this amiable suggestion ever put into practice.

*

For many months Joseph Rush disappeared from among his friends. It was not known to Mrs Wager that, among the people who took care of Mrs Rush and her child, Henry was the main, though a secret, benefactor. Neither did she learn, long after, by what instrumentality Joseph received a new start in life. It had been her devout hope that no such chance would ever be granted him; that he would remain an outcast, and drag his wife down to the gutter. Darling 'Muriel' would have gloated over the certainty of such a prospect for her sweet 'May.' Yet the fact was, that on a certain day two men encountered by appointment in a retired place, and, as they beheld each other, one of these men could not restrain his tears, whilst the other grasped him strongly by the hand.

'It's all right, Joe. I was a cursed fool to behave to you as I did. Women! women!'

And the other, hearing himself addressed in honest words of friendly encouragement, looked up again, and once more hoped.

THE FATE OF HUMPHREY SNELL

At seven years old Humphrey Snell was brought from his village home to live in London. The part of Essex to which the family belonged was falling into desolation. Thomas Snell, by trade a wheelwright, could hardly keep the wolf from the door; he had three boys to bring up, and, like his neighbours, he saw no hope but in the roaring city of refuge. Father, mother, and children housed themselves in three small rooms, somewhere near Caledonian Road.

The step was not so rash as in many similar cases. Snell had useful acquaintances, and found work. In time the two elder boys began to help with their earnings; James, the hope of the family, advanced himself at a large carriage-builder's, and his brother Andrew, working for a dealer in second-hand furniture, learned how to buy for little what might be sold for much. Humphrey, a more difficult lad to manage, entered the postal service as a telegraph messenger.

For one thing, Humphrey had more brain than muscle, and brain of the quality which does not easily command a price in open market. At school they called him a boy of promise, but his promises were not always fulfilled, for whenever he got the chance, he idled. As a craftsman, he would never be worth his salt, and the arts of money-making had no allurement for him. His delight was to escape from London streets and catch a glimpse of the country – no easy thing for a boy without pocket-money, but attainable now and then at the cost of walks which overtaxed his strength. Thomas Snell, who had not a good word for rural life, dealt harshly with the lad in this matter. 'Fields? What do you want with fields? Can you live on grass?' And when Humphrey returned from one of his rambles at a late hour, mud besmirched, with his pockets full of berries, he learnt the taste of the rod. However, it was necessary to find some occupation for him which afforded plenty of exercise in the open air, so said the hospital doctor who treated Humphrey for a small ailment. For a few months he ran about as an errand boy; but in the end, at his own suggestion, he succeeded in a higher aim, and donned the post-office uniform.

This, of course, represented the toga virilis*, and Humphrey was granted a few pence out of his weekly pay. When spring came round he spent the money on rail or tram-car. Sunday morning saw him make for the nearest exit from town, and as time went on, the growth of his legs enabled him to cover greater distances, till at length, from the limit of a threepenny ride he walked as far as to his old home, the Essex village of which he had never ceased to talk with affectionate remembrance. There he found kinsfolk: an old woman, his mother's aunt, who lived with her unmarried son, a market gardener in a small, poor way. They welcomed him, for Humphrey was a tall, comely lad, and pleasant to talk with; he had warm affections, generous instincts, and thought of himself with a rare modesty. Twice or thrice that summer the visit was repeated.

Humphrey's growth had been too rapid; his strength did not keep pace with it, and he began to suffer in health. This was a serious anxiety, for the time drew near when he would have to undergo the medical examination for night duty, with the benefit, if he passed, of an increased pay. Through the winter it seemed probable that his career in this direction was closed; but with the spring – as always – he experienced a revival of health and spirits. The sight of the first green leaf did him more good than all the medicine he had been taking, and when put to the doctor's test, he passed without objection.

In his brief hours of leisure, when a flight from town was impossible, he merely idled. Books did not much attract him; when he opened one he was sure to come upon something or other which took such possession of his thoughts, or so affected his imagination, that he went off into dreaminess, and for that day read no more. No young man ever had less interest in the life about him. For male companionship he cared little; and girls, though he sometimes admired them from a distance, always frightened him at close quarters. His mother called him a booby, for his small money-earning power, in comparison with that of the other sons, tried her patience. And a booby he thought himself; every year he grew shyer and had less to say in the family circle. James and Andrew shook their heads after trying to converse with him of such things as delighted their souls – profit and loss, the theatres and music-halls, the pleasures of the street.

'He'll get chucked one of these days,' Andrew remarked to his father, as they smoked together over a pot of old Burton.

'We shall have him on our 'ands.'

Yet they were not actively unkind to Humphrey – decent people, they could not pick a quarrel with one so amiably disposed. For all his sharpness at school, they thought he must have a 'weak place.' How otherwise explain the fact that a fellow of his age would walk himself to death for the sake of gathering a few flowers, which he pressed in sheets of paper and stored away as if they were worth money ? He had a collection of this rubbish, and Mrs Snell declared that it bred fleas. Humphrey never attempted to explain his unaccountable taste ; as yet, perhaps, he was unable to make any defence which even to himself would have seemed valid. He went his way in silence, and by habitual gentleness apologised for his unprofitable character.

At the age of nineteen another crisis lay before him : he must now face the medical examination which admits to the rank of postman, with the splendid salary of eighteen shillings a week. Of late his health had given him very little trouble, and it seemed unlikely that he would fail to satisfy the doctor; yet it so befell that, on the day of trial, he came home with abashed and dejected countenance. It was all over with him : the doctor had discovered so many points of constitutional weakness that Humphrey could not possibly be passed : he must resign the service.

'I told you we should have him on our 'ands,' said Andrew Snell, when the family met to consider this catastrophe.

Distress and apprehension made the poor lad really ill. Some disorder of the heart, hitherto obscurely manifested, took a bad turn, and he was obliged to attend a hospital. Week after week he led a life of silent misery under his parents' eyes ; there was no saying whether he would ever again be able to work for his living, and at his age to what, indeed, could he turn ? Mrs Snell lectured him by the hour on his bygone opportunities. He had only himself to thank for this disaster; it was a judgment upon him for his waste of time in running about after flowers and berries and suchlike childish things. If he had any sense of shame he would burn all that dirty stuff that cumbered his room. And Humphrey straightway did so, feeling he could do no less.

Thus might he have perished, but a kindly hand interposed. His relative in Essex, the market gardener, happened to come to town; he saw Humphrey, and in his private talk with him learnt what was the lad's desire. Thereupon he proposed to the parents that Humphrey should go back into the country with him, and try the effect upon his health of living there for a month or so. Thomas Snell agreed, and was willing to pay two or three shillings a week for his son's support.

Now this countryman, Doggett by name, sympathised in a half-articulate way with Humphrey's passion for the study of nature, and old Mrs Doggett so far inclined the same way that she had become a village authority on medicinal herbs; her teas and potions, cordials and fomentations enjoyed much credit among the neighbours. By this good woman's advice Humphrey threw away the pint bottle of physic he had brought with him from the hospital, and followed a course of homely remedies which Mrs Doggett prescribed and administered. To his boundless joy he rapidly grew better; before long he could walk miles without undue fatigue, and once more he gave himself up to the delight of searching wood and meadow and lane for plants that were still strange to him.

In talk with Mrs Doggett he called to mind that not far from his home in London was the shop of a herbalist. Now, how did that man procure his stock of herbs? Would he be willing to pay money for plants of a useful kind, such as one might collect here in Essex? Mrs Doggett had no doubt that he would. She knew of men who got a sort of living, at all events in the summer months, by going about herb-gathering and then selling to the shops. She believed there were a good many such shops in London and in other large towns. This information supplied Humphrey with so much matter for thought that he went out and brooded for a whole day. The result was that, not very long after, he privately journeyed up to London, carrying with him a bundle of 'herbs' of the rarer sorts, and so presented himself at the shop he knew of. Mrs Doggett's opinion proved correct: he could sell his plants though for a very small sum; and by conversing with the herbalist, he got hints as to the species it would best pay him to collect. So, with careful avoidance of his family, he returned to the village, still deeply brooding, and conscious of a hope he durst not confess.

The season was autumn. Doggett, who made a bare living by his agricultural work, had a scond pursuit, by which through the winter months he was accustomed to earn a little. He made a rough kind of basket, which could be sold in quantities at a neighburing town. Humphrey, whose dread of a return to London inspired him with unwonted energy, put the question to his relative whether, if he mastered the simple art of basket-making, it would be possible for him to earn food and lodging till next spring. Doggett favoured the idea; such food and lodging as he could offer might very well be paid for in that way. Thereupon Humphrey took a great resolve. He would never go back to London. In one way and another, so it appeared, he could keep himself alive amid the scenes he loved; a crust by the hedge-side and a draught from the stream were sufficient to him, and for clothing he need take but little thought. Thus, too, he might hope to grow strong in body and escape the doom with which he had been threatened.

From this day began a life of strange independence, of rare contentment; a life such as the philosopher might admire and envy; possible only to a nature endowed in high simplicity, and intellectual fervour. It lasted for seven years; so long a respite had Humphrey ere the fate of which he never dreamed confronted him.

In London there are some three-score herbalists, men and women whose business, however obscure, is not unprofitable. They supply old-fashioned remedies to poor people by whom the habits or traditions of a rural origin are still preserved; and not seldom thrive by common quackery among the merely ignorant. With many of these tradesfolk Humphrey came to have dealings; from all parts of the country he supplied them with the herbs they wanted, and received his money by post wherever he chanced to be. It brought him the barest livelihood, but that was all he asked. The warm nights of summertide he spent, as often as not, in field or coppice; at other times a wayside inn gave him shelter. Through county after county, north, south, east and west, he pursued his joyous pilgrimage, saddening only when the fall of the leaf admonished him that he must turn towards the Essex village which was his home in winter. Sickness he knew not; that became a far off memory, blended with the dreamy thought of his

life as a messenger in London streets. He had the supreme
happiness of earning bread at the same time that he pursued a
beloved study. Without so much as glancing at a book, he stored
his mind with knowledge of flower and fern and tree. Apart from
the plants he sold, names were of little account to him; his
untrained intellect cared nothing for the classifications of science,
though with opportunity he would doubtless have acquired all
that the books could teach, and have added to them from the
riches of his own observation. He marked the signs of kindred,
and made distinction of families in original, often uncouth, terms;
but, after all, each plant was to him an end in itself, a thing to be
watched and cherished for its beauty, to be recognised with joy as
often as his eyes fell upon it. His memory was wonderfully ten-
acious; after these seven summers it formed a floral map of the
country traversed by him, and only in this way did he recall his
wanderings. As much as possible he avoided intercourse with men,
though gentle and friendly as ever when brought into their company. His appearance, in spite of rude clothing, was anything but
repellent, for the comeliness of his boyhood still appeared in the
man's lineaments; he was browned with breeze and sunshine, had
long, thick hair of the chestnut shade, a beard roughly trimmed,
soft, large eyes. From the habit of bending earthward, he walked
with a slight stoop, but his frame was well knit and hardy.

On the close of the seventh summer, when trees were changing
hue, but as yet no leaf had fallen, Humphrey found himself at a
great distance from the friendly dwelling which would, as usual,
shelter him through the months of gloom. He was at the foot of
the Mendips, a district hitherto unknown to him. After a hot
day, spent in idling about a spot that pleased him, he set forth
at sundown to walk for a few hours on the road he had resolved
to follow. This led him to the city of Wells, which he reached
about ten o'clock. So clear a moon shone in the heavens that he
had been able to observe the wayside plants by its light. It irked
him to think of seeking a comfortless bed in some poor tavern
on such a night as this. He would pass through the town, and in
the meadows beyond find a free resting place, where no one
would interfere with him.

The streets were all but silent. He crossed the market place,
and issued from it by an old porch, wondering at the quaint
appearance of everything about him. When he came forth again
into the moonlight his wonder changed to astonishment, for he

was in the Cathedral Close, and before him stood the lofty front of an edifice more majestic than he had ever beheld. Humphrey knew nothing of Wells, save that it was a little market town; he had never heard of the Cathedral, and could not surmise its historic significance* ; but the scene impressed him strongly, and there he remained for a long time, in solitude and silence, his imagination moved by the glories of earth and heaven.

Slowly compassing the cathedral, he came within sight of the Bishop's Palace; here again wonder and awe arrested him, so strangely beautiful was the scene. He proceeded with soft step, as if afraid of intruding where such as he had no admission, towards the great trees that overhang the moat, and gazed at the ivied wall with battlements clear cut against the sky. A sound of rushing water fell on his ears; he paced onwards, and discovered the white moonlit torrent leaping from St Andrew's well*, which for centuries has poured its flood around the episcopal stronghold.

Here was the verge of open country – broad meadows gently rising to wooded hills. The town lay hidden by the ancient structures whereat he marvelled. No ordinary habitation could be seen, and not a sound was audible, save that music of the rushing water. Feeling no desire of sleep, and reluctant to turn away, Humphrey retraced his steps along the moat. On reaching the corner where the rank of great elms began, he saw a female figure standing by, or rather leaning against the nearest trunk; the attitude was one of distress – arms raised and head bent. Startled, he moved aside, and was endeavouring to pass without drawing attention, when the person suddenly faced him; in the shadow of the trees he could only ascertain that she was of girlish appearance, but he distinctly heard a sob escape her, and his curiosity turned to compassion. Perhaps his mood, which was far from worldliness, prompted him to indulge the simple impulse of humanity; the gloom, no doubt, aided an unusual boldness. Be that as it may, Humphrey stepped forward with the purpose of asking if he could be of help. But, even as his lips parted, courage failed him. He would have drawn back again; but the girl, surprised at his approach, said, in a frightened voice, 'What do you want?'

'Nothing. I was only going to ask if you could tell me what this place is.'

Uneducated man as he was, Humphrey had at all times a softness of utterance which mitigated the defects of his pronunciation; moreover, such thoughts as were native to him, and such a life as he had led for years past, could not but endow him with speech very different from that of the class he belonged to. At present the sympathy he felt made his tones peculiarly gentle and reassuring. After a moment's hesitation, and with an obvious effort to command herself, the girl answered his inquiry, even addressing him with a respectful 'Sir.' The tears in her eyes, no doubt, helped the darkness to disguise Humphrey's costume. Her own tongue declared her of humble birth and a native of this county.

Humphrey thanked her, and again wished to go his way, yet he stood hesitating. The Cathedral clock struck eleven.

'It's getting late,' he said, as the girl also remained motionless. 'You're going home, aren't you?'

'I want to, Sir; but—'

Her voice broke, and she was ready to begin crying again. Apart from its note of distress, the voice itself affected the listener in a way that was very strange to him. He wished to hear it once more.

'Don't call me "Sir"! I'm only a common man, as you'd see if it was daylight. Is it anything you can tell a stranger?'

'It isn't my fault,' sobbed the girl. 'They've turned me out, and I don't know where to go. I've got a little money, but I don't like to go to an inn 'cause they might know me and it 'ud look funny. It ain't my fault; I don't know what to do. I haven't done nothing—'

She seemed to be about eighteen, and betrayed a weakness of character even in excess of the failing common to her kind; her manner was childish, and could not have excited suspicion in the most experienced observer. Humphrey Snell, whose seven and twenty years represented the minimum of experience with regard to women, felt a profound pity as he listened to her; and therewith blended that other vague emotion stirred by the first sound from her lips – an emotion which reminded him of early manhood, when he was wont to shrink from girls and yet to worship afar off. He began to speak more freely; to urge that she should not remain out of doors at so late an hour. The dialogue was prolonged, and presently Humphrey learned all the particulars of the distressful story. Disentangled from a confusion of superfluous words, feeble ejaculations, repetitions endless, and periods of indiscoverable connection, the narrative can be briefly set forth. This young woman, having long ago lost her parents, had for three years been in service at Bristol; her only home was the house of a married sister, Mrs Davis, who lived at Wells. Now, for chosen friend she had a sister of her brother-in-law, Jenny Davis by name, who also took service in Bristol; and this, as it turned out, was anything but a happy circumstance, for Miss Davis one day disappeared from her situation, and left behind her some disagreeable rumours. Arriving in search of his sister, the man from Wells made inquiries which threw an unpleasant light not only on her behaviour, but also on that of her friend Annie Frost, who was under notice to leave her situation. Annie, after living alone in Bristol for some weeks, obtained another place, but kept it only a short time. 'It wasn't my fault,' she declared. 'I did nothing.' The latter statement might be true enough; doubtless it accounted for Annie's failure to procure another engagement. Having all but exhausted her money, she took a ticket for Wells, and presented herself at her sister's house. Mrs Davis received her coldly, and could not promise hospitality; it depended upon her husband, who would not be home till late that night. When Davis returned, he was somewhat the worse for liquor; without a moment's hesitation, he turned his sister-in-law out of the house, forbidding her, with many oaths, ever to show her face there again.

Humphrey, fully believing all that the girl said in her own defence, was overcome with indignation. He urged her to go back to the house and make another appeal. Surely her own sister would not let her be driven out into the street. Annie was persuaded to act on this advice, and they walked together in the direction of her relative's abode, which was not far off. On coming forth from shadow into moonlight, the companions exchanged a look, and Humphrey beheld the face he might have pictured – foolishly pretty, with round eyes and baby lips, and neither nose nor chin to speak of; on the whole, good-natured in expression, and even through the traces of tears displaying a coquettish self-consciousness.

Watching from a discreet distance, he saw the girl in long parley with someone who opened the door to her. At length she entered, and Humphrey turned away with a sigh of vast relief. That night he did not lie down to rest; the hours passed very quickly, and morning broke before he had time to think of sleep. The next day found him a changed man. He paid no heed to the promise of the sky, always his first care; he walked the lanes without a glance at what grew there; he forgot the necessity of eating. A voice was in his ears, and before his mind's eye shone a face upturned in moonlight.

On the second day he still lingered near to Wells. At sunset, as on the evening before, he paced the shadowed walk by the Bishop's Palace, and there, with a great leap of his heart, he encountered Annie Frost. Her eyes cast down, she stood still as he approached her. They talked for some minutes; Annie related her difficulties and trials, which she declared unendurable. The Davises grudgingly allowed her to stay beneath their roof till she could find employment, but she must be quick about it. While speaking, she cast rapid glances at her casual acquaintance, and seemed to pay more attention to his features than to his poor and travel-worn garb. Humphrey uttered scarce half a dozen words, and when she left him he walked rapidly away.

A fortnight later he was still in this neighbourhood. Every evening at sunset he had loitered near the moat, and several times had been rewarded by a meeting with Annie Frost. They had walked together over the fields. Humphrey, when he ventured to give an account of himself, perceived with a tremor of exquisite surprise that the girl willingly lent ear; at each meeting she grew more confidential, and seemed to regard him with a trust, an appealing simplicity, which thrilled him to the heart. Never in his life before had he revealed himself as to this girl. He imagined she understood him, that her mute attention meant sympathy. Yet of a sudden she asked: 'Don't you think you could earn more if you was to try?' Humphrey kept a silence, but said at length, absently, 'Yes, I dare say I might.'

Then Annie got a place, as general servant in a small house at Shepton Mallet. They met as though for the last time, and Humphrey was overcome with a profound melancholy. He listened to the girl's babble, sweeter now to his ear than ever song of lark on the uplands, or the ripple of a stream in ferny dells. She seemed to him a creature of exquisite modesty, of transparent truth; a child, yet a woman; pathetic in her pretty helplessness, yet worthy of any sacrifice a man could make for her.

'And shall I never see you again?' he faltered with throbbing heart.

Annie bit her lip and looked away.

'P'r'aps you'll be coming here again.'

'If I could — if I found—'

He stammered, and stood still in the darkness. Annie sighed, then murmured with touching sincerity :

'I should like to see you wearing better clothes.'

A silence.

'I'll write to you,' murmured Humphrey. 'I might have something to say—'

He offered to shake hands ; Annie gave the tips of her fingers. He turned away ; Annie moved to his side again.

'You will write ?'

'You'd really like me to ?'

'I never get a letter from nobody.'

'Yes, I'll write you a letter, and as soon as I can.'

So they parted, and Humphrey in that hour set forth upon his eastward journey. By dawn he had walked thirty miles along the highroad. Then he slept under a hedge ; and, in the afternoon, when he had munched his dinner of bread and blackberries, plodded on once more.

Farewell the tranquil mind ! All he thought of now was to travel as quickly as possible to his friends in Essex that he might take counsel with them about a purpose he had conceived, even as he sought their advice as to a momentous step nearly eight years ago. A dread misgiving haunted his hours of weariness, but after sleep he arose with a thrill of rapturous resolve. His blood ran turbid ; he cooled his burning forehead in a wayside stream. Ingenuous as a child, he never debated with himself the significance of what had befallen him ; his only question was whether he could achieve the undertaking he had in view. He yielded to his passion as to an uncontrollable, inscrutable force of nature. Right or wrong, wise or foolish, choice he had none. Of course, it seemed to him that his desire was the height of wisdom, for he loved with virgin heart.

The Essex village could not forward his projects. Here was no employment for him by which he could earn more than subsistence. Doggett shook a despondent head ; with him things were going cheerlessly, and he talked of having to seek a home elsewhere. The old mother lay sick unto death, and Humphrey could not trouble her with worldly things. Tortured by delay, he turned his thoughts to London. James and Andrew had continued to thrive ; Thomas Snell and his wife enjoyed repose in their green old age. Between them they might surely help the wanderer to such moderate security as he aimed at.

'Just what I always said,' Andrew remarked. 'All these years you've disgraced yourself leadin' a tramp's life, and now you expect us to find a berth for you. A nice sort of chap you are!'

To his mother Humphrey confided the facts of the case. Mrs Snell was interested and asked some scores of questions, pertinent and other. But she regarded her youngest son as an amiable lunatic, and could not take his wishes seriously. Meanwhile, he had written twice to Annie, in the second letter begging for a reply, but none came – possibly she could not write. Weeks passed, and he worked at basket-making. His life was devastated: he had no joy in the priceless past, and was agonised with dread of the future lest his supreme desire should never be granted him. Many and desperate were the schemes he projected. At length, when he was on the point of setting forth to walk into Somerset, careless if he begged by the way, there came a letter from Andrew, which enclosed a newspaper cutting. 'Is this any use to you?' wrote his brother. 'It's a club that a friend of mine belongs to. Jim and me wouldn't mind helping you with the money if you really meant settling down.' The advertisement to which Humphrey's attention was drawn ran thus:

'Steward and Stewardess wanted to take charge of a Workman's Club – members four hundred – to keep the place clean, and serve at bar. Wages £1 15s. per week, with rooms, coal and gas. Cash security, £30. Apply –'

Instantly he started for London, and on the following day, with money borrowed from his relatives, he travelled by rail to Shepton Mallet, where he spent twenty-four hours. He returned to London, frantic with alternate exultation and fear. His suspense was prolonged for a week; then the committee of the Workman's Club solemnly announced to him that his application would be favourably considered, if he and his wife were ready to enter upon their duties on that day fortnight.

Annie, whose handwriting was decipherable only by a lover's eyes, answered his news by return of post:

'Send me money to come i shall want all i have for my things i cant tell you how delited I feal but its that sudin it taks my breth away with heepes of love and—'

There followed a row of crosses, which Humphrey found it easy to interpret. A cross is frequently set upon a grave; but he did not think of that.

AN INSPIRATION

About six o'clock, just as Harvey Munden came to the end of his day's work, and grew aware that he was hungry, some one knocked at the outer door — a timid knock, signalling a person of no importance. He went to open, and saw a man whose face he remembered.

'What is it this time?' he asked good-humouredly.

'Well, sir, I should like, if you will allow me, to draw your attention to an ingenious little contrivance — an absolute cure for smoky chimneys.'

The speaker seemed to be about forty; he was dressed with painful neatness, every article of his clothing, from hat to boots, exhibiting some trace of repair. He stood with his meagre form respectfully bent, on his drawn features a respectful smile, and prepared to open a small hand-bag — so strikingly new that it put its bearer to shame. Harvey Munden observed him, listened to his exposition, and said at length:

'When do you knock off work?'

'Well, sir, this is probably my last call to-day.'

'Come in for a minute, then. I should like to have a talk with you.'

Respectfully acquiescent, the man stepped forward into the comfortable sitting-room, which he surveyed with timid interest. His host gave him a chair by the fireside, and induced him to talk of his efforts to make a living. Brightened by the cheeriness of the surroundings, and solaced by an unwonted sympathy, the hapless struggler gave a very simple and very lamentable account of himself. For years he had lived on the petty commission of petty sales, sometimes earning two or three shillings a day, but more often reckoning the total in pence.

'I'm one of those men, sir, that weren't made to get on in the world. As a lad, I couldn't stick to anything – couldn't seem to put my heart into any sort of work, and that was the ruin of me – for I had chances to begin with. I've never done anything to be ashamed of – unless it's idleness.'

'You are not married?'

His eyes fell, and his smile faded; he shook his head. The other watched him for a moment.

'Will you tell me your name? Mine is Munden.'

'Nangle, sir – Laurence Nangle.'

'Well, Mr Nangle, will you come and dine with me?'

Abashed and doubtful, the man drew his legs further beneath the chair and twisted his hat. There needed some pressure before he could bring himself to accept the invitation; improbable as it seemed, he was genuinely shy; his stammered phrases and a slight flush on his cheeks gave proof of it.

They descended together to the street, and Munden called a hansom; ten minutes' drive brought them to the restaurant, where the host made choice of a retired corner, and quietly gave his directions. Nangle's embarrassment being still very observable, Munden tried to put him at ease by talking as to any ordinary acquaintance, of the day's news, of the commonest topics. It was not possible to explain himself to his guest, to avow the thought which had prompted this eccentric behaviour; Nangle could not but regard him with a certain uneasiness and suspicion; but by dint of persistence in cheerful gossip he gradually fixed the smile upon the face of his shabby companion, and prepared him to do justice to the repast.

Failure in that respect would not have been due to lack of appetite. When soup was set before him Nangle's lips betrayed their watery eagerness; his eyes rolled in the joy of ancicipation. Obviously restraining himself, and anxious not to discredit his host by any show of ill-breeding, he ate with slow decorum – though his handling of the spoon obeyed nature rather than the higher law. Having paused for a moment to answer some remark of Munden's, he was dismayed by the whisking away of his plate.

'But – I – I hadn't finished—'

The waiter could not be called back, and Munden, by treating the incident jocosely, made it contribute to his guest's equanimity. When wine was poured out for him Nangle showed a joyous suffusion over all his changing countenance; he drew a deep breath, quivered at the lips, and straightened himself.

'Mr Munden' – this when he had drunk a glass – 'it is years since I tasted wine. And ah! how it does one good! What medicine is like it?'

'None that I know of,' jested Harvey, 'though I've had wine uncommonly like medicine.'

Nangle laughed for the first time – a most strange laugh, suggesting that he had lost the habit, and could not hit a natural note. Feeling the first attempt to be a failure, he tried again, and his louder voice frightened him into silence.

'What is your opinion?' asked Munden, smiling at this bit of character. 'Is it possible for a shy man to overcome the failing, with plenty of practice?'

'Do you ask that because of anything you have noticed in me?'

'Well, yes. It rather surprises me, after all your experience, that you are still unhardened. How do you manage to call at people's houses and face all sorts of—'

'Ah! you may well ask! Mr Munden, it's a daily death to me; I assure you it is. I often stand at a door shaking and trembling, and can scarcely speak when it opens. I'm the last man to succeed in this kind of thing; I do it because I can't do anything else. But it's awful, Mr Munden, awful; and I get no better. I know men who never feel it; they'd laugh in my face if I spoke of such a thing. But all my life I've suffered from want of self-confidence. If it hadn't been for that—'

He broke off to help himself from a dish offered at his shoulder. The waiter's proximity startled him, and for a few moments he ate in silence – ate with manifest hunger, which he did not try to disguise; for the influences of the fortunate hour had warmed his heart and were giving him courage. Munden set a fair example, himself no despicable trencherman. After an *entrée* of peculiar savour, Nangle found it impossible to restrain his feelings.

'I never in all my life ate anything so good,' he murmured across the table.

Munden observed the growth of a new man, born of succulent food and generous wine. The characteristics of the individual thus called into being promised amusement; it was clear that they would be amiable and not unrefined. Semi-starvation and a

hated employment had not corrupted the original qualities of
Laurence Nangle; rather, these qualities had been frozen over,
and so preserved. They were now rapidly thawing, and the
process, painful to him at first, grew so enjoyable that delight
beamed from his eyes.

At dessert he talked without self-consciousness, and was led
into reminiscence. Munden had chanced to mention that he was
a Yorkshireman.

'And so am I!' exclaimed Nangle; 'so am I. But I came away
when I was a little lad, and I've never been there since. Do you
know Colchester? That's where I grew up and was educated. I
hadn't a bad education; most men would have made more use
of it. But something happened when I was a young man – it
seemed to floor me, and I've never quite got over it.'

'A love affair, I dare say?'

Nangle looked away and slowly nodded several times. Then
he drank with deliberation, and smacked his lips. A glow was
deepening on his hollow cheeks.

'Yes, you are right. I could tell you a strange thing that
happened to me only a few days ago. But, first of all, I should
like to know – *why* did you ask me to dine with you?'

'Oh, an inspiration.'

'You thought I looked hungry. Yes, so I was; and the dinner
has done me good. I feel better than I have done for years – for
years. I could tell you a strange thing—'

He paused, a shade of troublous agitation passing over the
gleam of his countenance. After waiting for a moment Munden
asked whether he smoked.

'When I can afford it, which isn't very often.'

They rose and went to the smoking-room. Nangle's step had
the lightness, the spring of recovered youth. He selected a cigar
with fastidious appreciation; buoyantly he declared for cognac
with the coffee. And presently the stream of his talk flowed on.

'Yes, I had a very good education at a private school – a
commercial school. You don't know Colchester? I went into the
office of a woolstapler – Cliffe was his name; our best friend,
and always very kind to me. I didn't get on very well – never
was such a fellow for making mistakes and forgetting addresses,
and so on. I was an idle young dog, but I meant well – I assure
you I meant well. And Mr Cliffe seemed to like me, and asked
me to his house the same as before. I wish he hadn't; I should

have done better if he'd been a little hard with me. He had a daughter – Ah, well; you begin to see. When I was one-and-twenty, she was nineteen, and we fell in love with each other. We used to meet in a quiet place just outside the town – you don't know Colchester, or I could tell you the spot. I happened to be down there a year or two ago, and I went and sat in the old place for a whole day. Ah, well ! – Lucy Cliffe ; I've only to say the name, and I go back – back— It makes me young again.'

His eyes grew fixed ; the hand in which he held his cigar fell. A deep sigh, and he continued :

'I believe her father would have helped us, one way or another ; but Mrs Cliffe spoilt all. When it came out, there was a fearful to-do. Lucy was what you may call rich ; at all events, she'd be left comfortably off some day. As for me – what prospects had I ? Mr Cliffe talked kindly to me, but he had to send me away. He got me a place in London. Lucy wrote me a letter before I went, and said she must obey her parents. We were like each other in that : soft, both of us ; hadn't much will of our own. And so we never saw each other again – not till a few days ago.'

'She married some one else, no doubt ?'

'Yes, she did. And I knew all about it, worse luck ; I'd rather have lost sight of her altogether. She married the brother of a friend of mine ; well, not a friend, but an acquaintance, who was in London when I came, twenty years ago. She married three years after our parting, and I've heard of her from James Dunning (that's her brother-in-law's name) off and on ever since. I used to have a good opinion of Dunning, but I know better now. He's a rough, selfish brute !'

The last words were uttered with startling vehemence. Nangle clenched his fist, and sat stiffly, quivering with excitement. Munden subdued a smile.

'A long time back, nearly four years, this fellow Dunning told me that his brother had just died. Lucy was left with her daughter, the only child she'd had ; and they lived at Ipswich. Since then, I've met Dunning only once or twice, and when I asked him about Lucy, he just said she was going on as usual, or supposed she was. He told a lie, and I half guess the reason of it. The other day – do you know Prince of Wales Road, Kentish Town ? You've heard of it. Well, I was going along Prince of Wales Road, in the usual business way, and I knocked at the door of a largish, respectable-looking house. The minute I'd knocked the door opened; it was a lady just coming out — dressed in black. She looked at me, and I looked at her. I had a queer feeling, and there seemed to be something of the same on her side. I was just going to say something, when she asked me who it was I wished to see. I had only to hear her voice, and I knew I wasn't mistaken. But I didn't dare to speak; I stood staring at her, and she stood just as still. At last I somehow got out a word — "I think you are Mrs Dunning?" — "And you," she said all of a tremble, "you are Laurence Nangle." Then she turned round to the door and asked me to come in. And we sat down in a dining-room, and began to talk. You can't imagine how I felt. It was like talking in a dream; I didn't know what I said. Lucy hadn't altered very much — nothing like as much as I should have expected in twenty years. She seemed so young I could hardly believe it. Of course she's only about thirty-eight, and has lived all her life in comfort. But it's wonderful she should have known *me*, after all I've gone through. I must seem more like sixty than forty—'

'Not at present,' remarked the listener. And truly, for the warm, animated face before him was that of a comparatively young man.

'Well, I felt bitterly ashamed of myself, dressed as I was, and peddling from house to house. She kept staring at me, as if she couldn't get over her astonishment. Had she never heard of me? I asked. Yes, she had, every now and then. James Dunning had told her I was a commercial traveller, or something of that kind. Then I asked if she was living here, in Kentish Town. Yes, she was; with James Dunning and his wife. "And your daughter as well?" I asked. Then she began to cry, and told me her daughter had been dead for nearly two years, and she was quite alone, but for the Dunnings, who were very kind to her. She had come to live with them after her daughter's death. And she told me her husband had left her very well off, but what was the use of it when all her family was gone? — And just then we were disturbed by some one coming into the room; a flashy sort of young woman, I guessed her to be Dunning's wife, and I was right. Lucy — I can't help calling her Lucy — stood up, and looked nervous; and of course I stood up too. "I didn't know anyone was here," said her sister-in-law, looking very hard at me. "It's some one I used to know," said Lucy. "Oh, then I won't intrude." – Lucy couldn't say any more. She was ashamed of me, after all. But I felt a good deal more ashamed of myself, and I choked something about being in a hurry, and got out of the room. Neither of them tried to stop me. When I'd let myself out at the front door, I walked off like a madman, running into people because I didn't see them, and talking to myself, and going on straight ahead, till I came to my senses somewhere out Hampstead way.'

'I hope that isn't the end of the story,' said Munden, as he cut the tip of a second cigar.

'I only wish it was,' returned his guest, frowning and straightening himself as before. 'Now, you know something about me, Mr Munden – I mean, you can form some notion of the man I am from what I have told you. And do you think that I could do such a mean thing as go to that lady – her I call Lucy, for old-time sake – in the hope of getting money from her ? Do you believe it of me ?'

'Assuredly not.'

'I thank you for your saying so. It came about like this. I did a foolish thing. Two days after that meeting I had to be in Kentish Town again, and late in the evening I passed near Prince of Wales Road. Well, I was tempted. I couldn't resist the wish to go by that house where she lives. And when I got near it, in the dark, I stood still ; some one was playing a piano inside, and I thought it might be Lucy. I stood for a minute or two – and all at once a man came up from behind me and stared in my face. James Dunning it was. "Halloa !" he said. "Then it *is* you, Nangle. I just thought it might be. And what are you doing here ?" I couldn't understand his way of speaking, and I hadn't any words ready. "Now, look here, Nangle," he went on, drawing me away by the arm ; "you've found out that my sister-in-law is living with us. I didn't want you to know, because I couldn't trust you, and after what happened the day before yesterday I see I was right. Of course they told me. Now I want you to understand that my sister-in-law can't be troubled in this way. I suppose you're spying here on the chance that she may come out ; I'm glad I happened to find you at it. If you're in low water I don't mind lending you half-a-crown, but you'll keep out of Prince of Wales Road, or I shall know how to deal with you.' There, that's what he said to me. I wasn't man enough to strike him as I ought to have done ; I've always been poor-spirited. I just told him in a few hot words what I thought of his behaviour, and went off, feeling devilish miserable, I can assure you."

Munden reflected. There was silence for a little.

'Do you suppose,' asked the host at length, 'that Mrs Dunning – the widowed lady – regarded you with any such suspicion ?'

'Not for one moment,' cried Nangle.

'No ? and isn't it possible that you misunderstood her when you thought she was ashamed of you ? From what you have told me of her character—'

'Yes,' interrupted the other eagerly, 'no doubt I was wrong in that. She felt like I did – a sort of shame, a sort of awkwardness ; but if I had stayed she'd have got over it. I'm sure she would. I was a fool to bolt like that. It gave James Dunning's wife a chance of thinking of me as her husband does. It's all my fault.'

'And another thing. You take it for granted that James Dunning accused you of wanting to beg or borrow from his sister-in-law. Doesn't it occur to you that he might be afraid of something else – something more serious from his point of view ?'

'I don't quite understand.'

'Why, suppose that when the widowed lady talked to him about you she showed a good deal more interest in you than James Dunning approved ? Suppose she even asked for your address, or something of that kind ?'

Nangle fixed a gaze on the speaker. His eyes widened to express an agitating thought.

'You think – that – is possible ?'

'Well, not impossible.'

'And that fellow – is afraid – Lucy might—'

'Precisely. In all likelihood that would be very disagreeable to Mr and Mrs James Dunning. She is a widow in easy circumstances, without children, without near relatives—'

'You are right !' murmured Nangle slowly. 'I see it now. That's why he has been afraid of me. And he must have had some reason. Perhaps she has spoken of me. It seems impossible – after all these years—'

He sank back, and stared into vacancy with glowing eyes.

'In your position,' said Munden, 'I should take an early opportunity of revisiting Prince of Wales Road.'

'How *can* I ? Think of my poverty ! How can you advise such a thing ?'

'It behoves you,' continued the other, with much gravity, 'to clear your character in the eyes of that lady. In justice to yourself—'

'Again you are right! I will go to-morrow.'

'It seems to me that this is a case for striking while the iron is hot. It's now only eight o'clock, and give me leave to say that you will never be so able to justify yourself as this evening. A hansom will take you to Kentish Town in half an hour.'

Nangle started up – the picture of radiant resolve.

'I have just half-a-crown in my pocket, and that's how I'll use it! Thank you! You have made me see things in a new light. I feel another man! And if I find that what you hinted at is really the case, shall I hesitate out of false shame? Which is better for Lucy: to live with those people, always feeling sad and lonesome, or to find a real home with the man she loved when she was a girl – the man who has loved her all his life?'

'Bravo! This is the right – the heroic vein.'

In five minutes they had quitted the restaurant. They found a hansom, and, as he leapt into it, Nangle shouted gallantly to the driver: 'Prince of Wales Road, Kentish Town!' Impossible to recognize the voice which but two hours since had murmured respectfully at Harvey Munden's door. 'Come and see me to-morrow,' Munden called to him, and a hand waved from the starting cab.

Munden was entertained, and something more. Partly out of kindness, in part from curiosity, he had given a good dinner to a poor devil oppressed with ills; he desired to warm the man's chilly blood and to improve its quality; he wished to study the effects of such stirring influence in this particular case. And it seemed probable that he had achieved a good deal more than the end in view. It might come to pass that a good-humoured jest would change incalculably the course of two lives.

It happened that on the morrow he was obliged to go out of town. On returning late at night he found in his letter-box a hand-delivered note, with the signature, 'Laurence Nangle.' Only a couple of lines to say that Nangle had called twice, and that he would come again in a day or two. 'Yours gratefully,' he wrote himself, which possibly signified the news Munden hoped for.

Nearly a week went by, and again at six o'clock Munden was summoned to the door by a knock he recognized. There stood

Mr Nangle – *quantum mutatus*!* In his hand no commercial bag, but a most respectable umbrella; on his head an irreproachable silk hat; the rest of his equipment in harmony therewith. The disappearance of an uncomely beard had struck a decade from his apparent age; he held himself with a certain modest dignity, and did not shrink from the scrutiny of astonished eyes.

'Come in! Delighted to see you.'

He entered, and for a moment seated himself, but his feelings would not allow him to keep a restful position. Starting up again, he exclaimed:

'Mr Munden, what can a man say when he's in debt for all that makes life worth living?'

'It depends whether the creditor is man or woman.'

'In my case, it's both. But if it hadn't been for *you*—'

His voice failed him.

'I was right, was I?'

'Yes, you were right. I'll tell you about it. I got out of the cab at the end of Prince of Wales Road, and walked to the house. I knocked at the door. A servant came, and I told her I wished to see Mrs Dunning – the widow lady. I'd hardly spoken when James Dunning came out of a room; he had heard my voice. "What's the meaning of this?" he said in his brutal way, pushing up against me. "Didn't you understand me?" "Yes, I did, and better than you think. I have come to see a lady who happens to live in your house—" And just then I saw Lucy herself at the back of the hall. I brushed past Dunning, and went right up to her. "Mrs Dunning, I wish to speak to you. Will you let me? Or do you want me to be turned out of the house like a beggar?" "No, no!" She was white as a sheet, and held out her hand to me, as if she wanted protection. "It's all a mistake. You must stay – I want you to stay!" James's wife had come forward, and she was staring at me savagely. "Where can we talk in private?" I asked; and I didn't let go Lucy's hand. Then, all of a sudden, Dunning turned about; you never saw such a change in a man. "Why, Lucy, what's the matter? I thought you didn't wish to see Mr Nangle. You've altogether misled us." I looked at Lucy, and she was going red – and then I saw tears in her eyes. "Go into the drawing-room, Nangle," said Dunning. "It's all a misunderstanding. We must talk it over afterwards." So I went into the room, and Lucy came after me, and I shut the door—'

He stopped with a choke of emotion.

'Excellent, i' faith,' said Munden beaming.

'Do you suppose,' continued the other, gravely, 'that I could ever have done that if it hadn't been for your dinner? Never! Never! I should have crept on through my miserable life, and died at last in the workhouse; when all the time there was a woman whose own happiness depended on a bit of courage in me. She'd never have dared to show a will of her own; James Dunning and his wife were too strong for her. Cowards, both of us – but I was the worst. And you put a man's heart into me. Your dinner – your wine – your talk! If I hadn't gone that night, I should never have gone at all – never!'

'I knew that.'

'But what I can't understand is – *why* did you ask me to dine with you? Why? It's like what they call the finger of Providence.'

'Yes. As I told you – it was an inspiration.'

THE FOOLISH VIRGIN*

Coming down to breakfast, as usual rather late, Miss Jewell was
surprised to find several persons still at table. Their conversation
ceased as she entered, and all eyes were directed to her with a
look in which she discerned some special meaning. For several
reasons she was in an irritable humour; the significant smiles,
the subdued 'Good mornings,' and the silence that followed, so
jarred upon her nerves that, save for curiosity, she would have
turned and left the room.

Mrs Banting (generally at this hour busy in other parts of the
house) inquired with a sympathetic air whether she would take
porridge; the others awaited her reply as if it were a matter of
general interest. Miss Jewell abruptly demanded an egg. The
awkward pause was broken by a high falsetto.

'I believe you know who it is all the time, Mr Drake,' said
Miss Ayres, addressing the one man present.

'I assure you I don't. Upon my word, I don't. The whole thing
astonishes me.'

Resolutely silent, Miss Jewell listened to a conversation the
drift of which remained dark to her, until some one spoke the
name 'Mr Cheeseman'; then it was with difficulty that she
controlled her face and her tongue. The servant brought her an
egg. She struck it clumsily with the edge of her spoon and asked
in an affected drawl : 'What are you people talking about ?'

Mrs Sleath, smiling maliciously, took it upon herself to reply.

'Mr Drake has had a letter from Mr Cheeseman. He writes
that he's engaged, but doesn't say who to. Delicious mystery,
isn't it ?'

The listener tried to swallow a piece of bread and butter, and
seemed to struggle with a constriction of the throat. Then,
looking round the table, she said with contemptuous pleasantry :

'Some lodging-house servant, I shouldn't wonder.'

Everyone laughed. Then Mr Drake declared he must be off, and rose from the table. The ladies also moved, and in a minute or two Miss Jewell sat at her breakfast alone.

She was a tall, slim person, with unremarkable, not ill-moulded features. Nature meant her to be graceful in form and pleasantly feminine of countenance; unwholesome habit of mind and body was responsible for the defects that now appeared in her. She had no colour, no flesh; but an agreeable smile would well have become her lips, and her eyes needed only the illumination of healthy thought to be more than commonly attractive. A few months would see the close of her twenty-ninth year; but Mrs Banting's boarders, with some excuse, judged her on the wrong side of thirty.

Her meal, a sad pretence, was soon finished. She went to the window and stood there for five minutes looking at the cabs and pedestrians in the sunny street. Then, with the languid step which had become natural to her, she ascended the stairs and turned into the drawing-rom. Here, as she had expected, two ladies sat in close conversation. Without heeding them, she walked to the piano, selected a sheet of music, and sat down to play.

Presently, whilst she drummed with vigour on the keys, some one approached; she looked up and saw Mrs Banting; the other persons had left the room.

'If it's true,' murmured Mrs Banting with genuine kindliness on her flabby lips, 'all I can say is that it's shameful – shameful!'

Miss Jewell stared at her.

'What do you mean?'

'Mr Cheeseman – to go and – —'

'I don't understand you. What is it to me?'

The words were thrown out almost fiercely, and a crash on the piano drowned whatever Mrs Banting meant to utter in reply. Miss Jewell now had the drawing-room to herself.

She 'practised' for half an hour, careering through many familiar pieces with frequent mechanical correction of time-honoured blunders. When at length she was going up to her room, a grinning servant handed her a letter which had just arrived. A glance at the envelope told her from whom it came, and in privacy she at once opened it. The writer's address was Glasgow.

My Dear Rosamund

[began the letter], I can't understand why you write in such a nasty way. For some time now your letters have been horrid. I don't show them to William because if I did he would get into a tantrum. What I have to say to you now is this, that we simply can't go on sending you the money. We haven't it to spare, and that's the plain truth. You think we're rolling in money, and it's no use telling you we are not. William said last night that you must find some way of supporting yourself, and I can only say the same. You are a lady and had a thorough good education, and I am sure you have only to exert yourself. William says I may promise you a five pound note twice a year, but more than that you must not expect. Now do just think over your position—

She threw the sheet of paper aside, and sat down to brood miserably. This little back bedroom, at no time conducive to good spirits, had seen Rosamund in many a dreary or exasperated mood; to-day it beheld her on the very verge of despair. Illuminated texts of Scripture spoke to her from the walls in vain; portraits of admired clergymen smiled vainly from the mantelpiece. She was conscious only of a dirty carpet, an ill-made bed, faded curtains, and a window that looked out on nothing. One cannot expect much for a guinea a week, when it includes board and lodging; the bedroom was at least a refuge, but even that, it seemed, would henceforth be denied her. Oh, the selfishness of people! And oh, the perfidy of man!

For eight years, since the breaking up of her home, Rosamund had lived in London boarding-houses. To begin with, she could count on a sufficient income, resulting from property in which she had a legitimate share. Owing to various causes, the value of this property had steadily diminished, until at length she became dependent upon the subsidies of kinsfolk; for more than a twelvemonth now, the only person able and willing to continue such remittances had been her married sister, and Rosamund had hardly known what it was to have a shilling of pocket-money. From time to time she thought feebly and confusedly of 'doing something,' but her aims were so vague, her capabilities so inadequate that she always threw aside the intention in sheer hopelessness. Whatever will she might once have possessed had evaporated in the boarding-house atmosphere. It was hard to believe that her brother-in-law would ever withhold the poor five pounds a month. And — what is the use of boarding-houses if not to renew indefinitely the hope of marriage?

She was not of the base order of women. Conscience yet lived in her, and drew support from religion; something of modesty, of self respect, still clad her starving soul. Ignorance and ill-luck had once or twice thrown her into such society as may be found in establishments outwardly respectable; she trembled and fled. Even in such a house as this of Mrs Banting's, she had known sickness of disgust. Herself included, four single women abode here at the present time; and the scarcely disguised purpose of every one of them was to entrap a marriageable man. In the others, it seemed to her detestable, and she hated all three, even as they in their turn detested her. Rosamund flattered herself with the persuasion that she did not aim merely at marriage and a subsistence; she would not marry any one; her desire was for sympathy, true companionship. In years gone by she had used to herself a more sacred word; nowadays the homely solace seemed enough. And of late a ray of hope had glimmered upon her dusty path. Mr Cheeseman, with his plausible airs, his engaging smile, had won something more than her confidence; an acquaintance of six months, ripening at length to intimacy, justified her in regarding him with sanguine emotion. They had walked together in Kensington Gardens; they had exchanged furtive and significant glances at table and elsewhere; everyone grew aware of the mutual preference. It shook her with a painful misgiving when Mr Cheeseman went away for his holiday and spoke no word; but probably he would write. He had written – to his friend Drake; and all was over.

Her affections suffered, but that was not the worst. Her pride had never received so cruel a blow.

After a life of degradation which might well have unsexed her, Rosamund remained a woman. The practice of affectations numberless had taught her one truth, that she could never hope to charm save by reliance upon her feminine qualities. Boarding-house girls, such numbers of whom she had observed, seemed all intent upon disowning their womanhood; they cultivated masculine habits, wore as far as possible male attire, talked loud slang, threw scorn (among themselves at all events) upon domestic virtues; and not a few of them seemed to profit by the prevailing fashion. Rosamund had tried these tactics, always with conscious failure. At other times, and vastly to her relief, she aimed in precisely the opposite direction, encouraging herself in feminine extremes. She would talk with babbling naïveté, exaggerate the languor induced by idleness, lack of exercise, and consequent ill-health; betray timidities and pruderies, let fall a pious phrase, rise of a morning for 'early celebration' and let the fact be known. These and the like extravagances had appeared to fascinate Mr Cheeseman, who openly professed his dislike for androgynous persons. And Rosamund enjoyed the satisfaction of moderate sincerity. Thus, or very much in this way, would she be content to live. Romantic passion she felt to be beyond her scope. Long ago – ah! perhaps long ago, when she first knew Geoffrey Hunt—

The name as it crossed her mind, suggested an escape from the insufferable ennui and humiliation of the hours till evening. It must be half a year since she called upon the Hunts, her only estimable acquaintances in or near London. They lived at Teddington, and the railway fare was always a deterrent; nor did she care much for Mrs Hunt and her daughters, who of late years had grown reserved with her, as if uneasy about her mode of life. True, they were not at all snobbish; homely, though well-to-do people; but they had such strict views, and could not understand the existence of a woman less energetic than themselves. In her present straits, which could hardly be worse, their counsel might prove of value; though she doubted her courage when it came to making confessions.

She would do without luncheon (impossible to sit at table with those 'creatures') and hope to make up for it at tea; in truth, appetite was not likely to trouble her. Then for dress. Wearily she compared this garment with that, knowing beforehand that all were out of fashion and more or less shabby. Oh, what did it matter! She had come to beggary, the result that might have been foreseen long ago. Her faded costume suited fitly enough with her fortunes – nay, with her face. For just then she caught a sight of herself in the glass, and shrank. A lump choked her: looking desperately as if for help, for pity, through gathering tears, she saw the Bible verse on the nearest wall: 'Come unto me—' Her heart became that of a woeful child: she put her hands before her face, and prayed in the old, simple words of childhood.

As her call must not be made before half-past three, she could not set out upon the journey forthwith; but it was a relief to get away from the house. In this bright weather, Kensington Gardens, not far away, seemed a natural place for loitering, but the alleys would remind her too vividly of late companionship; she walked in another direction, sauntered for an hour by the shop windows of Westbourne Grove, and, when she felt tired, sat at the railway station until it was time to start. At Teddington, half-a-mile's walk lay before her; though she felt no hunger, long abstinence and the sun's heat taxed her strength to the point of exhaustion; on reaching her friends' door, she stood trembling with nervousness and fatigue. The door opened, and to her dismay she learnt that Mrs Hunt was away from home. Happily, the servant added that Miss Caroline was in the garden.

'I'll go round,' said Rosamund at once. 'Don't trouble—'

The pathway round the pleasant little house soon brought her within view of a young lady who sat in a garden chair, sewing. But Miss Caroline was not alone; near to her stood a man in shirt sleeves and bare-headed, vigorously sawing a plank; he seemed to be engaged in the construction of a summer-house, and Rosamund took him at first sight for a mechanic, but when he turned round, exhibiting a ruddy face all agleam with health and good humour, she recognised the young lady's brother, Geoffrey Hunt. He, as though for the moment puzzled, looked fixedly at her.

'Oh, Miss Jewell, how glad I am to see you!'

Enlightened by his sister's words, Geoffrey dropped the saw, and stepped forward with still heartier greeting. Had civility permitted, he might easily have explained his doubts. It was some six years since his last meeting with Rosamund, and she had changed not a little; he remembered her as a graceful and rather pretty girl, with life in her, even if it ran for the most part to silliness, gaily dressed, sprightly of manner; notwithstanding the account he had received of her from his relatives, it astonished him to look upon this limp, faded woman. In Rosamund's eyes, Geoffrey was his old self, perhaps a trifle more stalwart, and if anything handsomer, but with just the same light in his eyes, the same smile on his bearded face, the same cordiality of utterance. For an instant, she compared him with Mr Cheeseman, and flushed for very shame. Unable to command her voice, she stammered incoherent nothings; only when a seat supported her weary body did she lose the dizziness which had threatened downright collapse; then she closed her eyes, and forgot everything but the sense of rest.

Geoffrey drew on his coat, and spoke jestingly of his amateur workmanship. Such employment, however, seemed not inappropriate to him, for his business was that of a timber merchant. Of late years he had lived abroad, for the most part in Canada. Rosamund learnt that at present he was having a longish holiday.

'And you go back to Canada?'

This she asked when Miss Hunt had stepped into the house to call for tea. Geoffrey answered that it was doubtful; for various reasons he rather hoped to remain in England, but the choice did not altogether rest with him.

'At all events' – she gave a poor little laugh – 'you haven't pined in exile.'

'Not a bit of it. I have always had plenty of hard work – the one thing needful.'

'Yes – I remember – you always used to say that. And I used to protest. You granted, I think, that it might be different with women.'

'Did I?'

He wished to add something to the point, but refrained out of compassion. It was clear to him that Miss Jewell, at all events, would have been none the worse for exacting employment. Mrs Hunt had spoken of her with the disapprobation natural in a healthy, active woman of the old school, and Geoffrey himself could not avoid a contemptuous judgment.

'You have lived in London all this time?' he asked, before she could speak.

'Yes. Where else should I live? My sister at Glasgow doesn't want me there, and – and there's nobody else, you know.' She tried to laugh. 'I have friends in London – well, that is to say – at all events I'm not quite solitary.'

The man smiled, and could not allow her to suspect how profoundly he pitied such a condition. Caroline Hunt had reappeared; she began to talk of her mother and sister, who were enjoying themselves in Wales. Her own holiday would come upon their return; Geoffrey was going to take her to Switzerland.

Tea arrrived just as Rosamund was again sinking into bodily faintness and desolation of spirit. It presently restored her, but she could hardly converse. She kept hoping that Caroline would offer her some invitation – to lunch, to dine, anything; but as yet no such thought seemed to occur to the young hostess. Suddenly the aspect of things was altered by the arrival of new callers, a whole family, man, wife and three children, strangers to Rosamund. For a time it seemed as if she must go away without any kind of solace; for Geoffrey had quitted her, and she sat alone. On the spur of irrational resentment, she rose and advanced to Miss Hunt.

'Oh, but you are not going! I want you to stay and have dinner with us, if you can. Would it make you too late?'

Rosamund flushed and could scarce contain her delight. In a moment she was playing with the youngest of the children, and even laughing aloud, so that Geoffrey glanced curiously towards her. Even the opportunity of private conversation which she had not dared to count upon was granted before long; when the callers had departed Caroline excused herself, and left her brother alone with the guest for half an hour. There was no time to be lost; Rosamund broached almost immediately the subject uppermost in her mind.

'Mr Hunt, I know how dreadful it is to have people asking for advice, but if I might – if you could have patience with me—'

'I haven't much wisdom to spare,' he answered, with easy good nature.

'Oh, you are very rich in it, compared with poor me. And my position is so difficult. I want – I am trying to find some way of being useful in the world. I am tired of living for myself. I seem to be such a useless creature. Surely even I must have some talent, which it's my duty to put to use! Where should I turn? Could you help me with a suggestion?'

Her words, now that she had overcome the difficulty of beginning, chased each other with breathless speed, and Geoffrey was all but constrained to seriousness; he took it for granted, however, that Miss Jewell frequently used this language; doubtless it was part of her foolish, futile existence to talk of her soul's welfare, especially in tête-à-tête with unmarried men. The truth he did not suspect, and Rosamund could not bring herself to convey it in plain words.

'I do so envy the people who have something to live for!' Thus she panted. 'I fear I have never had a purpose in life – I'm sure I don't know why. Of course I'm only a woman, but even women nowadays are doing so much. You don't despise their efforts, do you ?'

'Not indiscriminately.'

'If I could feel myself a profitable member of society ! I want to be lifted above my wretched self. Is there no great end to which I could devote myself ?'

Her phrases grew only more magniloquent, and all the time she was longing for courage to say : 'How can I earn money ?' Geoffrey, confirmed in the suspicion that she talked only for effect, indulged his natural humour.

'I'm such a groveller, Miss Jewell. I never knew these aspirations. I see the world mainly as cubic feet of timber.'

'No, no, you won't make me believe that. I know you have ideals !'

'That word reminds me of poor old Halliday. You remember Halliday, don't you ?'

In vexed silence, Rosamund shook her head.

'But I think you must have met him, in the old days. A tall, fair man – no ? He talked a great deal about ideals, and meant to move the world. We lost sight of each other when I first left England, and only met again a day or two ago. He is married, and has three children, and looks fifty years old, though he can't be much more than thirty. He took me to see his wife – they live at Forest Hill.'

Rosamund was not listening, and the speaker became aware of it. Having a purpose in what he was about to say, he gently claimed her attention.

'I think Mrs Halliday is the kind of woman who would interest you. If ever any one had a purpose in life she has.'

'Indeed ? And what ?'

'To keep house admirably, and bring up her children as well as possible, on an income which would hardly supply some women with shoe-leather.'

'Oh, that's very dreadful !'

'Very fine, it seems to me. I never saw a woman for whom I could feel more respect. Halliday and she suit each other perfectly ; they would be the happiest people in England if they had any money. As he walked back with me to the station he talked about their difficulties. They can't afford to engage a good servant (if one exists nowadays), and cheap sluts have driven them frantic, so that Mrs Halliday does everything with her own hands.'

'It must be awful.'

'Pretty hard, no doubt. She is an educated woman – otherwise, of course, she couldn't, and wouldn't manage it. And, by the by' – he paused for quiet emphasis – 'she has a sister, unmarried, who lives in the country and does nothing at all. It occurs to one – doesn't it ? – that the idle sister might pretty easily find scope for her energies.'

Rosamund stared at the ground. She was not so dull as to lose the significance of this story, and she imagined that Geoffrey reflected upon herself in relation to her own sister. She broke the long silence by saying awkwardly :

'I'm sure I would never allow a sister of mine to lead such a life.'

'I don't think you would,' replied the other. And, though he spoke genially, Rosamund felt it a very moderate declaration of his belief in her. Overcome by strong feeling, she exclaimed :

'I would do anything to be of use in the world. You don't think I mean it, but I do, Mr Hunt. I—'

Her voice faltered ; the all important word stuck in her throat. And at that moment Geoffrey rose.

'Shall we walk about ? Let me show you my mother's fernery ; she is very proud of it.'

That was the end of intimate dialogue. Rosamund felt aggrieved, and tried to shape sarcasms, but the man's imperturbable good humour soon made her forget everything save the pleasure of being in his company. It was a bitter-sweet evening, yet perhaps enjoyment predominated. Of course, Geoffrey would conduct her to the station ; she never lost sight of this hope. There would be another opportunity for plain speech. But her desire was frustrated ; at the time of departure, Caroline said that they might as well all go together. Rosamund could have wept for chagrin.

She returned to the detested house, the hateful little bedroom, and there let her tears have way. In dread lest the hysterical sobs should be overheard, she all but stifled herself.

Then, as if by blessed inspiration, a great thought took shape in her despairing mind. At the still hour of night she suddenly sat up in the darkness, which seemed illumined by a wondrous hope. A few minutes motionless ; the mental light grew dazzling ;

she sprang out of bed, partly dressed herself, and by the rays of
a candle sat down to write a letter:

Dear Mr Hunt,

Yesterday I did not tell you the whole truth. I have nothing to live
upon, and I must find employment or starve. My brother-in-law has
been supporting me for a long time – I am ashamed to tell you, but I
will – and he can do so no longer. I wanted to ask you for practical
advice, but I did not make my meaning clear. For all that, you did
advise me, and very well indeed. I wish to offer myself as domestic help
to poor Mrs Halliday. Do you think she would have me? I ask no
wages – only food and lodging. I will work harder and better than any
general servant – I will indeed. My health is not bad, and I am fairly
strong. Don't – don't throw scorn on this! Will you recommend me to
Mrs Halliday – or ask Mrs Hunt to do so? I beg that you will. Please
write to me at once, and say yes. I shall be ever grateful to you.

> Very sincerely yours,
> ROSAMUND JEWELL

This she posted as early as possible. The agonies she endured in
waiting for a reply served to make her heedless of boarding-
house spite, and by the last post that same evening came
Geoffrey's letter. He wrote that her suggestion was startling.
'Your motive seems to me very praiseworthy, but whether the
thing would be possible is another question. I dare not take
upon myself the responsibility of counselling you to such a step.
Pray, take time, and think. I am most grieved to hear of your
difficulties, but is there not some better way out of them?'

Yes, there it was! Geoffrey Hunt could not believe in her
power to do anything praiseworthy. So had it been six years
ago, when she would have gone through flood and flame to win
his admiration. But in those days she was a girlish simpleton;
she had behaved idiotically. It should be different now; were it
at the end of her life, she would prove to him that he had
slighted her unjustly.

Brave words, but Rosamund attached some meaning to them.
The woman in her – the ever-prevailing woman – was wrought
by fears and vanities, urgencies and desires, to a strange point
of exaltation. Forthwith, she wrote again: 'Send me, I entreat
you, Mrs Halliday's address. I will go and see her. No, I can't
do anything but work with my hands. I am no good for anything
else. If Mrs Halliday refuses me, I shall go as a servant into some

other house. Don't mock at me; I don't deserve it. Write at
once.'

Till midnight she wept and prayed.

Geoffrey sent her the address, adding a few dry words: 'If
you are willing and able to carry out this project, your ambition
ought to be satisfied. You will have done your part towards
solving one of the gravest problems of the time.' Rosamund did
not at once understand; when the writer's meaning grew clear,
she kept repeating the words, as though they were a new gospel.
Yes! she would be working nobly, helping to show a way out
of the great servant difficulty. It would be an example to poor
ladies, like herself, who were ashamed of honest work. And
Geoffrey Hunt was looking on. He must needs marvel; perhaps
he would admire greatly; perhaps – oh, oh!

Of course, she found a difficulty in wording her letter to the
lady who had never heard of her, and of whom she knew
practically nothing. But zeal surmounted obstacles. She began
by saying that she was in search of domestic employment, and
that, through her friends at Teddington, she had heard of Mrs
Halliday as a lady who might consider her application. Then
followed an account of herself, tolerably ingenuous, and an
amplification of the phrases she had addressed to Geoffrey
Hunt. On an afterthought she enclosed a stamped envelope.

Whilst the outcome remained dubious, Rosamund's behaviour to her fellow-boarders was a pattern of offensiveness. She
no longer shunned them – seemed, indeed, to challenge their
observation for the sake of meeting it with arrogant defiance.
She rudely interrupted conversations, met sneers with virulent
retorts, made herself the common enemy. Mrs Banting was
appealed to; ladies declared that they could not live in a house
where they were exposed to vulgar insult. When nearly a week
had passed Mrs Banting found it necessary to speak in private
with Miss Jewell, and to make a plaintive remonstrance. Rosamund's flashing eye and contemptuous smile foretold the
upshot.

'Spare yourself the trouble, Mrs Banting. I leave the house to-
morrow.'

'Oh, but—'

'There is no need for another word. Of course, I shall pay the
week in lieu of notice. I am busy, and have no time to waste.'

The day before, she had been to Forest Hill, had seen Mrs

Halliday, and entered into an engagement. At midday on the morrow she arrived at the house which was henceforth to be her home, the scene of her labours.

Sheer stress of circumstance accounted for Mrs Halliday's decision. Geoffrey Hunt, a dispassionate observer, was not misled in forming so high an opinion of his friend's wife. Only a year or two older than Rosamund, Mrs Halliday had the mind and the temper which enable woman to front life as a rational combatant, instead of vegetating as a more or less destructive parasite. Her voice declared her; it fell easily upon a soft, clear note; the kind of voice that expresses good humour and reasonableness, and many other admirable qualities; womanly, but with no suggestion of the feminine gamut; a voice that was never likely to test its compass in extremes. She had enjoyed a country breeding; something of liberal education assisted her natural intelligence; thanks to a good mother, she discharged with ability and content the prime domestic duties. But physically she was not inexhaustible, and the laborious, anxious years had taxed her health. A woman of the ignorant class may keep house, and bring up a family, with her own hands; she has to deal only with the simplest demands of life; her home is a shelter, her food is primitive, her children live or die, according to the law of natural selection. Infinitely more complex, more trying, is the task of the educated wife and mother; if to conscientiousness be added enduring poverty, it means not seldom an early death. Fatigue and self-denial had set upon Mrs Halliday's features a stamp which could never be obliterated. Her husband, her children, suffered illnesses; she, the indispensable, durst not confess even to a headache. Such servants as from time to time she had engaged merely increased her toil and anxieties; she demanded, to be sure, the diligence and efficiency which in this new day can scarce be found among the menial ranks; what she obtained was sluttish stupidity, grotesque presumption, and every form of female viciousness. Rosamund Jewell, honest in her extravagant fervour, seemed at first a mocking apparition; only after a long talk, when Rosamund's ingenuousness had forcibly impressed her, would Mrs Halliday agree to an experiment. Miss Jewell was to live as one of the family; she did not ask this, but consented to it. She was to receive ten pounds a year, for Mrs Halliday insisted that payment there must be.

'I can't cook,' Rosamund had avowed. 'I never boiled a potato in my life. If you teach me, I shall be grateful to you.'

'The cooking I can do myself, and you can learn if you like.'

'I should think I might wash and scrub by the light of nature ?'

'Perhaps. Good-will and ordinary muscles will go a long way.'

'I can't sew, but I will learn.'

Mrs Halliday reflected.

'You know that you are exchanging freedom for a hard and a very dull life.'

'My life has been hard and dull enough, if you only knew. The work will seem hard at first, no doubt, but I don't think I shall be dull with you.'

Mrs Halliday held out her work-worn hand, and received a clasp of the fingers attenuated by idleness.

It was a poor little house; built – of course – with sham display of spaciousness in front, and huddling discomfort at the rear. Mrs Halliday's servants never failed to urge the smallness of the rooms as an excuse for leaving them dirty; they had invariably been accustomed to lordly abodes, where their virtues could expand. The furniture was homely and no more than sufficient, but here and there on the walls shone a glimpse of summer landscape, done in better days by the master of the house, who knew something of various arts, but could not succeed in that of money-making. Rosamund bestowed her worldly goods in a tiny chamber which Mrs Halliday did her best to make inviting and comfortable; she had less room here than at Mrs Banting's, but the cleanliness of surroundings would depend upon herself, and she was not likely to spend much time by the bedside in weary discontent. Halliday, who came home each evening at half-past six, behaved to her on their first meeting with grave, even respectful, courtesy, his tone flattered Rosamund's ear; and nothing could have been more seemly than the modest gentleness of her replies.

At the close of the first day, she wrote to Geoffrey Hunt: 'I do believe I have made a good beginning. Mrs Halliday is perfect and I quite love her. Please do not answer this; I only write because I feel that I owe it to your kindness. I shall never be able to thank you enough.'

When Geoffrey obeyed her and kept silence, she felt that he acted prudently; perhaps Mrs Halliday might see the letter, and know his hand. But none the less she was disappointed.

Rosamund soon learnt the measure of her ignorance in domestic affairs. Thoroughly practical and systematic, her friend (this was to be their relation) set down a scheme of the day's and the week's work; it made a clear apportionment between them, with no preponderance of unpleasant drudgery for the new-comer's share. With astonishment, which she did not try to conceal, Rosamund awoke to the complexity and endlessness of home duties even in so small a house as this.

'Then you have no leisure?' she exclaimed, in sympathy, not remonstrance.

'I feel at leisure when I'm sewing – and when I take the children out. And there's Sunday.'

The eldest child was about five years old, the others three and a twelvemonth, respectively. Their ailments gave a good deal of trouble, and it often happened that Mrs Halliday was awake with one of them the greater part of the night. For children Rosamund had no natural tenderness; to endure the constant sound of their voices proved, in the beginning, her hardest trial, but the resolve to school herself in every particular soon enabled her to tend the little ones with much patience, and insensibly she grew fond of them. Until she had overcome her awkwardness in every task, it cost her no little effort to get through the day; at bedtime she ached in every joint, and morning oppressed her with a sick lassitude. Conscious, however, of Mrs Halliday's forbearance, she would not spare herself, and it soon surprised her to discover that the rigid performance of what seemed an ignoble task brought its reward. Her first success in polishing a grate gave her more delight than she had known since childhood. She summoned her friend to look, to admire, to praise.

'Haven't I done it well? Could you do it better yourself?'

'Admirable!'

Rosamund waved her blacklead brush and tasted victory.

The process of acclimatisation naturally affected her health. In a month's time she began to fear that she must break down; she suffered painful disorders, crept out of sight to moan and shed a tear. Always faint, she had no appetite for wholesome food. Tossing on her bed at night, she said to herself a thousand times, 'I must go on, even if I die!' Her religion took the form of asceticism, and bade her rejoice in her miseries; she prayed constantly, and at times knew the solace of an infinite self-glorification. In such a mood she once said to Mrs Halliday:

'Don't you think I deserve some praise for the step I took?'

'You certainly deserve both praise and thanks from me.'

'But I mean – it isn't everyone who could have done it? I've a right to feel myself superior to the ordinary run of girls?'

The other gave her an embarrassed look, and murmured a few satisfying words. Later in the same day she talked to Rosamund about her health, and insisted on making certain changes which allowed her to take more open-air exercise. The result of this was a marked improvement; at the end of the second month Rosamund began to feel and look better than she had done for several years. Work no longer exhausted her. And the labour in itself seemed to diminish – a natural consequence of perfect co-operation between the two women. Mrs Halliday declared that life had never been so easy for her as now; she knew the delight of rest in which there was no self-reproach. But, for sufficient reasons, she did not venture to express to Rosamund all the gratitude that was due.

About Christmas, a letter from Forest Hill arrived at Teddington; this time it did not forbid a reply. It spoke of struggles, sufferings, achievements. 'Do I not deserve a word of praise? Have I not done something, as you said, towards solving the great question? Don't you believe in me a little?' Four more weeks went by, and brought no answer. Then one evening, in a mood of bitterness, Rosamund took a singular step; she wrote to Mr Cheeseman. She had heard nothing of him, had utterly lost sight of the world in which they met; but his place of business was known to her, and thither she addressed the note. A few lines only: 'You are a very strange person, and I really take no interest whatever in you. But I have sometimes thought you would like to ask my forgiveness. If so, write to the above address, my sister's. I am living in London, and enjoying myself, but I don't choose to let you know where.' Having an opportunity on the morrow, Sunday, she posted this in a remote district.

The next day, a letter arrived for her from Canada. Here was the explanation of Geoffrey's silence. His words could hardly have been more cordial, but there were so few of them. On nourishment such as this no illusion could support itself; for the moment Rosamund renounced every hope. Well, she was no worse off than before the renewal of their friendship. But could it be called friendship? Geoffrey's mother and sisters paid no

heed to her; they doubtless considered that she had finally sunk
below their horizon; and Geoffrey himself, for all his fine
words, most likely thought the same at heart. Of course they
would never meet again. And for the rest of her life she would
be nothing more than a domestic servant in genteel disguise –
happy were the disguise preserved.

However, she had provided a distraction for her gloomy
thoughts. With no more delay than was due to its transmission
by way of Glasgow, there came a reply from Mr Cheeseman:
two sheets of notepaper. The writer prostrated himself; he had
been guilty of shameful behaviour; even Miss Jewell, with all
her sweet womanliness, must find it hard to think of him with
charity. But let her remember what 'the poets' had written about
Remorse*, and apply to him the most harrowing of their
descriptions. He would be frank with her; he would 'a plain
unvarnished tale unfold.'* Whilst away for his holiday he by
chance encountered one with whom, in days gone by, he had
held tender relations. She was a young widow; his foolish heart
was touched; he sacrificed honour to the passing emotion. Their
marriage would be delayed, for his affairs were just now
anything but flourishing. 'Dear Miss Jewell, will you not be my
friend, my sister? Alas, I am not a happy man; but it is too late
to lament.' And so on to the squeezed signature at the bottom
of the last page.

Rosamund allowed a fortnight to pass – not before writing,
but before her letter was posted. She used a tone of condescension, mingled with airy banter. 'From my heart I feel for you,
but, as you say, there is no help. I am afraid you are very
impulsive – yet I thought that was a fault of youth. Do not give
way to despair. I really don't know whether I shall feel it right
to let you hear again, but, if it soothes you, I don't think there
would be any harm in your letting me know the cause of your
troubles.'

This odd correspondence, sometimes with intervals of three
weeks, went on until late summer. Rosamund would soon have
been a year with Mrs Halliday. Her enthusiasm had long since
burnt itself out; she was often a prey to vapours, to cheerless
lassitude, even to the spirit of revolt against things in general,
but on the whole she remained a thoroughly useful member of
the household; the great experiment might fairly be called
successful. At the end of August it was decided that the children

must have sea air; their parents would take them away for a fortnight. When the project began to be talked of, Rosamund, perceiving a domestic difficulty, removed it by asking whether she would be at liberty to visit her sister in Scotland. Thus were things arranged.

Some days before that appointed for the general departure, Halliday received a letter which supplied him with a subject of conversation at breakfast.

'Hunt is going to be married,' he remarked to his wife just as Rosamund was bringing in the children's porridge.

Mrs Halliday looked at her helper – for no more special reason than the fact of Rosamund's acquaintance with the Hunt family; she perceived a change of expression, an emotional play of feature, and at once averted her eyes.

'Where? In Canada?' she asked, off-hand.

'No, he's in England. But the lady is a Canadian. I wonder he troubles to tell me. Hunt's a queer fellow. When we meet, once in two years, he treats me like a long lost brother; but I don't think he'd care a bit if he never saw me or heard of me again.'

'It's a family characteristic,' interposed Rosamund with a dry laugh.

That day she moved about with the gait and the eyes of a somnambulist. She broke a piece of crockery, and became hysterical over it. Her afternoon leisure she spent in the bedroom, and at night she professed a headache which obliged her to retire early.

A passion of wrath inflamed her; as vehement – though so utterly unreasonable – as in the moment when she learnt the perfidy of Mr Cheeseman. She raged at her folly in having submitted to social degradation on the mere hint of a man who uttered it in a spirit purely contemptuous. The whole hateful world had conspired against her. She banned her kinsfolk and all her acquaintances, especially the Hunts; she felt bitter even against the Hallidays – unsympathetic, selfish people, utterly indifferent to her private griefs, regarding her as a mere domestic machine. She would write to Geoffrey Hunt, and let him know very plainly what she thought of his behaviour in urging her to become a servant. Would such a thought have ever occurred to a gentleman! And her poor life was wasted, oh! oh! She would soon be thirty – thirty! The glass mocked her with savage truth. And she had not even a decent dress to put on. Self-neglect had made her appearance vulgar; her manners, her speech, doubtless, had lost their note of social superiority. Oh, it was hard! She wished for death, cried for divine justice in a better world.

On the morning of release, she travelled to London Bridge, ostensibly *en route* for the north. But, on alighting, she had her luggage taken to the cloak room, and herself went by omnibus to the West End. By noon she had engaged a lodging, one room in a street where she had never yet lived. And hither before night was transferred her property.

The next day she spent about half of her ready money in the purchase of clothing – cheap, but such as the self-respect of a 'lady' imperatively demands. She bought cosmetics; she set to work at removing from her hands the traces of ignoble occupation. On the day that followed – Sunday – early in the afternoon, she repaired to a certain corner of Kensington Gardens, where she came face to face with Mr Cheeseman.

'I have come,' said Rosamund, in a voice of nervous exhilaration which tried to subdue itself. 'Please to consider that it is more than you could expect.'

'It is! A thousand times more! You are goodness itself.'

In Rosamund's eyes the man had not improved since a year ago. The growth of a beard made him look older, and he seemed in indifferent health; but his tremulous delight, his excessive homage, atoned for the defect. She, on the other hand, was so greatly changed for the better, that Cheeseman beheld her with no less wonder than admiration. Her brisk step, her upright bearing, her clear eye, and pure-toned skin contrasted remarkably with the lassitude and sallowness he remembered; at this moment, too, she had a pleasant rosiness of cheek which made her girlish, virginal. All was set off by the new drapery and millinery, which threw a shade upon Cheeseman's very respectable, but somewhat time-honoured, Sunday costume.

They spent several hours together, Cheeseman talking of his faults, his virtues, his calamities, and his hopes, like the impulsive, well-meaning, but nerveless fellow that he was. Rosamund gathered from it all, as she had vaguely learnt from his recent correspondence, that the alluring widow no longer claimed him; but he did not enter into details on this delicate subject. They had tea at a restaurant by Notting Hill Gate; Miss Jewell appearing indefatigable, they again strolled in unfrequented ways. At length was uttered the question for which Rosamund had long ago prepared her reply.

'You cannot expect me,' she said sweetly, 'to answer at once.'

'Of course not ! I shouldn't have dared to hope—'

He choked and swallowed; a few beads of perspiration shining on his troubled face.

'You have my address; most likely I shall spend a week or two there. Of course you may write. I shall probably go to my sister's in Scotland, for the autumn—'

'Oh ! don't say that – don't ! To lose you again – so soon—'

'I only said "probably"—'

'Oh, thank you ! To go so far away – and the autumn; just when I have a little freedom; the very best time – if I dared to hope such a thing—'

Rosamund graciously allowed him to bear her company as far as to the street in which she lived.

A few days later she wrote to Mrs Halliday, heading her letter with the Glasgow address. She lamented the sudden impossibility of returning to her domestic duties. Something had happened. 'In short, dear Mrs Halliday, I am going to be married. I could not give you warning of this, it has come so unexpectedly. Do forgive me ! I so earnestly hope you will find some one to take my place, some one better and more of a help to you. I know I haven't been much use. Do write to me at Glasgow and say I may still regard you as a dear friend.'

This having been dispatched, she sat musing over her prospects. Mr Cheeseman had honestly confessed the smallness of his income; he could barely count upon a hundred and fifty a year; but things might improve. She did not dislike him – no, she did not dislike him. He would be a very tractable husband. Compared, of course, with—

A letter was brought up to her room. She knew the flowing commercial hand, and broke the envelope without emotion. Two sheets – three sheets – and a half. But what was all this ? 'Despair . . . thoughts of self-destruction . . . ignoble publicity . . . practical ruin . . . impossible . . . despise and forget . . . Dante's hell . . . deeper than ever plummet sounded . . . forever ! . . .' So again he had deceived her ! He must have known that the widow was dangerous; his reticence was mere shuffling. His behaviour to that other woman had perhaps exceeded in baseness his treatment of herself; else, how could he be so sure that

a jury would give her 'ruinous damages' ? Or was it all a mere
illustration of a man's villainy ? Why should not she also sue for
damages ? Why not ? Why not ?

The three months that followed were a time of graver peril,
of darker crises, than Rosamund, with all her slip-slop experiences, had ever known. An observer adequately supplied with
facts, psychological and material, would more than once have
felt that it depended on the mere toss of a coin whether she kept
or lost her social respectability. She sounded all the depths
possible to such a mind and heart – save only that from which
there could have been no redemption. A saving memory lived
within her, and, at length, in the yellow gloom of a November
morning – her tarnished, draggle-tailed finery thrown aside for
the garb she had worn in lowliness – Rosamund betook herself
to Forest Hill. The house of the Hallidays looked just as usual.
She slunk up to the door, rang the bell, and waited in fear of a
strange face. There appeared Mrs Halliday herself. The surprised
but friendly smile at once proved her forgiveness of Rosamund's
desertion. She had written, indeed, with calm good sense, hoping
only that all would be well.

'Let me see you alone, Mrs Halliday. How glad I am to sit in
this room again ! Who is helping you now ?'

'No one. Help such as I want is not easy to find.'

'Oh, let me come back ! I am *not* married. No, no, there is
nothing to be ashamed of. I am no worse than I ever was. I'll
tell you everything, the whole silly, wretched story.'

She told it, blurring only her existence of the past three months.

'I would have come before, but I was so bitterly ashamed. I
ran away so disgracefully. Now I'm penniless – all but suffering
hunger. Will you have me again, Mrs Halliday ? I've been a
horrid fool, but – I do believe – for the last time in my life. Try
me again, dear Mrs Halliday !'

There was no need of the miserable tears, the impassioned
pleading. Her home received her as though she had been absent
but for an hour. That night she knelt again by her bedside in the
little room, and at seven o'clock next morning she was lighting
fires, sweeping floors, mute in thankfulness.

Halliday heard the story from his wife, and shook a dreamy,
compassionate head.

'For goodness' sake,' urged the practical woman, 'don't let
her think she's a martyr.'

'No, no ; but the poor girl should have her taste of happiness.'

'Of course I'm sorry for her, but there are plenty of people more to be pitied. Work she must, and there's only one kind of work she's fit for. It's no small thing to find your vocation – is it ? Thousands of such women – all meant by nature to scrub and cook – live and die miserably because they think themselves too good for it.'

'The whole social structure is rotten !'

'It'll last our time,' rejoined Mrs Halliday, as she gave a little laugh and stretched her weary arms.

ONE WAY OF HAPPINESS

Here and there in the more populous London suburbs you will find small houses built with a view to the accommodation of two families beneath the same roof. Considering the class of people for whom this advantage was contrived, the originator of the idea showed a singular faith in human nature. It does, however, occasionally happen that two distinct households prove themselves capable of living in such proximity for a certain time without overt breach of the peace – nay, with a measure of satisfaction on both sides. This was the case with the Rippingilles and the Budges. Rippingille, salesman at a large boot warehouse, and Budge, a coal-merchant's clerk, were young men of sober disposition, not incapable of modest mirth, content with their lot in life, and rarely looking more than a month or two ahead. Their wives did not lack corresponding virtues. Granted the female privilege of believing (and telling each other) that they might have married much more brilliantly if they had waited longer, and the necessary relaxation of abusing their husbands when a dinner was ill-cooked or babes gave trouble, Mrs Budge and Mrs Rippingille discharged their domestic duties as well as could be reasonably expected. They talked in a high key, laughed in a scream, and bade defiance to care with a very praiseworthy resolution. The Rippingilles had three young children, the Budges had two. It was not always possible for the two families to take their annual holiday at the same time; this year circumstances were favourable, and the parents planned a joint expedition to the seaside. Long and warmly did they discuss the attractions of half a dozen popular resorts; the final vote was for Brighton. They would leave home on Saturday afternoon; spend Sunday, Monday (the August Bank Holiday) and Tuesday by the seashore, and on Wednesday return. Thursday morning must see the bread-winners back at their respective places of business.

Mrs Budge and Mrs Rippingille had a clear fortnight in which to make their preparations and to talk inexhaustibly about the glories of Brighton. Both had been to Brighton before, but neither of late years. They lived in a crescendo of joyous excitement; from room to room they interchanged high-pitched remarks, jests, ejaculations.

'Louie! this time next week – eh!'

'Jist be at London Bridge, shan't we? Oh my! Say, Annie—'

One was in a top bedroom, the other in the wash-house, and at this moment the shrieks of two infants made them inaudible to each other; but they continued to vociferate with shrill merriment.

'Now look 'ere,' observed Rippingille, gravely, one night when the children were all in bed, and the elders had assembled, as was their habit, for a common supper. 'About the apartments.' It would never have occurred to Rippingille to say 'rooms' or 'lodgings.' His stress on 'apartments' held the listeners silent whilst he reflected. 'We mean 'aving comfort, understand, and we've got to pay for it. But we're not going be be 'ad.'

No, no; certainly not. All were determined not to be imposed upon. The ladies vied in screeching their reasonable demands. Two double-bedded rooms and a comfortable parlour; the cost not to exceed thirty shillings.

'And mind you,' Budge succeeded at length in remarking, with impressive severity, 'no hextras. Not a single bloomin' hextra! I know what that means, if they begin the game. Why, Tom Leggatt and me, we was once together down at Ramsgate—'

He was not allowed to finish the reminiscence; a chorus of awful experiences clamoured him down. In a quarter of an hour's time, when the others had paused breathless, Budge repeated, as though it were a novel remark:

'Mind you, not a single bloomin' hextra!'

Thereupon renewal of shrieks, and for another fifteen minutes all was vociferous confusion.

The purchase of a new jacket by Mrs Budge, whereas Mrs Rippingille could not afford that luxury, caused a slight heart-burning between the two; but they outlived it. All the children had some new garment, showy, inexpensive, purchased without any regard to durability or the wearer's comfort. Rippingille bought a straw hat, a yellow waistcoat, and a pair of sand shoes; his friend purchased a guinea suit of tweeds, and a blue necktie, relying upon an old cricket cap for the completion of his seaside costume. On the Friday night all, children included, donned their holiday attire, and ran about the house inviting each other's compliments.

Not without much discussion was it decided how they and their luggage should be transported to London Bridge station; time had to be considered, as well as money, and there seemed to be no avoiding the expense of a cab. Solemnly the precise fare was calculated. Convinced against their will that the outlay would be smaller by sixpence or so than if any other course were adopted, the ladies none the less resented this tax upon the holiday fund; notwithstanding high spirits, they looked sourly at the cabman. Rippingille, with the two eldest children – for the cab could not be made to hold all – went by omnibus.

Brighton was reached about five o'clock. Mrs Budge's baby, probably objecting to a bottle of half-churned milk, screamed vigorously most of the way, and by Mrs Rippingille was secretly voted a nuisance; but in all other respects the journey proved enjoyable. For the third-class carriage had its complement of passengers, all going to Brighton for a holiday, all noisily talkative and joyously perspiring. Much solid food and a liberal supply of liquid refreshment were consumed *en route*. Thus fortified, the happy band could postpone thoughts of a meal until they had discovered the suitable lodging, on which quest they set forth at once from the station. The sun shone gloriously; the street pavements were hot and dry; if necessary, two or three hours could be devoted to inspection of apartments.

At house after house they tried, not, of course, with a view of the sea or anywhere near it; the highways and byways along which they trudged might well have been part of some London suburb, save, perhaps, for an unusual freshness in the air. The wonted noises, the familiar accents, everywhere protected these Londoners against the unpleasant feeling of strangeness. Numbers of people strayed hither and thither on the same errand as themselves; every snatch of talk that fell upon their ears was concerned with rent of 'apartments.' And, indeed, their undertaking promised to be not a little wearisome; rents were mostly, from their point of view, exorbitant, or, if reasonable, covered but mean accommodation. At first, the whole party invaded each house. Presently, Mrs Budge, overtired with the burden of her infant, had to lag behind a little; and with her two little girls, who had begun to cry, Mrs Rippingille grew cross, but could still enjoy a scornful laugh in the face of extortionate landladies. The men supported each other in boisterous good humour.

'All right, Annie,' shouted Budge to his pallid wife. 'We've got the night before us, and miles of apartments to choose from.'

'Cheer up, old girl,' Rippingille called out to his own spouse. 'We won't be bested. Like a shrimp tea before we go on again?'

But the children (the eldest only six years old) could hardly drag their little limbs along; wails arose, and the mothers, nervously unstrung, had to threaten a slap, or even a 'hiding.'

'I say, Tom,' remarked Budge to his male companion quietly, 'we shall have to take the first where there's room enough. I'm about done up.'

Rippingille nodded, and with an air of cheery resolve they made for the next house which showed a card in the window.

Here, by good luck, three rooms were vacant, but one only was double-bedded. The landlady, however, professed her willingness to put in a sofa each night, and provide it with bedclothes.

'Well,' said Budge to his wife, 'I could sleep on the sofa and you and the children in the bed.'

'Of course you could,' exclaimed Mrs Rippingille, eager to get housed, and fairly content with the chamber which was designed for her and her family. 'I've often slep' on a sofa myself, and slep' sound too.'

At this there was a general roar of laughter, with no special meaning. The terms were now inquired, and on this point followed a vigorous contest. For the rooms, until evening on Wednesday, the landlady asked thirty shillings – and extras.

'Now see here, Mrs What's-yer-name,' cried Rippingille, in what he meant for a perfectly civil tone, 'we don't pay no hextras. It's got to be hinclusive – understand? Kitchen fire, candles, boots, and every blessed thing. We'll pay you thirty bob and not grumble, if you give us no cause. But no extras – see?'

All talked, or rather shouted, at once; there was a deafening uproar. The wives, tired out as they were, thoroughly enjoyed this combat of tongues, and the landlady, after a brave struggle against overwhelming odds, yielded with a good grace. She had never taken so little before; but as she could see that the babies, bless 'em, were crying to go to bed – well, she wouldn't hold out. But half the sum must be paid in advance; that she made a rule.

Budge went back to the railway station to fetch a tin box, in which both families had packed their indispensable belongings. Rippingille set forth to purchase the groceries and other articles of food. The ladies, until their luggage arrived, closely examined each of the rooms, and tried to keep the children quiet. Relieved from weary prolongation of their walk, and gratified by a conquest of the landlady, they were in the mood for finding everything admirable. Impossible, they agreed, to have done better. The place was clean; the beds looked comfortable; they were not more than twenty minutes' walk from the beach.

'I don't know what you think, Annie, but I call this first-rate. Did you see the picture of the Queen and all her fam'ly in my bedroom?'

'And look at those lovely hartificial flowers! Why, you feel you want to be smelling at 'em. I don't know what you think, but I'm a-goin' to enjoy myself!'

The first disappointment was the unpunctuality of supper, which, ordered for nine o'clock, was served at a quarter to ten. The children being in bed, their parents at length sat down to the meal with keen appetite, and soon recovered good humour. Budge had brought in with him a bottle of Irish whisky, Rippingille a bottle of rum; these stood unopened upon the sideboard, an exhilarating promise for half an hour before bedtime. It gave the ladies some concern to discover that the cupboard in which they would keep their grocery had no lock; at table they discussed this matter from every point of view, and came to the decision that a very careful watch must be kept upon the various parcels. Mrs Budge hit upon an ingenious device; when sugar, coffee, tea, and the rest had been opened, she should mark, with a pencil, the exact position of each packet upon the shelf, so as to ensure immediate detection of any tampering with the goods. Mrs Rippingille suggested that all edibles should be kept under lock and key in the bedroom; but, besides the inconvenience of this method, there was a certain delight attaching to the anticipation of sternly convicting their landlady, in case of fraud.

At half-past ten they sallied forth to taste the sea air. In a street hard by, in front of a busy public-house, they were arrested by a crowd gathered around negro melodists, and here they feasted their souls with music until the hat began to circulate, which sped them onwards. Arrived at the sea front, they found abundant life of the kind most pleasing to them : a thronged highway, resounding with virile shout and feminine squeal, with refrains of the music-hall, and every such noise as inspirits the children of a great capital. In spite of the fatigue which made their limbs ache, the happy wives and mothers leapt about like girls, screamed mirthfully at each other, thumped their husbands' backs, and declared a thousand times that this was the height of human bliss. On their return the spirit bottles were exultantly opened, and each one drank a stiff, sweet, steaming tumbler. Ordinarily very temperate people in the matter of strong beverage, they felt it incumbent upon them to indulge a little at the seaside. Rippingille pretended to be overcome and staggered about the floor with low comedy monologue. This brought the evening to a splendidly hilarious close, and they paired off for rest with laughter which made the house ring.

They awoke to Sunday. Not only this, but the weather had suffered an unfortunate change; the sky was gloomy and threatened rain. Breakfast, ordered for nine, could not be obtained until nearly an hour later. The children were troublesome and very noisy; the ladies had a bad headache, and began to complain loudly of various discomforts. To complete the cheerlessness of the morning, rain actually began to fall just as breakfast was finished.

'I tell you what it is,' exclaimed Rippingille, voicing the general sentiment, 'we're going to be better waited on than this, and the landlady's got to understand that.' He spoke while the servant was in the room. 'I don't call that fish properly fried – what do you say ?'

Budge was the person appealed to, and he assented vigorously, adding that, if dinner wasn't brought up at the right time, he would know the reason why.

'We've got eighteen people in the 'ouse to cook for,' remarked the servant impartially and casually.

All answered together that this had nothing to do with them, that they hadn't come here to waste time, and that they weren't the sort to pay money for what they didn't get. It was added that the bedrooms swarmed with fleas, and that the bedclothes were insufficient, with many another pointed complaint. But the servant merely smiled, and went her way.

With the aid of umbrellas, the whole party reached the parade, and found seats in a shelter. Budge and Rippingille, to ward off low spirits, engaged in horseplay, and were so far successful that at dinner-time all went back through the rain with resolute display of mirth. But the day was unpropitious. Mrs Budge, on scrutinizing the cupboard, protested that the bag of loaf sugar had been interfered with; there followed an unpleasant scene with the servant; the landlady herself could not be assailed, for she declined to come upstairs. Rain, squabbling, chastisement of children, and occasional words between the two ladies brought Sunday to its close. Happily, there remained the half-hour devoted to steaming tumblers, and this paid for all. Budge sang a song about waiting till the clouds roll by, and hearty voices joined him in the chorus. No one could honestly say that the day seemed lost.

On Monday morning the landlady began reprisals. Meeting Mrs Rippingille on the stairs, she complained of the noise that the five children made. A lady below (the word was meaningly emphasized) had been unable to sleep since seven o'clock this morning, owing to the tumult. 'Tell the lydy,' answered Mrs Rippingille tartly, 'she'd better git up earlier; it's good for her 'ealth.' And this retort kept the holiday makers in exuberant spirits till dinner-time. For the first time they got down on to the beach; they rolled about, and pelted each other; spades and buckets were bought for the elder children. They talked about bathing, but, on the whole, it seemed better to save their money for more certain delights. 'Paddling' could be enjoyed free of expense; and remarkable figures did the two young women present as they ran hither and thither on the edge of the tide – their petticoats pinned up outside their dresses. Budge and Rippingille, reclining pipe in mouth, watched with a genial grin.

Dinner, obtained only after repeated and furious ringing at the bell, came up infamously cooked; the huge slab of steak was tough as leather, and swam in water of a yellowish hue. Mrs Rippingille, who had visited the butcher's this morning, declared that a good half-pound had been feloniously cut off below stairs. Messages of savage insult were sent to the landlady, but satisfaction ended here. It was some relief, however; and, after all, the cooking could not be very much worse than that to which our friends were accustomed at home.

In the afternoon, Mrs Budge, whose baby had an attack of some complaint incidental to its time of life, offered to take care of all the children, whilst the other three elders went in search of enjoyment. This took the form of a ten-mile drive in a public brake, where they sat squeezed and perspiring amid some thirty people. The sun blazed; chalky dust hung in a perpetual cloud about the vehicle; it was hardly possible to get a handkerchief out of one's pocket; but gaiety defied everything. On the way home, Mrs Rippingille, red as a peony with heat and laughter and many quenchings of thirst, consulted the comfort of her neighbours by sitting on Mr Budge's knee; ceaseless joking as to Mrs Budge's state of mind if she knew what was going on kept all three in a roar. The absent lady, meanwhile, having administered remedies to her infant, was walking about the main streets of Brighton, enjoying the sight of the Bank Holiday crowd; the baby she carried in her arms, and the other children followed her. They wanted to play on the beach, but Mrs Budge said it was too far, and for her own part she preferred the pavement.

Over the steaming tumblers that night a vow was registered that, on the morrow, they would have better attendance and better cookery, or know the reason why. As soon as the children awoke, they were encouraged to make the utmost possible noise; to stamp and jump and throw over the furniture, and yell at the top of their voices. This had the desired effect; it brought up the landlady at breakfast. Before she could speak, the angry woman was overwhelmed with vilification. Presently Rippingille voiced the general demand.

'We haven't come here to be bested, and just you bear that in mind! If this kind of thing goes on we won't pay – not a bloomin' penny – understand? You've got to cook our meals proper and to time – see? What do you tike us for? Why, the beds ain't even shook up. And do you call these boots cleaned? It's himposition, that's what it is.'

The combat was too unequal; in spite of her great command of 'language,' the landlady retreated. The lodgers, flushed with

victory, sallied forth under a cloudy sky, and betook themselves
to the pier, where they attended a popular concert. Dinner, for
the first time, was ready almost at the appointed hour, and
somewhat better prepared than hitherto; pæans rose round the
table.

'They always try it on,' cried Budge. 'You've got to show 'em
you won't stand it.' And he chanted a verse of the last song they
had heard upon the pier.

Afterwards, all went for a sail in a yacht, and all were
lamentably ill. Rain came on; it soaked the holiday garments,
and led to all manner of unpleasantness among the three score
people packed on board. After a low-spirited tea, the two men,
foreseeing an evening of domestic discord, silently vanished, and
did not reappear until eleven o'clock. They had been to the
theatre. As it happened, their wives had found an excellent
opportunity for assailing the landlady, and were again victorious; so things passed off better than might have been expected,
and over the usual tumblers all unkindness was forgotten.

Wednesday dawned; the end of their holiday. Though breakfast was very late and very bad, no one seemed in the mood to
make an uproar. Mrs Rippingille busied herself with a scheme
for packing and carrying away every smallest remnant of every
purchased eatable; this must be done before she left the house
for the morning's amusement, or servant and landlady would
pillage without fear. Having swept the cupboard, she went
briskly forth to purchase dinner. The meal was to consist of
fried eggs and bacon, with a rice pudding to follow.

'And just you mind what I say' – thus she addressed the
servant on her return with the provisions – 'if this dinner isn't
properly cooked, you'll remember it. And tell your missis that.'

The menial grinned broadly, but made no answer.

Swift is the flight of happy hours and days. Everyone
remarked, at intervals through the morning, that they seemed
only just to have come to Brighton; yet to-night must see them
home again. The children, whose enjoyment had been considerably less keen than that of their elders, wore gloomy faces at the
thought of return; but the suggestion of donkey riding once
more exhilarated the whole company. Great and small mounted
for a gallop, and their yells rang along the beach. Other delights
followed. As dinner-time approached their hunger grew fierce;
the thought of delay was frenzy. A stampede upstairs announced

their arrival, and rendered needless the loud ring of the sitting-room bell.

Nor had they to wait. The red-nosed servant appeared in a few minutes, panting with the heavy tray. Her lips rigidly set, she put down the dish of eggs and bacon. In the same moment Mrs Rippingille, who had stepped forward to judge the cookery, uttered an indignant shriek. Her companions rushed to the table, and in union vociferated, not without cause, for the dish made a gruesome display; in place of succulent rashers lay blackened fragments scarce to be recognized as bacon, and the fried eggs were mere bits of greasy leather. Frightened at the results of her mischief, the servant fled; before she reached the kitchen the bell had begun to ring, and it rang incessantly, with ear-piercing clangour, until the landlady, who had just returned from a brief expedition on a matter of business, angrily confronted her lodgers.

'Look at that, woman !' they roared. 'What do you call that ?'

The landlady could not pretend that complaint was unjustified. She happened to be particularly anxious to get rid of these people, as their rooms were already let to more desirable tenants, who desired to enter into possession as early as possible.

'I don't want to have no more words with you,' she began, as soon as she could make herself audible. 'There's been a accident, and I tell you what I'll do. If you'll leave after dinner, instead of after tea, I'll take the price of that dinner off what you owe me. How much did the stuff cost ?'

The lodgers exchanged glances and reflected. It was possible to make a meal of a sort upon what lay before them, and the offered compensation would be clear gain. Not one had sufficient acuteness to see that, if they could claim damages at all, no condition need attach to the demand. After ten minutes' vehement debate they agreed upon terms, and promised to quit the house in an hour's time. Then, sharp set as wolves, they fell upon the base provender. Luckily, the rice pudding made a tolerable appearance; it vanished almost as soon as it reached the table.

They lingered about the shore and the streets till nearly sunset; the eating-house tea was universally declared the best meal they had had at Brighton. Every heart beat with a proud joy in the thought of two shillings deducted from their landlady's bill, compensation for a dinner, which, after all, they had thoroughly enjoyed. Nothing could have happened more luckily; the money saved, and the victory over a letter of lodgings, crowned their holiday. They talked of the affair at home and among their friends for many a month, and to the end of their lives it will be a sunny reminiscence.

A FREAK OF NATURE

No more respectable man paid rates in Holloway. His house stood in a street unbroken by shop or licensed victualler's; a street with railings and areas, and only one genteel notice of Apartments to let; where tradesmen called for orders, and the itinerant vendor of coals or vegetables had no chance of a customer.

Mr Brogden looked back upon sixteen years of married life; his age was now forty, and he had eight children. It was one of the sights of the street, when, on a Sunday morning, Mr and Mrs Brogden set forth for church, drawing after them their retinue of five youngsters, – the three of tenderest years being left at home for the maid-of-all-work to look after whilst she cooked the dinner. All were so nicely dressed, a pattern to Holloway households: from the father's silk hat (antiquated in form, but well preserved) to the pretty shoes of the youngest girl. Mrs Brogden's attire could not be called fashionable, but it was faultlessly neat, and such as became a self-respecting matron who has her regular seat half way down the nave. Such families, linked together, make the back-bone of English civilisation.

On Monday morning, be the weather what it might, Mr Brogden issued from his front door at an unvarying moment, cast a glance at the front of the house to see that windows were clean and curtains orderly, and walked to Holloway station, whence he had a season ticket to the City. From half-past nine to half-past five he sat in the offices of a well-known firm; and on his return by a specified train tea-dinner awaited him. At ten o'clock he went to bed.

When the sun chanced to shine, he would often have preferred to travel Citywards on the top of a Nag's Head omnibus; but this might not be. And for the simple reason that Mr Brogden could not afford the fare. His expenses were calculated, year in year out, down to the uttermost farthing; an uncovenanted tuppence would have thrown the budget into disorder. Literally, Mr Brogden durst not spend one halfpenny in gratification of a mere whim. Only by the exercise of severest economy, by the pursual of inflexible routine, could he hope to find himself solvent at the year's end. As it was, he owed nothing; and the possibility of an increase of salary helped him to face the probability of more children, and the growing demands of those already born.

Mrs Brogden was a thin, anaemic, yet wiry woman, somewhat younger than her husband. Her rigid sense of duty forbade moping and checked outbursts of temper, but was not inconsistent with ceaseless chatter in a high, querulous tone. She had altogether lost the habit of fondling her children, and for many years had uttered no word of affection to their father. This did not signify a dislike either of him or them; life had brought about such [a] state of affairs, that was all. To bear and nurse a new baby was a matter of the strictest business, to be dutifully discharged, with occasional reference to the will of God, and much more than occasional fault-finding with things domestic. Neither did Mr Brogden pretend to conjugal or paternal fervour. The phrase 'my dear' fell from his lips as a matter of course; he never addressed his wife unfeelingly, and gave her all the help that his other engagements allowed; but it was long, long, since her proximity had caused him a soft emotion, and very often indeed her voice, her countenance, told severely upon his nerves. The first child, and the second, had touched his heart; but now he regarded all with a weary kindness, or a harassing sense of responsibility.

Physically he was not a strong man, and for the last year or two he had been conscious of internal troubles which seemed to menace his mechanic health. A nervous disorder, perhaps; possibly something connected with the stomach. He dieted himself, but without appreciable result. Nowadays, when he rose of a morning, he generally had a slight headache, and sometimes his hand shook in an unpleasant way. Fits of mental abstraction began to worry him; he would unaccountably lose hold of a train of thought, or be unaware of remarks addressed to him. Undoubtedly, too, his wife and the children were more trying to his patience; he found himself, now and then, on the point of exclaiming angrily. The weekly revision of household accounts gave him special annoyance, accompanied as it was by Mrs Brogden's remarks on the behaviour of tradespeople and the quality of their wares.

One Saturday evening, when Mrs Brogden was discussing a grocer's bill, he suddenly experienced the strangest sensation. His brain seemed to rotate, and he clutched the table to prevent his body from likewise going round. Then a quivering fell upon his limbs, and his teeth chattered.

'Stop ! Please stop !' he exclaimed, staring half wrathfully, half fearfully, at his wife.

'What's the matter ?'

'I don't feel well. I can't bear this. Those bills will drive me mad.'

Mrs Brogden was rather indignant than alarmed.

'Oh, if you choose to let the grocer charge threepence for loaf-sugar—'

He sprang up, and walked about the room.

'I must go out for a little turn. It's a rush of blood to the head, I think. Please don't talk to me – *don't* !'

He hurried into the passage, seized his hat, and went forth. After a walk along Seven Sisters' Road, his strange seizure passed away. When he came home again, Mrs Brogden had gone to bed. As usual, he lay down beside her in silence.

But not to sleep. His mind was possessed with unwonted reminiscences ; boyhood and bachelor days came vividly back to him. He saw himself a young fellow of somewhat warm temperament, and ambitious of success in life. He remembered peccadilloes, utterly forgotten in the routine of respectable existence. A certain Lizzie – fie ! And the night when he and a sportive friend tied a cord at hat-height across a gloomy suburban street. Then his resolves to become rich ; the certainty that he would some day ride in his carriage ; the municipal dignities he might attain.

Mrs Brogden breathed heavily. The baby cried for a minute, but went to sleep again.

In the morning he felt too unwell for church-going. All day long he struggled with a distressing inability to command his thoughts, which ran in the most singular directions for the thoughts of a respectable man – on Sunday, too. In the afternoon he took a long walk, all down Caledonian Road ; but his spirits were none the better for it, and perhaps were not likely to be. At nightfall, when Mrs Brogden was putting children to bed, he again rose at a sudden impulse, and stole from, rather than left, the house. To go out on Sunday without explanation to his wife was an unheard-of proceeding; he felt inspirited, oddly enough, by the sense of audacity.

This time he took the Camden Road direction, and after walking for half an hour he turned into a decent by-street, short and ill-lighted. Here the gleam of a polished door-bell caught his eye, and forthwith an extraordinary temptation awoke in him. He looked up and down the street, and saw no figure. In an instant, as though constrained by [an] irresistible motive, he gave a strong pull at the bell-handle; then rapidly strode away and vanished round the near corner.

He was in a glow. That astounding prank had somehow done him good; it seemed to clear an obsruction from his brain. He laughed quietly and naturally, and felt disposed to skip.

In another deserted street, the spirit of mischief again demanded indulgence. This time it was a doctor's bell that he rang; and knowing that the door would be quickly opened, he sped off in delicious alarm. He ran almost into the arms of a policeman, just round the corner, and instantly, without a thought, exclaimed to him: 'Do you know there's a dreadful fire in Tottenham Court Road?'

'No, sir. Whose place?'

'Don't know. I only saw it from a distance. I'm in a hurry.'

Now his craving for sensation was appeased. At a brisk pace he returned to Holloway. On admitting himself with his latch-key, he found Mrs Brogden standing before him in the passage, her countenance indignant and wondering.

'I've had a walk, and feel better for it.'

His peremptory utterance had the natural effect. Mrs Brogden remonstrated with him for a full hour; to her the unusual was presumably the improper, and she told her husband in three score different ways that she could not understand him. Brogden did not give ear; his thoughts caused him so much amusement that with difficulty he refrained from chuckling.

But next day the headache and unsteadiness of hand were worse than ever. On his return from business, he felt most seriously out of sorts, and his wife at length perceived that he was unwell.

'I think a day or two of rest would put me up. Rest and change. In fact, I can't rest without change. I've a good mind to ask leave, and go down to my brother's.'

Mr Brogden's brother lived at a little town in Wiltshire, and throve in a drapery business; it was some years since the two had met. After long discussions spread over a couple of days, with the result that Brogden felt himself, in all seriousness, on the verge of lunacy, he was permitted by his wife to take this step, if he could be spared from the office. Never before had he sought an undue holiday; his employers freely granted him a week. And by an early train he travelled from Paddington.

The first sight of open country afforded him vast relief. To see the end of London was like shaking off a burden which had all but crushed him. Privately he had determined to see a medical man, down in Wiltshire. Of course it worried him to think of the money he was spending; somehow it must be made up by retrenchments. But better this than to break down altogether – like certain men he had known. Some ailment of the nerves, beyond a doubt. And really, remembering last Sunday, had he not been dangerously near insanity? He could not confess those disgraceful proceedings to any doctor.

Now, the further he advanced upon his journey, the less inclined he felt to go straight to his destination. Air and movement inspired him with a longing for liberty, absolute independence, which he could not enjoy at his brother's house. How delightful to spend the night somewhere alone, say at a country inn! And why not? Just this one night; then to-morrow he would proceed as he had purposed, and send the promised note to his wife.

Almost without an effort, he alighted at an unknown place some twenty miles on the hither side of the town for which he was booked. He left his bag at the station, and walked off along a rustic road; enjoying himself, though with mingled tremors, as he had never done since the eclipse of his youth in marriage. For a couple of hours he rambled in utter carelessness of locality, scarcely observing the landscape, absorbed in his exultant freedom. 'Ah! this is doing me good. This is what I needed. No necessity for paying doctors, afer all. Already I am a new man.'

Appetite directed him at length to a pleasant village inn. He entered a room where two guests were dining: a middle-aged clergyman, with ruddy cheek and benevolent smile, and a well-dressed lad of about sixteen. They glanced at him; Mr Brogden removed his hat and bowed. He was wearing the ordinary City garb, and looked what he had every claim to be considered, a most respectable man of business. No hint of poverty appeared in his clothing; he even exhibited a gold watch-guard. As for Mr Brogden's features, they were as good as a letter of commendation from the Lord Mayor: honest in every line, impressed with habitual gravity, and suggesting a certain reputable shrewdness.

Whilst enjoying the homely meal set before him, he necessarily overheard the conversation of his fellow guests. It appeared that they were uncle and nephew, and they seemed, like Brogden himself, to be merely having a long country walk. The cleric talked very agreeably, revealing a cheery, sanguine disposition, and a pleasant simplicity of mind; his jokes were frequent and estimable, but not brilliant.

Above the fireplace hung a coloured picture which served as advertisement of somebody's whisky; it represented one of the great Californian pines, with a coach-way cut through the living trunk. The boy began to question his uncle about this prodigy of nature. Now, as it happened, Mr Brogden knew a City clerk who had travelled in California, and from him he had gathered much more information than the good clergyman seemed able to supply. He longed to join in the talk. A pint of good ale had warmed his brain; he was in the mood for companionship, and, more than that, felt an eagerness to appear a person of some importance – the joy which life had so seldom granted him. As he gazed at the picture, smiling, the clergyman noticed him, and spoke courteously.

'Possibly you know more about those noble trees, sir, than I do?'

Brogden, delighted, poured forth all he could remember, and his companions gave friendly ear.

'Have you travelled in that part of the world, sir?'

'Yes, sir; some years ago.'

Was it he himself, Mr Brogden of Holloway, who had spoken? Or had a devil taken possession of his tongue? – He dropped back in his chair, quaking, overwhelmed with shame.

'How very interesting!' said the country parson, with a glance at his nephew. 'I must say that I envy you.'

'I was there on business,' Brogden remarked, in a voice that still did not seem his own. And he added certain particulars, true of his acquaintance in the City.

The clergyman was talkative; in a quarter of an hour's time he, his nephew and Mr Brogden made a friendly trio. The conversation turned upon matters commercial, for Brogden had allowed it to be understood that he was a London man of business taking a holiday, and this obviously interested the genial cleric.

'Pray tell me now, sir,' said the latter, 'what are the chances of an intelligent youth in a merchant's office in London? The fact is, my nephew here has a wish to obtain such a position.'

'In a house, for instance, like Messrs Truscott & Windham's,' said Brogden, naming, with a smile, his own famous employers.

'Ha!' The clergyman looked pleased. 'That would be the kind of thing. But in those great houses I fear it is not possible to place a lad without special influence.'

Brogden felt something perilous in his blood; the same impulse which wrought upon him when he rang the door-bells the other night; a sensation of reckless daring, exquisite to the nerves.

'I should like to hear,' he said, with something of solemnity, 'whether this young gentleman has undergone any preparation for commercial life.'

The boy good-humouredly submitted to examination. Mr Brogden's brain whirled. Turning at length to the clergyman, he remarked quietly:

'Perhaps I had better mention that I am Mr Truscott, the present senior partner in the firm we spoke of.'

A mist was before his eyes; the blood sang in his ears. From step to step of deception he had proceeded without power to check himself. An abnormal vanity hungered within him. He had set himself on all but the highest pinnacle in the world when, through life, he had played a humble part. So dazed was his imagination at the frantic feat, that he could not perceive its enormity.

'Mr Truscott,' the clergyman was saying, 'I have great pleasure in making your acquaintance. Permit me to introduce myself. I am Mr Lamb, vicar of Dippingham.'

If ever a man, not strictly insane, transferred himself into someone else's personality, it was Mr Brogden at this moment. For one thing, he had always admired and honoured Mr

Truscott, and in the conduct of life had made him an exemplar. The great merchant was not only a power in the City; his private character commanded respect, and among his subordinates in business he had a reputation for singular generosity. Physically, it was true, Mr Brogden by no means resembled him; but the clerk gave not a thought to this detail; his fraud aimed only at impalpable profit. For the first time in his life he was the recipient of homage, and that from a clergyman of the Church of England. As a religious man, he doubtless ought to have felt that his crime of dishonesty was aggravated by that of sacrilege; but his state of mind permitted no such reflection. He walked on air; his head had become a sort of balloon.

'I find it absolutely necessary for my health,' – thus was he speaking, – 'to run down into the country every now and then and have a day's walking. It is the simplest and best remedy for little ailments which trouble me. I have walked over from' – he named the station, – 'and now I shall ramble back, and catch an evening train for London.'

Mr Lamb ventured a suggestion.

'I wish I could persuade you to take the other direction, and walk with us to Dippingham. The roads are delightful. There are local trains, by which you could reach Swindon – '

'Oh, with the greatest pleasure !'

So the trio left their inn. To Dippingham was a walk of about seven miles; they made it a leisurely ramble, which occupied the time from half-past two to half-past six on this bright summer afternoon. Out of delicacy, the clergyman had ceased to talk of his nephew's ambitions, but ever and anon Mr Brogden made a remark to the lad which indicated that he had not lost sight of this important matter. When they drew near to the little town, Mr Lamb begged that his friend would walk as far as the vicarage. There would be no difficulty in reaching Swindon in time for the last up train. Heedless of everything but his ecstatic illusion, Brogden cheerfully consented, and to the vicarage they bent their steps.

They were received by Mrs Lamb, a homely gentlewoman, and her widowed sister, mother of the boy. As dinner was ready, Brogden sat down with the family. Nor did he incur the least danger of betraying habits inconsistent with his assumed station; flawless respectability appeared in his manners no less than in his speech. For the entertainment and instruction of the ladies he was induced to relate once more his experiences in California. He inquired benevolently concerning the poor of the parish, and then – oddest of situations – began to talk about the hardships patiently endured by a certain most meritorious class in London, to wit the body of respectable clerks, whose income, without being miserable, was yet barely sufficient for the needs of a decent family.

'Such cases, I fear, admit of no remedy. A strict economic law regulates the salaries paid by employers. But I have known of painful instances. Happily, they sometimes come under one's personal notice, and then, of course, something can be done.'

Mr Lamb was led into talk of curates; and so the conversation drew on, until a little clock on the dining-room mantelpiece struck eight. Mr Brogden looked round. Was he not forgetting, he said, that he had a train to catch? This moment had been awaited by the vicar.

'Is it really imperative, Mr Truscott, that you should return to-night? It would give us such pleasure if you could stay – if we might offer you a room – '

Brogden began to suffer unpleasant symptoms. A half-painful languor was creeping over him. He felt unable to come to a decision. The morrow glimpsed upon his mind in awful shape. But while he stood thus vacillating, the vicar began to take it for granted that he would stay. As a matter of fact, it was no longer possible to return to London, and this Mr Lamb well knew. With pardonable zeal for his nephew's prospects, he was doing his utmost to cement the friendship with Mr Truscott, – pathetic illustration of unwonted guile in a most simple and worthy man.

They sat together in the study, and smoked. Brogden had sunk into taciturnity; by ten o'clock he found it difficult to utter even a monosyllable. He was thinking of his wife and children; his actual surroundings seemed visionary; he had an aching in his muscles, a dizziness of brain, a terrible and increasing weight at his heart. Of a sudden, he staggered, rather than rose, from the chair.

'Mr Lamb, I am afraid I have walked rather too far to-day. – I feel exceedingly tired – '

The vicar was all sympathetic attention. In a few minutes he conducted the great man to his chamber, where all possible arrangements had been made for a guest's comfort.

'In the morning,' said Brogden, absently, as they shook hands,
'I should like to speak again of our young friend.'

'Oh, thank you, thank you,' replied the vicar, genially. 'A
refreshing sleep to you, my dear sir!'

The door closed. Brogden stood in the middle of the room,
and stared about him. He had the appearance of a man who has
drunk too much, and who is passing from exhilaration to
despondency.

He glanced at pictures; turned to the bed and regarded it with
gloomy eye; began to pace slowly, with cautious step, between
the window and the door. Presently his legs shook and failed
him. He dropped upon a chair, let his hands fall upon his knees,
and sat like one overcome by misery.

Time passed. He heard the church clock, hard by, from
quarter to quarter. All sounds in the house had ceased. It was a
perfectly still night; not a rustle in the trees.

Midnight tolled. Then did Mr Brogden stand up, listen for a
moment, step with lightest foot towards the window, most
carefully draw up the blind. All dark without; no gleam visible
above or below. He unhasped the window; he tried, with
trembling hand, whether it was possible to raise the lower sash
soundlessly. Yes, it might be done. This was an old and well-
built house, without any of the makeshift appliances to which
he was accustomed in his London home.

The window was half open, when a thought of terror stayed
him. Did Mr Lamb keep a dog? He knew not whether this room
looked from the front of the house or the back; but he discerned
a garden, and some loud-voiced animal might be holding watch
over the vicarage.

That must be risked. But stop; what was he doing? He had
not extinguished the light. Someone might all the time be
observing him.

With sweat running from his forehead, he raised the window
sufficiently to allow of his getting through. The drop would be
a trifle in such a moment; twelve feet at most, and onto garden
ground. He fixed the respectable silk hat very firmly on his head,
braced his nerves, struggled somehow onto the outer sill; then
grasped the lower woodwork of the window desperately, and
allowed his legs to sink.

So hung he for half a minute, then fell. A heavy fall; but, as
he had anticipated, broken by the mould of a flower-bed. It

seemed to him that he had made an alarming noise. His hat had been jerked off, and, when the shock allowed him to stand, he looked vainly about him for this indispensable head-gear. Ah, he had stepped upon it; he turned and felt it crunch.

Squeezing the now dishonoured cylinder upon his head, he made off like a burglar surprised. Impossible to seek for paths and gateways. Before him was a low wall, and he surmounted it. Only to find himself deep in the mud of a ditch; but a moment released him, and he sped over a broad field. It must have been half an hour before he could find an issue; everywhere seemed to be impermeable hedges. Moreover, it began to rain; though his sweat-bath concealed this fact from him till the shower had become heavy. At length the gate was discovered, and he came out into a highway.

Until the sky flushed with dawn, he walked forward at his utmost pace; for the most part through open country, but now and then passing a hamlet or village. His watch had stopped, but by daybreak he knew that he must have travelled at least ten miles. And what was the use of this, when assuredly, in a few hours, the police would everywhere be looking out for him? Mr Lamb must necessarily conceive the worst opinion of him. Communication would instantly be made with the real Mr Truscott. A full description of his appearance, together with the fact of his absence from town, could not but excite his City acquaintances to a surmise of the truth. He had ruined himself and his family. Better to end by suicide, and so get the benefit of the assumption that he was a victim of lunacy.

Yes. He would drown himself in a river or pond. And straightway be began to look out for a suitable spot.

It was not hard to find, but the effort to carry out his resolve proved hard indeed. For two or three hours he sat or walked near the muddy river which promised an end of his woes; with every minute the possibility of such an act grew more remote. He felt faint with hunger. There was money in his pocket, and inns were near. Midway in the morning he entered a wayside tavern, and ate as he had not eaten since boyhood.

By dint of much manipulation, he had restored his hat to a shameful sort of shapelessness. Brushes, water, and such aids now removed the other signs of vagrancy. Yet what was the use? — he asked. To be sure, he had no actual reason to fear arrest; excitement had magnified the dangers of his flight from Dippingham. But of a certainty he was ruined. As he lacked the courage to die, he must face the consequences of living. Idle, now, to think of a visit to his brother. He desired to obliterate himself, to disappear; to earn laborious bread under a strange name, in a locality where he could never be recognized. Charity must provide for his wife and children.

Hitherto completely ignorant of his geographical position, he now learnt that aimless wandering had brought him within a few miles of Swindon. Projects he could not form, but he set off and walked to the railway station. His mind was still visionary; he had no grasp of the realities of life; and so it came to pass that, at Swindon, he took a ticket for Bristol, where, after nightfall, he hired an obscure lodging, saying to himself that he must begin life anew.

Three days after this, Mr Truscott, the busy merchant, received a letter which puzzled him. It was written by one of his numerous clerks, the Mr Brogden who was just now away on sick-leave, and dated from somewhere in the East End. 'Sir, I humbly entreat that you will grant me a private interview. I believe that I have been seriously ill, and that I was not responsible for the actions that have disgraced me. I earnestly beg that you will hear me in my own defence. I will come at any hour to any place you may appoint.' – Now Mr Truscott had heard nothing whatever of disgraceful actions on his clerk's part. On inquiring in the office, however, he gathered that Mr Brogden had not been quite like himself of late. So he replied to the letter by telegram, simply requesting Mr Brogden to call at his residence that evening.

The interview which accordingly took place was remarkable. At the first sight of his clerk, and on hearing the first words which the poor man poured forth, Mr Truscott had no doubt that he was dealing with a lunatic. But a quarter of an hour's conversation put the matter in another light. A man of intelligence and of sympathy, he gave close attention to the whole surprising story, and then put a few important questions relative to Mr Brogden's private life.

'Tell me frankly,' he said at length. 'What is your own explanation of these strange proceedings?'

Brogden could think and speak lucidly enough. He looked very disreputable, very wretched, undoubtedly ill; but the man's honesty was obvious.

'I fear, sir,' he replied in humble tones, 'that I must have been rather overstrained, in some way.'

'I think so too. And how do you feel, in mind, at present ?'

'Much better, sir,' Brogden answered with truth. 'Very much better.'

Mr Truscott surmised, what Brogden perhaps did not understand, that nature had revenged herself and was permitting the return of normality. He spoke kindly and judiciously. The clerk was to take a month's holiday at his employer's expense ; when the result was seen, they would have another talk. – And so it came about that, at the month's end, Mr Brogden resumed his position in the office, but with slightly increased salary. He was as trustworthy and respectable a man as ever.

Between Mr Truscott and the vicar of Dippingham there took place a friendly correspondence, satisfactory to both. It was not Mr Lamb who wrote first, and that singular story never became known outside the walls of the vicarage.

A POOR GENTLEMAN

It was in the drawing-room, after dinner. Mrs Charman, the
large and kindly hostess, sank into a chair beside her little friend
Mrs Loring, and sighed a question.

'How do you like Mr Tymperley ?'

'Very nice. Just a little peculiar.'

'Oh, he *is* peculiar ! Quite original. I wanted to tell you about
him before we went down, but there wasn't time. Such a very
old friend of ours. My dear husband and he were at school
together — Harrovians. The sweetest, the most affectionate
character ! Too good for this world, I'm afraid; he takes
everything so seriously. I shall never forget his grief at my poor
husband's death — I'm telling Mrs Loring about Mr Tymperley,
Ada.'

She addressed her married daughter, a quiet young woman
who reproduced Mrs Charman's good-natured countenance,
with something more of intelligence, the reflective serenity of a
higher type.

'I'm sorry to see him looking so far from well,' remarked Mrs
Weare, in reply.

'He never had any colour, you know, and his life . . . But I
must tell you,' she resumed to Mrs Loring. 'He's a bachelor, in
comfortable circumstances, and — would you believe it ? — he
lives quite alone in one of the distressing parts of London.
Where is it, Ada ?'

'A poor street in Islington.'

'Yes. There he lives, I'm afraid in shocking lodgings — it must
be *so* unhealthy — just to become acquainted with the life of
poor people, and be helpful to them. Isn't it heroic ? He seems
to have given up his whole life to it. One never meets him
anywhere; I think ours is the only house where he's seen. A

noble life! He never talks about it. I'm sure you would never have suspected such a thing from his conversation at dinner?'

'Not for a moment,' answered Mrs Loring, astonished. 'He wasn't very gossipy – I gathered that his chief interests were fretwork and foreign politics.'

Mrs Weare laughed. 'The very man! When I was a little girl he used to make all sorts of pretty things for me with his fret-saw; and when I grew old enough, he instructed me in the balance of Power. It's possible, mamma, that he writes leading articles. We should never hear of it.'

'My dear, anything is possible with Mr Tymperley. And such a change, this, after his country life. He had a beautiful little house near ours, in Berkshire. I really can't help thinking that my husband's death caused him to leave it. He was so attached to Mr Charman! When my husband died, and we left Berkshire, we altogether lost sight of him – oh, for a couple of years. Then I met him by chance in London. Ada thinks there must have been some sentimental trouble.'

'Dear mamma,' interposed the daughter, 'it was you, not I, who suggested that.'

'Was it? Well, perhaps it was. One can't help seeing that he has gone through something. Of course it may be only pity for the poor souls he gives his life to. A wonderful man!'

When masculine voices sounded at the drawing-room door, Mrs Loring looked curiously for the eccentric gentleman. He entered last of all. A man of more than middle height, but much bowed in the shoulders; thin, ungraceful, with an irresolute step and a shy demeanour; his pale-grey eyes, very soft in expression, looked timidly this way and that from beneath brows nervously bent, and a self-obliterating smile wavered upon his lips. His hair had begun to thin and to turn grey, but he had a heavy moustache, which would better have sorted with sterner linea-ments. As he walked – or sidled – into the room, his hands kept shutting and opening, with rather ludicrous effect. Something which was not exactly shabbiness, but a lack of lustre, of finish, singled him among the group of men; looking closer, one saw that his black suit belonged to a fashion some years old. His linen was irreproachable, but he wore no sort of jewellery, one little black stud showing on his front, and at the cuffs, solitaires of the same simple description.

He drifted into a corner, and there would have sat alone,

seemingly at peace, had not Mrs Weare presently moved to a seat beside him.

'I hope you won't be staying in town through August, Mr Tymperley?'

'No! – Oh no! – Oh no, I think not!'

'But you seem uncertain. Do forgive me if I say that I'm sure you need a change. Really, you know, you are *not* looking quite the thing. Now, can't I persuade you to join us at Lucerne? My husband would be so pleased – delighted to talk with you about the state of Europe. Give us a fortnight – do!'

'My dear Mrs Weare, you are kindness itself! I am deeply grateful. I can't easily express my sense of your most friendly thoughtfulness. But, the truth is, I am half engaged to other friends. Indeed, I think I may almost say that I have practically . . . yes, indeed, it amounts to that.'

He spoke in a thinly fluting voice, with a preciseness of enunciation akin to the more feebly clerical, and with smiles which became almost lachrymose in their expressiveness as he dropped from phrase to phrase of embarrassed circumlocution. And his long bony hands writhed together till the knuckles were white.

'Well, so long as you *are* going away. I'm so afraid lest your conscientiousness should go too far. You won't benefit anybody, you know, by making yourself ill.'

'Obviously not! – Ha, ha! – I assure you that fact is patent to me. Health is a primary consideration. Nothing more detrimental to one's usefulness than an impaired . . . Oh, to be sure, to be sure!'

'There's the strain upon your sympathies. That must affect one's health, quite apart from an unhealthy atmosphere.'

'But Islington is not unhealthy, my dear Mrs Weare! Believe me, the air has often quite a tonic quality. We are so high, you must remember. If only we could subdue in some degree the noxious exhalations of domestic and industrial chimneys! – Oh, I assure you, Islington has every natural feature of salubrity.'

Before the close of the evening there was a little music, which Mr Tymperley seemed much to enjoy. He let his head fall back, and stared upwards; remaining rapt in that posture for some moments after the music ceased, and at length recovering himself with a sigh.

When he left the house, he donned an overcoat considerably

too thick for the season, and bestowed in the pockets his patent-leather shoes. His hat was a hard felt, high in the crown. He grasped an ill-folded umbrella, and set forth at a brisk walk, as if for the neighbouring station. But the railway was not his goal, nor yet the omnibus. Through the ambrosial night he walked and walked, at the steady pace of one accustomed to pedestrian exercise: from Notting Hill Gate to the Marble Arch; from the Marble Arch to New Oxford Street; thence by Theobald's Road to Pentonville, and up, and up, until he attained the heights of his own salubrious quarter. Long after midnight he entered a narrow byway, which the pale moon showed to be decent, though not inviting. He admitted himself with a latchkey to a little house which smelt of glue, lit a candle-end which he found in his pocket, and ascended two flights of stairs to a back bedroom, its size eight feet by seven and a half. A few minutes more, and he lay sound asleep.

Waking at eight o'clock – he knew the time by a bell that clanged in the neighbourhood – Mr Tymperley clad himself with nervous haste. On opening his door, he found lying outside a tray, with the materials of a breakfast reduced to its lowest terms: half a pint of milk, bread, butter. At nine o'clock he went downstairs, tapped civilly at the door of the front parlour, and by an untuned voice was bidden enter. The room was occupied by an oldish man and a girl, addressing themselves to the day's work of plain bookbinding.

'Good morning to you, sir,' said Mr Tymperley, bending his head. 'Good morning, Miss Suggs. Bright! Sunny! How it cheers one!'

He stood rubbing his hands, as one might on a morning of sharp frost. The bookbinder, with a dry nod for greeting, forthwith set Mr Tymperley a task, to which that gentleman zealously applied himself. He was learning the elementary processes of the art. He worked with patience, and some show of natural aptitude, all through the working hours of the day.

To this pass had things come with Mr Tymperley, a gentleman of Berkshire, once living in comfort and modest dignity on the fruit of sound investments. Schooled at Harrow, a graduate of Cambridge, he had meditated the choice of a profession until it seemed, on the whole, too late to profess anything at all; and, as there was no need of such exertion, he settled himself to a life of innocent idleness, hard by the country-house of his wealthy and influential friend, Mr Charman. Softly the years flowed by. His thoughts turned once or twice to marriage, but a profound diffidence withheld him from the initial step; in the end, he knew himself born for bachelorhood, and with that estate was content. Well for him had he seen as clearly the delusiveness of other temptations! In an evil moment he listened to Mr Charman, whose familiar talk was of speculation, of companies, of shining percentages. Not on his own account was Mr Tymperley lured: he had enough and to spare; but he thought of his sister, married to an unsuccessful provincial barrister, and of her six children, whom it would be pleasant to help, like the opulent uncle of fiction, at their entering upon the world. In Mr Charman he put blind faith, with the result that one morning he found himself shivering on the edge of ruin; the touch of confirmatory news, and over he went.

No one was aware of it but Mr Charman himself, and he, a few days later, lay sick unto death. Mr Charman's own estate suffered inappreciably from what to his friend meant sheer disaster. And Mr Tymperley breathed not a word to the widow; spoke not a word to any one at all, except the lawyer, who quietly wound up his affairs, and the sister whose children must needs go without avuncular aid. During the absence of his friendly neighbours after Mr Charman's death, he quietly disappeared.

The poor gentleman was then close upon forty years old. There remained to him a capital which he durst not expend; invested, it bore him an income upon which a labourer could scarce have subsisted. The only possible place of residence – because the only sure place of hiding – was London, and to London Mr Tymperley betook himself. Not at once did he learn the art of combating starvation with minimum resources. During his initiatory trials he was once brought so low, by hunger and humiliation, that he swallowed something of his pride, and wrote to a certain acquaintance, asking counsel and indirect help. But only a man in Mr Tymperley's position learns how vain is well-meaning advice, and how impotent is social influence. Had he begged for money, he would have received, no doubt, a cheque, with words of compassion; but Mr Tymperley could never bring himself to that.

He tried to make profit of his former amusement, fretwork, and to a certain extent succeeded, earning in six months half a sovereign. But the prospect of adding one pound a year to his starveling dividends did not greatly exhilarate him.

All this time he was of course living in absolute solitude. Poverty is the great secluder – unless one belongs to the rank which is born to it; a sensitive man who no longer finds himself on equal terms with his natural associates, shrinks into loneliness, and learns with some surprise how very willing people are to forget his existence. London is a wilderness abounding in anchorites – voluntary or constrained. As he wandered about the streets and parks, or killed time in museums and galleries (where nothing had to be paid), Mr Tymperley often recognised brethren in seclusion; he understood the furtive glance which met his own, he read the peaked visage, marked with understanding sympathy the shabby-genteel apparel. No interchange of confidences between these lurking mortals; they would like to speak, but pride holds them aloof; each goes on his silent and unfriended way, until, by good luck, he finds himself in hospital or workhouse, when at length the tongue is loosed, and the sore heart pours forth its reproach of the world.

Strange knowledge comes to a man in this position. He learns wondrous economies, and will feel a sort of pride in his ultimate discovery of how little money is needed to support life. In his old days Mr Tymperley would have laid it down as an axiom that 'one' cannot live on less than such-and-such an income; he found that 'a man' can live on a few coppers a day. He became aware of the prices of things to eat, and was taught the relative virtues of nutriment. Perforce a vegetarian, he found that a vegetable diet was good for his health, and delivered to himself many a scornful speech on the habits of the carnivorous multitude. He of necessity abjured alcohols, and straightway longed to utter his testimony on a teetotal platform. These were his satisfactions. They compensate astonishingly for the loss of many kinds of self-esteem.

But it happened one day that, as he was in the act of drawing his poor little quarterly salvage at the Bank of England, a lady saw him and knew him. It was Mr Charman's widow.

'Why, Mr Tymperley, what *has* become of you all this time? Why have I never heard from you? Is it true, as some one told me, that you have been living abroad?'

So utterly was he disconcerted, that in a mechanical way he echoed the lady's last word: 'Abroad.'

'But why didn't you write to us?' pursued Mrs Charman, leaving him no time to say more. 'How very unkind! Why did you go away without a word? My daughter says that we must have unconsciously offended you in some way. Do explain! Surely there can't have been anything—'

'My dear Mrs Charman, it is I alone who am to blame. I . . . the explanation is difficult; it involves a multiplicity of detail. I beg you to interpret my unjustifiable behaviour as – as pure idiosyncrasy.'

'Oh, you must come and see me. You know that Ada's married? Yes, nearly a year ago. How glad she will be to see you again. So often she has spoken of you. When can you dine? To-morrow?'

'With pleasure – with great pleasure.'

'Delightful!'

She gave her address, and they parted.

Now, a proof that Mr Tymperley had never lost all hope of restitution to his native world lay in the fact of his having carefully preserved an evening-suit, with the appropriate patent-leather shoes. Many a time had he been sorely tempted to sell these seeming superfluities; more than once, towards the end of his pinched quarter, the suit had been pledged for a few shillings; but to part with the supreme symbol of respectability would have meant despair – a state of mind alien to Mr Tymperley's passive fortitude. His jewellery, even watch and chain, had long since gone: such gauds are not indispensable to a gentleman's outfit. He now congratulated himself on his prudence, for the meeting with Mrs Charman had delighted as much as it embarrassed him, and the prospect of an evening in society made his heart glow. He hastened home; he examined his garb of ceremony with anxious care, and found no glaring defect in it. A shirt, a collar, a necktie must needs be purchased; happily he had the means. But how explain himself? Could he confess his place of abode, his startling poverty? To do so would be to make an appeal to the compassion of his old friends, and from that he shrank in horror. A gentleman will not, if it can possibly be avoided, reveal circumstances likely to cause pain. Must he, then, tell or imply a falsehood? The whole truth involved a reproach of Mrs Charman's husband – a thought he could not bear.

The next evening found him still worrying over this dilemma.

He reached Mrs Charman's house without having come to any decision. In the drawing-room three persons awaited him: the hostess, with her daughter and son-in-law, Mr and Mrs Weare. The cordiality of his reception moved him all but to tears; overcome by many emotions, he lost his head. He talked at random; and the result was so strange a piece of fiction, that no sooner had he evolved it than he stood aghast at himself.

It came in reply to the natural question where he was residing.

'At present' – he smiled fatuously – 'I inhabit a bed-sitting-room in a little street up at Islington.'

Dead silence followed. Eyes of wonder were fixed upon him. But for those eyes, who knows what confession Mr Tymperley might have made? As it was . . .

'I said, Mrs Charman, that I had to confess to an eccentricity. I hope it won't shock you. To be brief, I have devoted my poor energies to social work. I live among the poor, and as one of them, to obtain knowledge that cannot be otherwise procured.'

'Oh, how noble!' exclaimed the hostess.

The poor gentleman's conscience smote him terribly. He could say no more. To spare his delicacy, his friends turned the conversation. Then or afterwards, it never occurred to them to doubt the truth of what he had said. Mrs Charman had seen him transacting business at the Bank of England, a place not suggestive of poverty; and he had always passed for a man somewhat original in his views and ways. Thus was Mr Tymperley committed to a singular piece of deception, a fraud which could not easily be discovered, and which injured only its perpetrator.

Since then about a year had elapsed. Mr Tymperley had seen his friends perhaps half a dozen times, his enjoyment of their society pathetically intense, but troubled by any slightest allusion to his mode of life. It had come to be understood that he made it a matter of principle to hide his light under a bushel, so he seldom had to take a new step in positive falsehood. Of course he regretted ceaselessly the original deceit, for Mrs Charman, a wealthy woman, might very well have assisted him to some not undignified mode of earning his living. As it was, he had hit upon the idea of making himself a bookbinder, a craft somewhat to his taste. For some months he had lodged in the bookbinder's house; one day courage came to him, and he entered into a compact with his landlord, whereby he was to pay for instruction by a certain period of unremunerated work after he became proficient. That stage was now approaching. On the whole, he felt much happier than in the time of brooding idleness. He looked forward to the day when he would have a little more money in his pocket, and no longer dread the last fortnight of each quarter, with its supperless nights.

Mrs Weare's invitation to Lucerne cost him pangs. Lucerne! Surely it was in some former state of existence that he had taken delightful holidays as a matter of course. He thought of the many lovely places he knew, and so many dream-landscapes; the London streets made them infinitely remote, utterly unreal. His three years of gloom and hardship were longer than all the life of placid contentment that came before. Lucerne! A man of more vigorous temper would have been maddened at the thought; but Mr Tymperley nursed it all day long, his emotions only expressing themselves in a little sigh or a sadly wistful smile.

Having dined so well yesterday, he felt it his duty to expend less than usual on to-day's meals. About eight o'clock in the evening, after a meditative stroll in the air which he had so praised, he entered the shop where he was wont to make his modest purchases. A fat woman behind the counter nodded familiarly to him, with a grin at another customer. Mr Tymperley bowed, as was his courteous habit.

'Oblige me,' he said, 'with one new-laid egg, and a small, crisp lettuce.'

'Only one to-night, eh?' said the woman.

'Thank you, only one,' he replied, as if speaking in a drawing-room. 'Forgive me if I express a hope that it will be, in the strict sense of the word, new-laid. The last, I fancy, had got into that box by some oversight – pardonable in the press of business.'

'They're always the same,' said the fat shopkeeper. 'We don't make no mistakes of that kind.'

'Ah! Forgive me! Perhaps I imagined—'

Egg and lettuce were carefully deposited in a little handbag he carried, and he returned home. An hour later, when his meal was finished, and he sat on a straight-backed chair meditating in the twilight, a rap sounded at his door, and a letter was handed to him. So rarely did a letter arrive for Mr Tymperley that his hand shook as he examined the envelope. On opening it, the first thing he saw was a cheque. This excited him still more; he unfolded the written sheet with agitation. It came from Mrs Weare, who wrote thus : —

My Dear Mr Tymperley,

After our talk last evening, I could not help thinking of you and your beautiful life of self-sacrifice. I contrasted the lot of these poor people with my own, which, one cannot but feel, is so undeservedly blest and so rich in enjoyments. As a result of these thoughts, I feel impelled to send you a little contribution to your good work — a sort of thank-offering at the moment of setting off for a happy holiday. Divide the money, please, among two or three of your most deserving pensioners; or, if you see fit, give it all to one. I cling to the hope that we may see you at Lucerne.

With very kind regards.

The cheque was for five pounds. Mr Tymperley held it up by the window, and gazed at it. By his present standards of value five pounds seemed a very large sum. Think of what one could do with it! His boots — which had been twice repaired — would not decently serve him much longer. His trousers were in the last stage of presentability. The hat he wore (how carefully tended!) was the same in which he had come to London three years ago. He stood in need, verily, of a new equipment from head to foot; and in Islington five pounds would more than cover the whole expense. When, pray, was he likely to have such a sum at his free disposal?

He sighed deeply, and stared about him in the dusk.

The cheque was crossed. For the first time in his life Mr Tymperley perceived that the crossing of a cheque may occasion its recipient a great deal of trouble. How was he to get it changed? He knew his landlord for a suspicious curmudgeon, and refusal of the favour, with such a look as Mr Suggs knew how to give, would be a sore humiliation; besides, it was very doubtful whether Mr Suggs could make any use of the cheque himself. To whom else could he apply? Literally, to no one in London.

Well, the first thing to do was to answer Mrs Weare's letter. He lit his lamp and sat down at the crazy little deal table; but his pen dipped several times into the ink before he found himself able to write.

'Dear Mrs Weare,' –

Then, so long a pause that he seemed to be falling asleep. With a jerk, he bent again to his task.

'With sincere gratitude I acknowledge the receipt of your most kind and generous donation. The money . . .'

(Again his hand lay idle for several minutes.)

'shall be used as you wish, and I will render to you a detailed account of the benefits conferred by it.'

Never had he found composition so difficult. He felt that he was expressing himself wretchedly; a clog was on his brain. It cost him an exertion of physical strength to conclude the letter. When it was done, he went out, purchased a stamp at a tobacconist's shop, and dropped the envelope into the post.

Little slumber had Mr Tymperley that night. On lying down, he began to wonder where he should find the poor people worthy of sharing in this benefaction. Of course he had no acquaintance with the class of persons of whom Mrs Weare was thinking. In a sense, all the families round about were poor, but – he asked himself – had poverty the same meaning for them as for him? Was there a man or woman in this grimy street who, compared with himself, had any right to be called poor at all? An educated man forced to live among the lower classes arrives at many interesting conclusions with regard to them; one conclusion long since fixed in Mr Tymperley's mind was that the 'suffering' of those classes is very much exaggerated by outsiders using a criterion quite inapplicable. He saw around him a world of coarse jollity, of contented labour, and of brutal apathy. It seemed to him more than probable that the only person in this street conscious of poverty, and suffering under it, was himself.

From nightmarish dozing, he started with a vivid thought, a recollection which seemed to pierce his brain. To whom did he owe his fall from comfort and self-respect, and all his long miseries? To Mrs Weare's father. And, from this point of view, might the cheque for five pounds be considered as mere restitution? Might it not strictly be applicable to his own necessities?

Another little gap of semi-consciousness led to another strange reflection. What if Mrs Weare (a sensible woman) suspected, or even had discovered, the truth about him? What if she secretly *meant* the money for his own use?

Earliest daylight made this suggestion look very insubstantial; on the other hand, it strengthened his memory of Mr Charman's virtual indebtedness to him. He jumped out of bed to reach the cheque, and for an hour lay with it in his hand. Then he rose and dressed mechanically.

After the day's work he rambled in a street of large shops. A bootmaker's arrested him; he stood before the window for a long time, turning over and over in his pocket a sovereign – no small fraction of the ready coin which had to support him until dividend day. Then he crossed the threshold.

Never did man use less discretion in the purchase of a pair of boots. His business was transacted in a dream; he spoke without hearing what he said; he stared at objects without perceiving them. The result was that not till he had got home, with his easy old footgear under his arm, did he become aware that the new boots pinched him most horribly. They creaked too: heavens! how they creaked! But doubtless all new boots had these faults; he had forgotten; it was so long since he had bought a pair. The fact was, he felt dreadfully tired, utterly worn out. After munching a mouthful of supper he crept into bed.

All night long he warred with his new boots. Footsore, he limped about the streets of a spectral city, where at every corner some one seemed to lie in ambush for him, and each time the lurking enemy proved to be no other than Mrs Weare, who gazed at him with scornful eyes and let him totter by. The creaking of the boots was an articulate voice, which ever and anon screamed at him a terrible name. He shrank and shivered and groaned; but on he went, for in his hand he held a crossed cheque, which he was bidden to get changed, and no one would change it. What a night!

When he woke his brain was heavy as lead; but his meditations were very lucid. Pray, what did he mean by that insane outlay of money, which he could not possibly afford, on a new (and detestable) pair of boots? The old would have lasted, at all events, till winter began. What was in his mind when he entered the shop? Did he intend . . . ? Merciful powers!

Mr Tymperley was not much of a psychologist. But all at once he saw with awful perspicacity the moral crisis through which he had been living. And it taught him one more truth on the subject of poverty.

Immediately after his breakfast he went downstairs and tapped at the door of Mr Suggs' sitting-room.

'What is it ?' asked the bookbinder, who was eating his fourth large rasher, and spoke with his mouth full.

'Sir, I beg leave of absence for an hour or two this morning. Business of some moment demands my attention.'

Mr Suggs answered, with the grace natural to his order, 'I s'pose you can do as you like. I don't pay you nothing.'

The other bowed and withdrew.

Two days later he again penned a letter to Mrs Weare. It ran thus :

The money which you so kindly sent, and which I have already acknowledged, has now been distributed. To ensure a proper use of it, I handed the cheque, with clear instructions, to a clergyman in this neighbourhood, who has been so good as to jot down, on the sheet enclosed, a memorandum of his beneficiaries, which I trust will be satisfactory and gratifying to you.

But why, you will ask, did I have recourse to a clergyman ? Why did I not use my own experience, and give myself the pleasure of helping poor souls in whom I have a personal interest – I who have devoted my life to this mission of mercy ?

The answer is brief and plain. I have lied to you.

I am *not* living in this place of my free will. I am *not* devoting myself to works of charity. I am – no, no, I was – merely a poor gentleman, who, on a certain day, found that he had wasted his substance in a foolish speculation, and who, ashamed to take his friends into his confidence, fled to a life of miserable obscurity. You see that I have added disgrace to misfortune. I will not tell you how very near I came to something still worse.

I have been serving an apprenticeship to a certain handicraft which will, I doubt not, enable me so to supplement my own scanty resources that I shall be in better circumstances than hitherto. I entreat you to forgive me, if you can, and henceforth to forget

Yours unworthily,
S. V. TYMPERLEY

HUMPLEBEE

The school was assembled for evening prayers, some threescore
boys representing for the most part the well-to-do middle class
of a manufacturing county. At either end of the room glowed a
pleasant fire, for it was February and the weather had turned to
frost.

Silence reigned, but on all the young faces turned to where
the headmaster sat at his desk appeared an unwonted
expression, an eager expectancy, as though something out of the
familiar routine were about to happen. When the master's voice
at length sounded, he did not read from the book before him;
gravely, slowly, he began to speak of an event which had that
day stirred the little community with profound emotion.

'Two of our number are this evening absent. Happily, most
happily, absent for a short time; in our prayers we shall render
thanks to the good Providence which has saved us from a
terrible calamity. I do not desire to dwell upon the circumstance
that one of these boys, Chadwick, had committed worse than
an imprudence in venturing upon the Long Pond; it was in
disregard of my injunction; I had distinctly made it known that
the ice was still unsafe. We will speak no more of that. All we
can think of at present is the fact that Chadwick was on the
point of losing his life; that in all human probability he would
have been drowned, but for the help heroically afforded him by
one of his schoolfellows. I say heroically, and I am sure I do not
exaggerate; in the absence of Humplebee I may declare that he
nobly perilled his own life to save that of another. It was a
splendid bit of courage, a fine example of pluck and promptitude
and vigour. We have all cause this night to be proud of
Humplebee.'

The solemn voice paused. There was an instant's profound

silence. Then, from somewhere amid the rows of listeners, sounded a clear, boyish note.

'Sir, may we give three cheers for Humplebee?'

'You may.'

The threescore leapt to their feet, and volleys of cheering made the schoolroom echo. Then the master raised his hand, the tumult subsided, and after a few moments of agitated silence, prayers began.

Next morning there appeared as usual at his desk a short, thin, red-headed boy of sixteen, whose plain, freckled face denoted good-humour and a certain intelligence, but would never have drawn attention amongst the livelier and comelier physiognomies grouped about him. This was Humplebee. Hitherto he had been an insignificant member of the school, one of those boys who excel neither at games nor at lessons, of whom nothing is expected, and rarely, if ever, get into trouble, and who are liked in a rather contemptuous way. Of a sudden he shone glorious; all tongues were busy with him, all eyes regarded him, every one wished for the honour of his friendship. Humplebee looked uncomfortable. He had the sniffy beginnings of a cold, the result of yesterday's struggle in icy water, and his usual diffident and monosyllabic inclination was intensified by the position in which he found himself. Clappings on the shoulder from bigger boys who had been wont to joke about his name made him flush nervously; to be addressed as 'Humpy,' or 'Beetle,' or 'Buz,' even though in a new tone, seemed to gratify him as little as before. It was plain that Humplebee would much have liked to be left alone. He stuck as closely as possible to his desk, and out of school-time tried to steal apart from the throng.

But an ordeal awaited him. Early in the afternoon there arrived, from a great town not far away, a well-dressed and high-complexioned man, whose every look and accent declared commercial importance. This was Mr Chadwick, father of the boy who had all but been drowned. He and the headmaster held private talk, and presently they sent for Humplebee. Merely to enter the 'study' was at any time Humplebee's dread; to do so under the present circumstances cost him anguish of spirit.

'Ha! here he is!' exclaimed Mr Chadwick, in the voice of bluff geniality which seemed to him appropriate. 'Humplebee, let me shake hands with you! Humplebee, I am proud to make your acquaintance; prouder still to thank you, to thank you, my boy!'

The lad was painfully overcome; his hands quivered, he stood like one convicted of disgraceful behaviour.

'I think you have heard of me, Humplebee. Leonard has no doubt spoken to you of his father. Perhaps my name has reached you in other ways?'

'Yes, sir,' faltered the boy.

'You mean that you know me as a public man?' urged Mr Chadwick, whose eyes glimmered a hungry vanity.

'Yes, sir,' whispered Humplebee.

'Ha! I see you already take an intelligent interest in things beyond school. They tell me you are sixteen, Humplebee. Come, now; what are your ideas about the future? I don't mean' – Mr Chadwick rolled a laugh – 'about the future of mankind, or even the future of the English race; you and I may perhaps discuss such questions a few years hence. In the meantime, what are your personal ambitions? In brief, what would you like to be, Humplebee?'

Under the eye of his master and of the commercial potentate, Humplebee stood voiceless; he gasped once or twice like an expiring fish.

'Courage, my boy, courage!' cried Mr Chadwick. 'Your father, I believe, destines you for commerce. Is that your own wish? Speak freely. Speak as though I were a friend you have known all your life.'

'I should like to please my father, sir,' jerked from the boy's lips.

'Good! Admirable! That's the spirit I like, Humplebee. Then you have no marked predilection? That was what I wanted to discover – well, well, we shall see. Meanwhile, Humplebee, get on with your arithmetic. You are good at arithmetic, I am sure?'

'Not very, sir.'

'Come, come, that's your modesty. But I like you none the worse for it, Humplebee. Well, well, get on with your work, my boy, and we shall see, we shall see.'

Therewith, to his vast relief, Humplebee found himself dismissed. Later in the day he received a summons to the bedroom where Mr Chadwick's son was being carefully nursed. Leonard Chadwick, about the same age as his rescuer, had never deigned to pay much attention to Humplebee, whom he regarded as stupid and plebeian; but the boy's character was marked by a generous impulsiveness, which came out strongly in the present circumstances.

'Hallo, Humpy!' he cried, raising himself up when the other entered. 'So you pulled me out of that hole! Shake hands, Buzzy, old fellow! You've had a talk with my governor, haven't you? What do you think of him?'

Humplebee muttered something incoherent.

'My governor's going to make your fortune, Humpy!' cried Leonard. 'He told me so, and when he says a thing he means it. He's going to start you in business when you leave school; most likely you'll go into his own office. How will you like that, Humpy? My governor thinks no end of you; says you're a brick, and so you are. I shan't forget that you pulled me out of that hole, old chap. We shall be friends all our lives, you know. Tell me what you thought of my governor?'

When he was on his legs again, Leonard continued to treat Humplebee with grateful, if somewhat condescending, friendliness. In the talks they had together the great man's son continually expatiated upon his preserver's brilliant prospects. Beyond possibility of doubt Humplebee would some day be a rich man; Mr Chadwick had said so, and whatever he purposed came to pass. To all this Humplebee listened in a dogged sort of way, now and then smiling, but seldom making verbal answer. In school he was not quite the same boy as before his exploit; he seemed duller, less attentive, and at times even incurred reproaches for work ill done – previously a thing unknown. When the holidays came, no boy was so glad as Humplebee; his heart sang within him as he turned his back upon the school and began the journey homeward.

That home was in the town illuminated by Mr Chadwick's commercial and municipal brilliance; over a small draper's shop in one of the outskirt streets stood the name of Humplebee the draper. About sixty years of age, he had known plenty of misfortune and sorrows, with scant admixture of happiness. Nowadays things were somewhat better with him; by dint of severe economy he had put aside two or three hundred pounds, and he was able, moreover, to give his son (an only child) what is called a sound education. In the limited rooms above the shop there might have been a measure of quiet content and hopefulness, but for Mrs Humplebee. She, considerably younger than her husband, fretted against their narrow circumstances, and grudged the money that was being spent – wasted, she called it – on the boy Harry.

From his father Harry never heard talk of pecuniary troubles, but the mother lost no opportunity of letting him know that they were poor, miserably poor ; and adding, that if he did not work hard at school he was simply a cold-hearted criminal, and robbed his parents of their bread.

But during the last month or two a change had come upon the household. One day the draper received a visit from the great Mr Chadwick, who told a wonderful story of Harry's heroism, and made proposals sounding so nobly generous that Mr Humplebee was overcome with gratitude.

Harry, as his father knew, had no vocation for the shop ; to get him a place in a manufacturer's office seemed the best thing that could be aimed at, and here was Mr Chadwick talking of easy book-keeping, quick advancement, and all manner of vaguely splendid possibilities in the future. The draper's joy proved Mrs Humplebee's opportunity. She put forward a project which had of late been constantly on her mind and on her lips, to wit, that they should transfer their business into larger premises, and give themselves a chance of prosperity. Humplebee need no longer hesitate. He had his little capital to meet the first expenses, and if need arose there need not be the slightest doubt that Mr Chadwick would assist him. A kind gentleman, Mr Chadwick ! Had he not expressly desired to see Harry's mother, and had he not assured her in every possible way of the debt and gratitude he felt towards all who bore the name of Humplebee ? The draper, if he neglected his opportunity, would be an idiot – a mere idiot !

So, when the boy came home for his holidays he found two momentous things decided ; first, that he should forthwith enter Mr Chadwick's office ; secondly, that the little shop should be abandoned and a new one taken in a better neighbourhood.

Now Harry Humplebee had in his soul a secret desire and a secret abhorrence. Ever since he could read his delight had been in books of natural history ; beasts, birds, and fishes possessed his imagination, and for nothing else in the intellectual world did he really care. With poor resources he had learned a great deal of his beloved subjects. Whenever he could get away into the fields he was happy ; to lie still for hours watching some wild thing, noting its features and its ways, seemed to him perfect enjoyment. His treasure was a collection, locked in a cupboard at home, of eggs, skeletons, butterflies, beetles, and I know not what. His father regarded all this as harmless amusement, his mother contemptuously tolerated it or, in worse humour, condemned it as waste of time. When at school the boy had frequent opportunities of pursuing his study, for he was in mid-country and could wander as he liked on free afternoons; but neither the headmaster nor his assistant thought it worth while to pay heed to Humplebee's predilection. True, it had been noticed more than once that in writing an 'essay' he showed unusual observation of natural things; this, however, did not strike his educators as a matter of any importance; it was not their business to discover what Humplebee could do, and wished to do, but to make him do things they regarded as desirable. Humplebee was marked for commerce; he must study compound interest, and be strong at discount. Yet the boy loathed every such mental effort, and the name of 'business' made him sick at heart.

How he longed to unbosom himself to his father! And in the first week of his holiday he had a chance of doing so, a wonderful chance, such as had never entered his dreams. The town possessed a museum of Natural History, where, of course, Harry had often spent leisure hours. Half a year ago a happy chance had brought him into conversation with the curator, who could not but be struck by the lad's intelligence, and who took an interest in him. Now they met again; they had one or two long talks, with the result that, on a Sunday afternoon, the curator of the museum took the trouble to call upon Mr Humplebee, to speak with him about his son. At the museum was wanted a lad with a taste for natural history, to perform at first certain easy duties, with the prospect of further advancement here or elsewhere. It seemed to the curator that Harry was the very boy for the place; would Mr Humplebee like to consider this suggestion? Now, if it had been made to him half a year ago, such an offer would have seemed to Mr Humplebee well worth consideration, and he knew that Harry would have heard of it with delight; as it was, he could not entertain the thought for a moment.

Impossible to run the risk of offending Mr Chadwick; moreover, who could hesitate between the modest possibilities of the museum and such a career as waited the lad under the protection of his powerful friend ? With nervous haste the draper explained how matters stood, excused himself, and begged that not another word on the subject might be spoken in his son's hearing.

Harry Humplebee knew what he had lost; the curator, in talk with him, had already thrown out his suggestion; at their next meeting he discreetly made known to the boy that other counsels must prevail. For the first time Harry felt a vehement impulse, prompting him to speak on his own behalf, to assert and to plead for his own desires. But courage failed him. He heard his father loud in praise of Mr Chadwick, intent upon the gratitude and respect due to that admirable man. He knew how his mother would exclaim at the mere hint of disinclination to enter the great man's office. And so he held his peace, though it cost him bitterness of heart and even secret tears. A long, long time passed before he could bring himself to enter again the museum doors.

He sat on a stool in Mr Chadwick's office, a clerk at a trifling salary. Everything, his father reminded him, must have a beginning; let him work well and his progress would be repaid. Two years passed and he was in much the same position; his salary had increased by one half, but his work remained the same, mechanical, dreary, hateful to him in its monotony. Meanwhile his father's venture in the new premises had led to great embarrassments; business did not thrive; the day came when Mr Humplebee, trembling and shamefaced, felt himself drawn to beg help of his son's so-called benefactor. He came away from the interview with empty hands. Worse than that, he had heard things about Harry which darkened his mind with a new anxiety.

'I greatly fear,' said Mr Chadwick, 'that your son must seek a place in some other office. It's a painful thing; I wish I could have kept him; but the fact of the matter is that he shows utter incapacity. I have no fault to find with him otherwise; a good lad; in a smaller place of business he might do well enough. But he's altogether below the mark in an office such as *mine*. Don't distress yourself, Mr Humplebee, I beg, I shall make it my care to inquire for suitable openings; you shall hear from me – you shall hear from me. Pray consider that your son is under notice to leave this day month. As for the – other matter of which you spoke, I can only repeat that the truest kindness is only to refuse assistance. I assure you it is. The circumstances forbid it. Clearly, what you have to do is to call together your creditors, and arrive at an understanding. It is my principle never to try to prop up a hopeless concern such as yours evidently is. Good day to you, Mr Humplebee; good day.'

A year later several things had happened. Mr Humplebee was dead; his penniless widow had gone to live in another town on the charity of poor relatives, and Harry Humplebee sat in another office, drawing the salary at which he had begun under Mr Chadwick, his home a wretched bedroom in the house of working-folk.

It did not appear to the lad that he had suffered any injustice. He knew his own inaptitude for the higher kind of office work, and he had expected his dismissal by Mr Chadwick long before it came. What he did resent, and profoundly, was Mr Chadwick's refusal to aid his father in that last death-grapple with ruinous circumstance. At the worst moment Harry wrote a letter to Leonard Chadwick, whom he had never seen since he left school. He told in simple terms the position of his family, and, without a word of justifying reminiscence, asked his schoolfellow to help them if he could. To this letter a reply came from London. Leonard Chadwick wrote briefly and hurriedly, but in good-natured terms; he was really very sorry indeed that he could do so little; the fact was, just now he stood on anything but good terms with his father, who kept him abominably short of cash. He enclosed five pounds, and, if possible, would soon send more.

'Don't suppose I have forgotten what I owe you. As soon as ever I find myself in an independent position you shall have substantial proof of my enduring gratitude. Keep me informed of your address.'

Humplebee made no second application, and Leonard Chadwick did not again break silence.

The years flowed on. At five-and-twenty Humplebee toiled in the same office, but he could congratulate himself on a certain progress; by dogged resolve he had acquired something like efficiency in the duties of a commercial clerk, and the salary he now earned allowed him to contribute to the support of his mother. More or less reconciled to the day's labour, he had resumed in leisure hours his favourite study; a free library supplied him with useful books, and whenever it was possible he went his way into the fields, searching, collecting, observing. But his life had another interest, which threatened rivalry to this intellectual pursuit. Humplebee had set eyes upon the maiden destined to be his heart's desire; she was the daughter of a fellow-clerk, a man who had grown grey in service of the ledger; timidly he sought to win her kindness, as yet scarce daring to hope, dreaming only of some happy change of position which might encourage him to speak. The girl was as timid as himself; she had a face of homely prettiness, a mind uncultured but sympathetic; absorbed in domestic cares, with few acquaintances, she led the simplest of lives, and would have been all but content to live on in gentle hope for a score of years. The two were beginning to understand each other, for their silence was more eloquent than their speech.

One summer day – the last day of his brief holiday – Humplebee was returning by train from a visit to his mother. Alone in a third-class carriage, seeming to read a newspaper, but in truth dreaming of a face he hoped to see in a few hours, he suddenly found himself jerked out of his seat, flung violently forward, bumped on the floor, and last of all rolled into a sort of bundle, he knew not where. Recovering from a daze, he said to himself, 'Why, this is an accident – a collision!' Then he tried to unroll himself, and in the effort found that one of his arms was useless; more than that, it pained him horribly. He stood up and tottered on to the seat. Then the carriage-door opened, and a voice shouted –

'Anybody hurt here?'

'I think my arm is broken,' answered Humplebee.

Two men helped him to alight. The train had stopped just outside a small station; on a cross line in front of the engine lay a goods truck smashed to pieces; people were rushing about with cries and gesticulations.

'Yes, the arm is broken,' remarked one of the men who had assisted Humplebee. 'It looks as if you were the only passenger injured.' That proved, indeed, to be the case; no one else had suffered more than a jolt or a bruise. The crowd clustered about this hero of the broken arm, expressing sympathy and offering suggestions. Among them was a well-dressed young man, rather good-looking and of lively demeanour, who seemed to enjoy the excitement; he, after gazing fixedly at the pain-stricken face, exclaimed in a voice of wonder –

'By Jove ! it's Humplebee !'

The sufferer turned towards him who spoke ; his eyes brightened, for he recognised the face of Leonard Chadwick. Neither one nor the other had greatly altered during the past ten years ; they presented exactly the same contrast of personal characteristics as when they were at school together. With vehement friendliness Chadwick at once took upon himself the care of the injured clerk. He shouted for a cab, he found out where the nearest doctor lived ; in a quarter of an hour he had his friend under the doctor's roof. When the fracture had been set and bandaged, they travelled on together to their native town, only a few miles distant, Humplebee knowing for the first time in his life the luxury of a first-class compartment. On their way Chadwick talked exuberantly. He was delighted at this meeting ; why, one of his purposes in coming north had been to search out Humplebee, whom he had so long scandalously neglected.

'The fact is, I've been going through queer times myself. The governor and I can't get along together ; we quarrelled years ago, there's not much chance of our making it up. I've no doubt that was the real reason of his dismissing you from his office – a mean thing ! The governor's a fine old boy, but he has his nasty side. He's very tight about money, and I – well, I'm a bit too much the other way, no doubt. He's kept me in low water, confound him ! But I'm independent of him now. I'll tell you all about it to-morrow, you'll feel better able to talk. Expect me at eleven in the morning.'

Through a night of physical suffering Humplebee was supported by a new hope. Chadwick the son, warm-hearted and generous, made a strong contrast with Chadwick the father, pompous and insincere. When the young man spoke of his abiding gratitude there was no possibility of distrusting him, his voice rang true, and his handsome features wore a delightful frankness. Punctual to his appointment, Leonard appeared next morning. He entered the poor lodging as if it had been a luxurious residence, talked suavely and gaily with the landlady, who was tending her invalid, and, when alone with his old schoolfellow, launched into a detailed account of a great enterprise in which he was concerned. Not long ago he had become acquainted with one Geldershaw, a man somewhat older than himself, personally most attractive, and very keen in business. Geldershaw had just been appointed London representative of a great manufacturing firm in Germany. It was a most profitable undertaking, and, out of pure friendship, he had offered a share in the business to Leonard Chadwick.

'Of course, I put money into it. The fact is, I have dropped in for a few thousands from a good old aunt, who has been awfully kind to me since the governor and I fell out. I couldn't possibly have found a better investment, it means eight or nine per cent., my boy, at the very least! And look here, Humplebee, of course you can keep books?'

'Yes, I can,' answered the listener conscientiously.

'Then, old fellow, a first-rate place is open to you. We want some one we can thoroughly trust; you're the very man Gelder-shaw had in his eye. Would you mind telling me what screw you get at present?'

'Two pounds ten a week.'

'Ha, ha!' laughed Chadwick exultantly. 'With us you shall begin at double the figure, and I'll see to it that you have a rise after the first year. What's more, Humplebee, as soon as we get fairly going, I promise you a share in the business. Don't say a word, old boy! My governor treated you abominably. I've been in your debt for ten years or so, as you know very well, and often enough I've felt deucedly ashamed of myself. Five pounds a week to begin with, and the certainty of a comfortable interest in a thriving affair! Come, now, is it agreed?'

Humplebee forgot his pain; he felt ready to jump out of bed and travel straightway to London.

'And you know,' pursued Chadwick, when they had shaken hands warmly, 'that you have a claim for damages on the railway company. Leave that to me; I'll put the thing in train at once, through my own solicitor. You shall pocket a substantial sum, my boy! Well, I'm afraid I must be off; I've got my hands full of business. Quite a new thing for me to have something serious to do; I enjoy it! If I can't see you again before I go back to town, you shall hear from me in a day or two. Here's my London address. Chuck up your place here at once, so as to be ready for us as soon as your arm's all right. Geldershaw shall write you a formal engagement.'

Happily his broken arm was the left. Humplebee could use his right hand, and did so, very soon after Chadwick's departure, to send an account of all that had befallen him to his friend Mary Bowes. It was the first time he had written to her. His

letter was couched in terms of studious respect, with many
apologies for the liberty he took. Of the accident he made light
– a few days would see him re-established – but he dwelt with
some emphasis upon the meeting with Leonard Chadwick, and
what had resulted from it.

'I did him a good turn once, when we were at school together.
He is a good, warm-hearted fellow, and has sought this opportunity of showing that he remembered the old time.'

Thus did Humplebee refer to the great event of his boyhood.
Having despatched the letter, he waited feverishly for Miss
Bowes' reply; but days passed, and still he waited in vain.
Agitation delayed his recovery; he was suffering as he had never
suffered in his life, when there came a letter from London,
signed with the name of Geldershaw, repeating in formal terms
the offer made to him by Leonard Chadwick, and requesting his
immediate acceptance or refusal. This plucked him out of his
despondent state, and spurred him to action. With the help of
his landlady he dressed himself, and, having concealed his
bandaged arm as well as possible, drove in a cab to Miss Bowes'
dwelling. The hour being before noon, he was almost sure to
find Mary at home, and alone. Trembling with bodily weakness
and the conflict of emotions, he rang the door bell. To his
consternation there appeared Mary's father.

'Hallo! Humplebee!' cried Mr Bowes, surprised but friendly.
'Why, I was just going to write to you. Mary has had scarlet
fever. I've been so busy these last ten days, I couldn't even
inquire after you. Of course, I saw about your smash in the
newspaper; how are you getting on?'

The man with the bandaged arm could not utter a word.
Horror-stricken he stared at Mr Bowes, who had begun to
express a doubt whether it would be prudent for him to enter
the house.

'Mary is convalescent; the anxiety's all over, but—'

Humplebee suddenly seized the speaker's hand and in confused words expressed vehement joy. They talked for a few
minutes, parted with cordiality, and Humplebee went home
again to recover from his excitement.

A note from his employers had replied in terms of decent
condolence to the message by which he explained his enforced
absence. To-day he wrote to the principal, announcing his
intention of resigning his post in their office. The response,

delivered within a few hours, was admirably brief and to the point. Mr Humplebee's place had, of course, been already taken temporarily by another clerk; it would have been held open for him, but, in view of his decision, the firm had merely to request that he would acknowledge the cheque enclosed in payment of his salary up to date. Not without some shaking of the hand did Humplebee pen this receipt; for a moment something seemed to come between him and the daylight, and a heaviness oppressed his inner man. But already he had despatched to London his formal acceptance of the post at five pounds a week, and in thinking of it his heart grew joyous. Two hundred and sixty pounds a year! It was beyond the hope of his most fantastic day-dreams. He was a made man, secure for ever against fears and worries. He was a man of substance, and need no longer shrink from making known the hope which ruled his life.

A second letter was written to Mary Bowes; but not till many copies had been made was it at length despatched. The writer declared that he looked for no reply until Mary was quite herself again; he begged only that she would reflect, meanwhile, upon what he had said, reflect with all her indulgence, all her native goodness and gentleness. And, indeed, there elapsed nearly a fortnight before the answer came; and to Humplebee it seemed an endless succession of tormenting days. Then—

Humplebee behaved like one distracted. His landlady in good earnest thought he had gone crazy, and was only reassured when he revealed to her what had happened. Mary Bowes was to be his wife! They must wait for a year and a half; Mary could not leave her father quite alone, but in a year and a half Mr Bowes, who was an oldish man, would be able to retire on the modest fruit of his economies, and all three could live together in London. 'What,' cried Humplebee, 'was eighteen months? It would allow him to save enough out of his noble salary to start housekeeping with something more than comfort. Blessed be the name of Chadwick!'

When his arm was once more sound, and Mary's health quite recovered, they met. In their long, long talk Humplebee was led to tell the story of that winter day when he saved Leonard Chadwick's life; he related, too, all that had ensued upon his acquaintance with the great Mr Chadwick, memories which would never lose all their bitterness. Mary was moved to tears, and her tears were dried by indignation. But they agreed that

Leonard, after all, made some atonement for his father's heartless behaviour. Humplebee showed a letter that had come from young Chadwick a day or two ago; every line spoke generosity of spirit. 'When,' he asked, 'might they expect their new bookkeeper. They were in full swing; business promised magnificently. As yet, they had only a temporary office, but Geldershaw was in treaty for fine premises in the City. The sooner Humplebee arrived the better; fortune awaited him.'

It was decided that he should leave for London in two days.

The next evening he came to spend an hour or two with Mary and her father. On entering the room he at once observed something strange in the looks with which he was greeted. Mary had a pale, miserable air, and could hardly speak. Mr Bowes, after looking at him fixedly for a moment, exclaimed –

'Have you seen to-day's paper?'

'I've been too busy,' he replied. 'What has happened?'

'Isn't your London man called Geldershaw?'

'Yes,' murmured Humplebee, with a sinking of the heart.

'Well, the police are after him; he has bolted. It's a long-firm swindle that he's been up to. You know what that means? Obtaining goods on false credit, and raising money on them. What's more, young Chadwick is arrested; he came before the magistrates yesterday, charged with being an accomplice. Here it is; read it for yourself.'

Humplebee dropped into a chair. When his eyes undazzled, he read the full report which Mr Bowes had summarised. It was the death-blow of his hopes.

'Leonard Chadwick has been a victim, not a swindler,' sounded from him in a feeble voice. 'You see, he says that Geldershaw has robbed him of all his money – that he is ruined.'

'He *says* so,' remarked Mr Bowes with angry irony.

'I believe him,' said Humplebee.

His eyes sought Mary's. The girl regarded him steadily, and she spoke in a low firm voice –

'I, too, believe him.'

'Whether or no,' said Mr Bowes, thrusting his hands into his pockets, 'the upshot of it is, Humplebee, that you've lost a good place through trusting him. I had my doubts; but you were in a hurry, and didn't ask advice. If this had happened a week later, the police would have laid hands on you as well.'

'So there's something to be thankful for, at all events,' said Mary.

Again Humplebee met her eyes. He saw that she would not forsake him.

He had to begin life over again – that was all.

THE SCRUPULOUS FATHER

It was market day in the little town; at one o'clock a rustic company besieged the table of the Greyhound, lured by savoury odours and the frothing of amber ale. Apart from three frequenters of the ordinary, in a small room prepared for overflow, sat two persons of a different stamp – a middle-aged man, bald, meagre, unimpressive, but wholly respectable in bearing and apparel, and a girl, evidently his daughter, who had the look of the latter twenties, her plain dress harmonising with a subdued charm of features and a timidity of manner not ungraceful. Whilst waiting for their meal they conversed in an undertone; their brief remarks and ejaculations told of a long morning's ramble from the seaside resort some miles away; in their quiet fashion they seemed to have enjoyed themselves, and dinner at an inn evidently struck them as something of an escapade. Rather awkwardly the girl arranged a handful of wild flowers which she had gathered, and put them for refreshment into a tumbler of water; when a woman entered with viands, silence fell upon the two; after hesitations and mutual glances, they began to eat with nervous appetite.

Scarcely was their modest confidence restored, when in the doorway sounded a virile voice, gaily humming, and they became aware of a tall young man, red-headed, anything but handsome, flushed and perspiring from the sunny road; his open jacket showed a blue cotton shirt without waistcoat, in his hand was a shabby straw hat, and thick dust covered his boots. One would have judged him a tourist of the noisier class, and his rather loud 'Good morning!' as he entered the room seemed a serious menace to privacy; on the other hand, the rapid buttoning of his coat, and the quiet choice of a seat as far as possible from the two guests whom his arrival disturbed, indicated a certain tact. His greeting had met with the merest murmur of reply ; their eyes on their plates, father and daughter resolutely disregarded him ; yet he ventured to speak again.

'They're busy here to-day. Not a seat to be had in the other room.'

It was apologetic in intention, and not rudely spoken. After a moment's delay the bald, respectable man made a curt response.

'This room is public, I believe.'

The intruder held his peace. But more than once he glanced at the girl, and after each furtive scrutiny his plain visage manifested some disturbance, a troubled thoughtfulness. His one look at the mute parent was from beneath contemptuous eyebrows.

Very soon another guest appeared, a massive agricultural man, who descended upon a creaking chair and growled a remark about the hot weather. With him the red-haired pedestrian struck into talk. Their topic was beer. Uncommonly good, they agreed, the local brew, and each called for a second pint. What, they asked in concert, would England be without her ale ? Shame on the base traffickers who enfeebled or poisoned this noble liquor ! And how cool it was – ah ! The right sort of cellar ! He of the red hair hinted at a third pewter.

These two were still but midway in their stout attack on meat and drink, when father and daughter, having exchanged a few whispers, rose to depart. After leaving the room, the girl remembered that she had left her flowers behind ; she durst not return for them, and, knowing her father would dislike to do so, said nothing about the matter.

'A pity !' exclaimed Mr Whiston (that was his respectable name) as they strolled away. 'It looked at first as if we should have such a nice quiet dinner.'

'I enjoyed it all the same,' replied his companion, whose name was Rose.

'That abominable habit of drinking !' added Mr Whiston austerely. He himself had quaffed water, as always. 'Their ale, indeed ! See the coarse, gross creatures it produces !'

He shuddered. Rose, however, seemed less consentient than usual. Her eyes were on the ground ; her lips were closed with a certain firmness. When she spoke, it was on quite another subject.

They were Londoners. Mr Whiston held the position of

draughtsman in the office of a geographical publisher; though his income was small, he had always practised a rigid economy, and the possession of a modest private capital put him beyond fear of reverses. Profoundly conscious of social limits, he felt it a subject for gratitude that there was nothing to be ashamed of in his calling, which he might fairly regard as a profession, and he nursed this sense of respectability as much on his daughter's behalf as on his own. Rose was an only child; her mother had been dead for years; her kinsfolk on both sides laid claim to the title of gentlefolk, but supported it on the narrowest margin of independence. The girl had grown up in an atmosphere unfavourable to mental development, but she had received a fairly good education, and nature had dowered her with intelligence. A sense of her father's conscientiousness and of his true affection forbade her to criticise openly the principles on which he had directed her life; hence a habit of solitary meditation, which half fostered, yet half opposed, the gentle diffidence of Rose's character.

Mr Whiston shrank from society, ceaselessly afraid of receiving less than his due; privately, meanwhile, he deplored the narrowness of the social opportunities granted to his daughter, and was for ever forming schemes for her advantage – schemes which never passed beyond the stage of nervous speculation. They inhabited a little house in a western suburb, a house illumined with every domestic virtue; but scarcely a dozen persons crossed the threshold within a twelvemonth. Rose's two or three friends were, like herself, mistrustful of the world. One of them had lately married after a very long engagement, and Rose still trembled from the excitement of that occasion, still debated fearfully with herself on the bride's chances of happiness. Her own marriage was an event so inconceivable that merely to glance at the thought appeared half immodest and wholly irrational.

Every winter Mr Whiston talked of new places which he and Rose would visit when the holidays came round; every summer he shrank from the thought of adventurous novelty, and ended by proposing a return to the same western seaside-town, to the familiar lodgings. The climate suited neither him nor his daughter, who both needed physical as well as moral bracing; but they only thought of this on finding themselves at home again, with another long year of monotony before them. And it was so good to feel welcome, respected; to receive the smiling reverences of tradesfolk; to talk with just a little well-bred condescension, sure that it would be appreciated. Mr Whiston savoured these things, and Rose in this respect was not wholly unlike him.

To-day was the last of their vacation. The weather had been magnificent throughout; Rose's cheeks were more than touched by the sun, greatly to the advantage of her unpretending comeliness. She was a typical English maiden, rather tall, shapely rather than graceful, her head generally bent, her movements always betraying the diffidence of solitary habit. The lips were her finest feature, their perfect outline indicating sweetness without feebleness of character. Such a girl is at her best towards the stroke of thirty. Rose had begun to know herself; she needed only opportunity to act upon her knowledge.

A train would take them back to the seaside. At the railway station Rose seated herself on a shaded part of the platform, whilst her father, who was exceedingly short of sight, peered over publications on the bookstall. Rather tired after her walk, the girl was dreamily tracing a pattern with the point of her parasol, when some one advanced and stood immediately in front of her. Startled, she looked up, and recognised the red-haired stranger of the inn.

'You left these flowers in a glass of water on the table. I hope I'm not doing a rude thing in asking whether they were left by accident.'

He had the flowers in his hand, their stems carefully protected by a piece of paper. For a moment Rose was incapable of replying; she looked at the speaker; she felt her cheeks burn; in utter embarrassment she said she knew not what.

'Oh! – thank you! I forgot them. It's very kind.'

Her hand touched his as she took the bouquet from him. Without another word the man turned and strode away.

Mr Whiston had seen nothing of this. When he approached, Rose held up the flowers with a laugh.

'Wasn't it kind? I forgot them, you know, and some one from the inn came looking for me.'

'Very good of them, very,' replied her father graciously. 'A very nice inn, that. We'll go again – some day. One likes to encourage such civility; it's rare nowadays.'

He of the red hair travelled by the same train, though not in the same carriage. Rose caught sight of him at the seaside station. She was vexed with herself for having so scantily acknowledged his kindness; it seemed to her that she had not really thanked him at all; how absurd, at her age, to be incapable of common self-command! At the same time she kept thinking of her father's phrase, 'coarse, gross creatures,' and it vexed her even more than her own ill behaviour. The stranger was certainly not coarse, far from gross. Even his talk about beer (she remembered every word of it) had been amusing rather than offensive. Was he a 'gentleman'? The question agitated her; it involved so technical a definition, and she felt so doubtful as to the reply. Beyond doubt he had acted in a gentlemanly way; but his voice lacked something. Coarse? Gross? No, no, no! Really, her father was very severe, not to say uncharitable. But perhaps he was thinking of the heavy agricultural man; oh, he must have been!

Of a sudden she felt very weary. At the lodgings she sat down in her bedroom, and gazed through the open window at the sea. A sense of discouragement, hitherto almost unknown, had fallen upon her; it spoilt the blue sky and the soft horizon. She thought rather drearily of the townward journey to-morrow, of her home in the suburbs, of the endless monotony that awaited her. The flowers lay on her lap; she smelt them, dreamed over them. And then – strange incongruity – she thought of beer!

Between tea and supper she and her father rested on the beach. Mr Whiston was reading. Rose pretended to turn the leaves of a book. Of a sudden, as unexpectedly to herself as to her companion, she broke silence.

'Don't you think, father, that we are too much afraid of talking with strangers?'

'Too much afraid?'

Mr Whiston was puzzled. He had forgotten all about the incident at the dinner-table.

'I mean – what harm is there in having a little conversation when one is away from home? At the inn to-day, you know, I can't help thinking we were rather – perhaps a little too silent.'

'My dear Rose, did you want to talk about beer?'

She reddened, but answered all the more emphatically.

'Of course not. But, when the first gentleman came in, wouldn't it have been natural to exchange a few friendly words? I'm sure he wouldn't have talked of beer to *us*.'

'The *gentleman*? I saw no gentleman, my dear. I suppose he

was a small clerk, or something of the sort, and he had no business whatever to address us.'

'Oh, but he only said good morning, and apologised for sitting at our table. He needn't have apologised at all.'

'Precisely. That is just what I mean,' said Mr Whiston with self-satisfaction. 'My dear Rose, if I had been alone, I might perhaps have talked a little, but with you it was impossible. One cannot be too careful. A man like that will take all sorts of liberties. One has to keep such people at a distance.'

A moment's pause, then Rose spoke with unusual decision –

'I feel quite sure, father, that he would not have taken liberties. It seems to me that he knew quite well how to behave himself.'

Mr Whiston grew still more puzzled. He closed his book to meditate this new problem.

'One has to lay down rules,' fell from him at length, sententiously. 'Our position, Rose, as I have often explained, is a delicate one. A lady in circumstances such as yours cannot exercise too much caution. Your natural associates are in the world of wealth; unhappily, I cannot make you wealthy. We have to guard our self-respect, my dear child. Really, it is not *safe* to talk with strangers – least of all at an inn. And you have only to remember that disgusting conversation about beer !'

Rose said no more. Her father pondered a little, felt that he had delivered his soul, and resumed the book.

The next morning they were early at the station to secure good places for the long journey to London. Up to almost the last moment it seemed that they would have a carriage to themselves. Then the door suddenly opened, a bag was flung on to the seat, and after it came a hot, panting man, a red-haired man, recognised immediately by both the travellers.

'I thought I'd missed it !' ejaculated the intruder merrily.

Mr Whiston turned his head away, disgust transforming his countenance. Rose sat motionless, her eyes cast down. And the stranger mopped his forehead in silence.

He glanced at her; he glanced again and again; and Rose was aware of every look. It did not occur to her to feel offended. On the contrary, she fell into a mood of tremulous pleasure, enhanced by every turn of the stranger's eyes in her direction. At him she did not look, yet she saw him. Was it a coarse face ? she asked herself. Plain, perhaps, but decidedly not vulgar. The red hair, she thought, was not disagreeably red; she didn't dislike that shade of colour. He was humming a tune; it seemed to be his habit, and it argued healthy cheerfulness. Meanwhile Mr Whiston sat stiffly in his corner, staring at the landscape, a model of respectable muteness.

At the first stop another man entered. This time, unmistakably, a commercial traveller. At once a dialogue sprang up between him and Rufus.* The traveller complained that all the smoking compartments were full.

'Why,' exclaimed Rufus, with a laugh, 'that reminds me that I wanted a smoke. I never thought about it till now; jumped in here in a hurry.'

The traveller's 'line' was tobacco; they talked tobacco – Rufus with much gusto. Presently the conversation took a wider scope.

'I envy you,' cried Rufus, 'always travelling about. I'm in a beastly office, and get only a fortnight off once a year. I enjoy it, I can tell you! Time's up today, worse luck! I've a good mind to emigrate. Can you give me a tip about the colonies?'

He talked of how he had spent his holiday. Rose missed not a word, and her blood pulsed in sympathy with the joy of freedom which he expressed. She did not mind his occasional slang; the tone was manly and right-hearted; it evinced a certain simplicity of feeling by no means common in men, whether gentle or other. At a certain moment the girl was impelled to steal a glimpse of his face. After all, was it really so plain? The features seemed to her to have a certain refinement which she had not noticed before.

'I'm going to try for a smoker,' said the man of commerce, as the train slackened into a busy station.

Rufus hesitated. His eye wandered.

'I think I shall stay where I am,' he ended by saying.

In that same moment, for the first time, Rose met his glance. She saw that his eyes did not at once avert themselves; they had a singular expression, a smile which pleaded pardon for its audacity. And Rose, even whilst turning away, smiled in response.

The train stopped. The commercial traveller alighted. Rose, leaning towards her father, whispered that she was thirsty; would he get her a glass of milk or of lemonade? Though little disposed to rush on such errands, Mr Whiston had no choice but to comply; he sped at once for the refreshment-room.

And Rose knew what would happen; she knew perfectly.

Sitting rigid, her eyes on vacancy, she felt the approach of the young man, who for the moment was alone with her. She saw him at her side : she heard his voice.

'I can't help it. I want to speak to you. May I ?'

Rose faltered a reply.

'It was so kind to bring the flowers. I didn't thank you properly.'

'It's now or never,' pursued the young man in rapid, excited tones. 'Will you let me tell you my name ? Will you tell me yours ?'

Rose's silence consented. The daring Rufus rent a page from a pocket-book, scribbled his name and address, gave it to Rose. He rent out another page, offered it to Rose with the pencil, and in a moment had secured the precious scrap of paper in his pocket. Scarce was the transaction completed when a stranger jumped in. The young man bounded to his own corner, just in time to see the return of Mr Whiston, glass in hand.

During the rest of the journey Rose was in the strangest state of mind. She did not feel in the least ashamed of herself. It seemed to her that what had happened was wholly natural and simple. The extraordinary thing was that she must sit silent and with cold countenance at the distance of a few feet from a person with whom she ardently desired to converse. Sudden illumination had wholly changed the aspect of life. She seemed to be playing a part in a grotesque comedy rather than living in a world of grave realities. Her father's dignified silence struck her as intolerably absurd. She could have burst into laughter ; at moments she was indignant, irritated, tremulous with the spirit of revolt. She detected a glance of frigid superiority with which Mr Whiston chanced to survey the other occupants of the compartment. It amazed her. Never had she seen her father in such an alien light. He bent forward and addressed to her some commonplace remark ; she barely deigned a reply. Her views of conduct, of character, had undergone an abrupt and extraordinary change. Having justified without shadow of argument her own incredible proceeding, she judged everything and everybody by some new standard, mysteriously attained. She was no longer the Rose Whiston of yesterday. Her old self seemed an object of compassion. She felt an unspeakable happiness, and at the same time an encroaching fear.

The fear predominated ; when she grew aware of the streets

of London looming on either hand it became a torment, an anguish. Small-folded, crushed within her palm, the piece of paper with its still unread inscription seemed to burn her. Once, twice, thrice she met the look of her friend. He smiled cheerily, bravely, with evident purpose of encouragement. She knew his face better than that of any oldest acquaintance; she saw in it a manly beauty. Only by a great effort of self-control could she refrain from turning aside to unfold and read what he had written. The train slackened speed, stopped. Yes, it was London. She must arise and go. Once more their eyes met. Then, without recollection of any interval, she was on the Metropolitan Railway, moving towards her suburban home.

A severe headache sent her early to bed. Beneath her pillow lay a scrap of paper with a name and address she was not likely to forget. And through the night of broken slumbers Rose suffered a martyrdom. No more self-glorification! All her courage gone, all her new vitality! She saw herself with the old eyes, and was shame-stricken to the very heart.

Whose the fault? Towards dawn she argued it with the bitterness of misery. What a life was hers in this little world of choking respectabilities! Forbidden this, forbidden that; permitted – the pride of ladyhood. And she was not a lady, after all. What lady would have permitted herself to exchange names and addresses with a strange man in a railway carriage – furtively, too, escaping her father's observation? If not a lady, what *was* she? It meant the utter failure of her breeding and education. The sole end for which she had lived was frustrate. A common, vulgar young woman – well mated, doubtless, with an impudent clerk, whose noisy talk was of beer and tobacco!

This arrested her. Stung to the defence of her friend, who, clerk though he might be, was neither impudent nor vulgar, she found herself driven back upon self-respect. The battle went on for hours; it exhausted her; it undid all the good effects of sun and sea, and left her flaccid, pale.

'I'm afraid the journey yesterday was too much for you,' remarked Mr Whiston, after observing her as she sat mute the next evening.

'I shall soon recover,' Rose answered coldly.

The father meditated with some uneasiness. He had not forgotten Rose's singular expression of opinion after their dinner at the inn. His affection made him sensitive to changes in the girl's demeanour. Next summer they must really find a more bracing resort. Yes, yes; clearly Rose needed bracing. But she was always better when the cool days came round.

On the morrow it was his daughter's turn to feel anxious. Mr Whiston all at once wore a face of indignant severity. He was absent-minded; he sat at table with scarce a word; he had little nervous movements, and subdued mutterings as of wrath. This continued on a second day, and Rose began to suffer an intolerable agitation. She could not help connecting her father's strange behaviour with the secret which tormented her heart.

Had something happened? Had her friend seen Mr Whiston, or written to him?

She had awaited with tremors every arrival of the post. It was probable – more than probable – that *he* would write to her; but as yet no letter came. A week passed, and no letter came. Her father was himself again; plainly she had mistaken the cause of his perturbation. Ten days, and no letter came.

It was Saturday afternoon. Mr Whiston reached home at tea-time. The first glance showed his daughter that trouble and anger once more beset him. She trembled, and all but wept, for suspense had overwrought her nerves.

'I find myself obliged to speak to you on a very disagreeable subject' – thus began Mr Whiston over the tea-cups – 'a very unpleasant subject indeed. My one consolation is that it will probably settle a little argument we had down at the seaside.'

As his habit was when expressing grave opinions (and Mr Whiston seldom expressed any other), he made a long pause and ran his fingers through his thin beard. The delay irritated Rose to the last point of endurance.

'The fact is,' he proceeded at length, 'a week ago I received a most extraordinary letter – the most impudent letter I ever read in my life. It came from that noisy, beer-drinking man who intruded upon us at the inn – you remember. He began by explaining who he was, and – if you can believe it – had the impertinence to say that he wished to make my acquaintance! An amazing letter! Naturally, I left it unanswered – the only dignified thing to do. But the fellow wrote again, asking it I had received his proposal. I now replied, briefly and severely, asking him, how he came to know my name; secondly, what reason I had given him for supposing that I desired to meet him again. His answer to this was even more outrageous than the first offence. He bluntly informed me that in order to discover my name and address he had followed us home that day from Paddington Station! As if this was not bad enough, he went on to – really, Rose, I feel I must apologise to you, but the fact is I seem to have no choice but to tell you what he said. The fellow tells me, really, that he wants to know *me* only that he may come to know *you*! My first idea was to go with this letter to the police. I am not sure that I shan't do so even yet; most certainly I shall if he writes again. The man may be crazy – he may be dangerous. Who knows but he may come lurking about the house? I felt obliged to warn you of this unpleasant possibility.'

Rose was stirring her tea; also she was smiling. She continued to stir and to smile, without consciousness of either performance.

'You make light of it?' exclaimed her father solemnly.

'O father, of course I am sorry you have had this annoyance.'

So little was there of manifest sorrow in the girl's tone and countenance that Mr Whiston gazed at her rather indignantly. His pregnant pause gave birth to one of those admonitory axioms which had hitherto ruled his daughter's life.

'My dear, I advise you never to trifle with questions of propriety. Could there possibly be a better illustration of what I have so often said – that in self-defence we are bound to keep strangers at a distance?'

'Father—'

Rose began firmly, but her voice failed.

'You were going to say, Rose?'

She took her courage in both hands.

'Will you allow me to see the letters?'

'Certainly. There can be no objection to that.'

He drew from his pocket the three envelopes, held them to his daughter. With shaking hand Rose unfolded the first letter; it was written in clear commercial character, and was signed 'Charles James Burroughs.' When she had read all, the girl said quietly –

'Are you quite sure, father, that these letters are impertinent?'

Mr Whiston stopped in the act of finger-combing his beard.

'What doubt can there be of it?'

'They seem to me,' proceeded Rose nervously, 'to be very respectful and very honest.'

'My dear, you astound me! Is it respectful to force one's acquaintance upon an unwilling stranger? I really don't understand you. Where is your sense of propriety, Rose? A vulgar, noisy fellow, who talks of beer and tobacco – a petty clerk! And he has the audacity to write to me that he wants to – to make friends with my daughter! Respectful? Honest? Really!'

When Mr Whiston became sufficiently agitated to lose his decorous gravity, he began to splutter, and at such moments he was not impressive. Rose kept her eyes cast down. She felt her strength once more, the strength of a wholly reasonable and half-passionate revolt against that tyrannous propriety which Mr Whiston worshipped.

'Father—'

'Well, my dear?'

'There is only one thing I dislike in these letters – and that is a falsehood.'

'I don't understand.'

Rose was flushing. Her nerves grew tense; she had wrought herself to a simple audacity which overcame small embarrassments.

'Mr Burroughs says that he followed us home from Paddington to discover our address. That is not true. He asked me for my name and address in the train, and gave me his.'

The father gasped.

'He *asked*— ? You *gave*— ?'

'It was whilst you were away in the refreshment-room,' proceeded the girl, with singular self-control, in a voice almost matter-of-fact. 'I ought to tell you, at the same time, that it was Mr Burroughs who brought me the flowers from the inn, when I forgot them. You didn't see him give them to me in the station.'

The father stared.

'But, Rose, what does all this mean? You – you overwhelm me! Go on, please. What next?'

'Nothing, father.'

And of a sudden the girl was so beset with confusing emotions that she hurriedly quitted her chair and vanished from the room.

Before Mr Whiston returned to his geographical drawing on Monday morning, he had held long conversations with Rose, and still longer with himself. Not easily could he perceive the justice of his daughter's quarrel with propriety; many days were to pass, indeed, before he would consent to do more than make inquiries about Charles James Burroughs, and to permit that aggressive young man to give a fuller account of himself in writing. It was by silence that Rose prevailed. Having defended herself against the charge of immodesty, she declined to urge her own inclination or the rights of Mr Burroughs; her mute patience did not lack its effect with the scrupulous but tender parent.

'I am willing to admit, my dear,' said Mr Whiston one evening, *à propos* of nothing at all, 'that the falsehood in that young man's letter gave proof of a certain delicacy.'

'Thank you, father,' replied Rose, very quiety and simply.

It was next morning that the father posted a formal, proper, self-respecting note of invitation, which bore results.

A DAUGHTER OF THE LODGE

For a score of years the Rocketts had kept the lodge of Brent Hall. In the beginning Rockett was head gardener; his wife, the daughter of a shopkeeper, had never known domestic service, and performed her duties at the Hall gates with a certain modest dignity not displeasing to the stately persons upon whom she depended. During the lifetime of Sir Henry the best possible understanding existed between Hall and lodge. Though Rockett's health broke down, and at length he could work hardly at all, their pleasant home was assured to the family; and at Sir Henry's death the nephew who succeeded him left the Rocketts undisturbed. But, under this new lordship, things were not quite as they had been. Sir Edwin Shale, a middle-aged man, had in his youth made a foolish marriage; his lady ruled him, not with the gentlest of tongues, nor always to the kindest purpose, and their daughter, Hilda, asserted her rights as only child with a force of character which Sir Edwin would perhaps have more sincerely admired had it reminded him less of Lady Shale.

While the Hall, in Sir Henry's time, remained childless, the lodge prided itself on a boy and two girls. Young Rockett, something of a scapegrace, was by the baronet's advice sent to sea, and thenceforth gave his parents no trouble. The second daughter, Betsy, grew up to be her mother's help. But Betsy's elder sister showed from early years that the life of the lodge would afford no adequate scope for *her* ambitions. May Rockett had good looks; what was more, she had an intellect which sharpened itself on everything with which it came in contact. The village school could never have been held responsible for May Rockett's acquirements and views at the age of ten; nor could the High School in the neighbouring town altogether account for her mental development at seventeen. Not without

misgivings had the health-broken gardener and his wife consented to May's pursuit of the higher learning; but Sir Henry
and the kind old Lady Shale seemed to think it the safer course,
and evidently there was little chance of the girl's accepting any
humble kind of employment: in one way or another she must
depend for a livelihood upon her brains. At the time of Sir
Edwin's succession Miss Rockett had already obtained a place
as governess, giving her parents to understand that this was
only, of course, a temporary expedient – a paving of the way to
something vaguely, but superbly, independent. Nor was pro-
motion long in coming. At two-and-twenty May accepted a
secretaryship to a lady with a mission – concerning the rights of
womanhood. In letters to her father and mother she spoke much
of the importance of her work, but did not confess how very
modest was her salary. A couple of years went by without her
visiting the old home; then, of a sudden, she made known her
intention of coming to stay at the lodge 'for a week or ten days.'
She explained that her purpose was rest; intellectual strain had
begun rather to tell upon her, and a few days of absolute
tranquillity, such as she might expect under the elms of Brent
Hall, would do her all the good in the world. 'Of course,' she
added, 'it's unnecessary to say anything about me to the Shale
people. They and I have nothing in common, and it will be
better for us to ignore each other's existence.'

These characteristic phrases troubled Mr and Mrs Rockett.
That the family at the Hall should, if it seemed good to them,
ignore the existence of May was, in the Rocketts' view, reasonable enough; but for May to ignore Sir Edwin and Lady Shale,
who were just now in residence after six months spent abroad,
struck them as a very grave impropriety. Natural respect
demanded that, at some fitting moment, and in a suitable
manner, their daughter should present herself to her feudal
superiors, to whom she was assuredly indebted, though
indirectly, for 'the blessings she enjoyed.' This was Mrs Rockett's phrase, and the rheumatic, wheezy old gardener uttered the
same opinion in less conventional language. They had no
affection for Sir Edwin or his lady, and Miss Hilda they
decidedly disliked; their treatment at the hands of these new
people contrasted unpleasantly enough with the memory of old
times; but a spirit of loyal subordination ruled their blood, and,
to Sir Edwin at all events, they felt gratitude for their retention

at the lodge. Mrs Rockett was a healthy and capable woman of not more than fifty, but no less than her invalid husband would she have dreaded the thought of turning her back on Brent Hall. Rockett had often consoled himself with the thought that here he should die, here amid the fine old trees that he loved, in the ivy-covered house which was his only idea of home. And was it not a reasonable hope that Betsy, good steady girl, should some day marry the promising young gardener whom Sir Edwin had recently taken into his service, and so re-establish the old order of things at the lodge?

'I half wish May wasn't coming,' said Mrs Rockett, after long and anxious thought. 'Last time she was here she quite upset me with her strange talk.'

'She's a funny girl, and that's the truth,' muttered Rockett from his old leather chair, full in the sunshine of the kitchen window. They had a nice little sitting-room; but this, of course, was only used on Sunday, and no particular idea of comfort attached to it. May, to be sure, had always used the sitting-room. It was one of the habits which emphasised most strongly the moral distance between her and her parents.

The subject being full of perplexity, they put it aside, and with very mixed feelings awaited their elder daughter's arrival. Two days later a cab deposited at the lodge Miss May, and her dress-basket, and her travelling-bag, and her holdall, together with certain loose periodicals and a volume or two bearing the yellow label of Mudie.* The young lady was well dressed in a severely practical way; nothing unduly feminine marked her appearance, and in the matter of collar and necktie she inclined to the example of the other sex; for all that, her soft complexion and bright eyes, her well-turned figure and light, quick movements, had a picturesque value which Miss May certainly did not ignore. She manifested no excess of feeling when her mother and sister came forth to welcome her; a nod, a smile, an offer of her cheek, and the pleasant exclamation, 'Well, good people!' carried her through this little scene with becoming dignity.

'You will bring these things inside, please,' she said to the driver, in her agreeable head-voice, with the tone and gesture of one who habitually gives orders.

Her father, bent with rheumatism, stood awaiting her just within. She grasped his hand cordially, and cried on a cheery note, 'Well, father, how are you getting on? No worse than usual, I hope?' Then she added, regarding him with her head slightly aside, 'We must have a talk about your case. I've been going in a little for medicine lately. No doubt your country medico is a duffer. Sit down, sit down, and make yourself comfortable. I don't want to disturb any one. About teatime, isn't it, mother? Tea very weak for me, please, and a slice of lemon with it, if you have such a thing, and just a mouthful of dry toast.'

So unwilling was May to disturb the habits of the family that, half an hour after her arrival, the homely three had fallen into a state of nervous agitation, and could neither say nor do anything natural to them. Of a sudden there sounded a sharp rapping at the window. Mrs Rockett and Betsy started up, and Betsy ran to the door. In a moment or two she came back with glowing cheeks.

'I'm sure I never heard the bell!' she exclaimed with compunction. 'Miss Shale had to get off her bicycle!'

'Was it she who hammered at the window?' asked May coldly.

'Yes – and she was that annoyed.'

'It will do her good. A little anger now and then is excellent for the health.' And Miss Rockett sipped her lemon-tinctured tea with a smile of ineffable contempt.

The others went to bed at ten o'clock, but May, having made herself at ease in the sitting-room, sat there reading until after twelve. Nevertheless, she was up very early next morning, and, before going out for a sharp little walk (in a heavy shower), she gave precise directions about her breakfast. She wanted only the simplest things, prepared in the simplest way, but the tone of her instructions vexed and perturbed Mrs Rockett sorely. After breakfast the young lady made a searching inquiry into the state of her father's health, and diagnosed his ailments in such learned words that the old gardener began to feel worse than he had done for many a year. May then occupied herself with correspondence, and before midday sent her sister out to post nine letters.

'But I thought you were going to rest yourself?' said her mother, in an irritable voice quite unusual with her.

'Why, so I am resting!' May exclaimed. 'If you saw my ordinary morning's work! I suppose you have a London newspaper? No? How *do* you live without it? I must run into the town for one this afternoon.'

The town was three miles away, but could be reached by train from the village station. On reflection, Miss Rockett announced that she would use this opportunity for calling on a lady whose acquaintance she desired to make, one Mrs Lindley, who in social position stood on an equality with the family at the Hall, and was often seen there. On her mother's expressing surprise, May smiled indulgently.

'Why shouldn't I know Mrs Lindley? I have heard she's interested in a movement which occupies me a good deal just now. I know she will be delighted to see me. I can give her a good deal of first-hand information, for which she will be grateful. You *do* amuse me, mother,' she added in her blandest tone. 'When will you come to understand what my position is?'

The Rocketts had put aside all thoughts of what they esteemed May's duty towards the Hall; they earnestly hoped that her stay with them might pass unobserved by Lady and Miss Shale, whom, they felt sure, it would be positively dangerous for the girl to meet. Mrs Rockett had not slept for anxiety on this score. The father was also a good deal troubled; but his wonder at May's bearing and talk had, on the whole, an agreeable preponderance over the uneasy feeling. He and Betsy shared a secret admiration for the brilliant qualities which were flashed before their eyes; they privately agreed that May was more of a real lady than either the baronet's hard-tongued wife or the disdainful Hilda Shale.

So Miss Rockett took the early afternoon train, and found her way to Mrs Lindley's, where she sent in her card. At once admitted to the drawing-room, she gave a rapid account of herself, naming persons whose acquaintance sufficiently recommended her. Mrs Lindley was a good-humoured, chatty woman, who had a lively interest in everything 'progressive'; a new religion or a new cycling-costume stirred her to just the same kind of happy excitement; she had no prejudices, but a decided preference for the society of healthy, high-spirited, well-to-do people. Miss Rockett's talk was exactly what she liked, for it glanced at innumerable topics of the 'advanced' sort, was much concerned with personalities, and avoided all tiresome precision of argument.

'Are you making a stay here?' asked the hostess.

'Oh! I am with my people in the country – not far off,' May answered in an offhand way. 'Only for a day or two.'

Other callers were admitted, but Miss Rockett kept the lead in talk; she glowed with self-satisfaction, feeling that she was really showing to great advantage, and that everybody admired her. When the door again opened the name announced was 'Miss Shale.' Stopping in the middle of a swift sentence, May looked at the newcomer, and saw that it was indeed Hilda Shale, of Brent Hall; but this did not disconcert her. Without lowering her voice she finished what she was saying, and ended in a mirthful key. The baronet's daughter had come into town on her bicycle, as was declared by the short skirt, easy jacket, and brown shoes, which well displayed her athletic person. She was a tall, strongly built girl of six-and-twenty, with a face of hard comeliness and magnificent tawny hair. All her movements suggested vigour; she shook hands with a downward jerk, moved about the room with something of a stride and, in sitting down, crossed her legs abruptly.

From the first her look had turned with surprise to Miss Rockett. When, after a minute or two, the hostess presented that young lady to her, Miss Shale raised her eyebrows a little, smiled in another direction, and gave a just perceptible nod. May's behaviour was as nearly as possible the same.

'Do you cycle, Miss Rockett?' asked Mrs Lindley.

'No, I don't. The fact is, I have never found time to learn.'

A lady remarked that nowadays there was a certain distinction in not cycling; whereupon Miss Shale's abrupt and rather metallic voice sounded what was meant for gentle irony.

'It's a pity the machines can't be sold cheaper. A great many people who would like to cycle don't feel able to afford it, you know. One often hears of such cases out in the country, and it seems awfully hard lines, doesn't it?'

Miss Rockett felt a warmth ascending to her ears, and made a violent effort to look unconcerned. She wished to say something, but could not find the right words, and did not feel altogether sure of her voice. The hostess who made no personal application of Miss Shale's remark, began to discuss the prices of bicycles, and others chimed in. May fretted under this turn of the conversation. Seeing that it was not likely to revert to subjects in which she could shine, she rose and offered to take leave.

'Must you really go?' fell with conventional regret from the hostess's lips.

'I'm afraid I must,' Miss Rockett replied, bracing herself under the converging eyes and feeling not quite equal to the occasion. 'My time is so short, and there are so many people I wish to see.'

As she left the house, anger burned in her. It was certain that Hilda Shale would make known her circumstances. She had fancied this revelation a matter of indifference; but, after all, the thought stung her intolerably. The insolence of the creature, with her hint about the prohibitive cost of bicycles! All the harder to bear because hitting the truth. May would have long ago bought a bicycle had she been able to afford it. Straying about the main streets of the town, she looked flushed and wrathful, and could think of nothing but her humiliation.

To make things worse, she lost count of time, and presently found that she had missed the only train by which she could return home. A cab would be too much of an expense; she had no choice but to walk the three or four miles. The evening was close; walking rapidly, and with the accompaniment of vexatious thoughts, she reached the gates of the Hall tired, perspiring, irritated. Just as her hand was on the gate a bicycle-bell trilled vigorously behind her, and, from a distance of twenty yards, a voice cried imperatively –

'Open the gate, please!'

Miss Rockett looked round, and saw Hilda Shale slowly wheeling forward, in expectation that way would be made for her. Deliberately May passed through the side entrance, and let the little gate fall to.

Miss Shale dismounted, admitted herself, and spoke to May (now at the lodge door) with angry emphasis.

'Didn't you hear me ask you to open?'

'I couldn't imagine you were speaking to *me*,' answered Miss Rockett, with brisk dignity. 'I supposed some servant of yours was in sight.'

A peculiar smile distorted Miss Shale's full red lips. Without another word she mounted her machine and rode away up the elm avenue.

Now Mrs Rockett had seen this encounter, and heard the words exchanged: she was lost in consternation.

'What *do* you mean by behaving like that, May? Why, I was running out myself to open, and then I saw you were there, and, of course, I thought you'd do it. There's the second time in two days Miss Shale has had to complain about us. How *could* you forget yourself, to behave and speak like that! Why, you must be crazy, my girl!'

'I don't seem to get on very well here, mother,' was May's reply. 'The fact is, I'm in a false position. I shall go to-morrow morning, and there won't be any more trouble.'

Thus spoke Miss Rockett, as one who shakes off a petty annoyance – she knew not that the serious trouble was just beginning. A few minutes later Mrs Rockett went up to the Hall, bent on humbly apologising for her daughter's impertinence. After being kept waiting for a quarter of an hour she was admitted to the presence of the housekeeper, who had a rather grave announcement to make.

'Mrs Rockett, I'm sorry to tell you that you will have to leave the lodge. My lady allows you two months, though, as your wages have always been paid monthly, only a month's notice is really called for. I believe some allowance will be made you, but you will hear about that. The lodge must be ready for its new occupants on the last day of October.'

The poor woman all but sank. She had no voice for protest or entreaty – a sob choked her; and blindly she made her way to the door of the room, then to the exit from the Hall.

'What in the world is the matter?' cried May, hearing from the sitting-room, whither she had retired, a clamour of distress-ful tongues.

She came into the kitchen, and learnt what had happened.

'And now I hope you're satisfied!' exclaimed her mother, with tearful wrath. 'You've got us turned out of our home – you've lost us the best place a family ever had – and I hope it's a satisfaction to your conceited, overbearing mind! If you'd *tried* for it you couldn't have gone to work better. And much *you* care! We're below you, we are; we're like dirt under your feet! And your father'll go and end his life who knows where, miserable as miserable can be; and your sister'll have to go into service; and as for me—'

'Listen, mother!' shouted the girl, her eyes flashing and every nerve of her body strung. 'If the Shales are such contemptible wretches as to turn you out just because they're offended with *me*, I should have thought you'd have spirit enough to tell them what you think of such behaviour, and be glad never more to serve such brutes! Father, what do *you* say? I'll tell you how it was.'

She narrated the events of the afternoon, amid sobs and ejaculations from her mother and Betsy. Rockett, who was just now in anguish of lumbago, tried to straighten himself in his chair before replying, but sank helplessly together with a groan.

'You can't help yourself, May,' he said at length. 'It's your nature, my girl. Don't worry. I'll see Sir Edwin, and perhaps he'll listen to me. It's the women who make all the mischief. I must try to see Sir Edwin—'

A pang across the loins made him end abruptly, groaning, moaning, muttering. Before the renewed attack of her mother May retreated into the sitting-room, and there passed an hour wretchedly enough. A knock at the door without words called her to supper, but she had no appetite, and would not join the family circle. Presently the door opened, and her father looked in.

'Don't worry, my girl,' he whispered. 'I'll see Sir Edwin in the morning.'

May uttered no reply. Vaguely repenting what she had done, she at the same time rejoiced in the recollection of her passage of arms with Miss Shale, and was inclined to despise her family for their pusillanimous attitude. It seemed to her very improbable that the expulsion would really be carried out. Lady Shale and Hilda meant, no doubt, to give the Rocketts a good fright, and then contemptuously pardon them. She, in any case, would return to London without delay, and make no more trouble. A pity she had come to the lodge at all; it was no place for one of her spirit and her attainments.

In the morning she packed. The train which was to take her back to town left at half-past ten, and after breakfast she walked into the village to order a cab. Her mother would scarcely speak to her; Betsy was continually in reproachful tears. On coming back to the lodge she saw her father hobbling down the avenue, and walked towards him to ask the result of his supplication. Rockett had seen Sir Edwin, but only to hear his sentence of exile confirmed. The baronet said he was sorry, but could not interfere; the matter lay in Lady Shale's hands, and Lady Shale absolutely refused to hear any excuses or apologies for the insult which had been offered her daughter.

'It's all up with us,' said the old gardener, who was pale and trembling after his great effort. 'We must go. But don't worry, my girl, don't worry.'

Then fright took hold upon May Rockett. She felt for the first time what she had done. Her heart fluttered in an anguish of self-reproach, and her eyes strayed as if seeking help. A minute's hesitation, then, with all the speed she could make, she set off up the avenue towards the Hall.

Presenting herself at the servants' entrance, she begged to be allowed to see the housekeeper. Of course her story was known to all the domestics, half a dozen of whom quickly collected to stare at her, with more or less malicious smiles. It was a bitter moment for Miss Rockett, but she subdued herself, and at length obtained the interview she sought. With a cold air of superiority and of disapproval the housekeeper listened to her quick, broken sentences. Would it be possible, May asked, for her to see Lady Shale? She desired to – to apologise for – for rudeness of which she had been guilty, rudeness in which her family had no part, which they utterly deplored, but for which they were to suffer severely.

'If you could help me, ma'am, I should be very grateful – indeed I should—'

Her voice all but broke into a sob. That 'ma'am' cost her a terrible effort; the sound of it seemed to smack her on the ears.

'If you will go into the servants' hall and wait,' the house-keeper deigned to say, after reflecting, 'I'll see what can be done.'

And Miss Rockett submitted. In the servants' hall she sat for a long, long time, observed, but never addressed. The hour of her train went by. More than once she was on the point of rising and fleeing; more than once her smouldring wrath all but broke into flame. But she thought of her father's pale, pain-stricken face, and sat on.

At something past eleven o'clock a footman approached her, and said curtly, 'You are to go up to my lady; follow me.' May followed, shaking with weakness and apprehension, burning at the same time with pride all but in revolt. Conscious of nothing on the way, she found herself in a large room, where sat the two ladies, who for some moments spoke together about a topic of the day placidly. Then the elder seemed to become aware of the girl who stood before her.

'You are Rockett's elder daughter?'

Oh, the metallic voice of Lady Shale! How gratified she would have been could she have known how it bruised the girl's pride!

'Yes, my lady—'

'And why do you want to see me?'

'I wish to apologise – most sincerely – to your ladyship – for my behaviour of last evening—'

'Oh, indeed!' the listener interrupted contemptuously. 'I am glad you have come to your senses. But your apology must be offered to Miss Shale – if my daughter cares to listen to it.'

May had foreseen this. It was the bitterest moment of her ordeal. Flushing scarlet, she turned towards the younger woman.

'Miss Shale, I beg your pardon for what I said yesterday – I beg you to forgive my rudeness – my impertinence—'

Her voice would go no further; there came a choking sound. Miss Shale allowed her eyes to rest triumphantly for an instant on the troubled face and figure, then remarked to her mother –

'It's really nothing to me, as I told you. I suppose this person may leave the room now?'

It was fated that May Rockett should go through with her purpose and gain her end. But fate alone (which meant in this case the subtlest preponderance of one impulse over another) checked her on the point of a burst of passion which would have startled Lady Shale and Miss Hilda out of their cold-blooded complacency. In the silence May's blood gurgled at her ears, and she tottered with dizziness.

'You may go,' said Lady Shale.

But May could not move. There flashed across her the terrible thought that perhaps she had humiliated herself for nothing.

'My lady – I hope – will your ladyship please to forgive my father and mother? I entreat you not to send them away. We shall all be so grateful to your ladyship if you will overlook—'

'That will do,' said Lady Shale decisively. 'I will merely say that the sooner you leave the lodge the better; and that you will do well never again to pass the gates of the Hall. You may go.'

Miss Rockett withdrew. Outside, the footman was awaiting her. He looked at her with a grin, and asked in an undertone, 'Any good?' But May, to whom this was the last blow, rushed past him, lost herself in corridors, ran wildly hither and thither, tears streaming from her eyes, and was at length guided by a maid-servant into the outer air. Fleeing she cared not whither, she came at length into a still corner of the park, and there, hidden amid trees, watched only by birds and rabbits, she wept out the bitterness of her soul.

By an evening train she returned to London, not having confessed to her family what she had done, and suffering still from some uncertainty as to the result. A day or two later Betsy wrote to her the happy news that the sentence of expulsion was withdrawn, and peace reigned once more in the ivy-covered lodge. By that time Miss Rockett had all but recovered her self-respect, and was so busy in her secretaryship that she could only scribble a line of congratulation. She felt that she had done rather a meritorious thing, but, for the first time in her life, did not care to boast of it.

CHRISTOPHERSON

It was twenty years ago, and on an evening in May. All day long there had been sunshine. Owing, doubtless, to the incident I am about to relate, the light and warmth of that long-vanished day live with me still; I can see the great white clouds that moved across the strip of sky before my window, and feel again the spring languor which troubled my solitary work in the heart of London.

Only at sunset did I leave the house. There was an unwonted sweetness in the air; the long vistas of newly lit lamps made a golden glow under the dusking flush of the sky. With no purpose but to rest and breathe, I wandered for half an hour, and found myself at length where Great Portland Street opens into Marylebone Road. Over the way, in the shadow of Trinity Church, was an old bookshop, well known to me: the gas-jet shining upon the stall with its rows of volumes drew me across. I began turning over pages, and – invariable consequence – fingering what money I had in my pocket. A certain book overcame me; I stepped into the little shop to pay for it.

While standing at the stall, I had been vaguely aware of some one beside me, a man who also was looking over the books; as I came out again with my purchase, this stranger gazed at me intently, with a half-smile of peculiar interest. He seemed about to say something. I walked slowly away; the man moved in the same direction. Just in front of the church he made a quick movement to my side, and spoke.

'Pray excuse me, sir – don't misunderstand me – I only wished to ask whether you have noticed the name written on the flyleaf of the book you have just bought?'

The respectful nervousness of his voice naturally made me suppose at first that the man was going to beg; but he seemed no ordinary mendicant. I judged him to be about sixty years of age; his long, thin hair and straggling beard were grizzled, and a somewhat rheumy eye looked out from his bloodless, hollowed countenance; he was very shabbily clad, yet as a fallen gentleman, and indeed his accent made it clear to what class he originally belonged. The expression with which he regarded me had so much intelligence, so much good-nature, and at the same time such a pathetic diffidence, that I could not but answer him in the friendliest way. I had not seen the name on the flyleaf, but at once I opened the book, and by the light of a gas-lamp read, inscribed in a very fine hand, 'W. R. Christopherson, 1849.'

'It is my name,' said the stranger, in a subdued and uncertain voice.

'Indeed? The book used to belong to you?'

'It belonged to me.' He laughed oddly, a tremulous little crow of a laugh, at the same time stroking his head, as if to deprecate disbelief. 'You never heard of the sale of the Christopherson library? To be sure, you were too young; it was in 1860. I have often come across books with my name in them on the stalls – often. I had happened to notice this just before you came up, and when I saw you look at it, I was curious to see whether you would buy it. Pray excuse the freedom I am taking. Lovers of books – don't you think— ?'

The broken question was completed by his look, and when I said that I quite understood and agreed with him he crowed his little laugh.

'Have you a large library?' he inquired, eyeing me wistfully.

'Oh dear, no. Only a few hundred volumes. Too many for one who has no house of his own.'

He smiled good-naturedly, bent his head, and murmured just audibly:

'My catalogue numbered 24,718.'

I was growing curious and interested. Venturing no more direct questions, I asked whether, at the time he spoke of, he lived in London.

'If you have five minutes to spare,' was the timid reply, 'I will show you my house. I mean' – again the little crowing laugh – 'the house which *was* mine.'

Willingly I walked on with him. He led me a short distance up the road skirting Regent's Park, and paused at length before a house in an imposing terrace.

'There,' he whispered, 'I used to live. The window to the right of the door – that was my library. Ah !'

And he heaved a deep sigh.

'A misfortune befell you,' I said, also in subdued voice.

'The result of my own folly. I had enough for my needs, but thought I needed more. I let myself be drawn into business – I, who knew nothing of such things – and there came the black day – the black day.'

We turned to retrace our steps, and walking slowly, with heads bent, came in silence again to the church.

'I wonder whether you have bought any other of my books ?' asked Christopherson, with his gentle smile, when he had paused as if for leave-taking.

I replied that I did not remember to have come across his name before ; then, on an impulse, asked whether he would care to have the book I carried in my hand; if so, with pleasure I would give it him. No sooner were the words spoken than I saw the delight they caused the hearer. He hesitated, murmured reluctance, but soon gratefully accepted my offer, and flushed with joy as he took the volume.

'I still have a few books,' he said, under his breath, as if he spoke of something he was ashamed to make known. 'But it is very rarely indeed that I can add to them. I feel I have not thanked you half enough.'

We shook hands and parted.

My lodging at that time was in Camden Town. One afternoon, perhaps a fortnight later, I had walked for an hour or two, and on my way back I stopped at a bookstall in the High Street. Some one came up to my side ; I looked, and recognised Christopherson. Our greeting was like that of old friends.

'I have seen you several times lately,' said the broken gentleman, who looked shabbier than before in the broad daylight, 'but I – I didn't like to speak. I live not far from here.'

'Why, so do I,' and I added, without much thinking what I said, 'do you live alone ?'

'Alone ? oh no. With my wife.'

There was a curious embarrassment in his tone. His eyes were cast down and his head moved uneasily.

We began to talk of the books on the stall, and turning away together continued our conversation. Christopherson was not only a well-bred but a very intelligent and even learned man. On his giving some proof of erudition (with the excessive modesty which characterised him), I asked whether he wrote. No, he had never written anything – never; he was only a bookworm, he said. Thereupon he crowed faintly and took his leave.

It was not long before we again met by chance. We came face to face at a street corner in my neighbourhood, and I was struck by a change in him. He looked older; a profound melancholy darkened his countenance; the hand he gave me was limp, and his pleasure at our meeting found only a faint expression.

'I am going away,' he said in reply to my inquiring look. 'I am leaving London.'

'For good?'

'I fear so, and yet' – he made an obvious effort – 'I am glad of it. My wife's health has not been very good lately. She has need of country air. Yes, I am glad we have decided to go away – very glad – very glad indeed!'

He spoke with an automatic sort of emphasis, his eyes wandering, and his hands twitching nervously. I was on the point of asking what part of the country he had chosen for his retreat, when he abruptly added:

'I live just over there. Will you let me show you my books?'

Of course I gladly accepted the invitation, and a couple of minutes' walk brought us to a house in a decent street where most of the ground-floor windows showed a card announcing lodgings. As we paused at the door, my companion seemed to hesitate, to regret having invited me.

'I'm really afraid it isn't worth your while,' he said timidly. 'The fact is, I haven't space to show my books properly.'

I put aside the objection, and we entered. With anxious courtesy Christopherson led me up the narrow staircase to the second-floor landing, and threw open a door. On the threshold I stood astonished. The room was a small one, and would in any case have only just sufficed for homely comfort, used as it evidently was for all daytime purposes; but certainly a third of the entire space was occupied by a solid mass of books, volumes stacked several rows deep against two of the walls and almost up to the ceiling. A round table and two or three chairs were the only furniture – there was no room, indeed, for more. The window being shut, and the sunshine glowing upon it, an intolerable stuffiness oppressed the air. Never had I been made so uncomfortable by the odour of printed paper and bindings.

'But,' I exclaimed, 'you said you had only a *few* books ! There must be five times as many here as I have.'

'I forget the exact number,' murmured Christopherson, in great agitation. 'You see, I can't arrange them properly. I have a few more in – in the other room.'

He led me across the landing, opened another door, and showed me a little bedroom. Here the encumberment was less remarkable, but one wall had completely disappeared behind volumes, and the bookishness of the air made it a disgusting thought that two persons occupied this chamber every night.

We returned to the sitting-room, Christopherson began picking out books from the solid mass to show me. Talking nervously, brokenly, with now and then a deep sigh or a crow of laughter, he gave me a little light on his history. I learnt that he had occupied these lodgings for the last eight years ; that he had been twice married ; that the only child he had had, a daughter by his first wife, had died long ago in childhood ; and lastly – this came in a burst of confidence, with a very pleasant smile – that his second wife had been his daughter's governess. I listened with keen interest, and hoped to learn still more of the circumstances of this singular household.

'In the country,' I remarked, 'you will no doubt have shelf room ?'

At once his countenance fell ; he turned upon me a woebegone eye. Just as I was about to speak again sounds from within the house caught my attention ; there was a heavy foot on the stairs, and a loud voice, which seemed familiar to me.

'Ah !' exclaimed Christopherson with a start, 'here comes some one who is going to help me in the removal of the books. Come in, Mr Pomfret, come in !'

The door opened, and there appeared a tall, wiry fellow, whose sandy hair, light blue eyes, jutting jawbones, and large mouth made a picture suggestive of small refinement but of vigorous and wholesome manhood. No wonder I had seemed to recognise his voice. Though we only saw each other by chance at long intervals, Pomfret and I were old acquaintances.

'Hallo !' he roared out, 'I didn't know you knew Mr Christopherson.'

'I'm just as much surprised to find that *you* know him !' was my reply.

The old book-lover gazed at us in nervous astonishment, then shook hands with the newcomer, who greeted him bluffly, yet respectfully. Pomfret spoke with a strong Yorkshire accent, and had all the angularity of demeanour which marks the typical Yorkshireman. He came to announce that everything had been settled for the packing and transporting of Mr Christopherson's library; it remained only to decide the day.

'There's no hurry,' exclaimed Christopherson. 'There's really no hurry. I'm greatly obliged to you, Mr Pomfret, for all the trouble you are taking. We'll settle the date in a day or two – a day or two.'

With a good-humoured nod Pomfret moved to take his leave. Our eyes met; we left the house together. Out in the street again I took a deep breath of the summer air, which seemed sweet as in a meadow after that stifling room. My companion evidently had a like sensation, for he looked up to the sky and broadened out his shoulders.

'Eh, but it's a grand, day! I'd give something for a walk on Ilkley Moors.'

As the best substitute within our reach we agreed to walk across Regent's Park together. Pomfret's business took him in that direction, and I was glad of a talk about Christopherson. I learnt that the old booklover's landlady was Pomfret's aunt. Christopherson's story of affluence and ruin was quite true. Ruin complete, for at the age of forty he had been obliged to earn his living as a clerk or something of the kind. About five years later came his second marriage.

'You know Mrs Christopherson?' asked Pomfret.

'No! I wish I did. Why?'

'Because she's the sort of woman it does you good to know, that's all. She's a lady – *my* idea of a lady. Christopherson's a gentleman too, there's no denying it; if he wasn't, I think I should have punched his head before now. Oh, I know 'em well! why, I lived in the house there with 'em for several years. She's a lady to the end of her little finger, and how her husband can 'a borne to see her living the life she has, it's more than I can understand. By—! I'd have turned burglar, if I could 'a found no other way of keeping her in comfort.'

'She works for her living, then?'

'Ay, and for his too. No, not teaching; she's in a shop in Tottenham Court Road; has what they call a good place, and earns thirty shillings a week. It's all they have, but Christopherson buys books out of it.'

'But has he never done anything since their marriage?'

'He did for the first few years, I believe, but he had an illness, and that was the end of it. Since then he's only loafed. He goes to all the book-sales, and spends the rest of his time sniffing about the second-hand shops. She? Oh, she'd never say a word! Wait till you've seen her.'

'Well, but,' I asked, 'what has happened? How is it they're leaving London?'

'Ay, I'll tell you; I was coming to that. Mrs Christopherson has relatives well off – a fat and selfish lot, as far as I can make out – never lifted a finger to help her until now. One of them's a Mrs Keeting, the widow of some City porpoise, I'm told. Well, this woman has a home down in Norfolk. She never lives there, but a son of hers goes there to fish and shoot now and then. Well, this is what Mrs Christopherson tells my aunt, Mrs Keeting has offered to let her and her husband live down yonder, rent free, and their food provided. She's to be housekeeper, in fact, and keep the place ready for any one who goes down.'

'Christopherson, *I* can see, would rather stay where he is.'

'Why, of course, he doesn't know how he'll live without the bookshops. But he's glad for all that, on his wife's account. And it's none too soon, I can tell you. The poor woman couldn't go on much longer; my aunt says she's just about ready to drop, and sometimes, I know, she looks terribly bad. Of course, she won't own it, not she; she isn't one of the complaining sort. But she talks now and then about the country – the places where she used to live. I've heard her, and it gives me a notion of what she's gone through all these years. I saw her a week ago, just when she had Mrs Keeting's offer, and I tell you I scarcely knew who it was! You never saw such a change in any one in your life! Her face was like that of a girl of seventeen. And her laugh – you should have heard her laugh!'

'Is she much younger than her husband?' I asked.

'Twenty years at least. She's about forty, I think.'

I mused for a few moments.

'After all, it isn't an unhappy marriage?'

'Unhappy?' cried Pomfret. 'Why, there's never been a dis-agreeable word between them, that I'll warrant. Once Christopherson gets over the change, they'll have nothing more in the world to ask for. He'll potter over his books—'

'You mean to tell me,' I interrupted, 'that those books have all been bought out of his wife's thirty shillings a week?'

'No, no. To begin with, he kept a few out of his old library. Then, when he was earning his own living, he bought a great many. He told me once that he's often lived on sixpence a day to have money for books. A rum old owl; but for all that he's a gentleman, and you can't help liking him. I shall be sorry when he's out of reach.'

For my own part, I wished nothing better than to hear of Christopherson's departure. The story I had heard made me uncomfortable. It was good to think of that poor woman rescued at last from her life of toil, and in these days of midsummer free to enjoy the country she loved. A touch of envy mingled, I confess, with my thought of Christopherson, who henceforth had not a care in the world, and without reproach might delight in his hoarded volumes. One could not imagine that he would suffer seriously by the removal of his old haunts. I promised myself to call on him in a day or two. By choosing Sunday, I might perhaps be lucky enough to see his wife.

And on Sunday afternoon I was on the point of setting forth to pay this visit, when in came Pomfret. He wore a surly look, and kicked clumsily against the furniture as he crossed the room. His appearance was a surprise, for, though I had given him my address, I did not in the least expect that he would come to see me; a certain pride, I suppose, characteristic of his rugged strain, having always made him shy of such intimacy.

'Did you ever hear the like of *that*!' he shouted, half angrily. 'It's all over. They're not going! And all because of those blamed books!'

And spluttering and growling, he made known what he had just learnt at his aunt's home. On the previous afternoon the Christophersons had been surprised by a visit from their relative and would-be benefactress, Mrs Keeting. Never before had that lady called upon them; she came, no doubt (this could only be conjectured), to speak with them of their approaching removal. The close of the conversation (a very brief one) was overheard by the landlady, for Mrs Keeting spoke loudly as she descended the stairs. 'Impossible! Quite impossibe! I couldn't think of it!

How could you dream for a moment that I would let you fill my house with musty old books? Most unhealthy! I never knew anything so extraordinary in my life, never!' And so she went out to her carriage, and was driven away. And the landlady, presently having occasion to go upstairs, was aware of a dead silence in the room where the Christophersons were sitting. She knocked – prepared with some excuse – and found the couple side by side, smiling sadly. At once they told her the truth. Mrs Keeting had come because of a letter in which Mrs Christopherson had mentioned the fact that her husband had a good many books, and hoped he might be permitted to remove them to the house in Norfolk. She came to see the library – with the result already heard. They had the choice between sacrificing the books and losing what their relative offered.

'Christopherson refused?' I let fall.

'I suppose his wife saw that it was too much for him. At all events, they'd agreed to keep the books and lose the house. And there's an end of it. I haven't been so riled about anything for a long time!'

Meantime I had been reflecting. It was easy for me to understand Christopherson's state of mind, and without knowing Mrs Keeting, I saw that she must be a person whose benefactions would be a good deal of a burden. After all, was Mrs Christopherson so very unhappy? Was she not the kind of woman who lived by sacrifice – one who had far rather lead a life disagreeable to herself than change it at the cost of discomfort to her husband? This view of the matter irritated Pomfret, and he broke into objurgations, directed partly against Mrs Keeting, partly against Christopherson. It was an 'infernal shame,' that was all he could say. And after all, I rather inclined to his opinion.

When two or three days had passed, curiosity drew me towards the Christophersons' dwelling. Walking along the opposite side of the street, I looked up at their window, and there was the face of the old bibliophile. Evidently he was standing at the window in idleness, perhaps in trouble. At once he beckoned to me; but before I could knock at the house-door he had descended, and came out.

'May I walk a little way with you?' he asked.

There was worry on his features. For some moments we went on in silence.

'So you have changed your mind about leaving London?' I said, as if carelessly.

'You have heard from Mr Pomfret? Well – yes, yes – I think we shall stay where we are – for the present.'

Never have I seen a man more painfully embarrassed. He walked with head bent, shoulders stooping; and shuffled, indeed, rather than walked. Even so might a man bear himself who felt guilty of some peculiar meanness.

Presently words broke from him.

'To tell you the truth, there's a difficulty about the books.' He glanced furtively at me, and I saw he was trembling in all his nerves. 'As you see, my circumstances are not brilliant.' He half-choked himself with a crow. 'The fact is we were offered a house in the country, on certain conditions, by a relative of Mrs Christopherson; and, unfortunately, it turned out that my library is regarded as an objection – a fatal objection. We have quite reconciled ourselves to staying where we are.'

I could not help asking, without emphasis, whether Mrs Christopherson would have cared for life in the country. But no sooner were the words out of my mouth than I regretted them, so evidently did they hit my companion in a tender place.

'I think she would have liked it,' he answered, with a strangely pathetic look at me, as if he entreated my forbearance.

'But,' I suggested, 'couldn't you make some arrangements about the books? Couldn't you take a room for them in another house, for instance?'

Christopherson's face was sufficient answer; it reminded me of his pennilessness. 'We think no more about it,' he said. 'The matter is settled – quite settled.'

There was no pursuing the subject. At the next parting of the ways we took leave of each other.

I think it was not more than a week later when I received a postcard from Pomfret. He wrote: 'Just as I expected. Mrs C. seriously ill.' That was all.

Mrs C. could, of course, only mean Mrs Christopherson. I mused over the message – it took hold of my imagination, wrought upon my feelings; and that afternoon I again walked along the interesting street.

There was no face at the window. After a little hesitation I decided to call at the house and speak with Pomfret's aunt. It was she who opened the door to me.

We had never seen each other, but when I mentioned my name and said I was anxious to have news of Mrs Christopherson, she led me into a sitting-room, and began to talk confidentially.

She was a good-natured Yorkshirewoman, very unlike the common London landlady. 'Yes, Mrs Christopherson had been taken ill two days ago. It began with a long fainting fit. She had a feverish, sleepless night; the doctor was sent for; and he had her removed out of the stuffy, book-cumbered bedroom into another chamber, which luckily happened to be vacant. There she lay utterly weak and worn, all but voiceless, able only to smile at her husband, who never moved from the bedside day or night. He, too,' said the landlady, 'would soon break down: he looked like a ghost, and seemed "half-crazed."'

'What,' I asked, 'could be the cause of this illness?'

The good woman gave me an odd look, shook her head, and murmured that the reason was not far to seek.

'Did she think,' I asked, 'that disappointment might have something to do with it?'

Why, of course she did. For a long time the poor lady had been all but at the end of her strength, and *this* came as a blow beneath which she sank.

'Your nephew and I have talked about it,' I said. 'He thinks that Mr Christopherson didn't understand what a sacrifice he asked his wife to make.'

'I think so too,' was the reply. 'But he begins to see it now, I can tell you. He says nothing but—'

There was a tap at the door, and a hurried tremulous voice begged the landlady to go upstairs.

'What is it, sir?' she asked.

'I'm afraid she's worse,' said Christopherson, turning his haggard face to me with startled recognition. 'Do come up at once, please.'

Without a word to me he disappeared with the landlady. I could not go away; for some ten minutes I fidgeted about the little room, listening to every sound in the house. Then came a footfall on the stairs, and the landlady rejoined me.

'It's nothing,' she said. 'I almost think she might drop off to sleep, if she's left quiet. He worries her, poor man, sitting there and asking her every two minutes how she feels. I've persuaded

him to go to his room, and I think it might do him good if you
went and had a bit o' talk with him.'

I mounted at once to the second-floor sitting-room, and found
Christopherson sunk upon a chair, his head falling forwards,
the image of despairing misery. As I approached he staggered to
his feet. He took my hand in a shrinking, shamefaced way, and
could not raise his eyes. I uttered a few words of encouragement,
but they had the opposite effect to that designed.

'Don't tell me that,' he moaned, half resentfully. 'She's dying
– she's dying – say what they will, I know it.'

'Have you a good doctor?'

'I think so – but it's too late – it's too late.'

As he dropped to his chair again I sat down by him. The
silence of a minute or two was broken by a thunderous rat-tat
at the house-door. Christopherson leapt to his feet, rushed from
the room; I, half fearing that he had gone mad, followed to the
head of the stairs.

In a moment he came up again, limp and wretched as before.

'It was the postman,' he muttered. 'I am expecting a letter.'

Conversation seeming impossible, I shaped a phrase preliminary to withdrawal; but Christopherson would not let me go.

'I should like to tell you,' he began, looking at me like a dog
under punishment, 'that I have done all I could. As soon as my
wife fell ill, and when I saw – I had only begun to think of it in
that way – how she felt the disappointment, I went at once to
Mrs Keeting's house to tell her that I would sell the books. But
she was out of town. I wrote to her – I said I regretted my folly
– I entreated her to forgive me and to renew her kind offer.
There has been plenty of time for a reply, but she doesn't
answer.'

He had in his hand what I saw was a bookseller's catalogue,
just delivered by the postman. Mechanically he tore off the
wrapper and even glanced over the first page. Then, as if
conscience stabbed him, he flung the thing violently away.

'The chance has gone!' he exclaimed, taking a hurried step or
two along the little strip of floor left free by the mountain of
books. 'Of course she said she would rather stay in London! Of
course she said what she knew would please me! When – when
did she ever say anything else! And I was cruel enough – base
enough – to let her make the sacrifice!' He waved his arms
frantically. 'Didn't I know what it cost her? Couldn't I see in

her face how her heart leapt at the hope of going to live in the country! I knew what she was suffering; I *knew* it, I tell you! And, like a selfish coward, I let her suffer – I let her drop down and die – die!'

'Any hour,' I said, 'may bring you the reply from Mrs Keeting. Of course it will be favourable, and the good news—'

'Too late, I have killed her! That woman won't write. She's one of the vulgar rich, and we offended her pride; and such as she never forgive.'

He sat down for a moment, but started up again in an agony of mental suffering.

'She is dying – and there, there, that's what has killed her!' He gesticulated wildly towards the books. 'I have sold her life for those. Oh! – oh!'

With this cry he seized half a dozen volumes, and, before I could understand what he was about, he had flung up the window-sash, and cast the books into the street. Another batch followed; I heard the thud upon the pavement. Then I caught him by the arm, held him fast, begged him to control himself.

'They shall all go!' he cried. 'I loathe the sight of them. They have killed my dear wife!'

He said it sobbing, and at the last words tears streamed from his eyes. I had no difficulty now in restraining him. He met my look with a gaze of infinite pathos, and talked on while he wept.

'If you knew what she has been to me! When she married me I was a ruined man twenty years older. I have given her nothing but toil and care. You shall know everything – for years and years I have lived on the earnings of her labour. Worse than that, I have starved and stinted her to buy books. Oh, the shame of it! The wickedness of it! It was my vice – the vice that enslaved me just as if it had been drinking or gambling. I couldn't resist the temptation – though every day I cried shame upon myself and swore to overcome it. She never blamed me; never a word – nay, not a look – of a reproach. I lived in idleness. I never tried to save her that daily toil at the shop. Do you know that she worked in a shop? – She, with her knowledge and her refinement leading such a life as that! Think that I have passed the shop a thousand times, coming home with a book in my hands! I had the heart to pass, and to think of her there! Oh! Oh!'

Some one was knocking at the door. I went to open, and saw

the landlady, her face set in astonishment, and her arms full of books.

'It's all right,' I whispered. 'Put them down on the floor there; don't bring them in. An accident.'

Christopherson stood behind me; his look asked what he durst not speak. I said it was nothing, and by degrees brought him into a calmer state. Luckily, the doctor came before I went away, and he was able to report a slight improvement. The patient had slept a little and seemed likely to sleep again. Christopherson asked me to come again before long – there was no one else, he said, who cared anything about him – and I promised to call the next day.

I did so, early in the afternoon. Christopherson must have watched for my coming: before I could raise the knocker the door flew open, and his face gleamed such a greeting as astonished me. He grasped my hand in both his.

'The letter has come! We are to have the house.'

'And how is Mrs Christopherson?'

'Better, much better, Heaven be thanked! She slept almost from the time when you left yesterday afternoon till early this morning. The letter came by the first post, and I told her – not the whole truth,' he added, under his breath. 'She thinks I am to be allowed to take the books with me; and if you could have seen her smile of contentment. But they will all be sold and carried away before she knows about it; and when she sees that I don't care a snap of the fingers— !'

He had turned into the sitting-room on the ground floor. Walking about excitedly, Christopherson gloried in the sacrifice he had made. Already a letter was despatched to a bookseller, who would buy the whole library as it stood. But would he not keep a few volumes? I asked. Surely there could be no objection to a few shelves of books; and how would he live without them? At first he declared vehemently that not a volume should be kept – he never wished to see a book again as long as he lived. But Mrs Christopherson? I urged. Would she not be glad of something to read now and then? At this he grew pensive. We discussed the matter, and it was arranged that a box should be packed with select volumes and taken down into Norfolk together with the rest of their luggage. Not even Mrs Keeting could object to this, and I strongly advised him to take her permission for granted.

And so it was done. By discreet management the piled volumes were stowed in bags, carried downstairs, emptied into a cart, and conveyed away, so quietly that the sick woman was aware of nothing. In telling me about it, Christopherson crowed as I had never heard him; but methought his eye avoided that part of the floor which had formerly been hidden, and in the course of our conversation he now and then became absent, with head bowed. Of the joy he felt in his wife's recovery there could, however, be no doubt. The crisis through which he had passed had made him, in appearance, a yet older man; when he declared his happiness tears came into his eyes, and his head shook with a senile tremor.

Before they left London, I saw Mrs Christopherson – a pale, thin, slightly made woman, who had never been what is called good-looking, but her face, if ever face did so, declared a brave and loyal spirit. She was not joyous, she was not sad; but in her eyes, as I looked at them again and again, I read the profound thankfulness of one to whom fate has granted her soul's desire.

MISS RODNEY'S LEISURE

A young woman of about eight-and-twenty, in tailor-made costume, with unadorned hat of brown felt, and irreproachable umbrella; a young woman who walked faster than anyone in Wattleborough, yet never looked hurried; who crossed a muddy street seemingly without a thought for her skirts, yet somehow was never splashed; who held up her head like one thoroughly at home in the world, and frequently smiled at her own thoughts. Those who did not know her asked who she was; those who had already made her acquaintance talked a good deal of the new mistress at the High School, by name Miss Rodney. In less than a week after her arrival in the town, her opinions were cited and discussed by Wattleborough ladies. She brought with her the air of a University; she knew a great number of important people; she had a quiet decision of speech and manner which was found very impressive in Wattleborough drawing-rooms. The headmistress spoke of her in high terms, and the incumbent of St Luke's who knew her family, reported that she had always been remarkably clever.

A stranger in the town, Miss Rodney was recommended to the lodgings of Mrs Ducker, a churchwarden's widow; but there she remained only for a week or two, and it was understood that she left because the rooms 'lacked character.' Some persons understood this as an imputation on Mrs Ducker, and were astonished; others, who caught a glimpse of Miss Rodney's meaning, thought she must be 'fanciful.' Her final choice of an abode gave general surprise, for though the street was one of those which Wattleborough opinion classed as 'respectable,' the house itself, as Miss Rodney might have learnt from the incumbent of St Luke's, in whose parish it was situated, had objectionable features. Nothing grave could be alleged against

Mrs Turpin, who regularly attended the Sunday evening service;
but her husband, a carpenter, spent far too much time at The
Swan with Two Necks; and then there was a lodger, young
Mr Rawcliffe, concerning whom Wattleborough had for some
time been too well informed. Of such comments upon her
proceeding Miss Rodney made light; in the aspect of the rooms
she found a certain 'quaintness' which decidedly pleased her.
'And as for Mrs Grundy,' she added, '*je m'en fiche*,' which
certain ladies of culture declared to be a polite expression of
contempt.

Miss Rodney never wasted time, and in matters of business
had cultivated a notable brevity. Her interview with Mrs Turpin,
when she engaged the rooms, occupied perhaps a quarter of an
hour; in that space of time she had sufficiently surveyed the
house, had learnt all that seemed necessary as to its occupants,
and had stated in the clearest possible way her present
requirements.

'As a matter of course,' was her closing remark, 'the rooms
will be thoroughly cleaned before I come in. At present they are
filthy.'

The landlady was too much astonished to reply; Miss Rodney's tones and bearing had so impressed her that she was at a
loss for her usual loquacity, and could only stammer respectfully
broken answers to whatever was asked. Assuredly no one had
ever dared to tell her that her lodgings were 'filthy' – any
ordinary person who had ventured upon such an insult would
have been overwhelmed with clamorous retort. But Miss
Rodney, with a pleasant smile and nod, went her way, and Mrs
Turpin stood at the open door gazing after her, bewildered
'twixt satisfaction and resentment.

She was an easy-going, wool-witted creature, not ill-disposed,
but sometimes mendacious and very indolent. Her life had
always been what it was now – one of slatternly comfort and
daylong gossip, for she came of a small tradesman's family, and
had married an artisan who was always in well-paid work. Her
children were two daughters, who, at seventeen and fifteen,
remained in the house with her doing little or nothing, though
they were supposed to 'wait upon the lodgers.' For some months
only two of the four rooms Mrs Turpin was able to let had been
occupied, one by 'young Mr Rawcliffe,' always so called, though
his age was nearly thirty, but, as was well known, he belonged

to the 'real gentry,' and Mrs Turpin held him in reverence on
that account. No matter for his little weaknesses – of which evil
tongues, said Mrs Turpin, of course made the most. He might
be irregular in payment; he might come home 'at all hours,' and
make unnecessary noise in going upstairs; he might at times
grumble when his chop was ill-cooked; and, to tell the truth, he
might occasionally be 'a little too free' with the young ladies –
that is to say, with Mabel and Lily Turpin; but all these things
were forgiven him because he was 'a real gentleman,' and spent
just as little time as he liked daily in a solicitor's office.

Miss Rodney arrived early on Saturday afternoon. Smiling
and silent, she saw her luggage taken up to the bedroom; she
paid the cabman; she beckoned her landlady into the parlour,
which was on the ground-floor front.

'You haven't had time yet, Mrs Turpin, to clean the rooms?'

The landlady stammered a half-indignant surprise. Why, she
and her daughters had given the room a thorough turn-out. It
was done only yesterday, and *hours* had been devoted to it.

'I see,' interrupted Miss Rodney, with quiet decision, 'that our
notions of cleanliness differ considerably. I'm going out now,
and I shall not be back till six o'clock. You will please to *clean*
the bedroom before then. The sitting-room shall be done on
Monday.'

And therewith Miss Rodney left the house.

On her return she found the bedroom relatively clean, and,
knowing that too much must not be expected at once, she made
no comment. That night, as she sat reading at eleven o'clock, a
strange sound arose in the back part of the house; it was a
man's voice, hilariously mirthful and breaking into rude song.
After listening for a few minutes, Miss Rodney rang her bell,
and the landlady appeared.

'Whose voice is that I hear?'

'Voice, miss?'

'Who is shouting and singing?' asked Miss Rodney, in a
disinterested tone.

'I'm sorry if it disturbs you, miss. You'll hear no more.'

'Mrs Turpin, I asked who it was.'

'My 'usband, miss. But—'

'Thank you. Good night, Mrs Turpin.'

There was quiet for an hour or more. At something after

midnight, when Miss Rodney had just finished writing half a dozen letters, there sounded a latch-key in the front door, and some one entered. This person, whoever it was, seemed to stumble about the passage in the dark, and at length banged against the listener's door. Miss Rodney started up and flung the door open. By the light of her lamp she saw a moustachioed face, highly flushed, and grinning.

'Beg pardon,' cried the man, in a voice which harmonized with his look and bearing. 'Infernally dark here; haven't got a match. You're Miss – pardon – forgotten the name – new lodger. Oblige me with a light? Thanks awfully.'

Without a word Miss Rodney took a matchbox from her chimney-piece, entered the passage, entered the second parlour – that occupied by Mr Rawcliffe – and lit a candle which stood on the table.

'You'll be so kind,' she said, looking her fellow-lodger in the eyes, 'as not to set the house on fire.'

'Oh, no fear,' he replied, with a high laugh. 'Quite accustomed. Thanks awfully, Miss – pardon – forgotten the name.'

But Miss Rodney was back in her sitting-room and had closed the door.

Her breakfast next morning was served by Mabel Turpin, the elder daughter, a stupidly good-natured girl, who would fain have entered into conversation. Miss Rodney replied to a question that she had slept well, and added that, when she rang her bell, she would like to see Mrs Turpin. Twenty minutes later the landlady entered.

'You wanted me, miss,' she began, in what was meant for a voice of dignity and reserve. 'I don't really wait on lodgers myself.'

'We'll talk about that another time, Mrs Turpin. I wanted to say, first of all, that you have spoiled a piece of good bacon and two good eggs. I must trouble you to cook better than this.'

'I'm very sorry, miss, that nothing seems to suit you—'

'Oh, we shall get right in time!' interrupted Miss Rodney cheerfully. 'You will find that I have patience. Then I wanted to ask you whether your husband and your lodger come home tipsy *every* night, or only on Saturdays?'

The woman opened her eyes as wide as saucers, trying hard to look indignant.

'Tipsy, miss?'

'Well, perhaps I should have said "drunk"; I beg your pardon.'

'All I can say, miss, is that young Mr Rawcliffe has never behaved himself in *this* house excepting as the gentleman he is. You don't perhaps know that he belongs to a very high-connected family, miss, or I'm sure you wouldn't—'

'I see,' interposed Miss Rodney. 'That accounts for it. But your husband. Is *he* highly connected?'

'I'm sure, miss, nobody could ever say that my 'usband took too much – not to say *really* too much. You may have heard him a bit merry, miss, but where's the harm of a Saturday night?'

'Thank you. Then it is only on Saturday nights that Mr Turpin becomes merry. I'm glad to know that. I shall get used to these little things.'

But Mrs Turpin did not feel sure that she would get used to her lodger. Sunday was spoilt for her by this beginning. When her husband woke from his prolonged slumbers, and shouted for breakfast (which on this day of rest he always took in bed), the good woman went to him with downcast visage, and spoke querulously of Miss Rodney's behaviour.

'I *won't* wait upon her, so there! The girls may do it, and if she isn't satisfied let her give notice. I'm sure I shan't be sorry. She's given me more trouble in a day than poor Mrs Brown did all the months she was here. I *won't* be at her beck and call, so there!'

Before night came this declaration was repeated times innumerable, and as it happened that Miss Rodney made no demand for her landlady's attendance, the good woman enjoyed a sense of triumphant self-assertion. On Monday morning Mabel took in the breakfast, and reported that Miss Rodney had made no remark; but, a quarter of an hour later, the bell rang, and Mrs Turpin was summoned. Very red in the face, she obeyed. Having civilly greeted her, Miss Rodney inquired at what hour Mr Turpin took his breakfast, and was answered with an air of surprise that he always left the house on week-days at half-past seven.

'In that case,' said Miss Rodney, 'I will ask permission to come into your kitchen at a quarter to eight to-morrow morning, to show you how to fry bacon and boil eggs. You mustn't mind. You know that teaching is my profession.'

Mrs Turpin, nevertheless, seemed to mind very much. Her generally good-tempered face wore a dogged sullenness, and she began to mutter something about such a thing never having been heard of; but Miss Rodney paid no heed, renewed the appointment for the next morning, and waved a cheerful dismissal.

Talking with a friend that day, the High School mistress gave a humorous description of her lodgings, and when the friend remarked that they must be very uncomfortable, and that surely she would not stay there, Miss Rodney replied that she had the firmest intention of staying, and, what was more, of being comfortable.

'I'm going to take that household in hand,' she added. 'The woman is foolish, but can be managed, I think, with a little patience. I'm going to *tackle* the drunken husband as soon as I see my way. And as for the highly connected gentleman whose candle I had the honour of lighting, I shall turn him out.'

'You have your work set!' exclaimed the friend laughing.

'Oh, a little employment for my leisure! This kind of thing relieves the monotony of a teacher's life, and prevents one from growing old.'

Very systematically she pursured her purpose of getting Mrs Turpin 'in hand.' The two points at which she first aimed were the keeping clean of her rooms and the decent preparation of her meals. Never losing her temper, never seeming to notice the landlady's sullen mood, always using a tone of legitimate authority, touched sometimes with humorous compassion, she exacted obedience to her directions, but was well aware that at any moment the burden of a new civilization might prove too heavy for the Turpin family and cause revolt. A week went by; it was again Saturday, and Miss Rodney devoted a part of the morning (there being no school to-day) to culinary instruction. Mabel and Lily shared the lesson with their mother, but both young ladies wore an air of condescension, and grimaced at Miss Rodney behind her back. Mrs Turpin was obstinately mute. The pride of ignorance stiffened her backbone and curled her lip.

Miss Rodney's leisure generally had its task; though as a matter of principle she took daily exercise, her walking or cycling was always an opportunity for thinking something out, and this afternoon, as she sped on wheels some ten miles from

Wattleborough, her mind was busy with the problem of Mrs
Turpin's husband. From her clerical friend of St Luke's she had
learnt that Turpin was at bottom a decent sort of man, rather
intelligent, and that it was only during the last year or two that
he had taken to passing his evenings at the public-house. Causes
for this decline could be suggested. The carpenter had lost his
only son, a lad of whom he was very fond; the boy's death quite
broke him down at the time, and perhaps he had begun to drink
as a way of forgetting the trouble. Perhaps, too, his foolish,
slatternly wife bore part of the blame, for his home had always
been comfortless, and such companionship must, in the long-
run, tell on a man. Reflecting upon this, Miss Rodney had an
idea, and she took no time in putting it into practice. When
Mabel brought in her tea, she asked the girl whether her father
was at home.

'I think he is, miss,' was the distant reply – for Mabel had
been bidden by her mother to 'show a proper spirit' when Miss
Rodney addressed her.

'You think so? Will you please make sure, and, if you are
right, ask Mr Turpin to be so kind as to let me have a word
with him.'

Startled and puzzled, the girl left the room. Miss Rodney
waited, but no one came. When ten minutes had elapsed she
rang the bell. A few minutes more and there sounded a heavy
foot in the passage; then a heavy knock at the door, and Mr
Turpin presented himself. He was a short, sturdy man, with hair
and beard of the hue known as ginger, and a face which told in
his favour. Vicious he could assuredly not be, with those honest
grey eyes; but one easily imagined him weak in character, and
his attitude as he stood just within the room, half respectful,
half assertive, betrayed an embarrassment altogether encouraging to Miss Rodney. In her pleasantest tone she begged him to
be seated.

'Thank you, miss,' he replied, in a deep voice, which sounded
huskily, but had nothing of surliness; 'I suppose you want to
complain about something, and I'd rather get it over standing.'

'I was not going to make any complaint, Mr Turpin.'

'I'm glad to hear it, miss; for my wife wished me to say she'd
done about all she could, and if things weren't to your liking,
she thought it would be best for all if you suited yourself in
somebody else's lodgings.'

It evidently cost the man no little effort to deliver his message; there was a nervous twitching about his person, and he could not look Miss Rodney straight in the face. She, observant of this, kept a very steady eye on him, and spoke with all possible calmness.

'I have not the least desire to change my lodgings, Mr Turpin. Things are going on quite well. There is an improvement in the cooking, in the cleaning, in everything; and, with a little patience, I am sure we shall all come to understand one another. What I wanted to speak to you about was a little practical matter in which you may be able to help me. I teach mathematics at the High School, and I have an idea that I might make certain points in geometry easier to my younger girls if I could demonstrate them in a mechanical way. Pray look here. You see the shapes I have sketched on this piece of paper; do you think you could make them for me in wood?'

The carpenter was moved to a show of reluctant interest. He took the paper, balanced himself now on one leg, now on the other, and said at length that he thought he saw what was wanted. Miss Rodney, coming to his side, explained in more detail; his interest grew more active.

'That's Euclid, miss?'

'To be sure. Do you remember your Euclid?'

'My own schooling never went as far as that,' he replied, in a muttering voice; 'but my Harry used to do Euclid at the Grammar School, and I got into a sort of way of doing it with him.'

Miss Rodney kept a moment's silence; then quietly and kindly she asked one or two questions about the boy who had died. The father answered in an awkward, confused way, as if speaking only by constraint.

'Well, I'll see what I can do, miss,' he added, abruptly, folding the paper to take away. 'You'd like them soon?'

'Yes. I was going to ask you, Mr Turpin, whether you could do them this evening. Then I should have them for Monday morning.'

Turpin hesitated, shuffled his feet, and seemed to reflect uneasily; but he said at length that he 'would see about it', and, with a rough bow, got out of the room. That night no hilarious sounds came from the kitchen. On Sunday morning, when Miss Rodney went into her sitting-room, she found on the table the

wooden geometrical forms, excellently made, just as she wished.
Mabel, who came with breakfast, was bidden to thank her
father, and to say that Miss Rodney would like to speak with
him again, if his leisure allowed, after tea-time on Monday. At
that hour the carpenter did not fail to present himself, distrustful
still, but less embarrassed. Miss Rodney praised his work, and
desired to pay for it. Oh! that wasn't worth talking about, said
Turpin; but the lady insisted, and money changed hands. This
piece of business transacted, Miss Rodney produced a Euclid,
and asked Turpin to show her how far he had gone in it with
his boy Harry. The subject proved fruitful of conversation. It
became evident that the carpenter had a mathematical bias, and
could be readily interested in such things as geometrical problems. Why should he not take up the subject again?

'Nay, miss,' replied Turpin, speaking at length quite naturally; 'I shouldn't have the heart. If my Harry had lived—'

But Miss Rodney stuck to her point, and succeeded in making
him promise that he would get out the old Euclid and have a
look at it in his leisure time. As he withdrew, the man had a
pleasant smile on his honest face.

On the next Saturday evening the house was again quiet.

Meanwhile, relations between Mrs Turpin and her lodger
were becoming less strained. For the first time in her life the
flabby, foolish woman had to do with a person of firm will and
bright intelligence; not being vicious of temper, she necessarily
felt herself submitting to domination, and darkly surmised that
the rule might in some way be for her good. All the sluggard
and the slattern in her, all the obstinacy of lifelong habits, hung
back from the new things which Miss Rodney was forcing upon
her acceptance, but she was no longer moved by active resentment. To be told that she cooked badly had long ceased to be
an insult, and was becoming merely a worrying truism. That she
lived in dirt there seemed no way of denying, and though every
muscle groaned, she began to look upon the physical exertion
of dusting and scrubbing as part of her lot in life. Why she
submitted, Mrs Turpin could not have told you. And, as was
presently to be seen, there were regions of her mind still
unconquered, instincts of resistance which yet had to come into
play.

For, during all this time, Miss Rodney had had her eye on her
fellow-lodger, Mr Rawcliffe, and the more she observed this

gentleman, the more resolute she became to turn him out of the house; but it was plain to her that the undertaking would be no easy one. In the landlady's eyes Mr Rawcliffe, though not perhaps a faultless specimen of humanity, conferred an honour on her house by residing in it; the idea of giving him notice to quit was inconceivable to her. This came out very clearly in the first frank conversation which Miss Rodney held with her on the topic. It happened that Mr Rawcliffe had passed an evening at home, in the company of his friends. After supping together, the gentlemen indulged in merriment which, towards midnight, became uproarious. In the morning Mrs Turpin mumbled a shamefaced apology for this disturbance of Miss Rodney's repose.

'Why don't you take this opportunity and get rid of him?' asked the lodger in her matter-of-fact tone.

'Oh, miss!'

'Yes, it's your plain duty to do so. He gives your house a bad character; he sets a bad example to your husband; he has a bad influence on your daughters.'

'Oh, miss, I don't think—'

'Just so, Mrs Turpin; you *don't* think. If you had, you would long ago have noticed that his behaviour to those girls is not at all such as it should be. More than once I have chanced to hear bits of talk, when either Mabel or Lily was in his sitting-room, and didn't like the tone of it. In plain English, the man is a blackguard.'

Mrs Turpin gasped.

'But, miss, you forget what family he belongs to.'

'Don't be a simpleton, Mrs Turpin. The blackguard is found in every rank of life. Now, suppose you go to him as soon as he gets up, and quietly give him notice. You've no idea how much better you would feel after it.'

But Mrs Turpin trembled at the suggestion. It was evident that no ordinary argument or persuasion would bring her to such a step. Miss Rodney put the matter aside for the moment.

She had found no difficulty in getting information about Mr Rawcliffe. It was true that he belonged to a family of some esteem in the Wattleborough neighbourhood, but his father had died in embarrassed circumstances, and his mother was now the wife of a prosperous merchant in another town. To his step-father Rawcliffe owed an expensive education and two or three starts in life. He was in his second year of articles to a Wattleborough solicitor, but there seemed little probability of his ever earning a living by the law, and reports of his excesses which reached the stepfather's ears had begun to make the young man's position decidedly precarious. The incumbent of St Luke's, whom Rawcliffe had more than once insulted, took much interest in Miss Rodney's design against this common enemy; he could not himself take active part in the campaign, but he never met the High School mistress without inquiring what progress she had made. The conquest of Turpin, who now for several weeks had kept sober, and spent his evenings in mathematical study, was a most encouraging circumstance; but Miss Rodney had no thought of using her influence over her landlady's husband to assail Rawcliffe's position. She would rely upon herself alone, in this as in all other undertakings.

Only by constant watchfulness and energy did she maintain her control over Mrs Turpin, who was ready at any moment to relapse into her old slatternly ways. It was not enough to hold the ground that had been gained; there must be progressive conquest; and to this end Miss Rodney one day broached the subject which had already been discussed between her and her clerical ally.

'Why do you keep both your girls at home, Mrs Turpin?' she asked.

'What should I do with them, miss? I don't hold with sending girls into shops, or else they've an aunt in Birmingham, who's manageress of—'

'That isn't my idea,' interposed Miss Rodney quietly. 'I have been asked if I knew of a girl who would go into a country-house not far from here as second housemaid, and it occurred to me that Lily—'

A sound of indignant protest escaped the landlady, which Miss Rodney, steadily regarding her, purposely misinterpreted.

'No, no, of course, she is not really capable of taking such a position. But the lady of whom I am speaking would not mind an untrained girl, who came from a decent house. Isn't it worth thinking of?'

Mrs Turpin was red with suppressed indignation, but as usual she could not look her lodger defiantly in the face.

'We're not so poor, miss,' she exclaimed, 'that we need send our daughters into service.'

'Why, of course not, Mrs Turpin, and that's one of the reasons why Lily might suit this lady.'

But here was another rock of resistance which promised to give Miss Rodney a good deal of trouble. The landlady's pride was outraged, and after the manner of the inarticulate she could think of no adequate reply save that which took the form of personal abuse. Restrained from this by more than one consideration, she stood voiceless, her bosom heaving.

'Well, you shall think it over,' said Miss Rodney, 'and we'll speak of it again in a day or two.'

Mrs Turpin, without another word, took herself out of the room.

Save for that singular meeting on Miss Rodney's first night in the house, Mr Rawcliffe and the energetic lady had held no intercourse whatever. Their parlours being opposite each other on the ground floor, they necessarily came face to face now and then, but the High School mistress behaved as though she saw no one, and the solicitor's clerk, after one or two attempts at polite formality, adopted a like demeanour. The man's proximity caused his neighbour a ceaseless irritation; of all objectionable types of humanity, this loafing and boozing degenerate was, to Miss Rodney, perhaps the least endurable; his mere countenance excited her animosity, for feebleness and conceit, things abhorrent to her, were legible in every line of the trivial features; and a full moustache, evidently subjected to training, served only as emphasis of foppish imbecility. 'I could beat him!' she exclaimed more than once within herself, overcome with contemptuous wrath, when she passed Mr Rawcliffe. And, indeed, had it been possible to settle the matter thus simply, no doubt Mr Rawcliffe's rooms would very soon have been vacant.

The crisis upon which Miss Rodney had resolved came about, quite unexpectedly, one Sunday evening. Mrs Turpin and her daughters had gone, as usual, to church, the carpenter had gone to smoke a pipe with a neighbour, and Mr Rawcliffe believed himself alone in the house. But Miss Rodney was not at church this evening; she had a headache, and after tea lay down in her bedroom for a while. Soon impatient of repose, she got up and went to her parlour. The door, to her surprise, was partly open; entering – the tread of her slippered feet was noiseless – she beheld an astonishing spectacle. Before her writing-table, his back turned to her, stood Mr Rawcliffe, engaged in the deliberate perusal of a letter which he had found there. For a moment she observed him; then she spoke.

'What business have you here?'

Rawcliffe gave such a start that he almost jumped from the ground. His face, as he put down the letter and turned, was that of a gibbering idiot; his lips moved, but no sound came from them.

'What are you doing in my room?' demanded Miss Rodney, in her severest tones.

'I really beg your pardon – I really beg—'

'I suppose this is not the first visit with which you have honoured me?'

'The first – indeed – I assure you – the very first! A foolish curiosity; I really feel quite ashamed of myself; I throw myself upon your indulgence.'

The man had become voluble; he approached Miss Rodney smiling in a sickly way, his head bobbing forward.

'It's something,' she replied, 'that you have still the grace to feel ashamed. Well, there's no need for us to discuss this matter; it can have, of course, only one result. To-morrow morning you will oblige me by giving notice to Mrs Turpin – a week's notice.'

'Leave the house?' exclaimed Rawcliffe.

'On Saturday next – or as much sooner as you like.'

'Oh! but really—'

'As you please,' said Miss Rodney, looking him sternly in the face. 'In that case I complain to the landlady of your behaviour, and insist on her getting rid of you. You ought to have been turned out long ago. You are a nuisance, and worse than a nuisance. Be so good as to leave the room.'

Rawcliffe, his shoulders humped, moved towards the door; but before reaching it he stopped and said doggedly:

'I *can't* give notice.'

'Why not?'

'I owe Mrs Turpin money.'

'Naturally. But you will go, all the same.'

A vicious light flashed into the man's eyes.

'If it comes to that, I shall *not* go!'

'Indeed?' said Miss Rodney calmly and coldly. 'We will see about it. In the meantime, leave the room, sir!'

Rawcliffe nodded, grinned and withdrew.

Late that evening there was a conversation between Miss

Rodney and Mrs Turpin. The landlady, though declaring herself horrified at what had happened, did her best to plead for Mr Rawcliffe's forgiveness, and would not be brought to the point of promising to give him notice.

'Very well, Mrs Turpin,' said Miss Rodney at length, 'either he leaves the house or I do.'

Resolved, as she was, *not* to quit her lodgings, this was a bold declaration. A meeker spirit would have trembled at the possibility that Mrs Turpin might be only too glad to free herself from a subjection which, again and again, had all but driven her to extremities. But Miss Rodney had the soul of a conqueror; she saw only her will, and the straight way to it.

'To tell you the truth, miss,' said the landlady, sore perplexed, 'he's rather backward with his rent—'

'Very foolish of you to have allowed him to get into your debt. The probability is that he would never pay his arrears; they will only increase, the longer he stays. But I have no more time to spare at present. Please understand that by Saturday next it must be settled which of your lodgers is to go.'

Mrs Turpin had never been so worried. The more she thought of the possibility of Miss Rodney's leaving the house, the less did she like it. Notwithstanding Mr Rawcliffe's 'family,' it was growing clear to her that, as a stamp of respectability and a source of credit, the High School mistress was worth more than the solicitor's clerk. Then there was the astonishing change that had come over Turpin, owing, it seemed, to his talk with Miss Rodney; the man spent all his leisure time in 'making shapes and figuring' – just as he used to do when poor Harry was at the Grammar School. If Miss Rodney disappeared, it seemed only too probable that Turpin would be off again to The Swan with Two Necks. On the other hand, the thought of 'giving notice' to Mr Rawcliffe caused her something like dismay; how could she have the face to turn a real gentleman out of her house? Yes, but was it not true that she had lost money by him – and stood to lose more? She had never dared to tell her husband of Mr Rawcliffe's frequent shortcomings in the matter of weekly payments. When the easy-going young man smiled and nodded, and said, 'It'll be all right, you know, Mrs Turpin; you can trust *me*, I hope,' she could do nothing but acquiesce. And Mr Rawcliffe was more and more disposed to take advantage of this weakness. If she could find courage to go through with the thing, perhaps she would be glad when it was over.

Three days went by. Rawcliffe led an unusually quiet and regular life. There came the day on which his weekly bill was presented. Mrs Turpin brought it in person at breakfast, and stood with it in her hand, an image of vacillation. Her lodger made one of his familiar jokes; she laughed feebly. No; the words would not come to her lips; she was physically incapable of giving him notice.

'By the bye, Mrs Turpin,' said Rawcliffe in an offhand way, as he glanced at the bill, 'how much exactly do I owe you ?'

Pleasantly agitated, his landlady mentioned the sum.

'Ah! I must settle that. I tell you what, Mrs Turpin. Let it stand over for another month, and we'll square things up at Christmas. Will that suit you ?'

And, by way of encouragement, he paid his week's account on the spot, without a penny of deduction. Mrs Turpin left the room in greater embarrassment than ever.

Saturday came. At breakfast Miss Rodney sent for the landlady, who made a timid appearance just within the room.

'Good morning, Mrs Turpin. What news have you for me ? You know what I mean ?'

The landlady took a step forward, and began babbling excuses, explanations, entreaties. She was coldly and decisively interrupted.

'Thank you, Mrs Turpin, that will do. A week to-day I leave.'

With a sound which was half a sob and half grunt Mrs Turpin bounced from the room. It was now inevitable that she should report the state of things to her husband, and that evening half an hour's circumlocution brought her to the point. Which of the two lodgers should go ? The carpenter paused, pipe in mouth, before him a geometrical figure over which he had puzzled for a day or two, and about which, if he could find courage, he wished to consult the High School mistress. He reflected for five minutes, and uttered an unhesitating decision. Mr Rawcliffe must go. Naturally, his wife broke into indignant clamour, and the debate lasted for an hour or two; but Turpin could be firm when he liked, and he had solid reasons for preferring to keep Miss Rodney in the house. At four o'clock Mrs Turpin crept softly to the sitting-room where her offended lodger was quietly reading.

'I wanted just to say, miss, that I'm willing to give Mr Rawcliffe notice next Wednesday.'

'Thank you, Mrs Turpin,' was the cold reply. 'I have already taken other rooms.'

The landlady gasped, and for a moment could say nothing. Then she besought Miss Rodney to change her mind. Mr Rawcliffe should leave, indeed he should, on Wednesday week. But Miss Rodney had only one reply; she had found other rooms that suited her, and she requested to be left in peace.

At eleven Mr Rawcliffe came home. He was unnaturally sober, for Saturday night, and found his way into the parlour without difficulty. There in a minute or two he was confronted by his landlady and her husband: they closed the door behind them, and stood in a resolute attitude.

'Mr Rawcliffe,' began Turpin, 'you must leave these lodgings, sir, on Wednesday next.'

'Hullo! what's all this about?' cried the other. 'What do you mean, Turpin?'

The carpenter made plain his meaning; he spoke of Miss Rodney's complaint, of the irregular payment (for his wife, in her stress, had avowed everything), and of other subjects of dissatisfaction; the lodger must go, there was an end of it. Rawcliffe, putting on all his dignity, demanded the legal week's notice; Turpin demanded the sum in arrear. There was an exchange of high words, and the interview ended with mutual defiance. A moment after Turpin and his wife knocked at Miss Rodney's door, for she was still in her parlour. There followed a brief conversation, with the result that Miss Rodney graciously consented to remain, on the understanding that Mr Rawcliffe left the house not later than Wednesday.

Enraged at the treatment he was receiving, Rawcliffe loudly declared that he would not budge. Turpin warned him that if he had made no preparations for departure on Wednesday, he would be forcibly ejected, and the door closed against him.

'You haven't the right to do it,' shouted the lodger. 'I'll sue you for damages.'

'And I,' retorted the carpenter, 'will sue you for the money you owe me!'

The end could not be doubtful. Rawcliffe, besides being a poor creature, knew very well that it was dangerous for him to get involved in a scandal; his stepfather, upon whom he depended, asked but a fair excuse for cutting him adrift, and more than one grave warning had come from his mother during the past few months. But he enjoyed a little blustering, and even at breakfast-time on Wednesday his attitude was that of contemptuous defiance. In vain had Mrs Turpin tried to coax him with maternal suavity; in vain had Mabel and Lily, when serving his meals, whispered abuse of Miss Rodney, and promised to find some way of getting rid of her, so that Rawcliffe might return. In a voice loud enough to be heard by his enemy in the opposite parlour, he declared that no 'cat of a school teacher should get the better of *him*.' As a matter of fact, however, he arranged on Tuesday evening to take a couple of cheaper rooms just outside the town, and ordered a cab to come for him at eleven next morning.

'You know what the understanding is, Mr Rawcliffe,' said Turpin, putting his head into the room as the lodger sat at breakfast. 'I'm a man of my word.'

'Don't come bawling here!' cried the other, with a face of scorn.

And at noon the house knew him no more.

Miss Rodney, on that same day, was able to offer her landlady a new lodger. She had not spoken of this before, being resolved to triumph by mere force of will.

'The next thing,' she remarked to a friend, when telling the story, 'is to pack off one of the girls into service. I shall manage it by Christmas,' and she added with humorous complacency, 'it does one good to be making a sort of order in one's own little corner of the world.'

NOTES

'Lou and Liz'

p. 1 **pure and free**: From a hymn by George F. Root (1820–95).

p. 1 **Monty Car–lo**: From the popular song by Fred Gilbert (1850–1903), 'The Man Who Broke the Bank at Monte Carlo':

> As I walk along the Bois Bou-long
> With an independent air,
> You can hear the girls declare,
> 'He must be a millionaire';
> You can hear them sigh and wish to die,
> You can see them wink the other eye
> At the man who broke the Bank at Monte Carlo.

Gilbert submitted the song to the well-known music-hall singer Charles Coborn (1852–1945), whose real name was Colin Whitton McCallum, and Coborn first turned it down, but later he bought the singing rights for a guinea. Although not an immediate success, the song had become very popular by 1891, when it was published by Francis, Day & Hunter, and Coborn is said to have made a good deal of money from it. Fred Gilbert's song was inspired by the exploits of Charles de Ville Wells who, achieving every gambler's dream, broke the bank at the Monte Carlo casino and later wrote a book about it.

p. 2 **As y're 'eppy**: Perhaps an echo from Dick Swiveller in chapter 2 of *The Old Curiosity Shop*: 'What is the odds so long as the fire of soul is kindled at the taper of conviviality, and the wing of friendship never moults a feather!' George Du Maurier was to write in *Trilby* (Part 1), which was published in 1894 – after Gissing published 'Lou and Liz' – 'Life ain't all beer and skittles, and more's the pity; but what's the odds, so long as you're happy?'

p. 3 **Surrey**: The Canterbury Theatre of Varieties at 143 Westminster Bridge Road, and the Royal Surrey Theatre, at 124 Blackfriars Road, where melodramas and farces were performed, and admission could be had from 6d. and 4d. respectively. Both eventually became cinemas. The Canterbury was destroyed during the Blitz in 1940; the Surrey had been pulled down six years earlier.

p. 3 **Rosherville**: Rosherville Gardens, Gravesend, where music, dancing and theatrical entertainments attracted crowds during the summer. Admission then cost 6d. The Gardens could be reached by rail or steamer.

p. 9 **Old Vic**: The Old Vic, Waterloo Road, was opened in 1818 as the Coburg Theatre. In 1833, after redecoration, it was reopened as the Victoria, in honour of the future queen. Usually it was given up to melodrama. 'The lower orders', Charles Mathews wrote, 'rush there in mobs, and in shirtsleeves, frantically drink ginger-beer, munch apples, crack nuts, call the actors by their Christian names, and throw them orange peel and apples by way of bouquets.' See *An Encyclopaedia of London*, edited by William Kent (London, 1937), p. 667.

p. 13 **mide for two**: From 'Daisy Bell', by Harry Dacre:

> Daisy, Daisy, give me your answer, do!
> I'm half crazy, all for the love of you!
> It won't be a stylish marriage,
> I can't afford a carriage,
> But you'll look sweet upon the seat
> Of a bicycle made for two!

Dacre was an author, composer and singer, who enjoyed considerable success at the turn of the century. Among his other songs were 'Ting-a-Ling', 'Dorothy Jean', 'While London's Fast Asleep' and 'As your hair grows whiter'.

'The Day of Silence'

p. 18 **Four-arf**: Half-ale, half porter, at fourpence a quart (slang).

'The Fate of Humphrey Snell'

p. 58 **toga virilis**: At Rome in republican times men's dress consisted of an inner garment, the *tunica*, and an outer one, the *toga*. It was made of white wool and semicircular in shape. One end of it nearly reached the ground in front, the other being thrown over the left shoulder. The *toga virilis*, worn by ordinary citizens, was entirely white, whereas the *toga praetexta*, worn by free-born boys until they reached manhood and by some priests and magistrates, was bordered with a purple stripe.

p. 62 **historic significance**: Wells was the seat of the government of the early kings of Wessex.

p. 63 **St Andrew's well**: An underground stream, the Water of Wells, or St Andrew's Stream, which comes from the springs.

'An Inspiration'

p. 78 **quantum mutatus!** Virgil, *Aeneid*, 2, 274 (*Quantum mutatus ab illo / Hectore qui redit exuvias indutus Achilli*: 'How was he changed from that Hector who wended homeward, clad in the spoils of Achilles').

'The Foolish Virgin'

p. 80 Matthew 25, 1–4. 'Then shall the kingdom of heaven be likened unto ten virgins, which took their lamps, and went forth to meet the bridegroom. And five of them were wise, and five were foolish. They that were foolish took their lamps, and took no oil with them: But the wise took oil in their vessels with their lamps.'

p. 96 **Remorse**: Gissing may have thought of passages such as these: 'Never pray more; abandon all remorse; / On horror's head horrors accumulate' (*Othello*, III, iii, 370–1); 'So farewell hope, and with hope farewell fear, / Farewell remorse: all good to me is lost; Evil be thou my Good' (*Paradise Lost*, Book IV, 108–10); 'Remorse, the fatal egg by pleasure laid' (Cowper, *Progress of Error*, 239).

p. 96 **A plain unvarnished tale unfold**: An echo from *Othello* I, i, 91: 'I will a round unvarnish'd tale deliver.'

'The Scrupulous Father'

p. 160 **Rufus**: Latin for red-haired, used ironically here.

'A Daughter of the Lodge'

p. 169 **Mudie**: Charles Edward Mudie (1818–90), the founder of the famous circulating library, the main branch of which was opened in Oxford Street in 1852, ten years after he began to lend books at his shop in Bloomsbury. Mudie's moral scruples in selecting his stock were not free from some hypocrisy; his influence amounted to a form of cultural dictatorship and was fought by various writers, notably George Moore. See Moore's *Literature at Nurse or Circulating Morals*, ed. Pierre Coustillas (1976), and Guinevere L. Griest, *Mudie's Circulating Library and the Victorian Novel* (1970).

GISSING AND HIS CRITICS

The following extracts cover some eighty years, ranging from the late 1890s, when the English press reviewed Gissing's first collection of short stories, *Human Odds and Ends* (Lawrence & Bullen, 1898), to 1981, with a sophisticated modern interpretation of 'Fleet-Footed Hester' by Adeline Tintner, an American critic mainly known for her influential analysis of Henry James's works. Other assessments of *Human Odds and Ends* and *The House of Cobwebs* (Constable, 1906) may be found in *Gissing: The Critical Heritage*, edited by Pierre Coustillas and Colin Partridge (Routledge & Kegan Paul, 1972), which contains a bibliography of unreprinted reviews. Joseph J. Woolf's *George Gissing: An Annotated Bibliography of Writings about him* (Northern Illinois University Press, 1974) offers further bibliographical references and abstracts of articles and reviews. Anybody anxious to view Gissing's short stories in context should consult *British Short Fiction in the Nineteenth Century: A Literary and Bibliographic Guide*, by Wendell V. Harris (Wayne State University Press, 1979).

'The World of Books', *Daily Mail*, 2 November 1897, p. 3

Very cleverly, though doubtless involuntarily, Mr George Gissing disarms adverse criticism by the mere title of his new collection of stories and sketches:

'Human Odds and Ends'

But for this title one might have said of these various episodes that they were too sketchy, that they had no crux in them, but were studies rather than stories, and that their positively photographic realism occasionally made them so ever-truthful to life as to be false to art. Regarded, however, as studies in intention, as portraits of individuals, and chronicles of incidents in their lives, these little more or less sordid dramas of workaday life are masterpieces of observation and literary simplicity and strength. In 'The Day of Silence', Mr Gissing has caught nature's trick of placing tragedy in the humblest reassuring commonplaces of every day, and yet sacrificing no jot of his impressiveness. 'Comrades in Arms' and 'An Inspiration', on the other hand, deal as cleverly with comedy. Yet it is comedy with a lurking pathos ; pathos, or grim misery, must always lurk around the few smiles which Mr Gissing permits to brighten his pages. He is a supreme literary artist, nevertheless, and even those people who shrink from reading of the darker side of life cannot afford to neglect him.

'Mr George Gissing's Last', *Daily News*, 26 November 1897, p. 9

Mr George Gissing is a curiously close observer. His intent study of human nature is almost entirely confined to that of the English middle class. *Human Odds and Ends* [is] a series of stories and sketches dealing with the trials and aims of members of that vast section of society. He flashes the somewhat cold light of his penetrating insight into strange spiritual nooks and crannies, and reveals the aims and deceptions of a laborious, usually sordid and snobbish, multitude, the large majority of whose members lead lives of tragic dulness, at once precarious and pretentious. We see portrayed in these pages successful and defeated journalists, writers of books, teachers, and other professional men and women – Bohemians who, because of their temperament, or from lack of character, have failed in the strenuous struggle for existence ; others again who have reached to the summit of their calling, and yet have lost all zest in life, their spirit swamped in the triviality and vulgarity of their surroundings. It is all done to the life. The impression left by this amazingly real presentation is at once depressing to the emotions and intellectually stimulating. Sometimes, as in the strong and reticent sketch 'The Day of Silence', Mr Gissing gives us a glimpse of a more dignified tragedy in the life of the labouring classes, simpler, saner, more appealing in its sorrowful sincerity. The picture, indeed, of the joys of the middle class is more depressing than that of its struggles and failures. Much in the volume reads like notes and jottings to be further amplified. If this book has not the significance of Mr Gissing's more sustained achievements, admirers of his work, and they are numerous and increasing, cannot afford to overlook it.

'Novel Notes', *Bookman* (London), December 1897, p. 106

How much more pitiful Mr Gissing has grown of the human beings he creates for us! He still shows them to us in hard, or sordid, or hopeless plights, and he reveals more and more his disbelief in hardship as a blessed influence. Poverty is mostly ugly, and to sensitive souls generally demoralizing. But sometimes, of late, he goes further and shows he cannot bear the thought of help being withheld in so much curable human misfortune, and his hand is stretched out in rescue. The hopeless, harmless wretch in 'An Inspiration', gets vitality and an awakening to an old romance and a new future by a dinner. Mr Mayhew, the hero of 'In Honour Bound', is saved from paying the uttermost farthing of a debt that would have dragged him down. The poor, tired woman of 'The Day of Silence' dies before the bodies of her husband and child are brought home. There are other lighter, more amusing stories. But such as tell of the struggle with fate, of the shadow of poverty and of unsympathetic presences, are the stronger and give the colour to the book. As a writer of short stories, Mr Gissing is advancing with rapid strides to a high place. There is no waste, there are no preambles, in his straightforward, forcible narratives of the life of the less fortunate today.

'New Leaves', *Sun* (Melbourne), 1 April, 1898, p. 4

These sketches, originally written for the lighter periodicals, are much less sombre in tone than usual with him. Some of them indeed are humorous and romantic, and extract these characteristics from the unlikely material which abounds in the sections of society to which his attention is chiefly devoted. He has a real genius to perceive and extract the comedy as well as the pathos of everyday incidents in the careers of commonplace individuals.

In this book [*Human Odds and Ends*], 'An Old Maid's Triumph', and 'Our Mr Jupp' are things that no other writer living could have done so well, if indeed there could be any who could have done them at all.

Thomas Seccombe, 'The Work of George Gissing: An Introductory Survey', *The House of Cobwebs* (1906), pp. xlviii–xlix

Whatever the critics may determine as to the merit of the stories in the present volume, there can be no question as to the interest they derive from their connection with what had gone before. Thus 'Topham's Chance' is manifestly the outcome of material pondered as early as 1884. 'A Lodger in Maze Pond' develops in a most suggestive fashion certain problems discussed in 1894. Miss Rodney is a reincarnation of Rhoda Nunn and Constance Bride. 'Christopherson' is a delicious expansion of a mood indicated in *Ryecroft* (Spring XII), and 'A Capitalist' indicates the growing interest in the business side of practical life, the dawn of which is seen in *The Town Traveller* and in the discussion of Dickens's potentialities as a capitalist. The very artichokes in 'The House of Cobwebs' (which, like the kindly hand that raised them, alas! fell a victim to the first frost of the season) are suggestive of a charming passage detailing the retired author's experience as a gardener. What Dr Furnivall might call the 'backward reach' of every one of these stories will render their perusal delightful to those cultivated readers of Gissing, of whom there are by no means a few, to whom every fragment of his suave and delicate workmanship 'repressed yet full of power, vivid though sombre in colouring', has a technical interest and charm. Nor will they search in vain for Gissing's incorrigible mannerisms, his haunting insistence upon the note of '*Dort wo du nicht bist ist das Glück*', his tricks of the brush in portraiture, his characteristic epithets, the *dusking* twilight, the *decently ignoble* penury, the *not ignoble* ambition, the *not wholly base* riot of the senses in early manhood. In my own opinion we have here in 'The Scrupulous Father', and to a less degree, perhaps, in the first and last of these stories ['The House of Cobwebs' and 'The Pig and Whistle'], and in 'A Poor Gentleman' and 'Christopherson', perfectly characteristic and quite admirable specimens of Gissing's own genre, and later, unstudied, but always finished prose style.

Arthur Waugh, 'Gissing's Short Stories', *Daily Chronicle*, 26 May 1906, p. 3

As for the stories themselves [as distinct from Thomas Seccombe's introductory survey], it would serve no good purpose to enumerate their emotions; and, indeed, where the whole art of the story-teller depends upon a temperamental impression, often of a very sensitive order, comment and description are apt merely to confuse the issues. The tales which strike us as being the most masterly of an entirely masterly collection are 'The Scrupulous Father', 'Christopherson', 'Topham's Chance', and 'Fate and the Apothecary'. The last-named is, perhaps, almost intolerable in its unflinching acceptance of the old Greek theory of Atè, but all the others have little wandering airs of humour, traversing their grey ways; and if, as Mr Seccombe seems to suggest, they belong to a wide field in the career of Gissing's activity, they certainly give one the impression that the larger canvases were apt to destroy the effect of some of those lighter touches which may still be traced by the careful reader in even so sombre a picture as that of *New Grub Street*.

Mr A. H. Bullen, one of Gissing's most discriminating admirers, has always maintained that his genius was seen to peculiar advantage in the short story, and a further study of *Human Odds and Ends*, combined with the recent reading of *The House of Cobwebs*, confirms me in the conviction that Mr Bullen's judgment is here, as so often elsewhere, infallibly sound.

'Novels and Stories', *Glasgow Herald*, 31 May 1906, p. 11

The more than Maupassant-like disdain of mere plot of the conventional 'story' is here [in *The House of Cobwebs*] unfettered by the prudential considerations which account for the happy endings of one or two of the longer novels; the occasional touches of romance are only the spasmodic revolts of a sensitive nature against the dingy horrors of scenes which he had trained himself to regard with the microscopic curiosity of a Hogarth; each tale but raises the curtain, as if by accident, upon the downward career of some picturesque dead-beat or underdog, some hapless round peg in a square hole, and lets it fall again with full regard to pictorial, but with scarcely any to dramatic, effectiveness; while the dignity of human nature is vindicated by the affectionate delineation in such stories as 'The Salt of the Earth' or 'A Charming Family', of people whose blind trustfulness and calamitous unselfishness would have earned the withering contempt of a Dr Smiles or a Dr Carnegie. A terse, mature, yet exquisitely unusual style, a descriptive accuracy which might be called photographic if it could be attained by any but a very great artist, and a psychological insight which, while it may be only the outcome of brooding self-analysis, is so admirably apportioned as to endow every one of his personages with an absolutely self-consistent individuality – such are the distinguishing features of this, as of all the best work, of a writer who hewing at the sodden dough of London proletarian existence with the chisel of a great craftsman, raised English fiction higher into the region of pure literature than any writer since Thackeray.

Conrad Aiken, 'George Gissing', *Dial*, December 1927, pp. 512–14

Gissing was very much ahead of his time. When one reflects that it is now almost a quarter of a century since he died, one reads this posthumous collection of his short stories [*A Victim of Circumstances*] with astonishment: for with only one or two exceptions these stories are strikingly, in tone and manner, like the sort of thing which, in the hands of such a writer as Katherine Mansfield, critics hailed as revolutionary. In most of these tales the 'story' amounts to little or nothing. If one compares them with the contemporary work of Hardy or Meredith or Henry James, one finds a difference as deep as that which severed Chekhov from Turgenev. Here is little or nothing of Hardy's habitual use of tragic or poetic background, his intermittent reference to the backdrop of the Infinite; here is none of Meredith's brilliant, and brilliantly conscious, counterpoint of comment, with its inevitable heightening of distance between the reader and the story; none of the exquisite preparation and elaboration of James. Much more than he admitted, or realized, Gissing *was* interested in 'human life'; it is above all for his uncompromising fidelity to his vision that we can still read him with pleasure and profit. He seldom shapes or heads his narrative as these others did, attaches less importance than they to dramatic climax. He is content with a bare presentation of a scene or situation.

To say that Gissing would have been liked by Chekhov is to say that he is a 'modern' – he is decidedly more modern than Hardy or James. James, of course, would have disapproved of him, as he disapproved of Mr Arnold Bennett, on the ground that he offered his reader a mere slice of life, the *donnée* without the working out. Whatever we may feel about that, and however much this sort of modernity may ultimately make Gissing appear old-fashioned, we must unquestionably accept him as an artist of the Chekhov generation, and a good one.

J. M. Mitchell, 'Notes on George Gissing's Short Stories',
Studies in English Literature (Tokyo),
March 1962, pp. 195–205

As a man who contracted two eminently unsuitable marriages which ground down his vitality, Gissing realized to the full the misery of a bad match. In 'A Lodger in Maze Pond' [*The House of Cobwebs*] Shergold, whose mischosen shop-girl wife is now dead and who has before him the prospect of cultured leisure – the Gissing idyll – after inheriting a fortune, expounds:

> Not one man in a thousand, when he thinks of marriage, waits for the ideal wife – for the woman who makes capture of his soul or even of his senses. Men marry without passion. Most of us have a very small circle for choice: the hazard of everyday life throws us into contact with this girl or that, and presently we begin to feel either that we have compromised ourselves, or that we might as well save trouble and settle down as soon as possible, and the girl at hand will do as well as another. More often than not it is the girl who decides for us.

It is Gissing himself speaking, and the self-justifying tone is interesting. Like many men whose vulnerability to women is greater than their discernment, Shergold relishes this philosophizing about matrimony. And Gissing makes him follow his own course and make a second unhappy marriage, this time to a sluttish servant.

Gissing's view of women was as ambivalent as one might expect in a man whose life was fraught with a longing for feminine grace and beauty, and who had behind him the harsh experience of his youthful marriage to an irredeemable Manchester prostitute. He tended to divide women into two classes – snares and paragons. Woman the snare has frequent appearances; she is particularly well exemplified in one of his less skilful stories, in which Gissing nevertheless put a lot of his own idealizing, 'The Fate of Humphrey Snell' [*A Victim of Circumstances*], where the pathetic hero, after finding a way of life as a herb-collector that is in keeping with his gentle nature and love of the country, becomes infatuated with a slut of a housemaid. When she accepts his rash proposal of marriage, she writes him a letter at the end of which 'There followed a row of crosses, which Humphrey found it easy to interpret. A cross is frequently set upon a grave; but he did not think of that.' Woman the paragon in Gissing's stories is often the devoted wife who stands by her husband in his profligacy or penury, as in 'The Light on the Tower' [*A Victim of Circumstances*] and 'Out of the Fashion' [*Human Odds and Ends*]. The latter concludes wistfully:

> Wife, housewife, mother – shaken by the harsh years, but strong and peaceful in her perfect womanhood. An old-fashioned figure, out of harmony with the day that rules, and to our modern eyes perhaps the oddest of the whole series of human odds and ends.

Gissing sees this lady's qualities as vestiges of a better age. One of the factors which make him so modern an author is this romantic feeling for the past, his anger with the present, and glum pessimism about the future.

In his short stories Gissing treated marriage as one of the trapdoors of calamity; he used the background of contented wedlock more often than not to pick out the incidental limitations. But there are exceptions to this generally discouraging picture. One is 'The Honeymoon' [*A Victim of Circumstances*], technically one of his most competent stories, where the incipient battle of wills between the newly married, and at first devoted, couple culminates in the wife's submission to her husband's greater mental powers. This wishful if positive conclusion to the tale, which was published in 1893, is an interesting piece of compensating for the author's disillusionment in his second marriage, to Edith Underwood, which took place in 1891.

[. . .] Three conditions – poverty, living in lodgings, and misalliance – supplied much of the stuff of Gissing's stories. But there are other varieties of frustration which he rendered in his morosely compassionate view of the human lot. Thwarted ambition, social or spiritual, the stultified hankering after a larger life – these are the key-notes to several of the short stories. In 'A Daughter of the Lodge' [*The House of Cobwebs*] May Rockett has shot up by education above the lodge-keeping station of her family; but when she comes home for a holiday and tries to flaunt her advantages, she is humiliated by the womenfolk of the big house. She is worth noting too as an instance of Gissing's understanding of the kind of woman who strove for emancipation. In 'Snapshall's Youngest' [*Stories and Sketches*] a dealer in second-hand furniture is mortified when his plan of marrying his third daughter to a real gentleman is frustrated – the elder two having married in their own class in spite of his expensive efforts to elevate them – , because the girl falls in love with a rich grocer's son. The fact that the suitor is blessed with an income of £1,500 a year does not make up for Snapshall's disappointment. (Gissing had an accurate sense of social gradations, a matter in which he inherited a sensibility from his lower middle class parentage. The novel, *Born in Exile*, which is autobiographical in spirit where not in fact, is about the attempts of the lowly-born but highly intelligent Godwin Peak to marry into the class which will supply the sophistication he longs for.) Gissing's stories are instinct with the hopeless longing of the unprivileged city-dweller for a more abundant life, with what he called in the novel, *Thyrza*, 'the hunger of an unshaped desire' [p. 111 of all one-volume editions].

Adeline R. Tintner, 'Gissing's "Fleet-footed Hester" :
The Atalanta of Hackney Downs', *Etudes Anglaises*,
October–December 1981, pp. 443–7

What made George Gissing 'interesting' and 'singular', as Henry James wrote, was his 'saturation' with the lowest middle-class elements of English society, making him '*The* authority in fact –

on a region vast and unexplored'.[1] Yet Gissing was saturated in the literature of ancient Greece and Rome as well. There are but a few pieces of his writing that exhibit a happy George Gissing, but when they occur they are ushered in under the rosy glow of the classical tradition. The prose of *Veranilda*, the novel left unfinished at his death (1903), recreating the sixth-century classical world, reflects Gissing's lovingly remembered historians of antiquity. *By the Ionian Sea* (1901), his account of a trip to the sites of his classical education, omits only those places to which he 'could attach no classical memory' and concentrates on a 'mood of elegant leisure', antipodal to the mood of most of his fiction, an atmosphere which made the whole classical world, unlike his actual world, dear to him. Immersed in it his writing loses its sense of 'grudge' (as Walter Allen puts it), its reflected resentments, and its sense of agitated depression. Rarely do we find it in the novels and only occasionally in the stories.

In one in particular, however, not only are the usually universal physical illnesses of the typical Gissing hero and heroine total eliminated, but the saga of a very healthy and active couple is seen under the aspect of a myth straight from the pages of Ovid. In 'Fleet-footed Hester' (1893), Gissing created his own metamorphosis in a modern version of a tale from Book x of Ovid's *Metamorphoses* [. . .] Hester who lived in Hackney has only her first name, as Atalanta, her classical prototype, had, and that a Roman one, the Latin version of the Persian name meaning 'star'. A comet would describe her more accurately because she was the first 'running' heroine in modern fiction.

Gissing even as a young student had been a great lover and scholar of Latin Poetry, winning academic distinction. He won exhibitions in Latin when he matriculated as a BA from Owens College. According to Morley Roberts their talks together 'were nearly always about ancient times, and of the Greeks and Romans'.[2] He added that Gissing saw in Italy not the land of the Renaissance but a land still peopled 'with such folks as . . . Horace and Theocritus had known'. In addition to these poets, his favorites included Virgil and Moschus. But unlike some who

---

[1] Henry James, *Notes on Novelists* (New York: Scribner's, 1914), p. 439.
[2] Morley Roberts, *The Private Life of Henry Maitland* (London: Richards Press, 1958), p. 47.

have read the classics in their student days, he never forgot them and we find in his *Diary* constant mention of Greek and Latin books. It is interesting in connection with the story that reading throughout his life Ovid and Catullus, the chief sources for the legend of Atalanta, he was specifically steeping himself in Ovid's *Metamorphoses* on a trip to Guernsey in August, 1889.[3] He, of course, read the Greek and Latin classics in the original languages as may be seen from his frequent quotations in his *Commonplace Book* now in the Berg Collection in New York, and his familiarity with the classics extended to his everyday life.

So by the time he came to write 'Fleet-footed Hester' ('fleet-footed' is itself a classical epithet), he had reread the *Metamorphoses* intensively during a leisurely vacation period, only a few years before. The tale from the *Metamorphoses* which serves as Gissing's model is told by Venus to her beloved Adonis and concerns a beautiful girl, Atalanta, 'who could outrun the swiftest men'. She will marry only the man who can defeat her on the running field, but if he loses he must expect death. Hippomenes, a beautiful and well-connected youth, falls in love with her and tells her that if he wins she will have as her mate the great-grandson of Neptune. She warns him about the chance he is taking in racing against her, but he relies on Venus to see him through, which she does, providing him with three golden apples with which he lures and distracts Atalanta who breaks her speed and allows him to win the race and her hand.

Gissing has taken the basic figure of Atalanta for his heroine, Hester, and Hippomenes for his hero, John Rayner, but he subjects the plot to a transformation suitable to 1893 and an environment of working-class people. In fact, part of the charm of the story resides just in the yoking together of two such opposites, the fate of an aristocratic heroine of Greek mythology and that of the 'h' dropping heroine of a pickle factory. The

[3] *London and the Life of Literature in Late Victorian England: The Diary of George Gissing, Novelist*, ed. by Pierre Coustillas (Lewisburg: Bucknell University Press, 1978).

He arrived in Guernsey on 20 August, and on the 23rd he had 'read a little in Ovid's "Amores"', and he read more the next two days. On the 29th he 'read some of the "Metamorphoses"' (D 162), and on 5 September he 'Read Ovid once more' (D 164). On 12 September he 'Read some "Metamorphoses"' (D 165).

great-grandson of Neptune has been metamorphosed into a
foreman at the gasworks, a very good thing indeed in Hackney
social distinctions. John Rayner is usually referred to by both
his names, as if he were entitled to special deference.

Gissing's story is about a young woman who racing in London
fields outstrips the men. Like Atalanta of whom 'It would be
hard to say, though, whether her speed or beauty earned more
praise', Hester also 'had a splendid physique' and 'Running was
her delight and glory'. Hester 'could beat all but the champion
runner of that locality'.[4] She attracts John Rayner, the foreman,
and becoming engaged to him she is forced by him not only to
give up her job but to stop running in public as not proper for
his fiancée. She disobeys the rules, however, and in anger they
break off their troth. For two years they refuse to see each other,
although both are so unhappy that their characters deteriorate
to the extent of John Rayner's going to pot in general and losing
his well paying job. The *abrutissement* of the formerly healthy,
athletic and beautiful couple seems to correspond to the punishment meted out by Venus in Ovid's tale after Hippomenes
desecrates her altar without having thanked her for helping him
win Atalanta's race. As a result, she turns her couple of lovers
into wild beasts [...] This Gissing translates into modern
terms. John's 'comely face had lost its tint of robust health; he
wore grimy rags; his home was anywhere and nowhere'. Hester
now also 'laughed noisily – a thing John had never known her
do'.

The Venus of Ovid becomes transformed into Mrs Heffron,
the young widow friend of Hester's who acts as the *deus ex
machina* of this story. She recognizes John in Victoria Park
sleeping on the grass in his beauty and points him out to Hester
who 'for nearly a minute gazed on him', showing that her
interest in him has been resuscitated to the extent that, to
reinvolve him with her, she provokes her new boyfriend to fight
him. John wins, a fact which reawakens her own sense of her
special running skill, and she follows after his victory with a
race of her own against herself. She runs one thousand yards in
four minutes and two seconds. This is to show the reader that

[4] Geoge Gissing, *A Victim of Circumstances and Other Stories* (London:
Constable & Co., 1927), p. 291.

she knows what speed she can still do and so will be able to undertake her great race against time for her man.

Following close on that demonstration Mrs Heffron (equipped with a Cupid, like her prototype, Venus, in the form of an ailing two-year-old child whose sex is left ambiguous) tells Hester that John is going to leave his job and sail for the Cape. The night before he is to go on the five-fifty morning train to Southampton, Hester relieves the night watch of the sick child and, encouraged by Mrs Heffron to leave with her former beau, she intends to meet the train after her sick bed stint is finished.

At this point the final act of the little drama is begun. Hester's race against time begins as soon as she realizes that the clock in Mrs Heffron's rooms was incorrect, since an unexpected stoppage reveals a loss of two hours. She must now make a trip of three miles in 'five and twenty minutes'. We are to read the story constantly at this point with our eye on the clock, as if we were spectators of a special kind of marathon. The conditions include a total lack of money on Hester's part so that any kind of cab solution to reach the train in time is out. There is no question but that Hester must run for it ! [...]

We must interrupt Hester's race to Waterloo station [...] to note that the chief difference between Ovid's tale and our story is that Hippomenes is running against Atalanta for his life, whereas Hester is running against time for her life's happiness. Hester has a twenty-five minute period allotted to her, but she is helped by the fact that the clock at the station is five minutes fast. 'She was in time but her eyes dazzled, and her limbs failed.' That's when John Rayner comes to her [...]

Gissing the classicist has used some of the attributes in the tale by Ovid and has transformed them into the realistic language and contemporary figures of his day, for in each tale the beautiful swift girl is running a race to decide the choice of her mate. In Ovid's version Hippomenes, whose stakes are the same as Hester's, is aided by a goddess; in Gissing's version Hester is aided by her widow friend. The racing beauty in Gissing's tale has her equivalents of the golden apples which cut into Atalanta's speed. They are the disturbances and delays caused by policemen, interfering carts, and faulty clocks, but they still allow her, unlike Atalanta, to win her race. Her role, therefore, is more like that of the suitor of Atalanta in Ovid's tale than like that of the mythological heroine herself. Her race is the reverse of the one in Ovid. In other ways, however, Gissing's heroine is like Ovid's, for she was like Atalanta, 'the pride of the Arcadian woodlands' and 'a noble savage' and, like her classical predecessor, boasts of 'an unconscious reserve' which 'kept her apart from the loose-tongued girls of the neighbourhood'. The Arcadian elements are maintained by Gissing allowing most of the action preliminary to Hester's great race against time to take place in Victoria Park, Hackney's 'Arcadian woodland', as it were. John Rayner's susceptibility to Hester is like Hippomenes's to Atalanta : 'It was her running . . . that excited him to an uneasy interest'.

In a way Gissing has also absorbed the poetic character of Ovid's classic, for his race divides itself into pseudostrophes into which the twenty-five minute race for a three mile coverage has been divided. The first strophe is marked by the time 5 :31 seen by Hester as she starts her race. This time is seen on the clock 'between the Bank and the Mansion House' : a 'clock pointed to one minute past the half hour'. We are given the exact topography, mapped out earlier in the day by Gissing's trial run. 'She knew that it was now a straight run to the street which led out of the Strand towards Waterloo Bridge.' In this strophe certain elements of the poet Ovid's interpretation are transformed into the poetic realism of 1893. Hester, who had put on some fancy clothes, 'pulled the boa from her neck', and then 'loosely knotted the boa round her waist'. This gesture creates a picture which comes to life in strophe two, and is marked by the time 5 :33–4 ('She had lost two or three minutes', for a constable had stopped her, but she frees herself). 'Like a spirit of the wind, the wind itself blowing freely along with her from the northeast – she swept round the great Cathedral [St Paul's] and saw before her the descending lights of Ludgate Hill' [. . .]

The third 'heat' or strophe takes place at 5 :40, for Hester gets on a cart which 'came out from Blackfriars' at 'Ludgate Circus' and now 'turned westward, going to Covent Garden'. The big clock of the Law Courts, 'like the hand of fate', points to 'twenty minutes before the hour'. She has ten minutes left to win her race against time. The fourth strophe takes us through the Strand, 'another great place of business'. She 'passed it like an arrow, and on and on !' The image, although surely proper to a fleet girl, is also directly taken from Ovid, 'The girl sped on / On winged feet, swifter than Scythian arrow'. She runs past

'Somerset House – Wellington Street', and comes upon 'the lights of Waterloo Bridge [. . .]'

The fifth and last strophe, or clocked interval, is when Hester spots the station before her. The time is now 'a minute past train time. Five minutes fast, had she known it. On, in terror and agony !' And then comes a sentence which seems more Elizabethan than classical, suggesting perhaps Golding's Elizabethan translation of Ovid, if not the play, *The Duchess of Malfi* : 'She was in time, but her eyes dazzled, and her limbs failed' [. . .] The final line is classical in a generalized way. 'And behind them the red rift of the eastern sky broadened into day'.

SUGGESTIONS FOR FURTHER READING

Annen, Ulrich, *George Gissing und die Kurzgeschichte*, Bern : Francke Verlag, 1973.

Coustillas, Pierre, 'Gissing's Short Stories : A Bibliography', *English Literature in Transition*, Vol. VII (1964), no. 2, pp. 59–72.

Coustillas, Pierre, and Bridgwater, Patrick, *George Gissing at Work : A Study of his Notebook 'Extracts from my Reading'*, Greensboro : ELT Press, 1988.

Enzer, Sandra Solotaroff, 'Maidens and Matrons : Gissing's Stories of Women', unpublished Ph.D dissertation, State University of New York at Stony Brook, 1978.

Gerber, Helmut E. (ed.), *The English Short Story in Transition 1880–1920*, New York : Pegasus, 1967.

Korg, Jacob, *George Gissing : A Critical Biography*, Seattle : University of Washington Press, 1963.

Parlati, Mary Aurelia, 'A Critical, Sociological and Technical Analysis of George Gissing's Short Stories and Sketches', unpublished Ph.D dissertation, Fordham University, 1970.

Reid, Ian, *The Short Story* (Critical Idiom Series), London : Methuen, 1977.

Stubbs, Patricia, *Women and Fiction : Feminism and the Novel 1880–1920*, Brighton : Harvester Press, 1979.